THE RISEN SERIES BOOK FOUR

COURAGE

A ZOMBIE APOCALYPSE HORROR STORY

COURAGE IS NOT A
GOAL. IT'S THE
NEED TO SURVIVE.

MARIE F CROW

Copyright

Courage is a work of fiction. All names, characters, locations, and incidents are the products of the author's imagination or are used fictitiously. Any resemblance to actual events, locales, or persons, living or dead, is entirely coincidental.

COURAGE: A NOVEL
Copyright © 2020 by Marie F. Crow
All rights reserved.

Editing by KP Editing
Cover Design by KP Designs
- www.kpdesignshop.com
Published by Kingston Publishing Company
- www.kingstonpublishing.com

Table of Contents

"Courage is not a goal set in the dark throes of desperation. It's the need to survive. It's the need to push through the fears and find the strength to face the perils ahead. It's not a brass ring to be claimed or a trophy to boast over. It's the personal level of discomfort we all must face when no outstretched arm is there to help you." ~ Helena Hawthorn

The screaming won't stop. They surround us with their panic-filled pleads begging for random help. The agony of the prolonging sounds of misery over the sight of so many lost to us forever tears my soul. Their minds are pierced with panic resulting from the confusion and helplessness over the sights left before their eyes. All of this is mixing with the moans of the wounded in a delicate recipe of death. It's the icing upon Death's birthday cake. It swirls with the red and crimson colors of the blood coating the hall and floor like a whipped topping. For today, there will be no celebrating of any birth in a manger. There was no bright star leading us to salvation last night. Today, the only celebration is being held by the wicked, walking Demi-Gods of life.

The ones to which we pretend to not hold homage. The ones whose wrath we fear just the same: Truth, Karma, Death, and Fate. These are the ones celebrating today. These are the ones dancing around us. They dance around us and along this hallway of suffering with bare feet of jubilation. Santa did not bring us gifts this year, but they did. Oh, how they did, and their holiday has just begun.

Chapter 1

Rhett rocks the limp body of my best friend in his arms like a small child with a broken doll. His pleadings are soft murmurings that fill the air like a priest's chants as he begs God for Aimes' life. He pleads with her to forgive him, but she won't answer. Her white-blonde hair with its faded pink streaks sweeps the floor with his movements. It makes her appear that much more fragile in his desperate embrace. So lost in his own grief, he will not let her go. He is too afraid of what it might mean to no longer hold her body to him.

Chapel has given up the fight to remove Aimes. Instead, he attempts to lean around Rhett to hold pressure to the wound that slowly spills her life, hot and red, between his fingers. His tears mingle with her blood as they fall from his face. They are just as hot and escape just as freely.

The same scene is being mirrored behind them as another set pleads over a fallen loved one. Simon is moaning his pain over the unresponsive body of his wife, Shelia. I watch their memories play out across his face with his hope for her survival. His words echo his love for her as he begs her to stay with him. In an attempt to keep her with him he begs for her to remember certain shared events of their life. I know that this is his attempt to mentally refuse the truth. There will be no more events for them.

Dolph is pressing his trembling hands to Shelia's shattered head. They are covered with more than just her blood from the damage that has been done. The dark, thick matter that has spilt around her and onto him is proof of which her bleeding can't be stopped or slowed until her heart exhausts its energy to fight. Dolph's hands shake with that fear as each pump of her heart is slowing a fragment at a time. She is making her escape from this world. There is no stopping her death, but they are not ready to accept it yet. Their queen has been captured, tortured, and now lies dying between them.

Ross stares blankly ahead with unfocused eyes. His breath is a rapid, short panting of pain with his wound seeping dark under Richard's hands. No one cries for Ross. No one mourns the possibility of *his* death. Richard is only trying to prevent it to give his conscience a rest from the guilt it would harbor if he simply walked away. He doesn't offer simple words of comfort to his friend. He is too focused on Shelia to have anything left for Ross, and Ross pretends to not notice that his death will slip by as ignored as he was by them in life.

There is another who no one is pressing their palms against. His life is already lost. J.D.'s blood flows without pausing onto the cold tiles around him, warming them and painting them with his death. His eyes still stare at me, pleading with me to accept his apology. I am locked in the deep depths of their betrayal. I'm still confused over the why of his actions. My body trembles with the aftershocks of what I have seen. My mind is stuck in a loop. It is a queen of details replaying the last moments with vivid accuracy. She holds every scene and sound with perfection, and like any cruel queen, she wields it with brutal authority.

Marxx is whispering something into my ear but I can't focus on his words. There is too much around me. It competes for my attention and I don't fully hear him. His voice mingles with the screams like nothing more than a buzzing sound. All of it swirls into a whirlwind of emotions inside of me. The panic and pain of what I am feeling bubbles in my chest. There are too many things to break my heart and I refuse to visit any one vision for too long, or I will run the risk of drowning with defeat. The moment that started it may have passed, but the hour still lingers. It's drawing out every second of torment in which it can celebrate; every second that can cost us so much more than what we have already lost.

I force my breathing to slow and each breath draws my walls back around me. My eyes begin to focus. I close down the many screams that fragrant the air with their trademark perfume of torment that this new world has shown us. I force past the smells sending my stomach into a fear-filled fluttering.

Fear is a poison. It finds a way inside your veins and burns away all self-confidence. It fills you with visions of false, foreshadowed futures and impregnates you with doom. J.D. has taught me that. The only antidote for his fear was courage, courage and love. I have to find both inside myself now if I want to survive this and protect the ones I love. I am Helena Hawthorn. I have lost one family already, and I will not let fear take another.

Marxx moves with me like an unspoken soul mate. He is cautious and protective of me. He feels my mood switch with this new determination. Like always, there will be time to cry and mourn later. Now, there is only enough time remaining to save a precious few. But which few?

Dolph's eyes tell me that Shelia is not one of those who can be saved. The green of his eyes flash between anger and sorrow as he accepts Truth's damage. With a reluctance that echoes through his body, he releases his hold on Shelia's wound and sags with the defeat of it. It triggers an outcry from Simon that can only come from the depths of a pure loss of a love. In his grief, he rocks Shelia's body, clutching her close. With his incomprehension of how to accept her death, he still pleads with her as his hands roam from her face to her skull.

Simon has lost everything today at the hands of one man. There are no words to give him. There is no embrace comforting enough to take this away. He is being shredded bitterly with rage and grief and there is nothing I can do but watch. A year ago, this holiday would have been spent around another tree with memory-making moments of love and laughter. The only memory this date will forever hold for him now will be the memory of blood-covered hands and pleadings that went unanswered.

Time is frozen for his family the way only Death's freezing grasp can master. A little girl will never grow up. A wife will never grow old. However, a husband and a father will be forced to carry on alone. Truth gives this gift to him today. This is the present that Death offers him, and his misery is the only acknowledgement they are wanting.

I wonder if Simon will now hear the haunting laughter of what he has lost. Will smells sneak up on him when his mind wanders too deep into the shadows which try to protect us from memories like this? When his eyes are closed, in the moment right before sleep takes him, will they be with him again whispering for his attention? Will he open his eyes, or like Chapel, will he just pray for them to go away?

Chapter 2

There are footsteps running towards us as the sun races against time with each bright ray it casts over the earth. Paula's face is sculpted into one of neutral compassion. She wears it like a shield, protecting her from what she has to do. It protects her emotions from the carnage around her. A carnage she will have to dive deep into as her duty demands. Every shattered life is a life she once held in her heart. A heart fighting against a calm exterior with every beat it creates.

Our eyes connect as she kneels down next to Aimes, and all sounds vanish in our silent communication. She is drawing out the moments left to her before seeing what is waiting. It is not just Aimes she is avoiding but also the men who are breaking in front of her as well.

What lingers in our nightmares is not always the obvious. Sometimes it is the little things, the little sounds and smells that will torment our minds long after the memories are made. This is one of those memories, and we are both trying to avoid as much storage of it as we can. As our eyes disconnect, the sounds pour forth again, and it is crippling as time continues to seep away.

There is nothing I can do for my childhood friend, and like a coward, I turn from her not wanting to hold the sight of her in my mind. My heart flutters with the pain of possibly losing her. I once prayed I would give anything for Lawless' return, but I never thought it would cost me her. We never really know who is truly listening to our prayers and who will call our bluffs.

I move to the only victim left without an active aide. Ross. Ross' eyes are dulled by his pain. They watch me from behind a thick haze of disinterest. He expects no help from those around him. He has already accepted his death with that realization. Watching him float on consciousness with fluttering eyes, I finally feel pity for the man who so many have used for their own goals and ambitions. These same people who now have forgotten him with the depths of their suffering.

Their goals and ambitions awoke beasts in men, causing a full circle of torment that Karma knows so well. This wheel is her world. She spins it as well as the Fates do with their golden scissors perched for the inevitable. Just like the Fates, she can cut lives short with her own reasons and justifications. She never asks, nor needs, to hear ours.

Ross' shirt is soaked with the blood from the wound to his stomach. The shirt no longer absorbs or blocks any of the blood that his heart beats in vain to produce. His heart is too stubborn to admit defeat, and with its refusal, the blood continues to slip away. It seems impossible that there is any left in his body with so much weighing heavily on the fabric of his clothing, turning the color of his shirt into a thick, dark, irregular cloud.

"I never meant…." Ross' face contorts with pain, locking the words on his tongue. He doesn't have to finish his thoughts. He knows I understand. He just needs to hear my words of acceptance to ease a different type of suffering he is feeling.

"I know. No one is innocent anymore, Ross. We have each made our mistakes thinking it was for the best for our own people and our own needs. None of us stopped to think what it might do to the other." I give him the full weight of my gaze. He deserves at least that much.

This man has been put in the middle of everyone's plotting. He has been used more than a pawn in a chess game; only his side was never a clear color of black or white. Their actions made him grey with blurred alliances and mistrust from both sides. Ross' shoulders were not used to bearing the weight of the blame. They were just used to carrying loads that others were too afraid to carry themselves. This man who gave up his ego so long ago in the simple attempt to save lives, now sits with his life being forgotten.

My hands press against the wound of his stomach and instantly the thick blood flows over them, coating them like vinyl gloves with a thick shine. Pressing firmly forces more to flow through my fingers like warm, wet sand. It flows with a life of its own, filling in the crevices and fine lines as it fights to escape. Everything about Ross is weary from the constant abuse and he is ready to let go.

"It's not so bad." My voice is barely a whisper, and with the strength of a feather, it holds no convincing powers.

"It's not so bad" is the same as telling someone "I'm fine". These statements are uttered when, in fact, things are very bad, and nothing is fine. This is what we say when we do not hold the strength to admit how very bad everything really is. This is all very bad, and he is not fine. However, you never admit that to people. White lies are at their finest in moments of deep dread and desperation.

"I've got it. Go help Aimes." The voice above me is cold and empty, where warmth and laughter vibrated only moments ago. Moments that now feel like days lost when we all stood celebrating his life.

Lawless' hand rests flat on my shoulder, pulling me away from Ross. It once touched me with kindness, but now it only holds authority. The void of his normal personality frightens me. It inspires no trust in me to leave Ross with him. It only warns of what is to come.

"I can save him," I hiss, through my clamped teeth.

"Hells..." Marxx echoes the same tone conveying the same statement that Lawless spoke. Ross' clock has run out. Promises are about to be kept.

"It's too late, Hells. Go help with Aimes." Lawless' tone holds no room for arguments, but when did that ever matter to me?

I have faced bigger monsters than Lawless and won. He may be the "prodigal son", but he doesn't carry the same bat as Daddy.

I ask him, "You want me to just let him die? Just to turn my back on what you are about to do?" If he wants to intimidate me, he is going to have to bring a bigger stick.

My face must have shown my defiance as Ross and I stare at one another. A simple shake of his head tells me of his acceptance, and I feel my heart break. I cry for Ross. I cry for a man no one else has taken the time to comfort. He reaches to touch my cheek, seeking the proof his eyes are telling him, and I feel a new trail from his fingertips. I bless his death with my tears. He blesses me with his blood.

"I want you to walk away, now," Lawless says. He has missed our silent exchange. He will think he has won this round, but Ross and I know different. We will always hold the truth like a guarded secret long after he is gone.

With my final good-bye, I place a soft kiss upon lips that once smiled brighter than the noon sun. "I forgive you," I whisper to those lips, and I leave him with Lawless and Marxx.

I don't glance back. I don't spare Ross the anger of those who surround him. My cowardice shames me.

"I promised you I would kill you one day," I hear Lawless tell him.

It's not the comforting good-bye I had left Ross with, but it is what Ross' last moments are. Those words and the long black barrel of Lawless' gun are his farewell from this world.

The shot echoes and I feel my whole-body flinch with it as if it were I under that barrel. I cry, not for the man who led us into that trap of a store, but for the man who I met that first day at the Welcome Center. The man who another had left behind, too concerned with his own safety. A man who continued to find himself placed between the two warring sides, never finding some place for himself. His shaggy brown hair that day hinted at the stress he was put through and continued to show the wear of never really being allowed in on either side of the battle. Did I seal his fate the day we met or was it Simon, Dolph, and Richard under an abandoned strip mall? Either way, another name is signed to the list of the dead. A list still growing and I am not sure if I have the courage to keep writing.

Chapter 3

There is only one left from J.D.'s madness. With how well Death is winning this game, I am not sure I want to play anymore. How do you beg Death for mercy? What flag do you wave signaling your surrender? Where is my pause button so I can hide for just a few moments? Life isn't equipped with those, and Death really doesn't care if you are unable to go on.

The steps between my friend and I seem to multiply by four with every two I take. My feet are weighing heavily with fear's quicksand. J.D.'s blank, begging eyes swim before mine. Carol's twisted body at the bottom of the stairs flashes before me. Ashley, with her innocence over-run by evil, falls again before my eyes. I can hear Conroy's screams for help like the roar of an ocean in my ears. Lilly, with her missing center, is staring at me surrounded by the halo of her death. With Aimes' image added to its pages, would my portfolio of failures now be complete?

With a firm voice to reach the wrecked minds of Rhett and Chapel, Paula is giving instructions attempting to turn them into her assistants. They have exposed Aimes' upper body to gather a better idea of the damage. Rhett's eyes refuse to rest upon her with his unease over the exposure. They dart from the black bag of tools of Paula's trade, back to Aimes, never lingering longer than needed to fulfill the task set to him. It's endearing to see him falter so if it were not for the circumstances around it.

Aimes would marvel in the fact of finally being the source of his discomfort. Her quick wit would dance with comments. Instead she is silent, grey, and the shocking contrast of it only adds to the fears that flutter inside me. All the times I have wished for her silence I would take them all back for just one bubble gum scented, smart-ass remark. Just for one eye roll giving finality to any argument with her silently expressed point of view. Please, God, don't take my friend. Please, don't deny me the chance to say the words that I have never said to her. I don't need to hold her memories in the days that are left for me. I need to hold her hand.

The white lace of her bra adds a frail beauty to the singed circle on her flesh. Paula's examination allows red rivers to flow into her cleavage, pooling around pale flesh before slipping free to cascade to the tiles around her body. The contrast of colors between the rivers of blood and her skin's tone stirs my soul to panic. The very imagery I was seeking to avoid with my weakness is laid before me, taunting me. I know if she dies here today on this cold floor, the memory of her fall will come find me tonight. It will replay a thousand times with my mind's wickedness.

"Paula?" My voice holds the questions my tongue won't form.

"I don't know. If I dig to retrieve it, I will cause more damage. Did it pass through anything?" Paula is not exaggerating about the damage risk. With each new twist or tug of the singed circle, more rivers form with different speeds and currents.

"No. Clean shot." Rhett's voice is the weakest I have ever heard. His coloring seems to be fading as the reds grow bolder.

"You are *absolutely* sure of that?" Paula asks. I can see some of the tension loosening from Paula's shoulders. The grim press of her lips is relaxing, allowing color to slowly return to them.

Rhett and Chapel only nod. They are not sure if she is relaxing because of good news or if she is giving up. The weightlessness in my knees is also afraid of her answer. The room is tilting as I wonder if Death is again dancing in victory.

Strong arms circle my waist. The man I feared was lost to me now supports us both in our moment of fear-laced truth that awaits the future of our friend. I wonder if J.D. is holding his breath with worry over what awaits her. In his moment of hell, did he know the outcome of his madness, or was he able to escape the knowledge of where his shots landed? I know without a doubt one of us joined the ranks of hell today. The only thing uncertain is if heaven will gain one too.

"I can't lose her," I whisper to Lawless, who is the only thing keeping me standing.

There is no return reply, just his arms that hold me a little tighter and a head that rests a little heavier on my shoulder.

Paula is either ignoring us on purpose, or has completely forgotten us with her concentration. She has taken the bag from Rhett, placing Chapel's hand over Aimes' wound with thick, white gauze. I want to assume this is a good thing. She wouldn't waste resources if Aimes was past saving, would she?

Marxx seeing Rhett's distress is giving him silent support with one hand on his shoulder while we wait. Rhett is a ticking time bomb of rage on normal days. Not even Marxx knows what to expect from his brother this dawn if we lose Aimes.

So much betrayal and pain has been placed before Rhett, and when the tears settle, there are no promises of how Rhett will handle it. We are a huddled group awaiting news of our pixie, surrounded by the wails of those already mourning the ones they have lost. How will any of us handle what today has brought?

"I think she will make it even with the blood loss. If it was a clean shot, with no added debris other than a small piece of fabric from her shirt, then the heat from the bullet will cauterize any vessels it landed near and sterilize the actual shot. From what I can see, the path didn't hit anything vital, but I will keep a close eye on her. If an infection doesn't set in, there is no reason she won't recover completely," Paula says, wasting no time in moving to stitching the wound. She lets her words float in the air, waiting for them to sink in with each one of us as a smile sneaks upon her face.

Aimes is going to be fine. It will be a slow recovery, but she is going to be fine! A slow smile of praise spreads to us as reactions vary. Chapel's head bends back, gazing at the ceiling with silent prayers of thanks to a God he still holds close. Rhett's head comes down and his body hangs limply with his fear and tension released. Marxx pats Rhett's back with his silent emotions expressed in comfort to his brother. Lawless and I are a silent world of nerves as we cling to each other with love for our friend. No one is brave enough to utter a word that risks breaking the first small strand of hope on this once happy holiday.

"We aren't out of the woods yet. She has lost a lot of blood and is very weak. Soon as I finish these stitches, we need to move her downstairs where she can rest, and I can keep a better eye on her. If an infection is going to set in, we will know it by tonight." Paula has never sugarcoated her words. She isn't going to sprinkle sweetness now.

"Just say when," Rhett says, moving the position of his body to support Aimes' fragile weight.

"Isn't this just perfect." The voice chills the celebration. Dolph, covered in his own red horror story, is standing near us holding a look that fills his face with a fire of injustice. "J.D. - your leader - kills over half of us but his little pink princess lives. I'm sure all those crying over their dead will be so comforted to hear the news." Dolph's anger is pulsing with heat and it covers each word with bitterness. All the shyness has left the man with his emotions being a knot of torment.

"Aimes had nothing to do with this. There is no reason to place this on her," Paula says. She is not the only one stunned by Dolph's words. Unfortunately, the moment she used to reprimand Dolph, allowed Rhett to recover.

"Anything they say to the news, you just let me know. I'll have a nice talk with them right after you and I finish our little chat," Rhett says. There is no mistaking the innuendos Rhett alludes to. If there are, the shading of his eyes and expression on his face will clear them up.

"If you'll excuse us, we have to take our princess downstairs. I'll be back with shovels for your queen," Lawless says. He knew the reaction his words would stir. He had already left my side to block Dolph's path to me with his body.

Dolph's anger erupts as he rushes towards Lawless. He swings with his closed fist and wide-open eyes like a man possessed. Lawless, having learned a lot about the man from their little boxing match in the gym, is able to dodge the attack. He lands his jabs upon Dolph's body as he moves, stealing the air from his lungs. They don't fight against Chapel separating them after the first round is exchanged as they once did. Their anger is of a different type, but the look in their eyes radiates the same hatred for the other.

"Let us get Aimes to safety. Then, we will come back. We will help. We will help with it all," Chapel says. He seeks to soothe the ache of so many deaths caused by our leader and the damage from Lawless' hateful words.

"If Simon had never accepted your help to begin with, this would never have happened! Why the hell would we want to accept it now?" Dolph's question finds no answers from Chapel, and with a shove to the only man trying to help, Dolph walks back to Simon who is still mourning the loss of his wife and child.

"He's right," Chapel, the bearer of all things guilt-related, says with remorse. "All of this, it's our fault. I thought at the time it would have been harsher to loot them and let them go than to come and see what was here. I was wrong."

"The fault rests with J.D., God rest his soul, not with you. Not with any of you. You would think you would understand the difference between the truth and words said in anger with how your group carries on." Ah, there is that cold slap we have come to expect from Paula's words. She says, "Let's get this girl downstairs before Lawless provokes anymore unnecessary mayhem."

The look she gives Lawless is one well-rehearsed from many years of mothering. She motions for Rhett to lift Aimes' unconscious body and he does so, letting his anger melt away with each inch he lifts with her in his arms. His eyes grow bright with his tears as he gazes down at her. Until now, I held no knowledge of how deeply he felt for her.

With my own glare to Lawless for what just happened, I follow Rhett and Paula down a hallway I wish I could avoid. I focus on the blood that falls to the floor with the delicacy of rose petals shaken from a flower. It leaves a red trail in their wake that I do my best to step around it. Step on a crack; break your mother's back. If you step on your friend's blood, what becomes of that?

I close my senses to the many broken bodies that still lay about. I ignore the ones huddled in mournful embraces and blaming eyes as Chapel's words keep repeating in my mind. With each death I pass, I wonder if it is another sin added to my soul.

Is all of this our fault? If we had let J.D. have his fun then, would they be suffering now? If his simple ego was appeased back at the Welcome Center, would there have been a need for it to be appeased here at the school? Paula said this was J.D.'s fault, but I am starting to agree with Chapel. It was not J.D. who wanted to be here. He wanted to leave, but I stopped him. I kept them here when they were so close to leaving, and these innocent people could have escaped his wrath. I thought Aimes was going to be the last entry into my portfolio of failures, but with each body I pass, the pages grow along with the nightmares that will haunt me.

Our eyes are rimmed with red. Our hands are soaked in red. We have spread red to everything we have touched. We are covered and surrounded by the deaths of those we knew. Like flowers at a headstone, the red stains will always serve as a silent reminder of what has happened here today. As the moans mount, I am signaling my surrender. Death has won the game. He has defeated us almost completely. I truly hope it is now over. I only hope he will let us hold onto the one small victory Rhett clutches in his arms as we begin to descend into the lower level of the high school.

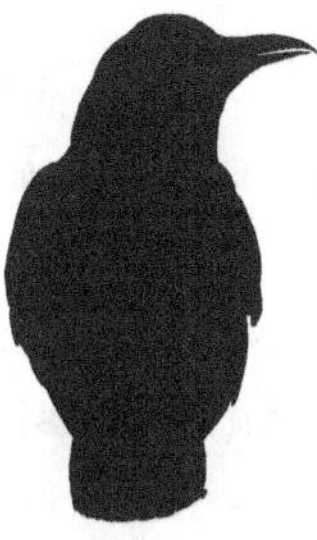

Chapter 4

The sun has finally crested the trees, sending its dazzling rays into the long windows of the bottom floor. The dead man with his broken neck seems more horrifying in the bright light of day. I refuse to glance at the woman who holds the proof we no longer need still planted in her chest. Her blood sticks to the bottom of my boots like glue in its cooled state. We trample it across the hallway, only spreading more of the red coloring I had hoped to escape. I have seen and smelled enough blood in one day alone to fill every day of a calendar with comments of its vision. After today, I have no desire to be reacquainted with it any time soon.

"Law, you left the gate open." Marxx motions with his head to the wide-open wooden doors of the courtyard to which Lawless stares at with a confused look.

"Pretty sure I didn't," Lawless says. He is lost in thought trying to force the memories from last night to the surface of his mind.

"Did they open themselves?" Marxx meant it as a jest, but no one is laughing. The mood shifts like an earthquake. We know what can open doors when others have had them closed.

"Give her to me," Marxx tells Rhett, and when he gains no response he says, "My arm is still bum. I can't fight them, but I can get her and Paula to safety."

"Wait, we don't even know if it really is them," Chapel pleads, trying to edge down the growing adrenaline.

"Take Hells." Lawless tells Marxx as he ignores the preacher's son. He is well aware of the risk that could be taking place.

"No," Rhett and I both speak the word together.

Turning his head to Marxx as he hands Aimes over to his protection. "We are down one already. She fights better than most men could anyway," Rhett says.

It is high praise from him. If only it was something I wanted to be praised for, though. Someone could tell me my hair looks nice today. That would be a better praise with how jumbled my nerves are. Yes, it is extremely "girly" and I'm okay with that.

"Anyone mind filling me in on who exactly "them" are?" Paula has gained enough insight to know whatever we are speaking of is dangerous. She just wants a better clarification on the matter.

"It's not who. It's what. The Risen." Chapel's words, even whispered to spare her a shock, caused her spine to straighten and eyes to widen. She knows the name he dubbed them months ago in a dirty bar of past lives. It was the first time we faced the truth of what was happening as a group, and since then, we have not been able to escape it.

"...but that is impossible. The chain gate should prevent them from entering. The wooden gate to the courtyard should block them if it fails. They can't open gates!" Paula stutters over the start of the sentence only to have her words crash into each other as it ends.

Trying to figure out who gets to tell her the truth of what the Risen can do, we stare at her. We know the facts well. We have seen them open doors. We have seen them fight in groups, silently sharing strategies to kill. We have seen them watch and wait, solving problems presented to them with their eyes. What chance does a fence, or a wooden-gated set of doors stand before them if they are motivated? None!

"You said so yourself, they keep pieces of their former selves. It allows them to think. It helps them figure out stuff. They adapt." It's Rhett who breaks the news to her, mumbling it while loading a fresh clip in his gun. His hands tremble a little from the many emotions he has endured today. I sense another roller coaster is about to start.

He is right. She said so herself when Marxx was bitten that they never truly die. Whatever was in the vaccine takes over the body. It shuts down the brain, making the person appear dead for moments in time until the new mind can take over. As she said, the vaccine takes over the host. It results in the pure hunters they are now where nothing alive is sacred. Not even their own family. That I remember only too well.

Her eyebrows speak the words her mouth does not. You can almost watch the conversation with just the face she is mentally holding. The scientist inside her must be fascinated with the results, but the humanitarian is struggling with the consequences. They had hoped to remove viruses from people. They have only managed to remove people with a virus.

"Marxx, follow behind me. Chapel and I will take the lead. Lawless, you and Hells keep our rear safe. Don't want anything sneaking up like a joke just when we think our shit is safe," Rhett barks the orders another man would have once given; my chosen father, J.D.

He was the man who kept us in line and encouraged us in a backhanded way. He was also our doom should we cross him. He taught us the meaning of the word "monster" this morning in his grief over the death of the prodigal son, Lawless. Lawless, who not only survived, but escaped the Risen and returned last night, only to be thrust into the chaos. It was he who then ended the life of J.D. with a single shot to his head, bringing the circle of Karma to a completion. Now he stands silent and brooding. His tongue is darting across his teeth as a sign of his growing anger or anxiety.

"Why?" Lawless' simple one-word question brings everyone to stare at us. "You heard what Dolph said. They don't want our help. Why do we keep offering it?"

"Because we are the good guys." Rhett tosses Lawless a spare clip, letting him know there is no room for argument.

Chapel half laughs looking at Rhett and asks him, "Since when?" He remembers the many past deeds they have done as a club.

"Since the real bad guys got a whole hell of a lot scarier than we are." Rhett chambers his gun, and the sound seems to echo against the plain, gray slate walls. He locks eyes with every man around him, sparing a few seconds of *and because I said so* with his face. It ends any further debates on the matter.

The resounding, agreeing chorus is the many echoes of chambered guns in response to his. Just like their Harleys, when one revs, they all rev. It has to be a boy thing. Their "boy thing" makes one thing plainly obvious to me. I don't have a gun. I am honestly about to bring a knife to a gunfight. I would have pointed that fact out, but the Risen left me no time.

The echoes from their guns proved to be a door knocker to the Risen. They inch slowly from the cafeteria, waiting for another clue to tell them where to turn. They have not seen us yet, but it will only be moments until their eyes begin to seek out what their ears no longer hear.

Seven of them stand now in the space between the cafeteria's open doors and the hall, but with the many sounds of shuffling, I know there are more. Their clothing is layers thick with stains from wear and death. Not only their death, but also the many they have brought to death. The stains swirl from rust colors to dark blacks as blood and earth mingle like a name branded upon them. Their bodies hold signs of abuse with broken fingers and torn flesh. Their flesh is spread, tainted, or bloated with decay. It holds all the shades rot can hold. If Death has ambassadors, the Risen would fill the position.

"You ready?" Lawless whispers his question to me, as I roll my eyes with frustration.

Knife to a gunfight and I'm on the front row. Tickets, please! I would love the chance to point out that Rhett wanted us on the back row, not the front!

Lawless takes the bullet from his chamber and tosses it high, sending it sailing across the herd, to hit against the wall across from us. At the sound of the sharp metallic ping, their heads turn in unison with an almost snap of attention, placing us now behind them. The first few branch off to examine the source of the noise as we hug the wall beside us, hoping to keep from their angle of sight. It is not enough. The rest still stay frozen in their statue form. I can mentally picture their eyes swaying, searching the shadows for their prey. The bullet does not bleed or have the flesh they desire. It will not hold their attention long.

"We have to get these doors closed. We can then play them off each side of the room with one group at the set of doors here and the set outside," Lawless whispers to me, as if we are wearing a matching set of knights-in-shining-armor outfits.

"You want to play Ping-Pong with the Risen?" My frustration is growing with my question and my knife is looking less and less useful with his answer.

"You have a better idea?" He meant to be serious with his question, but his sense of adventure just fills his face with mirth.

"No," I say, and I don't. This only pisses me off more.

"When I say run, run. Don't detour. Just hug the wall all the way down and get the doors closed," Lawless speaks to me as if his plan is brilliant, but I am seeing a lot of holes. I'm seeing holes that will eat me alive if given the chance.

"You want me to run right into the middle of them?"

My voice must vibrate with doubts as he smiles at me because he says, "Isn't that your normal plan?" His smile is so wide, that it makes an easy target and my knuckles itch to land a perfect bull's-eye.

"No," I say, with more bruised ego than anger, "it is not. It is just the way it happens."

"A lot," Marxx mutters, and I wonder when this conversation became a slapstick comedy hour. There are only rotting flesh-eaters ahead. Let's all stop to make some jokes!

"You ready?" Lawless' mirth is still abundant, wearing my trust a little thin.

"…or you could just wait for them to spot us while you two debate it til our deaths." Marxx sinks to the floor, supporting Aimes with his body as her weight pushes his damaged arm to its limit.

All of my anger fades as I realize my hesitation could be her death. If they spot us, Aimes cannot defend herself in this state. If we become over-ran, we would have to leave her as we fled. She would be left to them to destroy and feast. Survival isn't pretty anymore. Every day, we are taught a new lesson by it. I nod, signaling that I surrender again.

"Run," Lawless whispers.

It is such a small word to inspire so much fear. My legs falter with it before I can gain traction. My body falters with a last chance to save itself from what I am about to do again.

I hug the wall as close as I can, but still allow myself room to run. I know Lawless will be shooting over my shoulder to clear the biggest threats to me. He will have to wait though until I am closer than I want to be. The sooner he shoots, the sooner they will become aware.

My boot's flat heels click against the tiles as I see their heads cock in their hunting stage. They are attempting to use their ears to find a reason for the new noise, a noise that is slowly turning their heads towards me as I rapidly close the space between us. The glazed eyes from my nightmares will soon become focused on me. I can hear J.D. laughing in my mind, inspired by my constant mixture of "balls" and stupidity.

My hand finds the hilt of my hunting knife as easily as the knife finds the skull of the first target. It falls without a sound to signal the one in front of it to my presence, but my flesh gives me away. Each of us has a scent that is our own. A scent that we as humans no longer can notice, losing so much of the hunters we once were. The Risen are pure hunters, so they notice. They notice fast.

There is no gradual alert of me. They snap towards me, turning their bodies in whichever way they need to, with a sharp movement unlike anything I have seen from them before. The normal slow turning with strings is gone and replaced with a new attack. An attack they unleash with viciousness, reaching for me with hatred and hunger. I completely forget about the doors with them upon me.

Nails dig into my arm like a bird of prey's talons, preventing me from pulling away or risking more damage to my already pierced flesh. I scream with the fire-like pain and the female that holds me still smiles at me. My scream and the smell of my blood flowing to the floor around us bring forth a cry of victory from the cafeteria. It clenches my stomach tight and my body begins to sweat in panic. The only saving grace that I have is she only attacked my left arm. My right is still fully capable and proves it so as I arch my arm to connect the blade with her forehead.

Her eyes follow the blade and, at the last moment, she pulls me off-center with her talons, landing the blow as a deep gash to her cheek. She smiles at me as if to say, "*My turn,*" and she opens her jaw wide for her rebuttal.

Its black coloring and its rotting tissue from her many meals of blood-filled flesh surround me with the scent of plagues. All logic leaves me as I watch her. I could try to bring my knife back up, hoping to still land a blow, but she has almost twisted me with my arms crossed, using her body to counterbalance me. They shouldn't be able to plan this well. They shouldn't be able to fight this smart. I really should stop running into the middle of them.

The first shot finally comes, bouncing her head sideways with the hit. It explodes in a spray of carnage with the exit of the bullet and she falls limp. She tears the flesh of my arm with her fall and I follow her down out of sheer self-preservation. The shots come quicker now with our cover being blown. There is no reason to hold back. Unless you take into account the not limitless amount of ammo we have, but being at the bottom of a pile of rotting monsters again that are trying to eat me, I'm voting shoot now, worry later.

My arm feels limp as if it's on fire, but my job is to get the doors closed. I can do that with one hand. I use the cover fire to crawl to the open metal doors as more Risen are rushing out of them towards me.

Bodies are collapsing around me from the well-aimed shots. They bounce against the floor, leaving their eyes wide and staring at me. It unsettles my heart even more. Seeing the mass of horrors heading towards me unsettles it completely.

Wrestling my mind free from its enslavement of fear, I force my body to move again. Sliding across the floor to avoid taking a shot, I only come to kneeling to reach for the metal handles. The first door is easy. It closes with an eagerness compared to my own to block the running horde. The second door is held open with a wedge and my frantic pulling has managed to lodge it underneath the metal. Pushing the door open again, I kick at the crudely shaped wooden block, hoping to spin it enough so that it will slide and not become jammed again even as it laughs at my attempts. I am not standing tall enough to give me the leverage that I need. It only inches with each kick as the horde is closing the distance with my delay.

Lawless bounces the door off his palms with a thrust before turning his attention to the room. It gives the door the needed separation for me to pull the wedge free. He fires one shot into the room, hitting the one closest to the disappearing gap. Their bodies collide with the doors at the same instant they close, bowing them open before we can brace to close them again. Their pounding fists vibrate the metal, echoing through our palms.

Fingernails torture the paint as they claw, sending squeals of protest from the doors. The doors pop open with the many combined desires. I don't know how long he and I can hold them at bay.

Sensing my thoughts, Lawless grunts with the efforts to fight and says, "Rhett and Chapel have already gone around to the main courtyard. They are going to draw their attention from that entrance." He flips, using his back to brace better. "They will pick off what they can before shutting their doors. We will just keep repeating." He looks at me and asks, "Did you get an idea of how many are in there?"

"A lot. What if they are in the courtyard too?"

His face twists with his efforts as the doors pop open, bouncing us against the cold metal before we push them shut again. He says, "We didn't see any through the windows. Paula checked. She and Marxx are already headed for the gym with Aimes."

His words are chopped short with our bodies bouncing off the metal doors. My feet are losing against the slippery floor. They slide out from under me, made slick by the blood from upstairs on them and the blood that is now splashed in puddles around us. It leaves long, red trails smeared across the once grey, boring floor. I miss the boring floors and my mind wanders with the thought.

"Law, how thick do you think these doors are?" I ask.

He laughs a short sound of masculine amusement before saying, "I don't think they can dig through."

"Could a bullet?"

His amusement fades to one of shock with my question. "Shit," he says, and pulls us both to the floor as the first shot comes from the room behind us.

Chapter 5

The weight against the door halts, suspended between pushing and letting it fall back closed. The faces that once were covered with expressions of anger now slacken with their confusion. Their eyes are still glued to us between the gap in the doors, but they are no longer trying to reach through it. Their bodies still crave us. Their minds have just become more concerned with something else. Something they have learned is dangerous.

I can hear Rhett taunting them. The doors muffle his voice, but it still reaches me. "Here, freaks," he taunts them. "White meat or dark meat? I got them both for you right here. Come and get it!"

"Charming..." I whisper from the floor, mentally picturing the hand gestures he used to match his words. I can feel the gore sticking to me while the empty eyes from those we have already killed stare at me.

"Stay down," Lawless says. He pushes against my back to keep me from rising as the shots sound behind us.

I would almost rather take my chances with their bullets than to remain laying face-to-face with the bodies around us. When the shots slow, so does my heart.

"What are they doing?" I ask.

Lawless shrugs with a smile. "Wasn't blessed to have Superman for a dad, but knowing Rhett, he is reinventing duck, duck goose."

"I'm glad you find this all amusing."

His smile disappears at my tone. "Yeah, it's a laugh a minute around here," he says.

"Law, I didn't mean…" I stop, refusing to go on with his dedicated stare at the wall in front of us. He is straining to hear every noise from the other side of the doors and to not hear me at all.

here is no noise. The room is silent now. I worry we missed some signal saying it was our turn, or worse. Lawless' face wears the same concerns. He stares at the door over his shoulder as if he could see through it, demanding it to give up its secrets.

"It's cleared." Chapel's voice comes from down the hall, and it startles us both. He tells us, "Weren't as many as we thought, but we have a problem."

"What problem?" Lawless asks. The front of his shirt is as thick with the muck from the floor as mine. Like two twins of battle, we wait for the other two men to reach us.

"The other doors show signs of them. We locked the cafeteria to prevent any from sneaking back in," Chapel says once he reaches us.

"What do you mean "signs"?" I ask, but I really don't want to know. I never really want to know.

"Scratches, dents, that sort of thing," Rhett says, shrugging with his explanation as if it is just another day. I wish I had just a shot glass' worth of his crazy.

If I thought Lawless and I look like survivors of something horrible, I was wrong. Rhett is covered in dark splatters that cling to his arms and adds a shine to the leather vest. The spot where he held Aimes to him now blends with the new carnage. If battle carried a face, it would be his.

"Duck, duck, goose?" I repeat Lawless' idea while staring at the tall man covered in his venting. Lawless smirks, but the other two looks at each other before back at us. "Never mind," I say.

"What do you want to do?" Lawless recovers the conversation that I lured into paused confusion.

"Split up," Chapel suggests. "We need to make sure they aren't walking into a trap, but we can't leave until we make sure the things aren't all over the place."

Lawless nods and says, "Hells and I will cover down here. You two can catch up with the others and make sure they get Aimes to safety."

I nod in agreement and with the majority, except for one.

"No," Rhett tells us. "Hells and I will clean up down here. You and Chap go check on them."

Lawless starts to argue, but Rhett ignores him while inspecting my arm. I had forgotten about it with all that was going on, but now the burning pain flares back to life as I stare at it and he probes it with his fingers. Out of sight, out of mind.

"Gonna need to bind that," Chapel says, staring at the wound. "Looks like stitches later."

"Even more reason for you two to hurry up and make sure they made it." Rhett urges them forward with a glare and a hint of what may be happening to the others. It works. Law isn't happy about it, but it works.

He caresses my lower back as he passes by me, but we don't look at each other. Our death toll is mounting, even though it's still early in the day. We are both too afraid to admit the very real truth that this could be the last time we see one another. We don't have time for long goodbyes. Aimes and Marxx may be in danger, so every moment stalled could cost them – costing us.

Rhett rips the shirt from one of the dead bodies on the floor and shrugs with my disgust. He is completely honest with his voice when he says, "What? Not like he is using it. I prefer to keep a little something between me and them or I'd offer you mine."

"I don't think putting a dirty "rag" on an open wound is the best idea. Pretty sure I read that somewhere."

"Did you now? Well, Barbie, I would love to offer you something better, but we are kind of in the shit of it at the moment. We need to cover the smell of your blood, and this will do that, but I'll remind Paula to clean it really good for you if we live, okay?" He cinches the cloth tight with his last statement. I wince not only from the pain, but his tone, too.

He walks away from me in the opposite direction Chapel and Lawless took. The hall looms around us, suddenly much more alarming knowing that around any corner they could be waiting.

"What's the real reason you split us up like this?" I ask him, as I trail a few steps behind.

"He can't focus if you are near. He will be too worried about you and not have his mind on what is around him. We don't know how many made it in or how outnumbered we are."

"You are worried about us being outnumbered, but we split up anyway?" I ask, and he doesn't answer me. I guess I wasn't supposed to see the flaw in the plan so early. "You don't think he could keep me safe?"

Rhett chuckles as his eyes roam ahead of us. He is looking for anymore 'signs' letting the conversation remove the edge of the fear we are both feeling. He says with his predatory smile, "Sweetheart, you don't need anyone to keep you safe. You were kicking these things' ass while the rest of us were still trying to figure out what they were. I was more worried he wouldn't be able to keep himself safe. Love makes men into heroes, and heroes make good victims."

I don't want to talk about heroes or victims, so I focus on the task we have set and say, "The only other place this leads is the library and the main office. Simon keeps the office locked."

"Library it is."

"Library it is." I echo as its double doors come into view. The place where I once hid to avoid the man who stands in front of me may be hiding something else now, something even the pages of the books within could not contain.

Rhett stands motionless in front of the doors. It's hard to form a plan when one is blind to what is on the other side. I remember the layout. I am about to be Zombie Barbie again and my Ken is something more from a slasher film than a prince charming tale. It seems fitting.

"There is a block of space when you first enter where the librarian's desk sits. Once you have passed it, you have tables with chairs for reading in groups and the computer tables. The bookshelves follow behind them. They are floor to ceiling, but some shelves are half of the wall along the outside wall. I can lead us in," I say, trying to help him picture the room.

"Then ladies first," he says while smiling at me. I really hadn't counted on him taking me up on that offer.

I walk around him to center myself in front of the doors. One last deep breath to convince my heart and my mind that I can do this and away we go. The doors open slowly against my palm, revealing the room inch-by-inch. I'm starting to develop a serious phobia with double-metal doors.

No sound greets me. No snarling face jumps out to startle me. The room is silent and seems to be empty. "Seems" being the keyword and I would almost rather have them waiting for me at the door with dinner forks in their hands.

Rhett holds the door open for me with the "*I dare you*" smile still on his face. I used to wonder how his mind worked. I'm kind of over that.

I tell him, "I guess I don't have to worry about you being a hero."

"Sweetheart, what I have for you isn't love, but I'd be a victim all the same," he tells me. The humor is supposed to take the edge off what we are about to do. It gives us each a moment to prepare for what we are avoiding, the Risen.

"Don't let me die." I whisper to him, and take my first step into the room.

I feel his answer against my hair as he keeps the space tight between us. "Have I yet?" he asks me, and I can't argue with him. Well, at least not yet.

Chapter 6

I imagine something jumping out at me with every step I take. Like a twisted game of peek-a-boo, I picture them leaning out from a dark corner, but they don't. Monsters are never that accommodating.

Rhett motions to me that he will take one side of the many rows of long shelves while I am to walk parallel on the other side. His fascination with the splitting up idea goes against everything my heart is beating. You're supposed to divide and conquer the other side, not your own.

The windows of this room cast long shadows of the shelves with the sun's light. The shadows seem to reach out for us like the jagged claws of a great beast. The chairs I once lounged in appear to have aged with my absence. Thick pools of darkness now gather under the long tables. The room that was once my refuge is no longer my friend. It doesn't take us long to find out to whom it now belongs.

He stands with his back to us staring at a turning display of magazines. He might have been mistaken for someone scanning the many titles of gossip on another day, but this isn't another day. This is where his mind has shut off while he waits for something to hunt.

Rhett smiles with the irony of the man's pose. He whispers to me, "Think he reads the articles or just looks at the pictures?"

This ones' death is easy. Rhett takes full advantage of his blocked view with a casual walk to the man. With the same sense of nonchalant, he forces the blade of his large hunting knife into the back of the man's skull. It was a soundless death. Rhett is almost disappointed with the lack of danger. With the same ease and the same smile, he steps over the body as he searches for more with his big ole' bucket of crazy to keep him brave.

The next one is on my side of the shelves. She is wobbling back and forth. The motion follows her whole body in a lethargic sway. She stares at me a few moments before she actually sees me. It allows me to close the gap between us before she can attack. As her snarl spreads, my blade finds its mark. I watch gravity pull her from me as her eyes go back to dull and blank and it's another quick and clean kill. My heart begins to slow its pace with the smile that Rhett flashes to me. Have we finally caught a break or are the Demi-Gods just busy with someone else?

Rhett is already moving on like a silent killer. He said we are the good guys now because we are no longer the scariest things in this place. As I watch his face set with the joy of his hunt, I'm not so sure about that.

The snarl that escaped from the woman has gained the attention of the rest of the room. The room that I had thought to be empty is proving to be abundant. The Demi-Gods weren't busy with anyone else. They were just waiting until I was a better toy to be played with. The space between the shelves is starting to fill with sounds of them awakening. Grumbles and growls become something more menacing when their eyes find mine. What started as curiosity is now eagerness with their discovery. I stopped counting when the many divided rows became one. Actually, I stopped counting when I realized that if I kept counting, I would have started screaming.

Men and women of various backgrounds stare at me. Their clothing ranges from jeans and t-shirts to suits and ties, all stained and worn from what they have become now. The virus didn't discriminate between white or black, rich or poor. It turned them all. Now, they all kill with the same lack of segregation.

I can't stop my feet from going backward. My body has learned from my past experiences. It wants to endure no repeats. With Rhett nowhere to be found, my frantic heart pushes my nerves to their breaking point. My heart is beating so hard I can feel the vibrations through my body. My legs become soft with my fears, making my retreat clumsy. My first stumble excites them. They grow bolder in their stalking with almost- smiles and pre-victory sounds. It saps my resolve even more.

"Rhett!" I shout to someone, somewhere in the room, "Now would be a good time to see about that whole not-dying deal!"

The first row took my shout as an invitation to dinner and they rush me. My slow retreat has already brought me to the edge of one of the long tables. With a gymnastic skill that only fear can provide, I quickly mount and cross it to keep some away with the obstacle between us. The group is so over-eager to feed, it ruins their normal methodical hunting skills. They pile against the table, trying to force it to move with the sheer number of them, but the tables are bolted to the floor. It's not moving, not for them and not for me to keep it between us. I know it won't be long until they have figured out, they can simply move around it as I did. Once they do, I'm not sure what I will do.

Their outstretched arms reach for me. They swipe the air with anger over my elusiveness. The shouts that come from them are of rage-filled desperation. They are starving, drooling over the thoughts of food that is only inches away.

If there were less of them, I might be able to take a few down, but the clumped group stands too close for me to fight them. If I reach my arms in, my limbs will be torn apart like an overeager scavenger hunt for my flesh. My death would be quick as they set their teeth into my many veins.

I can't run and leave Rhett either. I am out of ideas and I'm out of options. When the first one starts to climb over the table, I know I am also out of time.

He crawls slowly over the table. He is testing it, but his eyes never leave me. It is a slow, predator climb, making my body become locked with tension. Behind him, the rest of his pack has stilled as they watch. They are also waiting to see if it works before following him. The tables creaking cocks his head, but he never stops. His destination is straight ahead of him. It's me.

He pulls away from the group. It is exactly what I needed. He is even gracious enough to come headfirst. Yes, those Demi-wenches are obviously not watching the show on this channel.

He senses the change in me. It's a subtle shift for both of us. He increases his speed and I increase my need to survive. I wait with my heart rushing in my ears for him to reach me. The white noise overcomes me. That simple, peaceful state-of-mind drowns out all sounds. It removes all my doubts and fears, replacing them with one simple logic - kill or be killed. It's nothing personal for him or for me. We both just want to survive.

His momentum brings him to me. I use his eagerness to counterbalance my lack of strength. With his help, I plant the blade into the space between the eyes that have watched me from his serial killer mind. It is not an instant death and I force the blade deeper into the skull to reach my target. It takes his brain a moment to catch up with the damage I have caused him. He stops, but his eyes still watch me until the false life that uses them fades completely. My victory dance becomes just a cry to battle.

They harbor no more hesitation and finally, Rhett doesn't either. Focusing their attention on me, the Risen never noticed the real threat standing directly behind them. Rhett is able to shoot into the clumped group, so they fall in short patterns of lines, like dominoes. His smile says it all. It says a little too much, and I duck as the barrel swings towards the center of the group.

As the last one falls, I watch his shoes wade through the piles. Their bodies roll when he kicks them as he passes through. I would like to think it's for safety reasons, but I'm sure a part of him just enjoys the act.

He kneels under the table to find me. I am staring into eyes that have not yet completely lost their predatory gleam. "What does that say about my aim when you feel the need to hide?" he asks me. "Hurt a man's pride like that…" he says. His smile is a good-natured jest, but Rhett always has a fine line that makes you pause before you return his smile.

He offers me a hand covered in the aftermath of the cafeteria like a dare. I stare at it, feeling my stomach roll from the many layers that cover it. Returning a shade of the same smile, I grasp it and allow him to pull me to him. You don't ever allow Rhett to find your weakness. He will turn it into a hobby, and as it is, he already knows plenty of things about me to keep him very busy if he so wanted.

"Took you long enough," I say to him. I'm not even trying to hide my annoyance over once again being the bait armed with only a hunting knife.

"Sorry," he tells me with a shrug, "takes time to line 'em up." He checks the remaining clip giving further reasons for delay and says, "I'm running low; didn't want to waste any shots."

For the third time today, I am surrounded by the dead and the clock has yet to strike noon. Some expressions must have peeked through the composure I am fighting to wear on my face. Rhett's eyebrow arches with a silent question, but I shake my head and head to the library door. If I allow myself this moment to break down, it will turn into hours, which we don't have.

"Stop."

It's one simple command; a short, hushed word he says, but with his tone, it holds the power of a bomb. We forgot one. She watches us while standing near the librarian's desk in a cardigan-covered dress that seems so painfully appropriate. Her blonde hair is still piled on her head from where she had looped it through her ponytail from days long ago. She has watched from her side of the room with silent self-preservation or plotting. Neither of those makes for a good ending.

Her arms are torn fragments of the flesh they once were. Her right cheek is shredded with claw marks and the connective tissue hangs in patterned holes peeking through to yellowing teeth like delicate crochet. Most people would be nervous about seeing her standing there. For some, it might even be terrifying. For Rhett, it is all amusement. He was made for a world of dark things and desperate moments. He was made for this world when it has broken so many others. Grabbing a book from one of the tables, he never pauses. He never slows his steps or alters his path. He may as well have been walking up to an old friend to say hello – or goodbye.

She doesn't fight him. She doesn't show any emotions at all as she watches him stalk towards her. When he raises his hand with the hardbound book, she accepts her death with the same blank face. Rhett smashes the spine of the book into her head, driving her to the ground with the force of it. Repeatedly, he forces it into the bones of her skull until they give way under his vengeance, crumbling underneath his assault and leaking the decaying fluids they once contained around her. What does it say about someone when the monsters view them as the bigger monster and simply accept death as unavoidable?

Rhett reads my confused look as something I'm feeling over the outcome, not the act. He shrugs, looking at the book in his hand that is now covered in thick pieces of the woman before dropping it to the floor. "It was a boring cover, anyway," he tells me before tearing the yellow cover with its black out-lined angle from the book and dropping it to the floor.

It lands perfectly by the dead librarian's hand as if the location was staged and not just another ironic twist life continues to offer us. Like a present or an apology, he shyly hands me the rest of the book that only days ago gave me comfort when no one else would. It's now topless and wet, exactly how Rhett enjoys his subject matters.

Chapter 7

"Do you even have a reason as to why we are still alive?" Rhett and I have walked our side finding only a few pairs of stragglers that were easy to kill, to his disappointment. With an insistence to be thorough, we even broke into the main office to be sure it was clear. That was the reason he gave, but we both knew he just enjoyed breaking in. Now covered in our blood, their blood, and others' blood, we run to hopefully find the rest of our family still alive with my question hanging between us.

"One," Rhett starts, "because we were born. Two, because we haven't died, yet." His face is completely serious with his answer. It reminds me why I don't come to Rhett for motivational speeches. He will simply kill the monster under the bed for you. He won't help you overcome your fear of it.

"Look," he tells me, "we survive because we are together, not because of you or me or anyone else alone, but because we take care of each other."

"What will we do now?" I ask him. I hadn't meant for it to be such a heavy question or that of one sounding like a child, but it is.

"I don't know. I really don't."

J.D. was many different things to many different people. His loss is the same combination. Mix the hanging fate of Aimes into that, and now there is no true north.

Chapel is sitting on one of the hallway's benches in front of the entrance to the gym. His head is lowered, cradled in his hands. We both take it as a bad sign. Rhett rushes through the doors, willing to face whatever the news may be, but not me. My legs are locked as I stare at Chapel. His lips are frantically moving with his internal thoughts. It doesn't take long for me to figure out that he is praying. I'm just too scared to ask for what or for whom.

"You okay?" I ask him. I hope it will give me an idea of what is waiting beyond the doors.

His voice is thick with cloaked emotions as he says simply, "Yeah."

"Does that work for you?"

He holds a hand out for me to take, lending me the strength that he and I both know that most of the time I just fake. "Yeah," he says again, gently leading me to sit beside him.

We sit side-by-side in silence, just allowing our presence to be the other's comfort. The preacher's son never turns his soul-seeing eyes to me, and I am grateful. I don't know what he would see right now.

"Why?" I ask, breaking the fragile silence first.

"Why what?"

"Why does it work for you?"

He sighs, bowing his head again and tells me, "We don't all have an Aimes in our life."

The mention of her name and the silence is a burden again. It's a heavy burden that crushes the wind from my lungs.

"Praying for you is like Aimes and I?" I whisper her name, afraid to speak it aloud as if it might be the last time I do.

He looks at me, feeling my question in his mind before answering it. "I can say what I need to say. Even the things I don't say, He knows. He doesn't judge either way."

"I thought the whole "judgment" thing went hand-in-hand with Him?"

"No," he says, looking at me with that gaze I was so afraid of moments ago, "that's mankind." There is a deep emotion to his voice that leaves no room for doubts about the life he has lived. I can't meet his eyes. Instead, I stare at his hands. I stare at the cross ring he always wears, which used to shine with the many white stones it holds. Now that shine is gone as the blood from my friend dries in every crevice it owns.

"Is Aimes…?" I can't say the word, but he knows what I am asking.

"No. Paula says she'll be fine. Just needs a few days to recover." He tucks my hair behind my ear and runs his knuckles tenderly down my cheek. That same thick voice tells me, "We have a lot of shit to do still. Perhaps it's best if you don't go in there, not yet. Let everything settle down inside you first."

Until this, we have all ignored Chapel. However, he was not the man who now sits here beside me, either. We have all had to change or be destroyed by what our lives have become. J.D. broke, but the man he viewed as our weakest link, strengthened. As he gives me words to excuse me from my fears, I can't imagine this life without him.

"She is sure that Aimes is going to be okay?"

"There's always a risk, but she's already gained some color back. It's a good sign, Hells." His voice is soft, comforting as he reassures me.

"I can't lose her." That sentence frees all of the emotions inside of me. Everything I have shut down and ignored rips forth in an exhale that shakes my body. I would collapse before God myself if He would spare her. I would blunder through every prayer I know if He would only hear me. I have offered my life to Death in exchange for hers already. I would give God the same trade if He cared.

Chapel crushes me to him. He hides me in the strength of his arms while I cry, rocking me into a peaceful place like the child I yearn to become again, safe and treasured. His heartbeat pounds against my ear with his own suffering. It's not just Aimes that has us clinging to each other, but J.D. and Shelia and all the other names seared into our hearts. Every new loss is the opening of wounds that never heal. The wounds left by those who have already gone. It is a reminder of all those we couldn't save and didn't save. When Death takes someone from you, he reminds you of all the others he stole too.

"I can't do it anymore," I whisper into his chest.

"You're the strongest person I know," Chapel says. I can feel the vibration of his words as they rumble in his chest. Somehow, it's comforting to a part of me that is very girly and that I very much dislike. "You just have to find the courage to get through each hour. Just focus on each hour. Soon, the hours will turn into days, the days into weeks and so forth until this is all over."

"What if it's never over?"

"Eventually Helena, it's over for us all."

His words startle me some. Like a prophecy of fate, you know it's coming, but you deny it. Somewhere down the long tunnels of my mind, I hear Lilly laugh, I smell the soft scent of Conroy's shampoo and I can see Ashley's blue eyes with their defeated tears. Eventually, it's over for us all.

"Pull it together," Chapel tells me, but it's not part of the pep talk. It's a warning. The muffled voices from behind the wall grow closer. Rhett is returning with the rest of what is left of our family.

I used my walls once to protect myself. Now, I use those same walls to protect them. The men have just left the bedside of our treasured pixie. They need strength now, not more sorrows.

Lawless holds the door for me after the rest have passed through. His eyebrows arch as he waits for me, confused by my delay. I'm just as lost, but not by confusion, by fears I have no words to explain. I can wade into death, but the thought of walking into a room where my best friend lies injured and suffering makes me powerless.

"We have to get upstairs," I say to him, as weak as a child in the dark. The disappointment on his face is searing. I watch as he stretches his neck, turning his face away from me as he chews back the words with which he wants to lash out.

"She's right. We don't know if any made it up there yet." Marxx nods, but he sees through me. His eyes stare at me intently as he says,

"We came across a few, but there should be more of them with the amount of damage Chapel was talking about."

"We found a crew in the library, but yeah, there should be more." Rhett's eyes have taken a far-off gaze as he tries to figure out where else the Risen could be. He says, "We left a gun with Paula and had her lock the doors. She should be good." Rhett shrugs, happy with his logic and ready to move on. Rhett's mind has a five-minute cycle. He is already thinking about the next possible task, killing.

"So, what's the plan?" Chapel's voice is still deep from his pain. It tugs at my own and I swallow against the burning pressure.

Marxx answers with his eyes still measuring me. He says, "Go upstairs. Check it out. We don't let them know what we found down here. They have enough shit to work through."

"Yup," Lawless says, as he pushes through the little group we have formed. "We wouldn't want to upset anyone." His double-edged words are sharp and the slice they leave on my heart makes me wince. He doesn't spare us a backward glance to see if we are following him and he doesn't care if we do or if we don't. Lawless has started the climb to the leadership of their crew. In their world, a strong leader doesn't hold your hand, he takes you by the throat and holds you in your place. That grasp reminds you of whom you respect not how to gain respect. I should be walking by his side, but he has left me behind with the guys as well. His grasp isn't around my neck. It's a much stronger hold. He has my heart, but it still leaves me choking just the same.

Chapel, the one of us who has adjusted the best to change, falls in behind him first. Marxx follows next leaving only Rhett and me to silently choose our path. Our faces both hold a look of concern, but his is a different set of eyes that watches. Feeling my stare, he slides those lethal eyes to me and lets me see a glimpse of his thoughts before he goes blank. Rhett will not bow down again. The man who monsters fear will not pay homage to their prince, and with J.D. gone, there might not be anyone who can keep our deadly master of games in line.

Chapter 8

The entrance to the hallway is the same as we had left it. The dead still stare out with their blank eyes and slack expressions. The Christmas tree's limbs have started to sag with the layers of crimson pulling them down. The fresh pine scent is tainted with the metallic undertones from the blood that covers it.

Do you know what day it is? Aimes' voice whispers through my mind, rattling my breath.

Rhett's hand roams my lower back as he pushes me forward. His eyes are still the blank, dangerous warning, but his hand with its stroking thumb lends me the comfort I need. I focus on the small, warm pattern of his thumb along my spine. I let his constant, gentle push guide me forward with each forced step. I have walked through so many things I wish I could erase from my mind. I have endured what others may have given up over and it's all wearing my heart raw and threadbare. A part of me craves the lost ability to submit and hide as I watched the days flow past with their constant pattern of predictability. I want to go back to that oblivious life. With as much as I want it, a part of me knows I can never be that girl again.

I lift my head and push down all the doubts that nag me. I lock the doors to all the rooms in my mind which threaten to open with their fanged demons. I slow my heart to the pattern of our steps, refusing to let it carry me into a panic. I can't go back so I might as well keep going forward. Even if forward is dark and frightening with its hidden agendas, I will meet it head on. Not because I want to, but because I have to.

Rhett smiles as he feels my spine stiffen under his palm. We don't acknowledge the intimate exchange out loud. We don't even look at each other. We simply fall in step and follow the rest of the group into the sobbing and the fight we both know is waiting for us. His hand falls from me, but not before his fingertips press against the lowest section of my back. This he does acknowledge with a wink from his pale, angry eyes.

The screams have drowned to the grief that only silence can accompany. All words have been used and have fallen short. Those who are embracing the ones who have lived in guilty gratitude and those who are lost in their memories of the ones they have lost divide the hallway. One common enemy unites them all - us.

Those once grateful, perhaps even envious of our little family, no longer harbor any admiration for us. They pull each other closer as we pass as if we could spread some disease of misfortune. Perhaps we could with how everything has played out. Some do not even try to hide their belief in our faults.

Marxx has to be restrained as one male spits at our feet as we pass. The man's grief has encased him with rage. He stands over the body of a dead female. He has arranged her to look as if she is sleeping with closed eyes and palms pressed to the floor. She is a modern-day Sleeping Beauty with her blonde hair fanned around her. In death, her skin tone still holds a pale ethereal entrancement and her lips cling to their pink tint even as it slowly fades. A simple kiss from a prince and it should spare this tragedy, but it won't. None of us are spared - not this father and not his daughter.

"You did this," the man shouts over the arms, pulling him from Marxx. He continues with his screaming, "You let him kill my daughter! We all saw how unstable he was. Why didn't you stop him?"

"We didn't know," Chapel lies. He lies with the bruising still on his face from his broken nose. He lies not with malice, but praying for mercy. Yearning for the punishment he feels he deserves; he has placed himself between Marxx and the man. Chapel will take the judgment. He craves it.

The man sneers with his rage into the face of Chapel. He stands toe to toe with the taller man with his anger giving him courage and says, "Isn't this what your type does? You kill, and prey on those you think weaker than you?"

Rhett laughs a deep chuckle as he wraps an arm around Chapel's shoulder. He blocks the view of Lawless pulling Marxx backward from the grieving father and says with his warning smirk, "Yeah man, that's what we do. We ride around town beefing with other MCs over territories, run drugs, all that crazy O.K. Corral shit just like whatever television show you've been watching." Rhett leans dangerously close and whispers beside the man's head, "It's a good thing that's all television bullshit because if you really thought we were like that, you'd know what I'd have to do to you now for spitting on a member of my club."

Rhett lets his words sink in as he pulls slowly away from the man to stare into his eyes. I watch as the emotions flicker across the man's face. He wants to hold on to his rage. He wants to stand firm and brave thinking it will be an act of justice to take out his anger on us, but another emotion that is harder to fight against slows his breathing and pulls him a slight step backward. Rhett smiles knowing he has the man now. I have learned from Rhett that you never back down to what you fear because once you have, you can never meet its eyes again and the man can't. Rhett played a game of truth or dare, and the man isn't willing to call dare, but Rhett is.

"Bury your daughter, man. Take care of your shit. I'm sorry for your loss, but if you ever pull something like that again…." Rhett lets the ending hang, and the silence says more than any words he might have chosen.

"I'm sorry." Chapel's voice holds the pain he is feeling, and it connects with the man. It's a verbal handshake of a greeting that no parent wants. With his voice, Chapel lets the other man know that he knows the man's suffering as only a father can. It's a balm to the man and he nods, but the anger is still a flicker of a candle's flame in his eyes.

Rhett pats Chapel's chest to signal the show is over. When Marxx looks to the man, I know it's not. It's just stalled until everyone can put the pieces of this day back together. Tomorrow, I'll worry about it tomorrow. Right now, I just want the chance to clean up today, a shower, a few hours of sleep, and Aimes' smiling face again. Marxx told me once that it was from me, she gained her strength. Standing here in the middle of a ring of hell, I'm not so sure he was right.

Her one-liners would have diffused this situation before the threats could have been shared. She would have had us shaking our heads with her mangled logic and forgetting we are deep in the puddles of the blood that are drying into shameful stains. Stains that no matter what Chapel may have told the man is are our fault. We knew this was going to happen. We underestimated J.D. and like so many others in his past, it could cost us everything; our home, our new bonds, our security, and our pixie – everything.

At one time, I would have told Marxx to grow up and stormed past them all. I would have taken the lead and left them to stew in their injured male pride. I was not this girl hanging in the back, huddled waiting with the choked breath, caged in fear over what they are going to do. That frustration is still with me. It's stalking the walls of my mind like a large cat with the dark thoughts that it whispers to me. I could focus on it, pulling it forward to shield the truth of how I am feeling, but I'm tired of being the fighter. I want to be just a survivor for one day, but that's not me. White flags are not my style even when they really should be.

My deep inhaled breath twitches Lawless' eyes to me as if he just remembered I was still here. It's the ignition I needed. "You boys done measuring your dicks? I'd like to check on Simon."

It's overly cruel for what has happened, I know, but it works. All eyes swing to me and I force my face to go blank. It deflates their puffed chests like an abused balloon. If I have learned anything from my time with G.R.I.T., it's that men don't respond well to subtle and we don't have a lot of time to waste. They really aren't amused by a lack of appreciation for their "manhood" either.

"Unless you're willing to hold the measuring stick, yeah, I'm good," Rhett tells me, with a new light to his eyes. His lips hold the trademark of trouble and when he looks to Lawless. I know it's not me he is toying with.

Lawless meets his stare and returns his own smirk with a head nod before saying, "Yeah, we all are friends here." Lawless pulls Marxx forward by the vest that unites them, never removing his stare from Rhett.

The cat in my mind roars with annoyance. It pushes me forward, lending my legs the prowling walk of its nature. "One big happy family," I say, as I walk through the cluster of them. "Let's go bury Daddy."

Their smiles melt. The corners of their mouths are pulled down, frowning over the momentarily forgotten event that has slipped from their minds. The clicking of my boots is the only sound in the hall now. I let it echo around me as I leave them behind.

"Changed my mind," I hear Rhett say behind me. "I'm afraid of what she might do with the measuring stick."

"That's why we don't give her a gun." Marxx' gruff voice is followed by their footsteps landing one more notch to my annoyance.

A thousand responses are crawling along with my tongue, but my bullshit meter is maxed already. He is right. If they had given me a gun when this all began, they would all probably have flesh wounds by now. Only flesh wounds, I promise. I bite back my bitterness and glance over my shoulder with a look that lets them know I heard them before heading towards the mourners with whom I am most concerned. I head towards the body of a man I called father as we leave a father behind.

Simon has laid his daughter, Kira, beside the body of his wife. He sits between them both, holding their hands with his head bowed. Someone has placed a cloth over Shelia's head. Her blood is a dark discoloration in the plaid-like patterns, but it shields Simon from having to stare at the ruins of his wife's once-perfect face. Kira has no covering. There is nothing to shield us from the deformed, tiny skull that rests tilted from the damage it has received. Her youthful perfection, just like her precious life, was forever stolen from her. Simon doesn't want this truth covered. He wants us all to see it, to really see it.

Dolph and I stare at each other over Simon. I am trying to put the missing pieces of time together by reading his face, but he shows me nothing. Richard stands near him with sadness pulling his shoulders low. The way his body sags, he looks as if the emotion has a greater sense of gravity than the pull of the earth. How do you comfort your friend who has lost his whole family in a matter of hours? My head swings to look at Chapel before I can stop myself. A lot of people say they are in their own private ring of hell daily. With Chapel having to watch his own story unfold over and over again, I know he really is.

I am aware the moment when Lawless and Rhett come into view for Dolph and Richard. I know because they no longer hold the posture of defeat. Their bodies rise as they inhale, pulling their heads and shoulders back. They come closer to Simon as if fearing what the other two males may say or do. When Simon notices their movement, he awakens from his grief-stricken trance and peers around with blinking eyes as if he had forgotten where he was. His mind was lost in the past to avoid traveling in the future. For him, it is now a future that will always be shaded with the shadows of his past.

"You're still here?" Simon's voice is flat and bare of any depths. It mirrors his face and eyes. "Figured you would have run off and left us to sort out the mess."

Dolph motions with a jab of his chin to where J.D. still lays in the pool of his blood. He looks directly to Lawless and asks, "Come to take out the trash?"

I don't know who moved to whom first because the explosion from Dolph's words was instant. Chapel and I have to brace against the floor to keep the groups apart as Simon watches with his empty eyes.

The shouting and accusations are disjointed and competing for damage as the two groups of men exchange them. Chapel and I shout amid the chaos, but it goes unheard. The tension that has been a stewing pot since the gym is finally boiling over having a real reason to fight.

Dolph stands chest-to-chest with Lawless as they stare, daring the other to take the first swing. Marxx is blocking Richard from the two men in a reverse style as Rhett had before.

Rhett blocked the man to settle down the fight, protecting Marxx. Marxx is blocking Richard to allow Lawless *to* fight. Marxx is protecting him, but for a different reason.

"Did you do this on purpose?" Dolph asks Lawless, baiting him into action. "You slink away in the night with some bullshit story of a close call just to see how this would all play out? You get the girl and leadership in one moment of lying glory."

"Yeah, that's what I did," Lawless tells him, smirking into the sneering face of Dolph. Lawless steps into that small fraction of space Dolph left between them. They are not just face-to-face anymore but almost cheek-to-cheek. He lowers his voice and asks, "What's the matter Dolph? You pissed because I'm back or are you pissed because I have *her* back?"

Dolph lifts his head, struck by what Lawless has asked, and looks to me before looking back to Lawless without realizing the action.

"Yeah, I know," Lawless says, leaning even closer to say into Dolph's ear, "I haven't got time to deal with you right now. So, you can either go back and stand in your corner and let us do the heavy lifting around here like you have been doing, or you can get your shit together and do something useful. I really don't care which option you choose, just stay out of my way. We have enough people to bury today, but what's a few more holes to dig if I have to." Lawless shrugs with his last words, expressing just how little it would affect him.

Marxx shoves Richard away and tells him, "That goes for you, too. I'll put you two lovebirds in one hole that way you can be stuck up his ass for an eternity."

"Let them do what they have to do," Simon's voice cuts through the tension with its dull edge before Richard can respond. "We can't do this on our own. There's just too many. What do you suggest?" Simon looks to Chapel for advice and it angers both Dolph and Richard, but they say nothing.

"We got those things downstairs. We have these people upstairs. The ground is already freezing. We are going to have to burn them all," Chapel says.

Richard's face and voice carry the shock he feels saying, "What do you mean, those things downstairs?"

"They found a way in." Rhett is leaning against the wall watching the action like a sideshow of entertainment when he answers the question. All he needs is a snack to fully enjoy himself. "We killed them."

"Jesus…" it is a soft mutter from Richard as he shakes his head.

Rhett chuckles and tells Richard, "Don't worry, we got it. Heavy lifting, right?" Rhett quotes Lawless, stroking the fire again back to its flickering heat.

"Enough, all of you!" I snap, verbally, and mentally. "Let's just get this done. Can you just for a few hours grow up, shut up, and man up so we can get this done?" My vision blurs behind the wall of tears that has formed. Hot and burning, they escape before I can blink them away. It's just too much. All of it is just too much.

Marxx comes to me, wrapping his arms around me, holding me. "Yeah, Hells, we can do that," he whispers into my hair. Marxx stepped up to comfort me, removing the option for Lawless or Dolph. Even as he says they can, he just proved they never will.

"We'll take the things out of the courtyard. Your group can start taking these bodies down into the courtyard. It keeps the two separate, and these people won't have to see it," Chapel offers the first real plan of action being just as weary as I am.

"…and J.D.?" Richard asks.

"We got him," Lawless' says, with a voice that dares the other man to say more.

He doesn't, but I know he wants to. It's such an easy setup for a cutting remark. It'll be one final triumphant blow for Richard's side. They know the problem though with landing a blow is not always from the blatant fallout. No, the real problem with throwing punches is you never know how hard the other person is willing to hit back. Like Christmas trees covered in blood, abandoned dolls and little children left dead along halls, you never really know how hard a person is willing to strike back until it's too late. It's too late for them. It's too late for you. It's just always too late.

Chapter 9

"Any thoughts on how we are going to get this done?" Marxx is staring at the many piles of Risen we have dragged into the cafeteria from our earlier morning rampage. We have smeared long lines of dark gore and blood in the process. It looks like a road map of homicidal roadways with how the streaks arch and cross over themselves. It smells of something much worse.

When they first started appearing, they smelled of death. They made the air heavy with it. Now, the degree of rotting has a different odor that is confusing to the senses. The mixture of a septic tank with the undertones of sickly-sweet acid burns my lungs. I gag as I pull the final bodies into the room as Rhett follows me with the librarian. Why he left her for last, I'm not brave enough to ask. Nor, do I want to venture a guess as to why he is positioning her folded arms perfectly over her chest. Some things with Rhett you just ignore with hopes the memory will fade away. Sometimes, the memories even do.

We stand there the three of us, staring at the many mutilated corpses with pieces of their remains still stuck to our hands and clothing. Somehow, we must carry them out into the open field which surrounds the school to burn them, sparing the sight from those who are trying to figure out the same problem above us.

"I'll pull the truck around," I say with a sigh my whole body feels, and the men nod with Rhett's eyes still for his librarian.

The cold winter wind is like ice to my flesh. The shock of it pulls me from my exhaustion and clears my head from the fog of stress and the lack of sleep and food. Snow gently swirls in the wind like tornados of frost. It lands in my hair and face, melting and leaving its wet stains behind. It reminds me of tears as if Mother Nature herself is walking with me in my desolate depression.

Aimes would love this. She would be spinning in circles, the center of a winter blending of season and laughter. She would be what this holiday is supposed to be – joyful.

Do you know what day it is? I do. It's the day I take the final step over the ledge of hope. There are no more rivers of denial for me to swim against. I will no longer wade in the deep pools of self-pity as I have been. This is our life now. One big fight for survival after the next, leaving us never knowing who the victim will be and who will be the ones left to bury them. I scream they scream, we all scream and when we do, we all sound the same, because eventually, it is over for us all.

Sitting in the truck, I want to scream. I want to scream into the dancing flakes around me that seeming to mock me with their imagined joy. I want to vent with my voice everything that I can't put a name to or pin a fault to someone. I want to scream, emptying the well of emotions that is overflowing with the amount that has filled me in just these few hours. I stare at the large black Harley with its dusting of white. The frost has formed veins on the chrome that spread with tiny, webbed fingers. The skull of their club stares back at me from the gas tank. Its smile is more menacing now that the bike has lost its owner. Like a horse gone wild, it's gloating over its freedom.

Putting my truck in gear, I ease out of the snow-rutted spot and angle the bed back towards the cafeteria doors. The tires slipped on the winter kissed cement, shuddering the beast. Inching the truck forward before trying to reverse again, I stare at that skull as we pass one another. It is an instant decision.

Slanting the long bed, I clip the front wheel of J.D.'s bike sending it to its side in a slow fall. The metallic scraping is satisfying to the bitter seed that is planted in my heart.

Do you know what today is? Yes Aimes, I do. It's National I'm-Over-It Day. It's a lot like Independence Day but instead of fireworks, we have bonfires of bodies.

Marxx motions me backward, lining the truck's bed's length with the steps into the building. Opening the door for me, he helps me down to the slick cement with a judging look in his eyes. His face is the mask of uncaring he normally wears. He looks to the fallen bike and back to me and asks, "Feel better?"

I shrug, ignoring his question. Did I feel better? No, not really, but every little moment of private malice takes a slight edge from the overwhelming discord.

The creaking of the bed's hinges summons Rhett to the door. He is covered in the streaks of blood and thick pieces of blowback from his many kills today and his eyes are dark pools of rage. If Aries were ever to hold a mortal body, Rhett would be the inspiration.

"Let's get this shit done," Rhett says, with a voice that makes the pit of my stomach clench.

"What did I miss?" I whisper to Marxx with my concerns.

Marxx lowers his head to see behind him without having to turn around. "Law and Chappy made it down with J.D. Upstairs voted he goes in the burn pile with the Risen instead of the one with people. Isn't going over well with the boys."

"…and you?"

Marxx raises his head slowly to look at me and says, "He made his choice. He went against the club putting us in danger. He went out alone. He goes out alone." The face that is staring at me is furrowed with his words. His voice makes the winter air feel warm in comparison. "But that little stunt," he says, nodding to the fallen bike, "might have been ill-timed."

I nod. "Maybe," I tell him. "It still felt good."

Marxx matches my nod and a slight smile pulls at the corner of his lips. "Maybe," he says.

The men have already started to drag the dead out. I watch as Marxx goes to wait by the truck to help lift the bodies into the bed. The men are behind their masks of boredom. Watching them one would think this task was no different than taking out bags of trash, not the bodies of things that once had ambitions for our deaths. The map of gore is now complete as it leads to the truck. It mars the perfection of the snow, and as much as it falls, it can't cover the tracks they make. The fight against the memory of the dead for Mother Nature and us, is a losing battle. The harder we try, the harder they supply us with proof that they are real.

Lawless lifts his head towards me in a nod as he shuts the truck's bed. "Take them out. Let's get this started."

I nod as I watch him walk away. His face is a carving of stone with his features set deep in emotionless lines. He is fighting against the exhaustion that his slumped shoulders and slow stride are expressing for him. His head rolls, stretching taut neck muscles and his eyes stare skyward longer than they should. I wonder what it is he is asking for from God. What does he pray for when the lights are gone, and the nights grow longer than any rope of hope he holds? Is it strength, courage, or just forgiveness and understanding?

He looks to me over his shoulder, when he feels my eyes on him. He cocks one eyebrow with a silent question, and I shake my head. I have too many questions and he doesn't have the time. I know who he is bringing out next. I know what will be waiting for Marxx and I when we return.

"Rhett," I call to the mock Aries staring into the back of the truck with eyes that have gone to another place. A dark place of which I don't want to ever be a guest. "I want his vest. Will you save it for me?"

Awareness comes back into those blue eyes. Their hue brightens as his mind travels back to the current time. "Yeah." He nods, still not fully himself. "I can do that." Just as quickly as he rose, he sinks back into the darkness that is Rhett and his eyes follow him into the pit.

"Let's go," Marxx calls from beside me in the truck, and I slide in with one last glance into the mirror. It reflects back an image that slices me and steals my breath. Those blue eyes lock with mine and from one corner a tear falls as the doors across from us in the courtyard open. It glides down a face lost in time with neither joy nor sorrow upon it.

Rhett has accepted what has happened as the bodies from upstairs are piled in white sheets all around the courtyard of various sizes and shapes. It's carved on his heart like the damage done to a tree's trunk and there is no escape from what he now knows. Death is the only escape left to us. Today is Rhett's Independence Day, too.

Marxx and I pick a spot a few feet from the courtyard walls. We are still aware of what could lurk, and we aren't willing to take the risk of venturing too far. We hold no tender care for the bodies that I push as he pulls from the truck. It strikes me odd, lost in my mental ramblings where conversation lulls, that these were once someone's loved ones too, but here we are shoving them out onto the lawn without any thoughts to their memories. There are no white sheets to spare us the sight of them or pay them any final respects. Only the thud and bounce their bodies make as Marxx drops them serves as their remembrance. You don't pray over what tries to kill you. You pray that it continues to fail.

With the final body freed from the truck, Marxx lifts his hand to help me down. My feet slip over the slick remains of the blood and he has to brace me to keep me from falling. He winces as my weight connects with his hands and I fall gracelessly into the pile of bodies. My arms keep me from landing fully into the face of the male at the top of the pile. His left eye is punctured from his death and it leaks grey, putrid fluid down his cheek that now dots my own face with the force of my landing. His ribs crack under my palms and it sounds like twigs snapping, but my stomach knows it's something much worse and reacts accordingly. His shoulders bounce as I press on him to escape and the motion swings his arms upward placing his hands on my hips like a lover welcoming me. Hands scoop me up and pull me against a warm chest before my screaming can start.

Lawless whispers into my ear, "I figured if I ever caught you cheating on me it would be with a better-looking guy." His breath is warm against my neck. It eases down some of the hysterics that were climbing up from the dark well of my mind. His words might have held a teasing nature, but his arms vibrate with how tight he holds me to him. "I got you," he whispers.

Marxx wipes away the clotted wetness from my face with the sleeve of his shirt. At the rate the day is going we'll be burning our clothes, too. "Sorry, Hells," he says to me. "My arm gave out."

"I'm good," my voice shakes. My body shakes. My mind and soul are riddled with crevices that threaten to splinter my mind, but I'm good I tell him. Like Chapel with his bruises, I'm good. Marxx and I nod at each other. Neither of us is willing to push the topic.

"I'm gonna' take the truck back," Marxx says, he is still nodding as he climbs into the cab. I can almost hear his mind working against him with petty insults for letting me fall.

"Let him go," Lawless says, feeling me try to turn in his arms. "We are all too thin right now for apologies or pity."

"…but it wasn't his fault."

Lawless shrugs, loosening his arms around me. "Point of view," he tells me, and I look at him. His dark brown eyes sway to me and a smile slowly spreads across his face. The smile that has always been his get-out-of-jail-free card still works. My lips curve despite my mood and I roll my eyes at him.

Patting his arm, he releases me from his safety net. I watch him slip back to being the protector as he scans the horizon for any threats.

"What's the plan?" I ask, watching him stare into the tree-dotted line around us.

His tongue swipes across his teeth as he does his trademark, sharp inhale. His hands slide into the pockets of his leather vest as he shrugs his shoulders. "Hell, if I know, Helena. There is not a whole lot of thought process to this."

"I was asking more of the big picture. What happens now?"

He never looks at me during our conversation. His eyes are too busy as they roam over the surrounding landscape to glance in my direction. "I can't see a big picture right now. I'm just trying to see to the end of today. Just let me get through today. We'll figure the rest of the shit out tomorrow."

I nod with his answer, respecting the honesty of his words. The truck's loud engine rumbles towards us and I watch him pull further into himself. His face sets into the bored, stone-like features the club wears when hiding their thoughts from the world. His hands come out from his vest and clasp at his waist, waiting for the others to arrive. The only tension he shows is the flexing of his arms as he grips and releases his fisted hands, but even that slows as the truck comes to park beside us. He asked to just let him get through today. I would have asked to just let me get through this. The rest of the day can't possibly hold anything more heartbreaking than what we are about to have to do. Could it?

Rhett and Chapel pull the wrapped body of J.D. from the bed of the truck. Lawless rolls his head at the sight, stretching his neck as he fights against his emotions. I reach out to him, but he sidesteps my hand, sparing me a brief glance as he heads to help carry the body. I watch, feeling like an intruder, as the four men carry the sheet-wrapped body away from the other pile. They look everywhere but at each other, relying on their once-tight bond to let them know what the other is thinking. They once moved and acted in perfect sync with each other, silently reading the other man's motives and moods from the many years they have survived as a family. Everything may feel like it is falling out from under us, but watching them I remember Rhett's words. *"We survive because we are together, not because of you or me or anyone else alone, but because we take care of each other."* Now, with the people inside the school drawing lines in the sand, each other is all we may have.

Rhett returns to where they have placed the body with a gas can that sloshes as he strides towards them. The red paint that is used for warning purposes tries to give one last clue as to what may happen once the match is sparked. The smell of the gas cuts through the acidic wasting of flesh. I have to bite my tongue to keep it still as protests expand in my chest like air. I don't want to watch. I don't want to see what is about to happen. I don't want to say good-bye to the man who has left me torn in two with my feelings for him. I lock my feet to the ground, refusing them the steps they want to take towards the sheet, but I don't try to hide the tears I feel licking their way down my face.

Chapel inhales, steadying his voice. Its deep pitch carries over the sounds of mourning from the inside the courtyard that play the perfect backdrop of a melody. "Gone is our Brother, a piece of our hearts. A silver tear to remember. A silver tear to pull us apart. Your memory we will cherish. Your body we now bury."

Lawless lights his cigarette, drawing a long inhale from it. The tip glows red as the heat travels through the ashes. He flicks it onto the sheet and exhales the thick smoke as the fire sparks to life. I watch the flames take J.D. They roar and snap, devouring the man who held the heavy burden of holding us together. A burden that in the end was too much to bear. In J.D.'s eyes, when he lost Lawless, he lost his world. Staring across the flames, I see the same fears on Law's face through the hazy heat and it's mixed with the bitterness of one who is left behind.

Rhett doesn't stay to watch the flames. He heads towards me with the same red warning can and splashes the pile near me, covering them with flammable liquid. My eyes bounce from the burning fire to the fire that is about to burn, not sure which is going to be worse. It's a crescendo of anguish with the splashing being the beat of the drum. Striking a match, Rhett lets the little stick fall, and the heat soars instantly. It's shocking how something of such a small size can cause such havoc. Like a wave, the flames flow forward overtaking the pile, covering it in the orange and yellows of itself. Rhett doesn't flinch from the heat. He doesn't step back from the black smoke that stretches upwards like long fingers reaching into the sky. The smoke that looks like souls fleeing from the twisted forms they have become. He stares into the flames at a woman who still wears a pink cardigan over her dress. Her blonde hair shaken loose from Marxx' treatment lies around her and catches the fire first.

The flames climb up her, slowly swallowing her body, but Rhett stares on. He stares at her the way the men are staring at the fire across from us. The same mixture of remorse and remembrance swirls in his eyes. Me? I'm just watching it all because if I stare at any one thing for too long, I might just dance in the flames myself.

Chapter 10

The greatest threat to a person's sanity is not always the monster they invent in dark corners staring back at them. Sometimes, it's the eyes of the people who think you are the monster staring at them. Right now, as we return to the courtyard, all eyes are on us. Maybe it's the bloodstained clothing that has more crimson than the original designs intended. Maybe it is the exhaustion that is stealing the color from our skin. It might be the black leather vests shining brighter than normal with the layers of gore that clings to them, or the vest that I am cradling like a teddy bear to ward off evil thoughts. Then again, it might just be Rhett. He has that effect on people. The words he dropped as the men lifted J.D.'s bike from its fallen position most likely didn't solve any of the trust issues the others seem to be having with us.

"How did this happen?" Lawless asks, staring at the dark Harley. He is looking for any imperfections in its frame. His fingers float over the high gloss of the metal searching for spots his eyes might miss. Marxx looks at me, cradling his arm, and we exchange a silent moment of plotting.

"Must have slipped," Marxx says shrugging, and it's a simple cover-up lacking any flare or in-depth planning.

Rhett looks to the other bikes and back to the one that stands in the center of their circle. I can almost feel the skull's eyes staring at me with blame. "Just his?" Rhett asks, with a voice that holds more accusation than question. He looks at the crowd who is standing across from us like a divided line of battle. "Just his?" he asks again, but that is not the question he is posing to the group.

Lawless follows the logic, standing to further add to the division and my heart sinks at what I may have caused.

"His is the heaviest. He was upset when he came back. He might have not had the stand all the way down…" My voice dies as my mind runs out of steam to fuel the argument.

"You really think they are brave enough to do that?" Chapel takes the dare to a different level. He isn't accusing them of doing it. He is accusing them of being too scared to do it. It brings the argument to a different thought, and yet, a whole circle of closing it, too.

"Nah. He's right. Isn't their style," Rhett says, as he pats Lawless as if to snap the other man out of the glare. Lawless doesn't awaken though. His eyes have found the man he would place the bet on, and that same man is staring back at him - Dolph.

"Larance," I whisper his name, with hopes that a gentle approach will bring him back around. He tilts his head in my direction, acknowledging my voice, but he doesn't look away from the other man. "It wasn't him." He gives me an eyebrow for my sentence, and I hear the words come from me before I am aware, I was going to say it. "I did it."

If I wanted his attention, I got it, his and the rest of the men. Marxx sighs with his hero attempt blown and Chapel smirks and coughs in hopes to cover the smile. Rhett and Lawless are not as amused.

Rhett takes a step closer to me, towering over me, and the sun casts him in a sudden shadow as if it is too scared to watch. "What?" It's one-word Rhett says to me, but it might as well have been a death threat in many languages. Chapel is already moving to me when Law places a fist on his chest to stop him. He is waiting like Rhett for me to explain.

How much of the truth do you tell a man who may just kill you for it? How far are you willing to spare your soul if your body is in harm's way?

"It was an accident," I start, rushing through every word I hold in my vocabulary that may save me. "I used to sit on it all the time and he would laugh at how I couldn't reach the ground. I just wanted…" My lies stall as Rhett's eyebrow rises.

"– that moment?" Lawless finishes for me and I pounce on the opening.

"Yes. That moment." I stare into a killer's blue eyes and lose all value to my soul. "I just wanted that moment, Rhett."

Lawless' fist melts like an ice sculpture on Chapel's chest, flattening itself in slow motion before it slips away. He comes to me and wraps those arms around me and even Rhett has to look away from my imagined weakness.

"Why didn't you just say so?" Rhett asks me, and I have to almost laugh with his question. Only half-hidden by Lawless can I look at Rhett and keep my composure.

"Doesn't matter," Marxx says, once again trying to cover my recklessness. "It's done and everything is fine. Can we get inside now?"

"Shouldn't we go over there?" Chapel asks, motioning with his head to the space across from us. The gap seems to have grown even further as we talked. "See if they need help or something?"

"All out of patience and marshmallows," Rhett says, with his first steps away from us. "I'm going in."

"How about bullets? You out of those?" Chapel's low voice crawls up my spine like fingernails. I shiver with it making Lawless pull me tighter to him.

"Running a little low," Rhett says. "Why?"

It's Marxx that answers him, not the preacher's son. "We missed some."

I don't know what is happening behind me. Whatever it is, it sets the men on edge. Lawless holds me like a man drowning, pulling my head to his neck. He whispers into my hair, "I want you to go inside.

Get to Aimes until someone comes for you. You don't come back. No hero shit."

I stiffen to argue with him, but he pulls me tighter, letting me know he isn't starting a debate. "Walk calmly in. Don't run until you have to." He pulls me from him with a sideways pushing motion. He doesn't want me to see whatever is behind me that has them rattled. "Marxx, get her in." Lawless is no longer whispering. His tone is harsh, sharp with his command.

"I should be out here with you." Marxx steps forward, his voice raw with the insult he feels has been given. I guess he feels overqualified for babysitting. Maybe he has forgotten the amount of trouble this baby can find for him.

Lawless turns to the taller man, giving him the full weight of his brown eyes. For a moment, they remind me of another set. A set that was steel-grey and just as angry under the surface. "You should do what you're told." Lawless doesn't yell. He doesn't let his voice climb even one pitch with his command. The steadiness of it gives it all the volume it needs.

For a moment, I think the two are going to argue, but Marxx nods with his jaw set. Taking me by the arm, he starts to pull me towards the door with his fingers taking out his anger on my skin.

"You really think they are on just that side?" I ask him, as he leads us away. I don't have to look to see what has started this. Like a kid who never lets on to understand the words their parents are spelling instead of saying, I know from what Lawless is sending me running from.

"I wasn't asked to think," Marxx tells me, still wounded from being sent away and his pride is making my arm pay for it.

"If you were to think, if you were to stop pouting like a child and think, would you think they are on just one side?"

His jaw slides side-to-side with his thoughts before he turns to me, "No. I don't."

"Looks like we get to have some fun, too." I smile at him. I smile letting it reach my eyes like a mischievous thought.

He stares at me, half dragging me still with a face that is searching mine. "My job is to get you to Aimes; to keep you girls safe. Your job is not to be a pain in my ass."

"Now Marxx," I smile again as he shoves me through a door into the school, "when have I ever been a pain in your ass?"

He doesn't have a chance to answer me. There is no charming come back to make me behave. He doesn't because as he opens his mouth, the screaming starts. It's a ripple effect of fears with one voice melding into more with each voice that joins the choir. It ranges in the highs of the females to the lows of males like sections of songs, but it is wordless melodies of what our days are now. We no longer need words to move us. Screaming seems to work just fine.

"You're not going to see Aimes, are you?" Marxx stares down at me with amusement and hesitation.

"No," I say to him, and we both smile with it.

The men have come to know me well. I'm not one to run and hide, praying for someone to come save me. I don't expect someone to take the bullet for me. I can light my own cigar and take it just fine on my own while bitching about it the whole time. I am more damned than I am damsel, and I don't cower in the corner from the big baddie or hide under the bed with my hand clamped over my mouth. Unless that big baddie is Rhett. Then all bets are off. Even Superman has his kryptonite.

"You have a plan?" he asks the question which has been repeated so many times today, as the passing hours are shaved down to seconds.

I glance behind me and watch the monsters that stalk us now overtake the area outside. I watch as those who try to run trip and fall with their feet clumsy in their haste to get away only to be set upon by greedy hands and starving mouths. I see all those people who were just moments ago staring at us with hate running to the very men they placed that hate on with prayers of salvation. I stare as the only ones Karma has left me head once again into the danger and dare Death for the third time today.

"Yeah," I tell Marxx, "the same plan I always have. Stay alive."

"Solid plan, but I was thinking of something with a touch more details." He is watching the start of a war outside with his mind racing for solutions. One man can start a war, but can only one end it?

I stare out the window with him, so close to where we used to sit and have our morning chats. The landscape is something much worse now. "If you have any suggestions, you should hurry." I prompt him into plotting.

"They can't shoot. They are running too low and there is too much risk of hitting someone -"

"- Not that Rhett would care."

"- Or your boy."

I ignore his tone and ask, "So? What is the plan?"

"If we don't take them from the other side, they will be overrun." He leaves it as simple as that. Simple, as if I should be grasping the hidden threat he has seen. Staring at the massacre, I do.

Following in his long stride, I slip into the leather vest they wear marking them as a group. The extra layers I wear of winter protection absorb some of the extra space left from the older man's size. The leather still wears the previous owner's scent like a denial of my right to wear it. For a flash of time, I can feel his corded arms around me like a ghostly hug, lending me the strength I will need to face what is waiting for us. His laughter once again floats behind the locked doors of my mind. He would not be surprised to find me back on the cement standing beside them. I have become either suicidal or stupid with illusions of grandeur. The inflamed wound on my left arm letting me know it's suicidal because my worn-out body has no illusions at all of what I am.

The screaming was muted behind the thick, grey walls. The safety glass constructed windows with its wire embedding dulled the colors of the murders. When Marxx opens the door, the safety blanket is stolen with savage brutality. Standing in the center of the chaos, there is nothing to soften what is happening all around me and my heart fights to stay the course. Its pattern is no longer the steady rhythm of a conqueror it had on the walk here. Now it is the pounding of a deserter.

The sights, the sounds, and the smells all add layer upon layer to the continued shocks to my confidence.

The burning bodies cloud the closed courtyard with smoke and wisp-like ashes that dance with the snow like demons with angels. The smell of the roasting flesh pairs with the copper blood as if Death walks in the past and present among us. He causes this loop of time where hope fades and depression has a hold on our hearts, robbing us of any possible victory.

"Helena!" Marxx' voice pulls me forward as my mind tries to hold me back. I don't need my mind for this. My body has learned long ago how to do this. We know what it takes to survive and as my blade finds the throat of the first glaring face, it's nothing personal. It's just them or us and today we are the good guys. Tomorrow, tomorrow we might all be dead.

The blood bubbles across the gash of the Risen's neck. Air that was trapped in his windpipe causes the blood to froth like thick coffee before it slides down his chest. Marxx finishes him when he drops to his knees with a quick kick to the head. It snaps the neck, leaving him a pile of useless limbs, but his eyes still watch us as we walk away.

Marxx grabs me by the vest I have placed upon me, pulling me to him. "You want to wear this, then act like it. You follow my lead, no hero bullshit." He has to shout over the screams of the dying and frightened. I nod, not trusting my tongue to obey me, but for it to say something that I might come to regret later. It does that sometimes.

With a shove, he turns from me and together we fill in the space needed that the other leaves, mirroring as we reduce the numbers of the Risen to make our way to the center where the rest of G.R.I.T. stands. I know the moment Lawless spots us through the weaving crowd. With his fist dripping from the assault he just landed, he mouths a word that I don't need to be near him to understand. That one syllable is easy to read on his lips even from this distance.

When Marxx loses a path through, he says the same word. This time, I am near enough to understand. We have fought our way into the eye of the deadly storm. My body that was once exhausted now quickens with the effort to survive. Adrenaline touches every muscle, feeding it with a false vigor. For a period, it fed me with a victory. As Marxx and I watched the circle we had cleared enfold us, I know it fed me lies.

Marxx is spinning, desperately slashing at the ones closest, trying to keep space between them and us. My hand is trembling as I clutch my knife in front of me. The blood falls from it, sprinkling the ground around me with the shaking of it. I don't look at the female inching towards me. She knows my body is giving out, something that hers will never do. She is waiting for it to happen with arms wide to block anyone else from taking me first. I don't want to see my death coming for me and when I feel Marxx stumble against me as they overtake him, I know this is how my life will end.

I don't hear the screaming anymore. I don't smell their deaths. There is nothing in this white noise of a moment. I have no fear. My heart holds nothing at all. I guess this is the peace people speak of when the last moments come for their loved ones.

She is just a hand's reach away now. Her steady eyes hold the same illusion of peace in them. She is no longer growling or threatening me. Like an executioner giving the condemned their time to prepare for the death that awaits them, she silently watches me.

I look to where I know the men were. Chapel is gone. He is lost among the crowd of murderous forms that feast from their kills. Rhett is pulling Lawless back into the school. There is so much ground lost between us, making it impossible for them to reach us in time and Rhett knows it. Lawless is screaming for me as he struggles against Rhett's arms, but the words don't reach me. I watch Simon leading as many as he can to safety as he watches so many of his friends being destroyed, but his eyes flicker one last time to the two burning white sheets.

One last time, I tell myself, *just one last time.*

Exhaling the air from my lungs, I set my blade tightly in my hand. For Lilly, for Ashley, for Conroy, for those they took from me-- just one last time I will fight. One last time before I let them take me, but if they want me, they are going to have to take me. I am going to make it very personal.

Chapter 11

With nothing left to lose, Marxx has drawn his gun and begins firing into the skulls of the ones on top of him. The rapid shots shatter the bones into dark sprays that drip down his face layering it like demonic tears. He is baptized by their blood, and like a sinner praying for salvation, he is saved. The woman who was so certain of my doom melts back to the savage her nature now claims. The deep growl starts in the back of her throat before erupting into a screaming snarl at me. Her eyes glow with the hate and hunger that guides them to find us.

The sounds of Marxx' firing propels her into rash action. I don't challenge my body. I brace, letting her weight take me down. She rides the blade down so when we both slam against the concrete it is propelled under her chin by the impact. I shove it the rest of the way into her, past the solid structure of her upper jaw. The jawbone makes the sound of crunching as the blade is forced through. It reminds me of candied brittle being snapped and crumbling into pieces as she becomes a heavyweight with her second life ended.

Marxx crawls to me as I roll her from me. My blade is wedged tight into the roof of her mouth making the last victory hers. "Leave it," he says. He is panting as his hand reaches out to me. His shoulder has been torn open over the joint of his arm leaving it limp. His face is thick with blood, leaving me unsure if it belongs to him or what he has killed. "I'm not going to die on my back." He holds his hand to me again, pleading with me without words.

I stand first, testing my quivering legs before I help him up. His body is as exhausted as mine is as I pull him to me. He sways, going pale beside me with unfocused eyes. He was my hero once when I needed to be saved. He was my protector when I felt the world had turned against me.

We survive because we are together, not because of you or me or anyone else alone, but because we take care of each other. The words echo inside me. *Just one more time.*

"Marxx, you want to wear this?" I ask him, grasping the leather vest watching him try to focus on me as if I were a mirage in the heat. "You follow my lead. No hero bullshit."

He smirks, swaying against me. "Sweetheart, I'm all out of bullshit and running low on hero." His voice is gruff with his normal gravel-like tone but now it also has the tone of defeat. Marxx has given up.

"Not yet you're not. Not yet…"

We are the only two left standing in a sea of stalking shapes. The silence now seems louder than the screams with just the guttural growls and deep throat callings of what stands around us. Those who are not stalking towards us linger over the fallen bodies not willing to leave their meal. The dark clumps they pull from the fallen are fresh and warm, simmering with the steam that escapes the ruined body cavities and it is enough to sate their hunger. Now they watch like macabre dinner theater guests as their companions come for us.

"Got a plan?" Marxx asks me with a growing smirk.

I have to chuckle as we stand here with no hope and fewer answers. "Yeah, the same one I always have."

"Stay alive," we say in unison, our voices filled with more amusement than we should have at the situation.

I shrug, wincing against the complaint of pain my shoulders scream with the movement. "Seems to be working so far."

Marxx hands me a small, serrated blade he keeps in a holster at his waist. "We'll see," he says to me. I take it giving him a smile as he places his last clip into his gun. "We'll see," he repeats again. We turn, ready to become either survivors or victims as Karma inhales a deep breath as she watches the show.

We stand back-to-back, inching our way to the window tinted black by the sun's rays that vibrates with blows from hidden fists. I know it is Lawless and Rhett screaming for us through the thick glass, willing us forward to them with their desperate commands. My mind's eye can see them pleading with us to make it to them. I can see their anguish having to watch us like ancient roman gladiators battling against death. I can hear their phantom screams pleading with any deity that is still listening for our lives. Seeing the many that lay torn and spread into nothing more than warm meat around me, I'm not sure there are any left to pray to, much less any to reach down a divine hand to save us.

Every step we take is mirrored by the Risen who follows us. Their legs twist with their movements to defy muscle commands following us in disjointed steps as if their lower body is disconnected from their spines. Their heads cock to each side in drawn-out actions to avoid having to move their eyes. They have spread around us again in the few seconds we took to collect ourselves.

I hear Marxx sigh seeing that they are not going to rush us, but wait for us to wear out and bring ourselves down. "If I run, they will follow me," Marxx says. His voice is so filled with grief and exhaustion that my mind fights to hold onto any last thoughts of making it.

"If you run, I'll follow," I tell him, shaking my head as Mother Nature kisses my face with her swirling snow. Even she is starting to accept the inevitable. "No more hero bullshit, remember?"

"They aren't going to rush us, Sweetheart. They are just waiting for us to fall."

"Then your ass had best stay on your feet."

Marxx chuckles, tripping due to his exhaustion and it causes the ones closest to him to open their eyes wide with excitement. Their voices rise with the hopes of this standoff ending. My legs threaten to give way and I have to focus on each step we take. My feet feel as if they are weighted, dragging instead of lifting with my sideways path to the vibrating window.

How many have we lost? How many are now around me lining the pathway with their spilled entrails and blood? The question brings my eyes to stare into the landscape around me. I watch as fists are punching into bodies, ripping pieces from the torn flesh. I see the many mouths that are dripping with blood as they chew from limbs that have been severed. Ashes from the burning fire whirl around me with the winter wind casting them in different directions. A light snowfall is dusting the same wind heavier than the ashes that battle against the pure white perfections. There, in the backdrop is Lilly in her white nightgown she loved. The same nightgown she wears when she haunts me.

I watch as she runs with a smile on her face across the spans of the courtyard. Her ghostly feet leave no tracks in the thin layer of snow. She runs, spinning and reaching for the winter flakes with tiny hands which used to hold mine. She turns to me; her blue eyes glowing with the joy of youth and reaches for me. Her hand pulls on my tired soul like a familiar handshake and I want to go to her.

"Helena," she calls to me. "Helena, come on." Her bell-like voice still holds the power to make me smile.

"Helena," her mouth moves with my name, but it is coming from behind me. "Helena, come on!" My shoulders shake with a rough hand that pulls at me. It's pulling me in the wrong direction. Lilly is in front of me, not behind me.

"Helena!" It's Marxx who is shouting my name and not the bell-like innocence of a five-year-old that I crave to answer. "Keep moving!"

Marxx' shouting has excited the one he has turned his back on. It lunges now, seeing an opportunity that was denied to him before. The weight of the attack takes Marxx to his knees beside me. It pulls me off balance and I land with one knee colliding into the cement. I turn to pull the attacker from his back, exposing my own.

I realize my mistake too late. Hands are upon me before I can brace for them. They force me onto my back, bending my body backward with my legs still stuck underneath me. I watch as the first face comes into view. I can hear Marxx screaming in pain just a few inches from me and I close my eyes to hide from Death. Just one last breath and I wait for it all to end. I wait for the pain that will free me from it all. The smell of their baby shampoo blocks out the scent of blood that clings to me after being surrounded by it for so long. The sounds of their laughter fill my ears, saving me from having to listen to Marxx' screaming death.

I can feel their hands pulling at me, trying to drag me in different directions like wild dogs fighting for their food. The first set of teeth bites into my shoulder, worrying the joint with tiny piercing blades, trying to tear through the winter coat. The pain tears a scream from my lungs. The feel of my blood from the reopened wound on my arm is warm, and it washes over me, stealing my breath, choking the screams in my throat. Sharp nails rake across my chest trying to tear away the layers of clothing like the peelings of fruit to expose the juice-filled pulp.

The winter coat is delaying their destruction and they become demented with the distraction. Their hands tear through the lining and its inner shell of padding with a frenzy, jerking my body with their desperation to feed. My legs are trapped underneath me. My arms are dead weights with fatigue. Not even the adrenaline that propels my heart into erratic rhythm can stimulate my body now. I am being forced to watch them find their way to my candy-red center because they are not content with the meat on my arms or the font of my neck. They want the sweet meat of my core. How many licks does it take to get to the center of one's spleen? I guess I am about to find out.

I close my eyes and scream. I scream into the wind and the snow that caresses me. I scream along with the man that lies somewhere near me, enduring the same death. I scream because there is nothing else, I can do. I am screaming so loud that I don't hear the car horn at first. I don't notice how their hands have stopped, prolonging my death even longer, and preventing my escape.

Feet rush towards me. Voices float over the thin strand left of my sanity as Lilly's and Conroy's laughter fills the darkness of my mind. Ashley's shadow shrouds my purgatory whispering into my ear. "Not yet. No, not yet. One more time," she says, as I feel my face splashed with thick wetness. I gasp with it, opening my eyes to squint against the sun. The shadow of a dark shape stands over me. I watch the outline kneel to me and a female voice says with laughter, "God is on your side today."

"There is no fucking God," I laugh, with my bitterness and watch as the dark outline expands, filling my whole vision with the growing shadow. I let the darkness take me. I let it all go. It's not children's laughter I hear now as my eyes flutter close. It's the Devil's. J.D. is laughing and I laugh right along with him.

Chapter 12

The grass underneath me is beautiful. The deep jades and emeralds of the greens blanket the ground, and the trees stand envious with their foliage of budding flowers. The grass blades are warm from the summer sun and bend around my bare feet, climbing into the spaces left between my toes as I walk to the many children in blinding, white clothing. They play with brightly colored inflated balls that soar into the air around them before being caught with fits of giggles. Their laughter is contagious, and I find myself joining in their game as a bystander. I clap for the boys who toss the vivid balls between each other and laugh with the girls who manage to "steal" those same toys with mischievous charm. They chase one another around with false anger and playful motives just as if they were back on the school's playground.

"They look happy," Marxx says, standing beside me with a genuine smile. He is without his vest or frowns, taking years and the hardened edge from his appearance. Seeing him widens my smile and I take his hand in mine as we watch the children play. "You look happy," he tells me, returning my smile.

"When was the last time you laughed like that?" I ask him, my eyes roaming the children with my twist of sad thoughts.

"It hasn't always been so bad."

"It hasn't always been so good."

He pulls on my hand and I follow the motion to stand facing him. His eyes stare at me with confusion and pity. He tells me, "It's not about the bad, Helena. You always cling to the worst, letting it overshadow any hope or good. When you look at the world, you don't see the sunshine. You cling to the rain. You think that makes you strong. You think this obsession of yours with the dark will spare you any misery. The truth is, Sweetheart, you cause your misery. You cling to it. You have to learn to let it go. Whatever it is you think you are hiding from; it won't go away until you let it go."

I look back to the children playing so innocently with their laughter and ignorance of suffering. "Marxx, you have no idea." I watch a girl's red pigtails hover in the air weightless as she spins in circles. She is dressed in the same white dress like her friends and it expands around her ankles as she spins. Conroy had called her Margaret. To me, she is the embodiment of my sins.

"You killed them," Marxx whispers it to me like a sinner exposed. He's right. I am.

"I had to."

"Did you?"

"It's not my fault. They would have killed me. They killed Ashley. They had Conroy." I am whispering, confessing the transgression like a sacrament my heart has repeated every day since it happened.

"…and what of Lilly? Where is Lilly, Helena?"

"Carol killed her."

"Where is Carol?'

"I killed her."

"You killed them all. If you hadn't been running late, you might have been able to be there to stop it. You know that."

My heart is punctured with the words I have not been strong enough to string together. The same words which Marxx now tortures me with.

He continues his torment, "You were with Lawless and Aimes, avoiding having to return to those kids. The kids have somehow become your responsibility by parents who hated you." He pulls me to his chest, and forces me to look at his face as it fills with rage. "It was never really about Leslie. You needed a reason to hate him because you hated yourself. You blame them both for your failures. You let them take the fall for what you couldn't face. It was so easy to crawl into that little hole of self-pity when the world was convinced you were the wronged, but you were really the culprit. You let them all die. Here, to think you labeled Aimes as the traitor when it was you. It's always been you, bitch!" He is screaming at me. He is screaming the words I have hidden from in my mind. The very words that whisper to me when the sun's warmth is gone and the dark of the lonely night forces you to face the many truths of your life.

"I didn't know…" My voice cradles the guilt and anguish that is as familiar to me as my shadow and it follows me just as closely.

"If you had, would you have gone home? If you had known what was waiting for you, would you have gone to those kids? Would those children be dead now or would they still be alive? Or, would you have stolen those few more hours with Lawless, letting them all fall to your weakness?" He is whispering to me now, daring me to finally see into the cavernous hole of myself.

My jaw hangs open with the truth I am too ashamed to admit; my secrets that have been the catalyst for it all. I have thought my biggest failure was not saving them, but it wasn't. My biggest failure was not wanting to, and I finally claim it. "No," I say aloud, letting my secret fly like a caged bird that has been living behind bars for too long. "No." My body sags with it finally being free.

Marxx lets me fall with disgust plain on his face and it shatters my already bleeding heart. Like the red glitter I had left in Carol's hair, the tiny shards of what is left of my heart are now cutting me even deeper with my shame.

I never wanted any of it. I never wanted to have to save them and if I could do it all over again, I would never return to that house to find them. I would have never started this journey, this trial by death and fire.

I fall to the ground and the greens darken around me. The blades of grass become like razors as I fall, slicing my legs and feet. The ground is so covered in blood that the red from it splashes onto my hands and arms. It sprinkles onto my face, burning me with molten warmth when I fall. I lift my hands to stare at them. I watch the blood climb, covering me in it like a living thing. The blood climbs up my body inch by inch coating me in red death.

"You're wrong, Helena. It *is* your fault, and their blood will forever be on your hands." Marxx stands over me with the same look of disgust, but now it is mixed with a hatred that burns hotter than the blood on my body.

I hold my hands up to him, pleading for his forgiveness with shoulder-shaking sobs. The blood drips from my arms, keeping vigil for each life I have taken. The children now stand around me. Their white clothing is dotted with the blood they have splashed through to find me. They are not the monsters that I killed. They never were. They were just children. They were never really dead and now they stand around me with judgment on their faces. As I watch, wounds form on them, bleeding like scarlet letters of my shame. I watch each stab I have placed on them form, adding more blood to the ground at their feet as it runs down their perfect legs and arms. It destroys the innocence of their glowing white clothes just as I destroyed the innocence of their glowing youths.

"I'm so sorry," I whispered, too weak with shame and sorrow to add any volume to my voice.

"Where is my mommy?" one asks me.

"I want my daddy!" one little girl cries out.

"When can we go home?" a little boy asks.

They fill the air with their innocent questions as each begins to cry and plead for help. Marxx turns to leave me, giving me his back to face my sins alone.

"Marxx!" I scream, begging for him to stay with me. Begging him to, but I know he won't. "Marxx…" I fill my lungs with his name over and over, but he never turns around. He never looks back at me as the children bleed around me with their white clothes becoming as ruined as I made them months ago.

"Marxx!" I scream again, and my eyes are blinded by a bright overhead light. I blink against the glare, pulling the room into focus through the tears giving it a haze.

"What?" His gruff voice comes from beside me and I am almost too afraid to turn my head. He is sitting on the examining table looking at me with confusion and amusement. His arm is suspended in a sling and butterfly bandages cover a raw, red line on his forehead. I sit up, looking at my hands as if they are not my own. I flip them from palm-to-top several times as my brain catches up to what has happened. My winter coat has been removed along with the vest I have claimed as my own. The shirt I wore over my tank top is missing. With just the tank top and jeans, and my now trademark scuffed boots, the room is chilling.

My shoulder is an uneven ring of shading from the bruising that has started. My arm bears testimony to Chapel's earlier suggestion for stitches. My stomach stings and lifting the tank top I see the crisscrossing of lines that look like fine paper cuts, but I am alive. I am alive and not on a grassy field with children bleeding from their death; deaths that I caused.

"It was just a dream. You were there and -" I close my mouth against the nightmare, letting the sleeping demons lie.

"Yeah, he was there, I was there, and a lion was there. Time to wake up, Dorothy. You're back in South Carolina." Rhett's voice cuts through my confusion with a welcoming hug. He grips me tight and says, "Thought you were told to get back here. When are you going to listen?"

"Not my strong point," I say to him with a smile. "Law and Chapel?" I ask, not seeing them in the room.

"With the crazies." He rubs the top of my head roughly and turns to leave, holding the door to the adjoining room open as he waits for Marxx and myself. He stares at me and leaves the things he wants to say in his eyes. His eyes tell me how I scared him. They speak of the thoughts he was enduring as he watched us through the window. His trembling hand shows how bad he wants to hold me, but whatever is waiting for the three of us through that door is preventing him from showing any of it.

"I thought you were the crazy one?" I ask him, pausing before going through the doorway.

"Different kind of crazy," Rhett lets his voice drop low while his smile reaches high. *Grinning Riders In Torment*, that is what they call themselves because sometimes all you can do is grin when the pain is too great when there is nothing else to be done. Rhett does that now. He grins at me and lets the imagined laughter cover over his true emotions.

"Where is Aimes?" I ask, trying to delay having to face the unknown.

Rhett nods with his head into the room I am stalling from facing. "Being prayed over."

"… by Chapel?"

Marxx exhales behind me placing his hand on my shoulder to guide me through the door. The memory of the nightmare is still too close to the surface and I flinch without meaning to. He drops his hand and puts on his mask refusing to let the sting of my action show.

"Not Chapel. Now move." Marxx falls back to his limited vocabulary and blank eyes and shoves me forward.

The large sports medicine room of the gym is filled with faces that make my chest ache with gratitude. Lawless meets me halfway and we hold on to each other as if it has been years since we were allowed to touch. We embrace as if years have kept me from his arms instead of a few hours, and if today had gone differently, it might have been true.

He has showered and wearing new clothes since he had commanded me to leave him. His skin smells of the gym's soap and the scent enfolds me as I cradle into the space of his neck and shoulder. I ignore the warnings of pain and cling to him, not letting even air come between our bodies. His warmth and his scent engulf me and it's the first real touch of his comfort I have had all day. It brings tears to my eyes that I blink to deny.

I stare over his shoulder into a room where people are waiting with nervous anxiety. Simon is to one side with Richard and Dolph. Dolph stares at his feet to avoid watching Lawless and me, and he is not the only one in the room who is not thrilled with our reunion.

Leslie leans against the wall somewhere between the middle of their group and ours with a space left between her and Rhett. I know who filled that space. It is empty because he is now in my arms and I can't stop the smile that spreads across my lips. Petty? Maybe.

Chapel is standing in the center of the room with Paula. They are keeping watch on Aimes who still sleeps with her coloring a pale imitation of her natural skin tone. In the middle of it all, stands a man and a woman who's smiles at first strike me as venomous. The woman stands watching us with clasped hands to her face as if praying in front of curved lips. The man is older than her. His hair is more salt than pepper, and the two-toned combination hints of his age. The wrinkles at the corners of his eyes along with his smile emphasize it even more. Something about them both makes me subconsciously pull closer to Law. It must have shown in my eyes.

"Now, is that any way to greet the woman who saved you?" the man asks me, taking steps towards us.

Hearing the footsteps behind him, Lawless straightens. He gives me one honest look before his face lights with false sincerity. The smile would be convincing if he hadn't shown me his true thoughts. He turns to the man saying, "We are all grateful you arrived when you did."

Leslie snorts, giving her opinion of the topic. It draws a smile from Rhett with slow, deliberate thoughts. With his arms crossed and half leaning on the wall, he leans over to whisper to her and whatever he said causes her breathing to quicken and her face to become frozen with worry. As much as I have hated today, at least I was able to avoid Leslie.

The man takes note of the interaction and I see him storing it for later use with a glance to his female counterpart.

"I see there is some tension in the room," the woman says as she tries to gauge on which side of the room, she wants to place her friendship. I don't blame her. They have just walked into a civil war and there is no peace treaty or Switzerland between our sides anymore. The closest thing we have to that would be Chapel and Paula, but they both have their spines and their thoughts on the matter. They just prefer to not share them until they have to. With the barbs behind Paula's words, I prefer that, too.

"Is she going to be okay?" I ask Paula, completely ignoring the new drama that wants to play.

"Judging by the number of comebacks she had for the situation a moment ago," Paula says. "I think she'll live."

Sidestepping from Lawless, I go to my friend and stare at the sleeping pixie. "She was awake?" Her face is slack in slumber and it is odd to see it without her normal mischievous grin. Her lips are missing the scent from her never-ending supply of bubble gum with its pink tint that matches the absent shine of her lip-gloss. I used to tease her when she was eighty and in a nursing home, she would be the only one there with neon streaked hair, lip-gloss and using gum as a currency like cigarettes in a prison. I spent days hating her, pushing her away with my demons whispering to me because of my self-loathing. If she doesn't recover, those will be days that I can never make up for.

Lawless rests his hands on my shoulders letting his thumb rub the tension that rests there with my thoughts. "Yeah, she asked about you. Told her you were resting off another hero-mode episode." His voice is light-hearted, but my ears also bear the undertone of annoyance.

"I couldn't just go and not try to help."

"I know," he tells me, and he sounds as tired as he looks. His thumbs press a little firmer into my shoulders and I know that his conversation isn't over. The strangers standing watching us may have just saved me twice today.

"Travis and Selma." Chapel takes up the lulled space of the fallen conversation using it to introduce the two who are content to just watch the show.

"Your friend is going to be fine." Selma glides towards me. Her body has the lean, well-toned look of someone who has never been idle in life. Her dark hair and matching eyes contradict the sweet smile that never seems to fully leave her lips. It's her eyes that give me more pause than those red lips. "We just have to pray. God, in His salvation, will allow her to live if it is His will."

My thoughts hover somewhere between amusement and irony. I ask her, "You really believe that?"

"The reason the dead walk is because you, like so many, do not. Don't you see?" She comes to me, grasping my hands. She is filled with concern about my doubts. It adds a flame to her eyes that glow with her convictions. "We put our faith in science. We worshiped mortals like they were angels. We turned our eyes from the only one who can save us while we spent our words on praises for another. So, He took His eyes from us. He took our comforts away, bringing us to our knees where we should have been all this time. He wants his children back. He wants the love we stole from Him." Her voice fills with joy with each word that falls from her lips. Her face comes alive with the joy her mind is picturing with her imagined rapture.

"What naughty children we must be for our glorious Father to punish us so." Rhett has his own smile, and it removes Selma's.

She recovers quickly, forcing her face to be pleasant and peaceful. For a moment, with her back to the rest of the room, I saw the woman she was hiding. She turns to Rhett and says, "You have lived a life born from the Devil's rib. You have walked side-by-side with him for so long that it clouds your heart with bitterness." She smiles at Rhett with compassion. "That's why He has led us here. That is why we arrived just when we were needed the most. You sent those souls to heaven and God used them to lead us here. What you saw as smoke, He saw as a beacon. He saw that you believed with some small part of you and now we are here to help guide you home."

Home, such a dangerous and deceiving word to behold now. That simple one-syllable strokes an emotion across every face when she says it. There is nothing anyone wants more now than a home.

The feeling of it is not lost on Rhett. He pulls his shoulders back and looks from Selma as his jaw works out his emotions with slight movements. When he looks at her again, there is something new in those blue eyes. Something that I had witnessed before when he stood in the snow staring at me from behind the truck and it was gone as fast as it sprung to life. "My GPS works just fine, woman, and it's pointed south, not north," Rhett tells her with a relaxed stance that vibrates with his tension.

"Your maps just haven't been updated recently." Selma's smile is candy-coated, daring Rhett to sample her sweetness. It's the fact that he doesn't that says more than any response he may have given her.

I look to Chapel and as usual he is watching with locked, silent concentration. Chapel doesn't hear conversation; he sees it. He sees it in a way that makes a person squirm and rethink every word they said in the mountainous valleys of the silence between exchanges. A part of me has come to understand that was one reason J.D. disliked the man so much. Our glorious father controlled through fear and it's hard to strike fear in someone who sees what's more than just skin deep.

Paula feels the tension mounting from years of having to harness people under tight reigns. Her "Betty Crocker" is slipping into more of a "Mommy Dearest" personality. The day hasn't been kind to any of us.

"Out." Heavy and threatening, Paula uses one word to disarm any more bombs from exploding today. "Out," she says again, when no one makes the first move. She doesn't yell or bark her request. It's more like a mother who has finally found the last moment of sanity. She is so calm that it is more frightening than if she was wielding weapons.

Like waves being pulled by gravity, each group falls back into its own, departing the room. Our little hybrid of a family pulls back into the room where I awoke with Marxx, the man who now watches Rhett with veiled eyes and thoughts. He places himself between Rhett and Lawless so he can better watch the taller man.

"What was that?" Marxx asks, swaying so that Rhett cannot look away from him.

"Nothing." Rhett shrugs, dismissing the missed mark he normally lands with joyous pride. "I'm tired and didn't feel like toying with the bitch."

Marxx' eyes roam Rhett's face, not fully believing him before he looks at Lawless asking, "You tired?"

I know the real question. I know what Marxx is asking without asking in their double-edged word game. Lawless does, too. "Yeah," Lawless says, settling the debate and backing down both men. "Not all of us got to take a little nap." With one move, he has placed both men on equal footing of behavior without either having to be directly called out. Both men understand their mistake and both men accept it.

Chapel places one arm over my shoulder, pulling me to his chest in a false embrace to mask the words he whispers into my ear. "He might just be able to handle it," he whispers.

I look to him as he walks past me, hiding my reaction and he winks before fully putting his back to me. He leaves the measuring contest to the other three men as he throws his body onto one of the examining tables to sleep. The blue cushioned bench doesn't give at all and it sounds as ungraceful as it looked.

In agreement with Paula's earlier mood and now Chapel's need to distance himself, I turn to leave, and I'm instantly met with disapproval. "Where are you going?" Lawless' cold tone twists its way up my spine, paralyzing any movement of my body.

"We might have had a nap, but we didn't get a shower," I called to him over my shoulder. Two can play at the "who's the biggest slacker" game.

"She sure is spending a lot of time alone with Marxx here, Law," Rhett says, and I can hear a bench sigh with weight. I can see his smile with his joke without having to look at him.

"So, let me get this straight. You have no witty comeback when a stranger is questioning your conviction and loyalties, but put you in a room with just us and your Mr. Funny Man suddenly? Wouldn't that make you the bitch?" I'd like to think my mark was struck, slapping the smile from his face. The problem with Rhett, one smile normally just replaces a different, darker one. I'm not turning around to check. Nope, I'm walking right through these doors and praying the barrier will save my skin and the time-lapse from the shower will remove the risk of returning. I have high hopes. It's a lot like dreams, but a lot more gullible.

"Hey," Lawless calls to me, as we pass through the doorway and the sound of his voice pulls Paula from tending to the wounded that I had not noticed before. Her face shows no welcome and her mood is better accented with her hands resting on her broad hips.

Lawless lowers his voice to avoid her wrath, but still pulls me to a stop with an unfriendly hand on my arm. "That shit you pulled, it almost cost you your life, again. How many more times until you start to think?"

"I was thinking."

"Don't even play the martyr here on me. I have zero patience for your hero-act. I tell you to do something, from now on, you do it." He steps close to me, his eyes bearing down on me and not an ounce of kindness is reflected in their brown depths. "No more bullshit, Helena. You want to kill yourself, use a gun. Don't place your suicide at someone's feet."

His words chill me. I can feel them as they make their mark like cold liquid sliding down my throat. They settle like rocks into the pit of my stomach and I have to look away from him. "I can't save you from yourself," he tells me, and his voice holds the pitch of exhausted concern.

"Never asked you to." I am raw and I have nothing in me to give him. There is no fight or forgiveness to be asked. I'm just raw with exposed nerves and fatigue.

"I know," he says, letting go of my arm with fingertips that linger until the last possible moment.

Months have passed since we stood at the Welcome Center and I watched the first chasm form between us. As I watch his hand fall from me, I fall back into that moment when I knew our romance was becoming wilted like beautiful flowers that once stood admired and cherished. I have clung to him with needs of being wanted and feeling safe. Those are things of childhood ghosts and now my ghosts are much more demanding of my sanity. I have bigger demons now that whisper to me. I don't know if either of us is strong enough to battle for what we once were with the scars we have each caused the other, but I want him to be.

"Come with me?" I shyly ask him so hesitantly, that he stiffens in front of me. I look to him to see his mask staring back at me. I watch him roll his shoulders with exaggerated tension as he looks away from me. I know what his answer is going to be before he says it.

"No," he says as softly as I asked. "Not this time." He kisses the top of my forehead, keeping his lips to me while he struggles to control his emotions. "Not this time," he whispers, still hovering over me, asking for understanding for what he cannot do.

"You made me a promise, once," I say to his chest, with how close he is holding me.

"I've made you a lot of promises." He pulls from me, leaving the meaning of what he said balancing on a razor's edge. I watch him leave me, and only when his back is fully to me, do I have the courage to let the first tear fall.

I thought I was brave. I thought I was strong. I thought I was saving him, but watching him walk from me, I know now that I was condemning myself. Like a shadow, he was walking with me when the sun was high. Now that darkness is starting to surround me, he is fading into the pitch of it and it's my fault. What do you say when the reason the ground under your feet is eroding is because of you? What do you say to the mirror when it's what is staring back at you that is causing your misery? If you go chasing after white rabbits, eventually you will fall from the world you know.

Chapter 13

The chilled water from overhead flows over my slumped, battered body. It pools in my contours before running freely down my thighs. It swirls in a red tide at my feet from the blood on my skin before draining away. It's transfixing to watch, with my thoughts a jumbled mess, trying to avoid the obvious.

Marxx never followed me, leaving me alone to sulk and swim in my self-enforced depression. Perhaps sleep called to him more than the need to be clean. Perhaps, like myself, he didn't want to be alone with me. Twice now, my actions have almost gotten him killed. That has to dent any desire to repair fraying bonds. If I were a man, he would punch me, ridding himself of his anger and we would then hug and leave it all behind us. I am a woman though, and men never know how to really handle us in a fallout. They don't feel right saying the words that skip across their tongues, so they avoid talking to us at all. I don't know what I would say to him, either. Sorry just doesn't seem heartfelt enough.

My mind is drowning in my thoughts when I feel the butterfly-like caress of fingers on my back. They descend down my back, drifting along my spine, and the gentleness of it rolls me to standing. Only

Lawless would be so bold as to touch me like this and I close my eyes, letting him wordlessly seduce me.

His fingernails from the other hand presses into the skin of my thigh, scraping upwards on the tender flesh and the sensation of pleasure and pain pulls a moan from me. His breath is directly on the back of my neck, quickening my breathing with the anticipation of his mouth. My body is already responding with tightening and swelling, growing warm with my desire for him. I know this position well and I am already imagining the feel of his hands on my hips, the sounds of his moaning with the rhythm of our bodies, and the shattering release we will share with how well he knows how to bring me.

His hand travels my stomach, expanding his fingers as they slowly reach lower and I shiver under his touch, encouraging him. I open my eyes to watch him touch me and a scream gags my throat.

These are not the memorized fingers of a lover, but the flesh-rotting extensions of decay. I struggle to free myself from the arm's embrace that I was just willingly leaning into. The mouth that I thought was waiting to kiss me licks the base of my neck. The tongue feels like a thick slug slipping along my flesh. A demonic guttural male sound comes from behind me as his fingers dig into my lower stomach, trying to peel me open like a present filled with hidden delights.

The same fingers that I thought I would watch with enchantment; I now stare at in misery as they begin to tear into me. Blood oozes from the wound under the nails before trickling down my legs. He is going to eviscerate me as I watch, unable to escape from his vice-like grip. I scream from the pain as he pulls me apart like delicate lace.

The blood that was once droplets now flows like a thin stream. I can taste the bile of my fear. The beating of my heart hammers in my ears when my need for survival takes over any squeamish logic that I would cater.

I no longer pull on his arm to free myself. I mimic his actions and begin to shred his arm with my nails. His is oblivious to any pain that motivates me to desperation. I pull strands of his skin away like the layers of rotten wood. His dark, black blood rushes over my hands the deeper I gouge, scooping out corroded tendons to expose the bone. His body has been months without proper nutrients and the bones fracture with my punishing assault. I plead with the forming fissures to separate before his toying becomes deadly. Already his fingers have lost some of their strength with the damage, but it is not enough. His fingers still wiggle into my stomach like worms eating away at me.

The sounds of his bones breaking like the snapping of a wishing bone give me hope. They fracture bit by bit as I punch against them letting my hope give the ball of my fist strength. It's rewarded when the arm hangs limply, suspended in the air only by the depths of my stomach the fingers have penetrated and what is left of the destruction of muscles I have caused.

The slug had been traveling my neck like it was ice cream. Now sensing something has changed, he pauses with the tip of it still wiggling against me, betraying his mind's command. With his arm broken, the pause buys me the time I need to escape. Slipping past the shower's curtain, I start to run as he grasps me by the hair. The sudden shift in momentum sends me falling backward with the slick tiles producing no traction. The collision leaves my head spinning, stunning me with dots of bright lights. I feel him before my vision clears enough to allow me to see him.

He is licking the cavern his fingers have made, drawing my blood into his mouth. He pins me with his weight while fixing his mouth over the jagged wound, sucking the raw meat allowing him to swallow the reward. With each swallow, he is chewing his way into me like a parasite burrowing deep into its victim. My head is spinning from the pain, making it hard to concentrate. The pain brings ragged screams fighting to escape my body from the torture as he fights to enter me.

I have no weapon. There is no object around me that I can see to save me. I can hear my flesh separating under his probing tongue. I can feel my blood flowing hot over me as it warms the tiles, scenting the room with coppery death. It churns with the smell of decay from my abuser like Halloween potpourri.

"You waiting for some white knight here, Barbie?" J.D. taunts me from a dark, shadowed corner of the room. "You best get a move on if you are thinking of making it out of this mess." His eyes watch me with the same twisted sense of humor he held in life.

"You're dead," I whisper to him with the numbness and shock starting to climb into my mind, like wisps of calming clouds.

He laughs and it touches my skin like static electricity. "Join the club, Barbie. Where are those balls of yours? Twice today you rolled over for these things like one of those sheep out there. Did you become a sheep on me?"

"No."

"You sure? Cause you ain't doing a whole lot right now, are you?" He is standing over me, watching my death like a science experiment with the same interest over the outcome. "Why don't you take that elbow of yours and see how well it fares against that skull of his? Unless you want to be cored like some deer for slaughter." He stands, shrugging as he does. "Don't matter to me. I'll be seeing you soon, either way."

"…not today."

He smiles at me the same smile that used to chill my blood. The same blood that now pools hot around me like a fountain. "…not today?" he asks me.

My body is limp and heavy. Living in some dream-like state, my mind has detached from my body with efforts to block the pain of the gnawing. Now, I am demanding that it accept everything that it is trying to hide from like a parent dragging a child to a dark room. It's dragging its feet and refusing to look, but we both have to. We both have to walk through that fear-filled doorway if we want to live.

My arm is the weight of a giant's. It moves with the same grace as I drag it up, allowing gravity and the sheer limpness of it to collide my elbow with the skull that nuzzles back-and-forth into my stomach like a slurping lover. Each collision brings my mind to the brink of the doorway with small steps of avoidance until we both crash through it. It leaves me screaming again with the pain.

The screams fill me with life and the desire for his death. I have done enough damage to him that he is aware of me again. With my elbow bleeding from my broken skin, and dripping black from the remains of his wound, he turns to lock those hazed eyes on mine.

His face is smeared in crimson-black shades and it takes me a moment to realize that he is wearing me. Against my own desire, I look to where he has lifted his head and I see that he has torn open my lower stomach like a medieval cesarean. My eyes grow as wide as the wound and he smiles at my reaction to my horror.

I wondered earlier how many licks does it take to get to my spleen? We aren't finding out, not today. My leg closest to his head bends, striking my knee against his temple and ricocheting his head from side-to-side. His hands slip on the now blood-slick tiles and falls back into the ruin of my stomach he made. It slows us both for a moment until I can clear the black spots from my vision. I roll, dumping him onto the floor and scream with the burning fire of pain the movement brings. He is locked in his mental prison with the sudden change from meal to the fighter as he watches me drag myself away from him. His eyes roll to the projected path I have put myself on, but he does not see me as a threat. I don't blame him. I am smearing blood and tearing myself further open with my escape. I can feel every raised edge of the bathroom's tiles like they are serrated knives. They steal my breath and my vision with my self-mutilation for survival.

I know what I have to reach. My vision is tunneled on the pile of my discarded clothing. They beckon to me from the depths of my darkness with whispers of hope. I can hear the pleading of the words they hold for me. All I have to do is reach them and it will all be okay, but they seem to escape further from me with each drag that I use to pull myself forward. They aren't beckoning me. They are taunting me.

"Come on girl, get that ass moving." J.D. is squatting by the pile, putting voice to the words that it lacks the ability to do to the event. "Oh shit, he's coming for ya' now, Sweetheart. You better move." J.D. laughs as he looks over my shoulder and I too look.

The Risen has grown bored with the delay. He is crawling towards me with a jerky one-armed motion without eagerness, but with patience. He has already fed today. I am just the late morning snack he was craving; warm, alive, and squirming in his mouth. Seeing him moving makes me move.

"Oh, it's on now. Look at him move. He wants your ass harder than Law does!" J.D. is shouting with amusement. His crude laughter weaves with his words.

"Fuck you," I say between my gritted teeth.

"Oh, watch out. She's got her bite back. What are you going to do, Barbie? You going to pull that limp body of yours over here and shut me up? You going to come make me?"

My anger claws back against the pain. I use it to push my body the last few inches even as it fights back to succumb to death.

"Come on, Sweetheart. Come on. Come get it." J.D. is filling the room with his boisterous voice as he claps, cruelly encouraging me to reach the pile and it drowns out the growling from behind me.

I reach for *it*. The *it* J.D. was taunting me to find. The *it* I stole from Lawless when he kissed me good-bye. The *it* he pretended not to notice missing from his back. The *it* now resting firmly in my hand with its loaded weight of welcoming satisfaction.

I roll onto my back and the Risen pauses, staring into the barrel of the gun. His face contorts to rage, and he screams at me. The trigger slides back and the skull disappears with a black spray from the many shots I fire. I fire until the clip is empty and with the body now a headless, soaked mess, I fall back to the tiles. I am exhausted, wracked with pain, and fighting to control my breathing between my silent sobs, but I am alive. So far, I am alive.

"Stay dead, J.D," I whisper to the memory and he laughs. It floats around the room like a phantom dancer flirting with the shadows. "Just stay dead."

The room explodes with shouting and movement. My name is in the jumbled mess of sounds, but it's Rhett's voice that I recognize first from my drifting torture. "When I pictured you nude, wet, and waiting for me on your back, it was always a little less gory."

"Liar," I barely whisper to him, with my mind crawling back into the safety of oblivion from shock.

"Maybe," he tells me, and I feel something warm drape across my body.

"Take a deep breath," Lawless coaxes me from behind my closed eyes. At least, I think they are closed. The blackness could be from my lack of desire to see anything, anymore.

"Why?" I ask him, with half-hearted interest. My mind is already gone, refusing to put any pieces of conversations together. I won't force it back to the doorway, again.

"I'm going to move you."

"That doesn't sound like a lot of fun."

Rhett laughs his deep male chuckle of danger. "Looking around here, your sense of fun worries even me."

Lawless lifts me, sending fire and ice scalding through my body. I swim between screams and nauseating white noise. I choose to skinny dip into the lake of white noise, letting it take over my senses. It locks my voice and lulls my body into thick limpness.

"Is she -" I hear Chapel start to ask, but Lawless clips his question short.

"No," he says, with conviction to spare and share with the rest of the room. "She wouldn't do that to me."

Just like a man to make my death all about his needs.

"You wouldn't do that to me," Lawless says again, and I know he is speaking to me as I feel us running to Paula. I know that he is trying to convince himself as well as me the need to believe in it. Personally, hanging limp and floating somewhere between the present and the past, he may be the only one.

There has to be that moment when you accept that your luck has run out. I have been balancing on the edge of death since it started, daring it to take me with my self-hatred spurring me into every fray under the false banner of bravery. It wasn't bravery that encouraged me to lure the crowd from Aimes; it was the fact I didn't deserve to live, and she did. It wasn't boldness that allowed me to step up to J.D.; it was the lack of caring what happened. It isn't confidence in Law's words that keeps me clinging to the thin veil of conciseness now; it's my defiance to let the laughing devil that now haunts me be correct. I'm not a heroine or a leader. I'm flawed, moody, and stubborn and that's all the luck that has kept me alive so far. Everything else, that's just Fate's cruel twist of my life for her amusement.

I know when we reach Paula's infirmary. The lights brighten the hue of darkness my eyes hold from pitch to silver. I know the moment he places me upon one of the tables as the white-hot pain eats my body, opening my eyes. Everything is hazy and blurred as if looking through a window of dirty glass. I can make out who-is-who only from my understanding of what their outlines should hold. My voice is still locked and already my head is starting to swim back into the darkness.

I feel more than I see as Lawless places himself near me amid the dark shadows and shapes. "Don't do this. Not after how far we have come. Don't you do this to me," his voice is crumbling, trembling with the same force as the hand that rests on the side of my face.

"Let her go," Paula's steady voice comes across from him. Lawless must have shared some look of confusion because I hear her say, "You don't want her awake for what I am going to have to do. She is missing tissue. I'm going to have to pack this wound before I can stitch it. This is not going to be easy. It's best if she just went under on her own. I don't have anything here for pain."

"Nothing?" It's Chapel now that speaks somewhere from the void.

I can almost picture Paula shaking her head in the long pause of her answer. "Nothing for the amount of pain that I am about to cause her," she says, and it's a rousing endorsement. I just can't wait to get started.

"…but she is going to make it?" Marxx, my personal super-hero, is somewhere to my left. I wonder if comic book heroes ever grow annoyed with having to keep saving the same female counterpart over-and-over again? Do they ever just want to shout, "Jesus Christ, when will you learn, woman?"

"…skin is greying. Her heartbeat is irregular. She pretty much bled out in there and if you don't let me get started, she may very well finish in here," Paula says, and I have lost some of the conversations with my mental debate. Am I going to make it?

There is a gentle kiss placed on my forehead. It stalls with the need to stay connected in some way. It's the same kiss Lawless gave to me before he walked away, and it is the same that he gives me now. "You like to prove people wrong. I think you do it just to piss people off. Do it now. Prove her wrong now," Lawless whispers to the skin he left his mark on, before I feel the heat of his body leave me. The missing warmth chills me in more ways than one.

"I know you're still here. You're a fighter to the end, but now, you have to give up. You need to let go, Helena. I'll do my best to keep you alive, but right now, you need to let go." Paula's voice is already slipping away.

I try to fight to hold onto it as if it held mass, but my mental fingers slide through it, falling like Alice into the hole. I am chasing white rabbits again and they have led me back into the darkness, right back into the same pitfall of irony.

"Helena? Helena, come play." It's Lilly's voice. It precedes the same scent of innocence that has become her perfume like a haunting record.

I'm back on the grassy field, but this time it is J.D. who is sitting on the hill waiting for me. He is chewing on one of the blades of grass, unaware of the razor-like edge that has sliced his lips. He is oblivious to the blood that is flowing from the corner of his mouth, and when he smiles at me, it only flows faster. It drips down his chin onto the leather vest that I know waits for me in another world. A world I have left behind with my rabbit hole of hell.

"I thought you said you weren't coming to see me today, Barbie?" he laughs, with his joke and all I can do is cry. If Marxx saw through the gate of my secrets, J.D. will destroy the vault that holds them.

As I stand with the grass already breaching the flesh of my feet and legs with each wind that sways the blades like saws, I watch the children and I listen to the laughter. I have to wonder, do the ghosts of my past haunt me or am I haunting them? Do I cling to them for fear of forgetting them or do they cling to me with the fears that I will forget what I have done to them? When J.D. stands with his bleeding mouth to come to me, I know it doesn't matter. We are all bound together now, through hell or paradise, we are together. The saints, the sinners, and myself, like a collection of broken toys for the gods' amusement in our purgatory.

Chapter 14

Time slips from me like sand in an hourglass or the hours wasted watching a predictable soap opera on television – whichever suits the situation better. Sometimes I can catch the fragments of conversations and I imagine what the words mean with comical glee. In the trapped darkness of my mind, I picture them dramatically acting out the things they are saying with forced emotions. Chapel and Paula have quite the romance, at least in my mind, anyway.

Sometimes there is just the shuffling silence of someone sitting next to me like a shadow that just hovers and watches the show. The shadows sometimes speak. They whisper encouragements to open my eyes or to give them something to let them know I can hear them. They tell me about what is going on and what moments I have missed. No one speaks of Aimes and I take notice of that. Does she lie beside me in her own dark well of dreams or has she escaped them to find security somewhere else far from any of us? Is she somewhere I seem to always be denied?

It's Dolph's shadow that is speaking to me now. He is telling me something that I know should be important, but my mind is already drifting back into the undertow of bliss. The harder I fight to stay in the long tunnel of his voice, the faster the current pulls at me.

"…know how much longer. They don't even pretend…" I hear him and a wave of nothing crashes over me, drowning him out. "It won't last much longer if…" Another wave before he starts again. "Lawless and Rhett won't back down. They both…" Like the rocking of the sea, his voice ebbs and flows around me. "It's going to shit, Helena. Simon said it was J.D. that held all of you together. Without him, they are just fighting with…"

I don't need to hear anymore. If I could roll my eyes, I would. Let me guess, the boys are being naughty, and you want me to bring them into line, again. End of the world, killing zombies, I'm one thread from a complete mental breakdown and I still have to muck through the miles of male ego. It's just another day in paradise and me without my fruity drink with its matching umbrella.

I have lost time again. The last time I left Dolph was speaking to me like I was an effigy of a holy relic with the powers to save mankind. Now, there is shouting. Angry male voices reverberate through the room. Instantly the part of me that has a romance with my middle finger starts to dive back down again, but the side of myself which relies on my humanity has to look at the car wreck stays awake with curiosity.

Lawless is shouting about something someone has done. I can hear things being thrown around the room with metallic clamoring when the objects land. Chapel and Marxx are trying to talk him down from the steep cliff he has climbed in his rage.

"This is what they want. You are playing right into their hands with this temperamental bullshit of yours," Marxx' gravel voice demands Lawless' attention. "You can't keep taking the bait."

"No, I'm just supposed to be spoon-fed their shit?" The objects have landed, but Lawless hasn't climbed from the cliff yet. It sounds more like he is ready to jump.

"You're supposed to walk away." Chapel weighs in from somewhere deeper in the room. He is letting Marxx do the subduing. I can't really fault him.

"*He* would never back down to them," Lawless stresses the word, hinting at the one we all know he speaks.

"*He* isn't here, and you are not him." Marxx doesn't back down from the man Lawless viewed as a father. "Don't become him. You won't like that road."

Stay dead J.D. Why can't you just stay dead? I'm almost afraid he will answer me shrouded in the darkness of the chamber I mentally occupy.

"You saying I don't have what it takes to be him?" Lawless asks.

"I'm saying you won't like being him. You're going to have to find your own way now, Brother. You don't have to live in his shadow anymore," Marxx says.

I put together the pieces of what is going on in the drawn-out silence. I imagine Lawless standing there with his hands in the vest pocket rebuilding the layers of his brick walls while Marxx and Chapel watch motionless, afraid to break the fragile mortar that holds him together. I can feel the weight of Chapel's eyes with how well trained they are to see into the corners of your soul that you either try to hide in or from him. I can feel them so well because it takes me a moment to realize that I am staring into them. My vision expands from the one pinpoint of his face to include the whole room. It's like wiping away the film from a window before you stare through it. You just never expect anyone to be staring back at you when you press your face to the glass.

"Hells?" Chapel calls my name, with more question than hello.

I blink, trying to keep him in focus and all the give-a-damn I can muster is, "What?" It's very lackluster, but somehow feels perfect.

"It's about time," Marxx chuckles, seeing my eyes swing to him. "Thought you had finally checked out on us."

"If only you were so lucky." I wince, trying to sit up and reluctantly admit defeat from the pain. Chapel rushes with a mini-skip like movement to get to me when he sees my curiosity over the wound.

"You don't want to do that," Chapel tells me. Marxx and Lawless are avoiding my gaze. It's bad. It's very bad.

"She's going to have to." Lawless looks to me with pity and yet a moment of guilt crosses the shadows of his eyes.

"What? No more bikinis?" I try to smile, but their faces scare me. These are men that have done the things most of us only threaten to do in moments of anger. They did it because they found it fun. They were blood-soaked and sin-tainted before it became a necessity to be so. Now, whatever is hidden under my gauze-wrapped lower stomach is making them cringe.

"You really want to do this?" Chapel is asking me with a warning undertone. Lawless is right, I always have to push my luck; me and my white rabbits.

Chapel removes the tape and I hiss as the blood-stuck gauze is lifted away. They were right. I should have listened. My lower abs are a gaping, vertical arch of red meat. The many stitches that try to pull the jagged flesh together wander down my stomach in a drunken swagger of a pattern. I have seen better stitches in Frankenstein movies, and I am feeling about as pretty as one of his brides.

"It kept getting infected. Paula had to keep removing more and more trying to find healthy tissue to save." Chapel recovers the wound hearing my uneven sigh. "It looks good now." His statement makes me wonder what it looked like before, but I think better of asking. See? I'm learning.

"Aimes?" I ask, happy to change the topic from my new accessory and myself.

"Good," Chapel finally smiles, and it spreads through the room like a candle's glow.

"Giving us all grief like normal." Lawless smirks and I know who has been her verbal punching bag. He comes to me with exhaustion weighing heavy on his shoulders. I guess I haven't missed that much at all. "What am I going to do with you?" he asks me half-teasing, half-angry.

"Spank me. It's the only way I'll learn," I tell him, with hopes to pull the teasing further to the surface than his anger. When his eyes warm with half-masked thoughts, I know I have won.

"On that note," Law's voice is ripe with unanswered desires. We are suddenly alone in the room, or we might as well as be for the lack of attention we have to spare for anyone else. His fingertips caress my face, rememorizing the map of my features like a man drowning and desperate for pleasant memories. "I'm sorry," he tells me, as he stares at his fingers to avoid my eyes. "I should have been there."

"You kept your promise."

He chuckles with remorse. "I shouldn't have to keep coming for you. I should already be there."

Shrugging I tell him, "I'm not an easy one to keep safe."

"That one we will agree on."

"Where did he come from? Where did any of them come from?" I ask the question that has twirled in my mind with my forced slumber. "We cleaned out the place."

"We never checked the second floor. We went right to the third. When they were bringing their dead down, it must have brought them down. We have found a few just roaming, but it's clear now."

I shift letting him sit beside me, but he isn't happy with just that little space once the invitation has been given. Like a gentle lover, he stretches out the length of his body, pressing it against my side. He cradles my head with his arm tucked under me while the other travels up and down my body with soothing measures. This is the side of Lawless that only I am allowed to see. In private moments like this, he is mine and not the man he has to become for others.

"How long?" I ask him, letting the waves of his fingers coast me out to a relaxing sea of safety.

"That you have been under?" He shrugs with his face. It's a gentle frown before relaxing again. "Almost three weeks. Paula said if you didn't wake up soon…" He stops, unable to continue and unable to look at my face. "You kept calling out for J.D. I never wanted him back more than I did then."

I don't have the heart to tell him that more than likely I was yelling for him to leave me alone in whatever state of purgatory he was walking with me. "I'm sorry," I tell him, and I feel like a coward.

He finally does shrug this time. "Don't blame you. He was always the one we went to when we needed someone to pull us through. He always knew what to do."

"It wasn't always the right thing" Is what my tongue wants to say. Instead, I say, "Yeah." I'm earning that gold medal of chicken shit today. Silver isn't as pretty, anyway. "Anything I should know about?" I bring the topic away from the man he sees as savior and I see as something between father and tormentor.

"Later," he whispers against the sensitive skin of my neck, "let me just be right here, right now."

Now who's the chicken? "You know that is not going to happen, right?"

He sighs with a mixture of a laugh and exhales. "Yeah, I had hoped, though."

"Last time I left you alone…" I leave the accusation unsaid between us. I'm holding my breath just the same as if I had asked about Leslie out loud.

His sigh is long and wounded. I can feel his whole body deflate with it. "I told you. I'm all in. No more running, Helena. I'll hold us both down if I have to, but no more running."

"So, is that a no or is the florist just out of white roses?" I ask, once again trying for humor to skirt having to face anything deeper. He bites my ear with gentle teeth, and I have to laugh before pulling free. "Who were you yelling about?"

"Rhett has made some new friends." Lawless settles deeper into the groove beside me, refusing to talk about it anymore. It doesn't take long before his breathing is a steady, calm pattern of slumber. It is the only thing that is calm.

I remember the look on Rhett's face when Selma had said that one word. That one word that we each hold dreams of with golden-lined aspirations. Did Rhett fall into his own rabbit hole or has he simply stepped to the side of Simon? Did the look of rooted angst the day when Lawless stepped up to lead bear poisonous fruit? How do you lure the beast back into a cage once it has tasted freedom? How far has Rhett taken his Independence Day and how many bonfires has it cost us? All of this rampages my mind with a new fear greater than the last with each new question that forms.

I want to be brave enough to wake the sleeping man at my side and ask it all, but I know that soon I will be facing them. Soon I will be out there, neck-deep in whatever has befallen while I was held in the confinement of my dark, unconscious delirium. It waits for me like a noose, and if I am to hang, let me steal what bliss that I can, while I can. Let me just be right here, right now.

Chapter 15

The whole place still wears the scars of what has happened. It's on the faces of those who still walk the halls like colorless outlines of their former selves. It's the conversations that hold whispers too afraid to speak for whom may be listening. The discoloration and irregular patterns along the floors and walls will forever stand as proof like monuments to the deaths that have happened. The air has the smells of brutality and frailty like a wind of forced change. The air is more suffocating than life-giving, and it carries the taste of madness; a madness that dresses itself up in the trappings of pearls and virginal whites tricking those around it with beguiled charm.

"Dear God." My jaw hangs with what is waiting in the courtyard.

"Pretty, huh?" Aimes says beside me, staring at the relic that has my attention. She had been waiting for Lawless and I when we awoke. By awoke, she was flicking her wet fingertips at us until the water startled Law awake enough that he fell from the bench with his sudden movement and the limited space it had. I had laughed watching him chase her around the room with his injured pride, a source of more amusement for her. After all that we have come through, I still felt that tinge of jealousy watching their easy friendship.

"What the Hell is it?" I ask her, as we walk through the cafeteria's war-beaten walls.

She exaggerates her eyes and wiggles her fingers saying, "Our salvation."

"Our what?"

"Your cavalry has a big cup of psycho they drink from. The worst part." She points to where a group of people stand and I spot a familiar face, "our psycho is doing shots of it."

Rhett stands amid the new group and when he smiles, I feel my stomach sour. There, in the middle of what I remember as burning piles of sheet-wrapped memories and decaying decimation has been transformed into rows of wooden pews leading to a wooden cross that looms in front of them. It casts a long shadow that feels more threatening than inspiring. The pews erected upon the scorched cement seem to mock what took place there. As if one could sit silently in revelations upon the remembrance of the murdered.

To further add to my misgivings, the cross looking to be made of tree trunks wears a white shroud draped across its extended arms like a white sheet once used to spare the sight of the dead. All around it mingling with smiles and welcoming embraces are those who came riding in with open arms of heroics with Rhett as their shiny new centerpiece.

"They have convinced everyone that God moves through them and they are here to save us by doing His work." Lawless crosses his arms, staring into a scene depicting a joyous reunion, not a place of earth that holds more tragedy than a place should. "The sheep almost worship them."

It's not the people he is glaring at, but someone who once stood by our side. Even with the tinted windows, Rhett looks over as if he can feel our eyes on him. Maybe he can.

"Sheep, huh?" I ask, remembering another man that dubbed them with that word. He shrugs at me with his face matching the motion.

"Our little Lawly has become quite the cranky guy with your departure." Aimes leans forward to glance past me where we three stand lined up. She sticks her tongue out at Lawless and he rolls his eyes with the fact. I'm guessing he has heard this speech before.

"Why do I have a feeling I am going to be blamed for a lot of this with my "departure"?" I ask her.

She smiles at me and I can feel the sarcasm coming. "Because you're just so purdy," she tells me, batting her eyes with false worship.

Chapel saves me when his arms drape over my shoulders pulling me to his chest. "Let her get back on her feet before you two send her back to hiding."

"Had any conversations with the man from Galilee, lately?" Lawless asks Chapel, while trying his best to not let his thoughts cross his face. He nods to Marxx when the man comes to stand beside him, but keeps his eyes forward.

"None worth repeating," Chapel answers, watching the crowd grow outside.

"You?" Lawless tilts his head to Marxx asking for his input.

"Why start now?" Marxx asks him, telling his opinion on the idea of religious rapture.

"Me either," Lawless says. He turns to look at Chapel and asks, "So, what does that make them?"

"Kool-Aid makes the world go 'round?" Aimes offers, tinting the tone of the conversation to more of her style.

Chapel is unmoved with her humor. The preacher's son won't be deterred, not by her or by whatever is assembling beyond us. "Faith makes the world go around. Kool-Aid just makes it more fun to watch," he sighs, and I can feel it expand his broad chest.

"How is this even possible?" I ask, still stuck on my confusion over how so much has changed in what, to me, feels like only hours.

"We lived in a time of smartphones and stupid people," Marxx grunts, showing he stands as annoyed as Lawless with the change of scenery.

Aimes sighs and it's never a good sign. "Yeah, I miss sexting," she says, as if it is the most normal thing to admit to missing. Sometimes, I really wish she would just smile and nod instead of sharing her special trademarked skills of conversation.

"Let's get this over with," Chapel says, with one final hug.

"Get what over with?" I ask, growing nervous watching Lawless stiffen.

"Why, silly, the cleansing of our souls." Aimes tilts her head, smiling at me with comical confidence. "We couldn't possibly risk the end-of-days with these black marks on our hearts."

"Why is it with every question I ask you, I just grow more confused?" I make a face at her and she returns the heart-felt gesture with one of her own.

"Because you're just so damn purdy," Marxx says, on the far end of our chain and it makes both Aimes and I laugh.

"I think I'll sit this one out." Lawless is unmoved by the laughter with his brown eyes still seeking the tall man that he once called Brother.

"You sat out of the last one and you remember how well that went over." Aimes' eyebrow is arched so high it looks purely cosmetic, but with her mouth set into a frown it is anything but false.

"She's right," Chapel says. "You need to sit with us and see how Travis handles it. Let him try to spin a new tale."

Marxx knows that Lawless holds no concern for how Travis sees him. He takes a different road. "You can keep Hells warm and piss Dolph off."

It works. Lawless smiles with the thought, but it's not a smile of affection. It's pure male ego wrapped in well-formed lips and reflected in amused eyes. Watching him, I feel like a goldfish won at a county fair and I just want to float to the bottom of the bag with hopes this new home offers some consolations.

"Let's get this over with," Lawless echoes the words with his new resolve.

Marxx bounces the door open with his palms letting the loud sound signal our arrival. Conversations lull to a dull undertone. The men never pause to glance around them but almost rudely take a converted pew. Marxx places his feet on the one in front of us motioning with his eyes for Aimes and I to sit on either side of his boots. Lawless and Chapel frame us so that the men look like hired security surrounding us. Of course, Aimes can't pass up the chance to unlace the heavy leather boots and Marxx lets her amuse herself. Half of Aimes' antics are out of nervous tension. The other half are just out of mischievous craziness stirred with boredom. No one likes it when she gets really bored.

Lawless stretches back so that his elbows support him on Marxx' bench. It places the two men side-by-side despite their different pews. It all looks very relaxed and bored, but I have seen this act before from them. They both stare at Rhett with that same uninterested look, letting him know as well the game they are playing. With their silent ways of speaking, they have let each other know that Lawless and Marxx will step up if something threatens us and Chapel has the duty of protection. What the hell has happened while I was recovering?

With the appearance of Travis, whom I remember briefly, the crowd recovers and begins to settle around the nearby pews. Simon takes the pew furthest from the front. He seems to have aged decades since I saw him last. His constant, flirting smile has been destroyed by what life has left of him. Dolph is sitting to one side of him, but Richard is missing and something about the way Dolph sits lets me know he is not just running late.

"Where is Richard?" I whisper to Aimes, as if we were really sitting in a sacred place of worship.

Aimes shakes her head at my question. She never looks up from the mess she is making of Marxx' laces. If there is a sudden need for Marxx to move, I don't think he will make it very far, but he says nothing, so her fingers keep toying.

"Lost him with your first suicide attempt," Lawless answers, never lowering his voice from a normal level of conversation.

"That was far from her first," Marxx counters. "You need to recount."

I turn to look at the two men who find themselves rather funny. "Really?" I hiss, and earn wider grins from my frustration.

Travis clears his throat with his level gaze locked in our direction. "If we may start?" he asks, not masking his annoyance.

Marxx blows him a loud kiss and Lawless has to duck his head to recover from his laughter. Oh father, how proud you would be if you were still here. Travis is not as amused, and he looks to Rhett who is standing at the edge of the raised pulpit. Rhett flexes his shoulders, pulling them back and his chest forward in a slow stretch. It's a silent challenge and it brings the humor in the men beside me to a stop, but it brings something else forward.

Lawless sits up, leaning onto his legs with a bowed back and a steady gaze, sending his own challenge. I'm not even bothering to see what Marxx has projected, but his boots no longer separate Aimes and me.

"Beloved, children of God, we come together tonight under the clear blue sky of our Lord to give praise and thanks to Him today." Travis' voice rings out over the courtyard. His widow peak of thick graying hair rustles in the breeze. His lips curve into a smile as he speaks. I think I have seen sharks wear the same grin. "Today, we have proof of His mercy. We hold vigils to His miracles. He has not forsaken us as so many of you have thought. No!" Travis comes from behind the attempt of a podium with emotions vibrating his voice. His words are inflaming him, and he hungers for that fire to spark in those around him. "You thought you walked in His shadow cast by His back turned to you. You feared He had removed your names from His heart, but today, today my brothers and sisters, we have proof of His steadfast devotion to us sinners."

"People actually believe this stuff?" I lean into Aimes to ask her with as silent as I can be and still be heard over his continued shouts of proclamations.

"Oh yeah," she whispers back.

"Does Rhett?" I ask, still huddled in our bubble of whispering.

"Hook, line and vagina."

"What?" I look to Rhett with her explanation with shock and baffled confusion. He meets my eyes with his blank face refusing to acknowledge me.

"He and Selma Whorepants are the new it couple. I have bets on a June wedding," she tells me, locking her eyes on Rhett who is trying to not watch us. Aimes, being the rock star that she is, lifts her middle finger towards him and runs her tongue up its length slowly before sucking it into her mouth. For a moment, a smirk pulls on his lips before he recovers, and those blue eyes go from amused to winter ice. "Look, I'm not saying Rhett is a sex addict. I'm just saying you never see Rhett and a virgin together in the same room."

"You never see me and Batman in the same room," Lawless says nonchalantly.

"No, but I have seen your wallet and you in the same room enough times to feel pretty confident that you are not a Wayne," Aimes says, beaming her mischief to the man beside us.

"How many people do you think live inside Rhett?" I ask, watching his rapid mood swings with curiosity.

"Depends on the alcohol," Lawless says, with the same lack of amusement for the man that the man now stares at us with.

With my attention focused on Rhett, I missed the fact that Travis has been making his way towards us or to where his ranting has been leading. Now, he stands beside Lawless with a smile that feels more predatory than a pilgrim. Have to give the man credit for bravery.

"What is the miracle I speak of? What is this holy icon of His guiding hand for you to reflect upon? For you to grasp in your moments of weakness?" Travis is staring right at me while he speaks, and I sense that this is all about to go wrong for one of us. If Karma holds true to her style of humor, it will be me.

He reaches for me and with that one motion Lawless and Marxx stand. Rhett is now moving towards us from the front, as Dolph is moving behind us. Chapel has already started scooting Aimes further from the eye of the storm; that eye being myself. Karma, she's a funny one.

Travis is either paying no attention to the tension he has started or simply enjoys the theatrics. He never pauses in his preaching. "Here among us once again is the heroine you have all come to love. This child of God who has placed herself in harm's way for your own safety with no thoughts for herself. The one who holds the hearts of these distressed men who are in need of her guidance back to their salvation." With each sentence, the crowd grows louder in agreement with his revelations. "She, who has been tested by these demons time and again only to stand taller with His love from each encounter. Is it not God's supremacy over these evils that lends her the courage to fight them? Is it not His halo of golden protection that encircles her like the Angel David to defeat the cruelty of the Devil? What other answer would you have, but His?" The courtyard erupts into shouts of joy with his sudden outburst of a question. The louder they grow the angrier the men around me become.

I bite my tongue against the sharp wit that cuts my mouth. If someone had been taking notes of my life, it's not Travis. I would place my faith in sadistic irony before a holy, guiding hand.

Travis reaches for me, pulling me to him to further his crusade. Lawless mimics the movement, keeping his shoulder between Travis and I. His hands are a relaxed clasping of his wrist at his waist, just waiting for use while Travis continues his aimed words. "We arrived here at the point in time when she was being tested the most. She was tested in the moment of saving not only you, but also her people as well. She was prepared to give in to the Devil's temptations of peace." The crowd murmurs with some imagined fear they feel. "Oh yes!" he tells them, raising their anxiety higher. "She had given over her body to the demons and her mouth to the Devil. Selma pulled her from the wreckage of her destruction only to hear the blasphemy fall from her damned, ruby lips." He points to the woman who bows her head with sadness letting her black hair fall around her shoulders in condolence. "She said unto her," Travis lowers his voice to hushed whisper to continue, "There is no fucking God," he yells, with the Devil's disjointed moment of evil enticements. But God didn't give up on her like how easily she was lured from Him. He sent us here right at that moment to guide her back to Him just as we have guided so many of you back to His love. He saved her with His glory, healing her broken body and soul so that she may return to you tested and tempered. Not once. Not Twice, but three times!" He turns from me, putting his back to Lawless and Marxx who hum a chord from the song with the same theme unmoved by the show.

Travis is counting on Rhett who stands beside him to keep the two men in line for the finale. That mistake might just cost us all.

"Children," he continues, "my brothers, my sisters, my friends do not judge the ones who pull from Him. Fear not the ones who ache to walk in the shadows of evil. Do not label them in their weakness and black hearts for we are here now. We are here to keep safe with His help what these men could not."

I felt the shift before it happened. As I lunged for Lawless, his hands shoved against the back of Travis, sending him to his knees. Stepping in front of Law to stop him, I forgot about Rhett. I forgot about the one who no longer caters to our security. So accustomed to him being beside me, I neglected his motives. Rhett, lost in the forward momentum never had time to stop his fist. It collides with my face, crumpling me with his strength and silencing the roar the courtyard had become with Travis' preaching. Time is suspended with the shock of what has happened. Kneeling on the cement, I have to wonder at what point did I switch from life's amusement to its piñata.

"Son of a bitch!" Aimes' voice fills the silence first. The strong arms of Chapel, who she is no match for no matter how angry she becomes, holds her against him. She is going to try to escape him just the same with her rage. "That is Helena you piece of shit! You hitting women now? You get a shiny new piece of ass and forget who you are? Do *they* even know who you are? Do your new holy rollers know about you like we do?"

"Shut up!" Rhett yells back at her.

"Or what?" she yells back, just as loud, like the Chihuahua of anger that she is. "You going to march over here and hit me, too? Does it make your new conquest wet to see you beat on your former friends? She sure seems to always be around when you grow brave."

Rhett steps forward to her and Lawless is there to block him. He stands chest to chest with the taller man and smiles into his face. "Dare you," Lawless says, and they lock eyes with the challenge.

I stand, swaying some with the sudden shift of the earth. "All of you shut up," I say, with more vindication than I feel. "It was an accident. It's my fault. I forgot that Rhett has turned his back on his family for a piece of ass when I stepped between them." I look into the blue eyes that turn to me bleeding into shades of sorrow and guilt. "Like I said, my fault for trusting him." I pull Lawless from Rhett and turn my back on him. "It won't happen again."

"See how she calms their beast? See how -" Travis stands, gearing up for another round of Who's-Your-Savior when my wit finally escapes.

"The snake charming is over for today, Travis." I lean close to his ear and sweetly say to him, "If you think they have a black heart, you had better hope God does reach down to guide me because you haven't seen anything yet. It wasn't God who guided me back from death. It was actually someone much, much closer to their nature."

Travis turns his head to speak to me. "I know of the man you deemed father," he says, and we are talking so close to each other's face our lips could touch like lovers.

"No, you don't," I say to those lips, that seem to reach for me with an unnamed hunger. "If you did, you wouldn't keep poking them like a child. Eventually, I'm going to let their beasts play and then you will really know about the man I deemed father, Travis," I say his name as close as I can to his lips, without touching them and I feel his response. He is hungry, amused, and somewhat taken aback by my boldness.

"Mommy's home," Aimes says and there is no missing the mischief in her voice.

"...and she's so damned purdy," Lawless says, pulling me to him with a proud smile.

Rhett watches me walk past him and I don't even look in his direction. He has made his choice of which side he now lives and sealed it with the mark on my face. When my anger and the pain from his fist fade, I will feel sadness over that fact. Right now, both are hot, burning me in their own way and that heat lends my legs the confidence to put him behind me even if my head is still swaying from the blow.

"Bye, Lover Boy. Say a prayer for me, would ya?" Marxx asks Rhett, dousing the exit with brighter flames before turning to follow me with Lawless in tow as they return to humming the song from The Commodores.

My family follows me away from the murmur of the people we leave in our wake, but I hadn't expected to see Dolph and Simon keeping pace in the reflection of the glass in the windows. I have no idea what this means for them or us and I'm not stopping to glance behind me to ask either set.

I have never learned to count my blessings. I choose to dwell in my disasters. Sometimes I wallow in them. Sometimes though, I hurl them like a Molotov cocktail and watch with enjoyment as they burn everything down around me. It's amazing the things we can use as a weapon against the ones we love.

My confidence falters as soon as I am past the metal doorway of the cafeteria. I let the pain of my face take me, giving away to the tears that it causes as I sit at one of the tables nearest to me. Aimes drops to her knees in front of me to examine the bruise I know will soon bloom on my cheek. "I guess, I should just be happy he missed the nose." I try to smile, to spread some cheer to the face that clouds with remorse in front of me.

"You know this will burn any bridge he might have held with them," Aimes says to me.

We look to the men huddled together in debate over what has occurred. I'm not sure why there is such an uproar. It really was a mistake, but if the blow had landed on Lawless like it was meant, there is no exaggeration to the chaos that would have ensued. A part of me has to wonder if that was Travis' goal. He stirred their angst with his touch and enticed it with his words. I just haven't put the puzzle together yet as to why.

"I think I pulled some stitches when I reached for Law." My stomach is searing me, cramping me with the pain.

"Sometimes it hurts to be so devoted to the ones we care for," Selma's voice startles Aimes and me. She has snuck up on us both from another entrance while we watched the men talk. She smiles seeing our unhappiness with her presence, but to be fair, it is not only directed at her. Leslie stands beside her like a blind acolyte worshiping her mistress with mimicked motions. "I think we got off on the wrong foot."

"Unless, that is the foot you are going to take out of your ass, nope, we good." Aimes smiles with her words like a beacon of goodwill and hospitality.

"I know it must be hard to see the one you coveted with another, but that is no reason we can't be friends." Selma has her own well-veiled venom, and it shocks me with her suggestion. "Just look at how well Larance and Leslie get along as an example."

Well, now she just wants to get hit. I stand ignoring the rush of heat-like pain it gives me and ask her, "This is a game to you and Travis, isn't it? You come into places with your bible verses and fake holy water to stir fear into people so that you can control them. Must really piss you two off we won't fold like everyone else has for you."

"You're wrong." Selma is calm and collected and she smiles at me. "You're not important enough to piss me off. You're not the only one who has been tested by your faith. He has brought me through the fire, and I stand firm in His purpose for me and for anything, or anyone, that stands in the way of that. I have already proven my dedication to Him with the triumph over the evil my life became. And now," she looks to Aimes who has lost some of her smirk when their eyes met, "He rewards me with a man like Rhett to keep me safe during the day and comforted at night." She leaves no illusions to her meanings. She has all but spray-painted across the floor a line from which she wants me to cross. She has said silently that Rhett is hers now and if I want him, I have to come take him. People should really be more careful of what they ask me to do. My mood swings are legendary.

"I think we have all had enough of yours and Travis' side-show." Dolph has come to see what our little "girl hour" is about, leaving those with hotter tempers to only stare after him.

"Selma here was just telling us how we could all still be best friends," I say, looking to Dolph, briefing him on the conversation.

Dolph laughs a deep male sound of dark humor, shaking his head. "You might want to rethink antagonizing this one," he says to Selma. "Travis is right about one thing. She isn't scared easily."

Selma smirks, giving me one more look-over before turning to leave with Leslie in tow, but I can't let her leave that easy. It just wouldn't be any fun.

"Selma, Rhett has something of mine, and I will be coming for it. I always come for what is mine and I always have it returned to me."

They both turn when they hear me, and I level a punctuated look to Leslie. Selma catches it and looks to her new worshiper with questions that I know she will demand answers to when they are from earshot. She won't allow me to see her curiosity.

I let them slip from view with the bitter taste on my tongue wanting to spread further misery. I wasn't bluffing with my threat, though. Before I had left Paula's tender care, I had asked where J.D.'s vest was. Lawless had told me with no joy that Rhett had taken it when they had found me in the shower area, and he had kept it along with his vest. Both of these actions are a festering layer to the wound Rhett has caused for the men. His vest is their problem, but J.D.'s vest is mine and I always have what is mine returned to me.

Chapter 16

We no longer call the third-floor home like the rest of the people who live here. Instead, they had moved to the second floor while I was recouping from my "departure". Everyone seemed to think at the time it was best to provide some space between the two groups who have now splintered to three – us, them, and the ones who hover somewhere in the middle.

"What is their story? The real story?" I ask Lawless, when it is just he and I alone in our new room.

"It changes with who is around," he sighs, slouching to the cot we once shared. "When they first got here, it was just some stroke of luck they found us. That luck became more and more divine as time went by."

"...and Rhett?"

"What's confusing about it? All a man wants is someone to love him and someone to protect. Selma provided both."

"Since when does Rhett care about love?" I ask, ignoring the underhanded build up.

"When he had to kill his best friend."

The silence in the room becomes a weighted burden which conversations seem to fall into. It's a heavy pressure of a loss of direction, leaving me searching for words to fill it. *How about them Braves?* "No one had a choice," is what I say, instead.

"We all have choices." Most would be swarmed with remorse over what has happened, but Lawless still hovers on the edge of rage that threatens to send him falling from the steep cliff of his anger like the man we speak of.

"He made his and forced ours." I keep my voice steady, unsure of which way this conversation will go and worried something I say will be what topples it into something worse.

"I don't remember you having to do anything," he tells me, and I sigh seeing how fast the toppling has started.

"Go on," I tell him. "I know you haven't done this with anyone yet, so let's go. Tell me all about it."

He just stares at me from the cot with his left leg bouncing rapidly. I watch his jaw saw back-and-forth with the words which are silently filling his mouth.

"Come on, Law. Tell me how unfair life is. Tell me how no one can possibly understand what you are feeling. Tell me how somehow this is your fault. Somehow, you should have done something to prevent it even though we both know no one could have stopped him. You don't stop J.D. You just get the hell out of his way."

"Did you talk to him? They said you talked to him before it happened."

"We sat in one of the bathrooms. I held his hand while he cried over you. Whatever J.D. was, he did love you. He never settled with the guilt of letting you run out that door without him."

"Did you know? Did you have any clue what he was going to do?" Lawless is staring at me, searching my face for some help with this wide hole he has been left in. So much has happened and, yet, this is the moment of time he is stuck mentally repeating. For him, the real reason J.D. killed the children isn't with J.D. at all. The fault is with

Lawless. In his mind, it was him who pushed the man to do the damage that set us on this path.

"Larance," I ease myself down beside him, fighting against the pain it causes my stomach. "You couldn't have known. No one really thought he would go that far. At most, we figured he would rough up a few people after daring them into a fight with insults. Marxx and Rhett would have to pull them all apart while Chapel played peacekeeper, just another Saturday night with the club. No one saw how deep J.D. was lost. Angry, stir-crazy, maybe just full crazy - I don't know - but not that volatile."

"You really believe that?" He is staring right at me now. He might as well be kneeling on his knees for me to absolve him from this shame. I'm going to have to lie to do it.

"Yeah, I really believe it." I don't blink. I don't cringe. I don't even have a smile to spare him. I just say what I have to say to help him through this loop of misery. When your hands are soaked in children's blood, what's one more sin to endure? "Rhett was pretty torn up, also."

Everything about Lawless changes with the name. The soft little boy is gone, and the walls of life have replaced him. His eyes cut away from me and stare into a far corner with his jaw working in anger again. I never stop to count my blessings.

"He didn't mean to hit me. This nice bruise should be yours," I tell him, trying to make a joke out of the land mine I have not just stepped on, but might as well be twirling upon with ballerina perfection.

"I know. When he hit you, Marxx grabbed me. In that split second, I was ready to kill him and he wasn't even looking at me. He never looked up at me. He was watching you. I saw everything across his face, but he didn't see Travis. Travis was watching me. It's what he wanted to happen. He wanted me to go after Rhett because then Marxx would follow, proving to them that everything he is saying about us is true." Lawless tilts his head to look at me. The dark amber of his eyes catches the light and glows. "What I am mad about most is that Rhett either doesn't see it, or doesn't want to see it. Up until he hit you, I figured he didn't see it. Watching him with you near, I think now, he just doesn't want to. Something broke inside of him with Aimes. He went darker than normal while you were gone. Whatever it is, they found it and now he's hiding from it."

Rhett darker than normal? I miss all the good party tricks. "What do you mean?'

"He would sit by you for hours. He wouldn't move. He wouldn't talk. He wouldn't let anyone else near you. He would just sit there staring at you. Aimes tried her best, but every inch she made, he just rebuilt. One day with Selma, and that's it. He never looked back."

"*Don't let me die*," I had whispered to him. "*Have I yet?*" was his whispered response. His hands were shaking when he held that door for me with Marxx shoving me through it. He sat beside me in the dark, watching over me with my whispers in his mind like his now circles mine. If memories could make noises with their interweaving of connections, the sound would be deafening. Lawless was right. Selma found something, and like the master manipulator that she is, she is having fun with it.

A soft knock on the door pulls both of our attention forward. Aimes with arched eyebrows of hope creeps into the room followed by two larger shadows. "So, how's it going?" she gingerly asks us with just as carefully placed steps towards the spare cot.

I'm not sure what was supposed to have been going so all I can do is stare at her with that question on my face.

"Aimes had bets settled if you had talked Lawless into a hug-it-out yet with Rhett since you're such the lady and all to save us." Marxx settles my mental debate with his explanation. He leans against the wall near the door like a supporting beam of the room.

"Once, twice, three times…" Aimes says and her smile is almost painful. I sense a new joke that will follow me. Wonder Bitch suddenly doesn't feel so awkward.

"From the one who has kept ending up being saved, that's funny," I tell the room, earning me different sounds of approval. It's nice to know they have noticed.

"So, what are we going to do with our little time bomb?" Marxx isn't asking me. He's looking to Lawless for answers with the tune of a score to settle.

"Let him go." Lawless spreads his arms wide, showing his palms as if asking, *what can we do?* "He has to make his own way just like we do. If this is the way he wants to go, let him."

"Just like that?" Marxx' gravel is buried in amusement and curiosity. The look he gives me lets me know exactly what he's curious about.

I shrug, letting his male mind wander down avenues I don't want to explore with him. His smile widens and I know the avenue is all downhill for him now.

"You're up and around for one day and the boy is making full sentences instead of just glares. Maybe Travis is right after all." Marxx stands tall with his smile growing to match his full height. He says, "Maybe we should send you over to play with his crew for a couple of hours." He winks at me, lowering his voice to a fun-filled whisper saying, "I'd like to watch."

"Hells and Selma?" Chapel asks, shaking his head slowly. "Now that would be something to watch."

I have nothing really to judge Selma by other than our few minutes of dare-you-dare-me earlier, but she has obviously given the men something to be cautious about. Even Aimes is shadowed with doubts at the mention of the name.

"I don't understand her deal. Why is she clinging to Rhett so hard?" I ask with no one offering anything useful about the woman other than the amusement to see her fall, which I have to admit that I too share.

"She seems to be Travis' right hand. No one sees him, or speaks to him, unless she approves it. She just walked in and somehow took over. No one even batted an eye at it." Aimes is flustered and beyond annoyed, but she's hiding something. We've been friends for too long for me not to catch the subtle hint she is glossing over. It's just a fact when Aimes is annoyed with someone, they become a pet project of one-liners and stick sharpening, not this hide-and-seek of meetings.

"We can't control Selma and we can't control Rhett," Lawless says, standing to stretch his lean frame filled with stress and anger-filled knots. Ending the debate, he strolls for the door not making eye contact with anyone. The watchful, thrill-seeking lighthouse I once knew is being rebuilt into something much more self-assured and angry. "Just stay out of their way until we figure out what we are going to do next with us. J.D. knew this would never work out for the long term. We should start thinking about that."

"J.D. made sure it wouldn't work out for the long term." Aimes lets the words fall before her mind can stop them. Her eyes dilate with the shock of hearing her speak them. She cringes from the man who has become frozen in front of her and she refuses to meet his gaze.

Marxx and Chapel are already moving forward with neither of them exactly sure what Lawless will do. I watch it all from the cot like a confused bystander, not really certain of what has happened, but nervous from the sudden tension surrounding me.

Lawless is still, like an animal before it attacks. His body is rigid with the coiled anger her words have twisted inside him. His head is only half turned to her, letting his eyes focus on her from a side view as if he too is worried what he may do if he really were to look at her.

"We all make choices." Lawless' words are slow and hissed between his teeth. I have never seen him talk to Aimes this way or look at her with such malice and I'm on my feet before I realize I am. His shoulders relax when he hears the cot move. It's not out of a sudden mood change. He knows I have a death wish and the brightly-colored hero cape to match. Marxx and Chapel might just wait and watch, but my buttons are pressed faster and more reckless than most.

He says to her, "Don't force me to make any of my own choices. We've already had this talk, remember?" He gives her his full gaze now and whatever she sees in it doesn't bring her any comfort.

Lawless doesn't wait for her to answer him. Her mouth is locked with pressed lips and it's enough for both of them. He leaves the room with Marxx and Chapel close at his heels and the air becomes breathable again. I had thought I had just lost days from healing from the shower. Now, I see I might as well have lost months with so much left being unsaid by hidden threats and glaring eyes. To say the sky is falling is an understatement. It has fallen and we are walking on it like broken glass that twists and tears the flesh we once were. It is leaving cuts no bandage will be able to heal with how deep it is wounding us all.

I have no idea what to say about the little show I just watched. She isn't offering any guidance either as we stand across from each other in a room that feels suddenly too large. "How's the shoulder?" I ask her, once again demonstrating why I have the gold medal when it comes to avoidance.

Her eyes are far away but she shrugs just the same with her mind running in two different locations. "Won't be passing through any security checks at airports, but I'm guessing that is no longer high on the to-do list anyway."

"Guess Daddy issues are higher these days."

Her eyes come into focus, looking at me with the weight of a thousand unsaid words. "You have no idea," she says before slumping back against the spare cot. It complains under the sudden weight and I half expect to see it fold with the amount of noise that comes from the worn springs. Her eyes twitch as she stares at the ceiling above us as if she is reading the words she can't find to speak. As the silence grows, my patience shrinks.

"So?" I finally ask, breaking the surrounding silence. I might as well have used a mallet with how she jumps at my voice.

"So what?" Aimes returns, still avoiding the conversation we both know is coming.

"So, what aren't you telling me?"

"What I had for breakfast?" she ventures, clinging to the last moments before the truth is out between us.

I don't say anything. I let the pressure of the silence and my stare build until I know her false strength will shatter. Her record for holding out in our years together is five minutes. It doesn't take that long this time.

"I had sex with Rhett." Her words are rushed and stacked on top of one another with such speed it takes me a moment to collect them. Even then, my mind can't put them in the correct order. Surely, I did not hear what my mind is telling me, she said.

"What?" I ask, not willing to trust my ears.

"I had sex with… Rhett…." Aimes holds the name in whispered confession letting the sentence drag between us.

I still can't believe it. I ask her again thinking it will magically change if I keep asking her to repeat herself. "What?" This time she will say something that makes sense. This time we will laugh over what I think she said.

"Really?" Aimes asks, and sits up to glare at me with exaggerated annoyance. "How many times do you want me to say it? I had sex with Rhett. I had sex with Rhett. I totally did Rhett." She throws her arms up in frustration and her eyebrows almost match the height.

I stutter a thousand responses that catch in my throat. None of them seem correct. They seem as mismatched as the woman and the man she just admitted to sleeping with. I can only sit staring at her until my mind chains something together.

"When?" I ask her and out of all the "W" questions I want to ask, this one seems the most fitting place to start and the least harmful to my brain.

She flops back on the cot making the springs curse with the abuse. A less secure woman would feel nervous over the marked complaint by the bed. Aimes is more worried about the conversation. Her eyes move more rapidly as she stares at the ceiling. The words she was reading now are full sentences as she picks and chooses which way to let this conversation head. This might just take the full five minutes.

"When I finally escaped from Paula, he was like my shadow. He was like always there. If I so much as winced, poof, there he was suddenly doing whatever I was trying to do for me. It was kind of nice at first, but it got old fast," Aimes says, reading the ceiling again like her favorite novel. "Plus, he and Law were always fighting. No matter what Law said, he had to disagree with him. He didn't just disagree.

He dared Law to call him out on it, but Law never did, and each time Rhett just grew angrier. It was like he wanted to fight with Law, but Law wasn't taking the bait. If Rhett wasn't trying to pick a fight or stalking me, he was sitting in the dark with you. Literally, in the dark. It was creepy," she pauses like the novel has abruptly stalled at the cliffhanger, and like an addicted reader, I grow frustrated left with my questions unanswered.

"…and?" I finally asked her, when her silence seemed to last longer than I could handle.

Her sigh is heavy. Like a high school girl waiting to hear the latest gossip, her full exhale of a sigh only adds to my mounting frustrations. "He was sitting in that dark room with you when I came to check on you one day. He was like crying. It was so odd and scary at the same time to see Rhett like that. He was so broken," she pauses, turning the page on the ceiling before speaking again. "I put my hand on his shoulder to give him comfort. It was totally innocent! He pulled me into his lap and…." her words fall off, leaving me leaning in to hear more, "…it just happened. I didn't go in thinking; hey I'm totally going to go get me some Rhett. It just happened and I let it. After that, he avoided me, and Selma went to work on him. She never lets me forget that fact."

"Wait, you had sex with Rhett while I was lying there?"

"Way to focus on the not important here."

"…but you did?"

"…but we did."

"…and now Selma is using it to tear you apart?"

"…and now Selma is using it to tear me apart."

"Glad we are both in agreement," I say, holding my head with my hands.

How did everything go so off course? How did in a matter of a few weeks everything become too tangled? Why is it with the world ending brutally all around us it still all boils down to who-is-sleeping-with-who in the constant never-ending circle of drama? We have people who were once normal turning cannibal, but please, let me focus on how to fix your love life. I have nothing better to do with my afternoon. Kill people trying to eat me, solve love lives and separate male bullshit. Yup, nothing exciting going on here.

"So, what are we going to do?" Aimes asks me with a voice as deflated as I feel.

"Don't know."

"Where was he buried?"

I'm startled by the sudden change in conversation. Like a scratched record, my mind is still skipping over her confession of having sex with Rhett and it keeps repeating her words. "Buried who?" I ask her, with the confession silently looping.

"J.D.," she says it, as if I should have known who she was talking about and I roll my eyes with her annoyance.

"We didn't bury him. We burned him just like everyone else."

"You should have buried him."

"What difference does it make?"

"When you bury people there is a spot to go to remember them. Now, there is nothing."

It seems Lawless isn't the only one with daddy issues. It's amazing how a man who lived a life's mission-based around revenge can still be missed. I suppose I shouldn't throw rocks when I live in a glass house so haunted by the past.

"You want me to take you there?" I hold my breath after I ask the question with hopes she will say no. I'm only kidding myself. I know what she is going to say.

"They wouldn't take me. They said it wasn't worth the risk. How would we get past them?" Aimes asks, and for the first time, I can hear the hint of mischief returning to her voice since we were left alone.

In-depth planning is not really my strong point. I prefer to run blindly into the thick of it and pray it works out. So far, for the most part, it seems to be working. Why change it?

"I'll think of something," I tell her and it's the best plan I have at the moment.

"We are so going to get in trouble," she says smiling.

"It's what I do best," I tell her.

Trouble and I have a complicated relationship. Like an addict who swears to never touch the substance again, I always do. I always end up right back at the very rock bottom I swear to avoid. As much as people complain about me being there, my addiction to trouble is what makes them always come to me for help first. I won't shy away from doing what has to be done because I'm not afraid of the fall. The long, dark tunnel that trouble leads us down doesn't frighten me. I'm comfortable in its darkness. That is what frightens me. When the darkest corners of humanity become your home, what does that say about your soul?

Chapter 17

Slipping past the main guards was easy. The fact the guards are made up of members of the new religious high order, and not our crew, is most likely what made that fact true. The fact they are the new home team favorite, and not Lawless and sidekicks, should worry me. Maybe because we are doing exactly what will bring their anger down upon us, and that I am once again blowing Death a kiss-laden dare. I don't think about the oddity of it. Some blessings come with the sparkling bows of obvious. Some slip past you only to become an afterthought. Whichever this one is, I'm just going to bow my head in silent thanks and worry about it later. I hope someone is taking notice because slowly, and one scar at a time, I'm learning.

My heart is in my throat as Aimes and I cling to the rough mortar of the grey bricks on the outside courtyard wall. The snow is slush under our boots. The weather in our part of South Carolina hardly ever reaches the cold temperatures needed during the day to keep it powder fresh. There is great irony in the truth of feeling like we are in hell in the summers only to be surrounded by slushies in the winters.

The blade I am gripping in my hand has become as much a part of my limited apparel as the boots now protesting against the watery abuse. My other hand is extended, palm flat against the bricks like a blind woman searching for answers as to what is around her. Unless the bricks are dripping with blood or hold the stains of murders past, they can't help me decipher any clues as to where the Risen might be lurking, but I cling to them just the same.

Aimes is my shadow. Her feet root into each print I am leaving. She slides along the wall as if she is a reflection of me. Her eyes are just as wide and scan the wooden barrier of the forest with the same determination as mine. We both know the risk we are taking. I just wonder if the man we are risking it for is worth it.

"It's just a little further," I whisper, worried over how far the winter wind will carry my voice. In the truck, it didn't seem this far. Now, we might as well have marked a place near Grit for the miles that seem to stretch to the little piece of land we used.

"You don't look so hot," Aimes whispers, staring at me as we slide along the wall.

"I'm fine," I tell her, remembering another woman who once called me on that lie.

"You look like you are half dead."

"I've been half dead. Compared to that, I'm fine," I tell her, ending the debate. She's right, though. I'm not fine. As I stare at the makeshift marker for J.D., my body is slick with sweat from nausea and pain. My stomach feels like it is on fire and aching at the same time from the wound. The two sensations are dueling to compete for my suffering like a badge of victory. I'm willing to call one a winner if it would lessen their battle. I point to the marker ahead of us and say, "Right there." It's not as exciting as anything Columbus might have said, but he didn't have flesh-eating people hiding around corners.

Aimes takes the lead now with her fascination for finding the spot like a knight looking for the Grail. I follow slowly behind her, already knowing what is there. She stands staring down at the ground covered in the disguise of snow that allows for it all to look so peaceful. I know what that lie is covering.

The sheet burned away quickly with its worn cotton threads. The heat of the fire, even with the accelerant of the gasoline, never reached the required heat to fully burn the body we left behind. Hiding underneath the thin layer of snow is J.D.'s scorched remains and I pray the sun is not cruel enough to melt the lie.

"We should have buried him. We would have a place to remember him. He would have liked that," Aimes says. She is sullen, staring at the attempt of a marker.

"That's a comfort for the living. The dead don't really care if you come or not. They are dead," Rhett says from behind us.

His voice doesn't startle me. It does Aimes. She spins with his voice like it belongs to some dark fear of hers. Since it's Rhett, it just might.

"What do you want?" Aimes asks, like a fragile child. Her voice is sad and hopeful at the same time.

Rhett looks away from us scanning the area around us and says, "Nothing." Everything about him says the opposite. "What are you two doing out here alone?" he asks, changing the subject.

"We were never really alone," I tell him, and earn a smile from the man with pride pulling at his lips. I have spent so long avoiding Rhett that I have learned to spot him a mile away. He has been following us since we entered the courtyard where he was mingling with the newly saved, or doomed, depending on your point of view. Some things haven't changed for either of us. "Selma tell you I was looking for you?" I ask him and watch his smile freeze and become a different animal.

"Nope," he says. He is daring me to call his bluff and I totally would if I was not already holding onto my own making me an easy target for him. "Have something you want to talk about?" he asks me, pushing the matter further.

"Yes, but not out here," I tell him, looking around fully aware of how exposed we are.

"Figures she wouldn't tell you. For someone so secure in the fact that she owns you, she sure does do a lot to keep you under her thumb," Aimes says. She crosses her arms glaring at Rhett. She has missed the innuendos and has chosen to take us down a much bumpier road. In her mind, she hovers somewhere between a discarded friend and scorned lover. The bite behind her words proves it to be true.

"It's not her thumb she keeps me under." Rhett's smile is genuine, and it adds to the ick factor of it all. Didn't I warn about calling the man's bluff when wounded?

"Either way, you admit you are now her little bitch," Aimes says, pressing the conversation forward. I mentally applaud her bravery because mentally is silent.

Rhett shrugs nonchalantly with the smile still stuck to his lips, but his hand twitches. It's a small, sudden spasm and most would never have seen it, but I do. Aimes might have too if she wasn't so lost in the turbulent storm of her emotions.

Rhett's eyes focus past Aimes on the marker before floating down to the thin layer of snow. His eyes swirl deepening and lightening their shade with emotions, but his face stays the passive blank mask of their training.

"One might think that I am finally not someone's little bitch," he says, and his eyes meet mine with private knowledge.

I'm starting to understand how Selma found his hidden buttons. It is starting to become clear how she was able to turn him from us. She just didn't count on a few things in her equation. There is a comfort in shared pain, and she can't measure the meters Rhett and I have swum together. Nor can she compete with the many different life vests we have shared to keep us from drowning. No matter the depths of her passion shared with him at night, we have all learned the dawn always comes, leaving us vulnerable to the light of the sun. It's when lovers can no longer ease your suffering, but only those who have shared the darkest hours of your life.

"He needs you," I say, watching the life return to the set of eyes holding me captive. "He may not know it, but he does. I know it. Chapel knows it."

He looks to Aimes when I leave her name from the list and her eyebrow arches as if a string had pulled it. She says, "I don't know what she is talking about."

"Do you need me?" Rhett asks her, with a voice that would shatter into thin pieces if pressed too hard. It completely steals any fight from her, relaxing her posture.

"Didn't concern you before." Marxx' voice does startle me. I was so lost in the domestic scene before me, I never heard him walk toward us. With his smile proudly displayed, that might have been his goal. "When will you learn to listen?" Marxx asks me. He boldly ignores the set of eyes watching him with unmasked hostility.

"When will you learn to keep her safe?" Rhett returns the question asked with an accusation of his own.

Marxx' head turns slowly to the man behind him. He never turns his shoulders making sure that his back is kept to Rhett. It's a screaming insult done silently without a single word needing to be said. "Last time I checked," Marxx says, in a voice deep with anger, "you made sure to let everyone know they weren't your problem anymore."

"It's so endearing to be coined a problem," Aimes says rolling her eyes.

I guess when it is, she and Rhett fighting that's okay, but should anyone else argue it is annoying. Good thing no one ever asks me my take on it all. Far as I am concerned, they are all annoying and there are not enough "time out" corners in the whole place in which to put them.

"You know what I meant." Marxx offers, but he doesn't take his eyes from the man he is poking with a stick. He is willing to put his back to him, but only as long as he can keep tabs on Rhett. Interesting to know.

"You're right," Rhett says. "They aren't."

The shock of his words radiates out like a bomb dropped leaving us all wounded from the shrapnel. The vulnerable side we saw of him has passed. Now Aimes and I are the ones stripped bare in front of him with the aftermath leaving us gasping. I look away from the man, not willing to let the sting of his words be seen reflected in my eyes. Aimes takes a different route with her emotions.

"I hope she swallows you whole," Aimes tells Rhett. Her voice is shaky with the damage from his words. "You and your stupid pride."

"She swallows me every night and it brings me great pride." Rhett leers with these words and I roll my eyes with how, once again, Aimes has been led into a pitfall of wordplay. It's one of his best games.

"We really have to learn better insults," Aimes concedes, as she watches Rhett walk away.

"We? Don't drag me into your fights," I answer, still staring into the forest border ignoring Marxx who is shuffling from amused to anger as he watches Rhett walk away and listening to our banter. "I stayed quiet."

"Yeah, I noticed. Thanks for the back-up there, gal pal."

"Anytime."

"You mean, anytime it doesn't involve Rhett?"

"Exactly."

"He really makes you that nervous, Hells?" Marxx is genuine in his interest but the uplifted corner of his mouth suggests that he is holding another emotion within. "You go toe-to-toe with those things, but Rhett makes you nervous?"

I know what to expect from the Risen. Their motives and desires remain constant no matter where we encounter them. They want us dead. It's rather simplistic.

Rhett's motives, not so much. You never know at which station the mood swings of his crazy train will stop. Some days, he may just make a complete round trip in one conversation. Whereas most times he isn't plotting your death directly, but that is always up in the air, too. The Risen, I understand. Rhett, not at all.

As I watch Lilly run a jagged path in-between the tree line, I know it's not just Rhett who confuses me with hidden desires. The dead seem to be just as twisted with their motives. *They are not dead. They never were.*

"Who is that?" Aimes whispers the question, as her eyes squint to fight against the sun's rays. It's amazing how far a whisper will carry when every moment is now swathed with last-minute dangers. Rhett pauses in his stride to see where Aimes is looking and when I follow their gaze, I'm shocked. Their eyes watch the apparition who stalks my mind play among the snow-hazed trees. I look to Marxx and see that he too is staring at her.

"You see her?" It's my turn to whisper. I don't do it out of fear of what I am seeing. I do it with the fears of what they are seeing. I know I'm one stumble from insanity if Aimes calls out to Lilly.

"Yeah, who is it?" Aimes squints her eyes harder trying to make out the damning details.

I am ready to answer her when Rhett curses under his breath and answers for me. "It's April," he says, and I want to argue with him.

I want to tell him how I am not amused by his joke, but I don't. See, I'm learning in leaps and bounds – whatever that means.

"When will you learn to keep her safe?" Marxx repeats the question that was asked of him and I can hear the smirk coating his words.

Speaking of "time out corners" I ask, "Who is April?" before I need to find a few.

"Selma's daughter," Marxx tells me, still wearing his smile.

I understand now why his question is so satisfying to him. I don't understand how a woman with such traits as she has could give birth to a blonde, ivory-skinned child running amok in the woods, but I admit that I might have slept through high school biology. Right now, I'm just satisfied that my personal ghosts are lying in wait to ambush me in the dark and not under the noon sun.

"You should probably go get her. You know, earn you some pink points with Selma for later," Aimes teases Rhett with her verbal jab, but her innuendo isn't easy for her to accept or to say.

"We should go get her," I say. At once, the three of them turn to me, mirroring the same expression of shock from my proposal. "All of us."

I don't stand still waiting to listen to their outburst of bickering. I do what I always do when I know I have stirred the pot. I walk away. I walk, hiding from those behind me the grimace of pain it causes me. I focus on putting one foot in front of the other with silent prayers that this won't become the time I am left to walk alone. Mostly, I'm just doing what I do best, chasing rabbits, and making up stuff as I go.

Chapter 18

"April!" Rhett shouts into the forest, with less than an ounce of concern for what may be lurking in it. The rest of us just hope with nervous, swaying eyes that his love affair with danger won't catch up with us. It most likely will.

From where April has squatted to draw with a broken branch in the dusting of snow, she gives Rhett one glance over her shoulder before she is off like a startled deer. With the same lack of concern, he displayed moments ago, Rhett is right behind her. He crashes through the trees trying to keep her in sight and we follow behind him, trying to keep him in our sight. It's the proverbial game of "follow the leader". Since the 'leader' is a scared little girl this might become the longest round of the game in my life.

The snow is thicker among the trees with their heavy branches blocking the sun's warmth. It's no longer the slippery mess but almost soft like a carpet under my boots. The vibrations from our running sends it cascading from above before the wind picks it up, swirling it like a snow globe around us. Quickly, the icy breath of Mother Nature steals the air from our lungs, cramping our sides. I surrender to the pain of my stomach, slowing my speed until my attempt to run is nothing more than an unflattering jog. Between me with my wounds, Aimes with hers still healing and Marxx unwilling to risk leaving us behind, the gap between Rhett and us grows.

We rest against the tree trunks, our lungs aching from the extent we have pushed our bodies in the winter weather. I'm grateful for the several packs a day lifestyle Marxx led before all of this. His panting is keeping him from saying the words his face is wearing as he stares at me.

To say that Rhett crashed through the forest before would be an understatement to the amount of noise he makes as he backtracks to us. "I lost her," Rhett says, and his hand does that same twitch from before.

"When you talked to this kid last," Aimes says, bent over to help reduce the cramp in her side as she pauses to take a few deep breaths before she can continue, "she didn't happen to say meep, meep at any time did she?"

Rhett wants to glare at her, but even his face is too tired to form the expression.

"It won't be hard to find her. We'll just track her in the snow," Marxx says, as he points to the trail we have left in our wake.

The relief his idea grants Rhett makes him exhale a long drawn-out sound. Rhett's shoulders sag with the release of his worry. For a brief exchange, the two men seem to bridge a crevice between them before they can remember which side of the line they now sit.

"We'll find her," Marxx tells him. He gives Rhett one solid pat on his chest when walking past. It's a small thing, hardly even an event at another time, but right here it's a miracle. Under the limbs of snow-hidden trees, it's a start.

It doesn't take Marxx long to discover her path. We zig and zag with her tiny footprints leading us along a twisting trail. When we exit from our shelter of trees, my heart drops. All of our questions as to where the Risen had come from lie expanding before us. It was only a matter of when, not if, they would come to test the brick walls of the high school. It was built in their backyards. A masterpiece of a suburban maze sat behind us the whole time.

The wooden privacy fence that separated the neighborhood from the tree line has been torn down in places. The missing wooden slats are broken and splintered as if a battering ram was taken to it. Shards of the boards lay scattered around our side of the divide with ruptured chaos. In some spots of the wooden mile, tops of the boards show the proof of what has happened with the dried, darkening evidence still staining them. This place should be filled with the sounds of children playing in the yards and the homes being tended to, but instead, there is just the crowing of the birds circling overhead.

"What is a bunch of crows called, again?" Aimes is staring at the same ominous sign as I am that something bad has happened here. Not that we need the birds to tell us what we have come to expect.

"A murder," Marxx says, answering her question with half-interest. His eyes are scanning for the lost trail of April's. Under the shelter of the trees, her little feet made perfect impressions where the snow was like a white carpet. Now under the sun's assault, the melting ice crystals are not deep enough to fully impact a print into.

"Well with that comfort-inspiring fact from Marxxipedia, who wants to go first?" Aimes asks.

I'm not shocked when her head turns to me first. Annoyed, but I'm not shocked.

It's Rhett who steps up to the fence first, calling over his shoulder, "I will. She's my responsibility."

We don't argue with him. Perhaps I would have if I wasn't fighting to cover the fact my legs are weak from the burning-like pain of my stomach. Its fire-laced aching is an agonizing remembrance of the dangers that might be waiting for us. It robs me of the self-confidence I once had and replaces my mind with cautions that never lingered there before.

With the first step through the splintered mess, I am nervous. I can feel my shoulders cramping with tension from the imagined pictures in my mind. The only sounds around us are the birds and the ice giving under our feet. I have learned silence is sometimes more frightening than a thousand screams. Screaming lets you know where the danger is waiting. It warns you, whereas silence keeps her secrets guarded until you are the one screaming.

"Here," Marxx calls out. It seems to be his own scream with how it violates the stillness, making even Rhett twitch with the abruptness of it. "She went this way." Marxx has somehow found the lost trail that went unseen by the rest of us. It is just indentions in the slush, but when looking at the whole area, it is easy to see how they line up to lead off in the direction of one of the backyards. It's like one of those pictures where you have to stare just right for the image to appear and Marxx has. He is still staring when he says, "She skipped past the first three homes and went for the one at the front of the cul-de-sac."

"Why?" Aimes asks, as if the melted mess holds that answer as well.

It doesn't and the look Marxx gives her confirms it.

"Let's go find out." Rhett doesn't leave time to stand around to form a plan. In his mind, the plan has been made. We find her and we go back. It seems simple enough and just how he likes plans to be. Apparently, I am not the only one who takes a while to learn things.

Every window we pass is blacked out with some material. The lower windows have boards nailed across them. Doors hold wooden beams of varying size and thickness like children playing at building forts. Wooden decks have been destroyed to supply the wooden hopes of protections and to help slow anything from making its way to the back doors. This was a group effort fulfilled by those who stood their ground here. These people went on with their lives in a fragile attempt of waiting this out. Now, the same people who once fortified these homes are either lying dead inside or worse. They may be the ones we burned. The Risen don't roam like cattle with mindless actions. It's only when something stimulates them to action do they travel. It would only make sense the ones that once stood like Death's army would come from a place so near. With April leading us behind enemy lines, I hope their numbers have been decreased.

"You've got to be kidding me," Marxx mumbles his disbelief, pulling my focus back to the house in front of us.

"Still leading the way?" Aimes asks Rhett. She is daring him as we stare at what only the sickest of minds could recreate.

The home is a sprawling one-story of pastel blue vinyl and red accent bricks. Streamers hang from the open back doorway alternating between faded shades of pink and yellowing white. The back yard is littered with brightly patterned paper. The pink gingham tablecloth is still sitting on the picnic table. It waves in the soft wind like a last attempt to call for help from someone dying before going still. Like one of the discarded bows wrapping all around the scene lays the half snow-buried dead. The children stare out at us with animal-scavenged skin and torn body cavities. Some still wear their pointed paper hats of pink and white.

The vinyl wears the smears from the attacks showing the escape path of those who tried to make it. In the middle of a celebration of life, Death came. It came with clawing hands and tearing teeth. It came and stole its victory, leaving the proof of its act to be witnessed for years to come and we haven't even gone inside yet.

Rhett climbs the stone steps to the open doorway with his blade in hand. He signals for us to give him a moment to look inside before we follow him. Seeing what is staring at us with unblinking eyes and weather-worn paper hats, I would rather take my chances inside.

The changing of seasons is evident on the tile floor of the room we enter. Water stains the entrance from the snow that has been blown in only to melt to form irregular markings. The house smells of a stagnant lake if lakes were decorated with streamers and sagging balloons taped to its edges.

The many handprints and long lines of dried darkness ruin the neutral colors chosen for the walls. I want to convince myself that it is only mud. The markings are nothing more than overzealous children and the natural damage they can cause. I want to convince myself of that, but I can't. I've seen too much since this all began to ever be able to lie about what the marks are and what they mean. These same experiences allow me to know that one of the many layers of what we are smelling means we are not alone. We just haven't found them yet, and they haven't found us, yet.

Both of the men are twitchy. Every noise we make pulls their shoulders taunt. Each doorway we pass is a building of courage to look into. When Marxx signals for us suddenly to stop, the snow might as well have been poured down our backs for the icy chill he gives us.

"Not that way." Marxx mouths the words, too afraid of how they might carry. He is staring at an arched entrance into a den. The taller house beside this one blocks the sun's light leaving the room in long shadows and an unwelcoming feel.

Rhett arches one eyebrow with his unformed question wondering what he isn't seeing that Marxx has. The way Marxx's eyes are darting around the home, I have a feeling he is seeing a lot that we aren't.

"No breeze," Marxx adds, just the smallest level of a voice to his words. We look to the streamers and see what we missed. The streamers are still swaying. The many pinks and decaying whites intermingle with each other with an invisible wind. The wind was not caused by nature, but by something else passing near them.

"April?" I mimic Marxx with my mouthed question refusing to add my voice to it.

"Don't know," Marxx answers, "but I'm not going that way until we check the rest of the house."

Rhett teeters on both sides of the fence about the plan. A part of him wants to rush into the den and either find the little girl or kill what is in there. I can watch the pros and cons of the plan work themselves out by the expressions on his face. Marxx leaves him to his demons, leading Aimes and I further into the house. Rhett follows, but he doesn't turn his back on the room and its shadowed secrets.

Down the long hallway, I watch as those who once lived here age from framed square to framed square. Sweet faced babies turn to toddlers who turn into children. The holidays come and go like a slideshow as I walk past. Halloweens to Christmases blend with birthdays all framed in their monuments of times gone by. With so many signs of the attacks around us, the smiling faces somehow appear that much more delicate.

Aimes stumbles into a wooden hall table. Mementos fall to the ground like porcelain explosions. Each crash seems louder than the first. The twisted irony is how they fall slowly, one after another, dragging out the duration of the sound. The silence that follows is engulfing. Each of us strains to hear any sounds from inside the home alerting us to dangers. When nothing moves, Rhett tears down a section of streamers and begins to beat Aimes with the thin paper. Watching her being mock assaulted with the crumbling pastel pieces breaks the tension that has been building. Marxx even finds himself joining in with the subdued laughter.

"Alright! Alright!" Aimes whispers, finally throws her hands up to shield herself from the paper. "Death by papercut was not my exit plan!"

"People plan that?" Rhett asks, giving me a heavy stare as he drops his sorry excuse of a battered weapon. My response is a middle finger before I turn to follow Marxx again on our hunt for a little girl who has mastered this whole hide-and-seek game as well as she did follow-the-leader.

"Hells, you and Aimes finish scouting out down here. Rhett and I will head upstairs," Marxx whispers. He is motioning with his head as if here and upstairs were hard to figure out in his directions.

The fact that I feel the need to give him the same answer as I gave Rhett means that I am recovering faster than expected. The fact that moving is still a small form of torture tells me that I have a long way to go still.

Aimes and I watch as the two men climb the stairs to the room over the garage. We don't move until the two men are out of sight and realize Marxx was serious about his idea. Leave us down here and the two men go upstairs? Surely, he was joking and any moment his head will pop down with his twisted smile asking, "Scared ya?" I think Aimes is, too. She tilts her torso to see up the stairs as if waiting for the same thing.

I unclip the blade from my side and whisper, "It looks like we are on our own."

"Think they will kill each other up there?" Aimes asks me, still doing the half-lean, trying to see up the dark stairs.

"I'm more worried about what may kill us down here."

"Yeah, I guess that is a bigger worry. If Marxx thought anything was really down here, he wouldn't have left us, right?"

"Riiight," I say to her, with a smile extending the vowel sound to further carry my disbelief.

"You could just lie to me." Aimes hisses behind me in a whisper as we begin to creep through the hallway again.

"You look very pretty today."

"I hate you..."

I feel my smile before I can stop it. The men have always had the friendships that gave them the strength they need to face their obstacles. For Aimes and myself, it is the same. Except that we don't use trash-talk and dares to build us up to walk into the unknown. We use humor. One last laugh before the hand comes out of the darkness to snatch you.

The shadows feel denser without Marxx leading the way. They seem to follow us without Rhett holding them at bay behind us. I can feel my hand tremble as it clutches the blade when we pass open doorways to bedrooms. I spare their darkened rooms one quick glance before moving past them. Just a moment of a pause to watch for movements or to listen to sounds before we are almost run by the opening. Zombie Barbie my ass.

The last room served as their living room. Its wide expanse has the feel of comfort that is minus the smears, the toppled frames, and general unease of an abandoned house. I feel as if we have made it through a carnival house of horrors and can finally exhale. There is nothing to jump out at us. No one has rushed at us from silent bedrooms. There have been no hands pushing through small spaces to grab us as we went past. With the front door standing wide and open to the daylight beyond it, my heart starts to settle into a normal pattern.

"Empty," Rhett barks from behind us, and both Aimes and I jump, releasing a half-muted scream. "Don't guess you two had any luck?"

"Define luck?" I ask, fighting to regain my breathing.

"Nothing ate us," Aimes says, with one palm to her chest, "but we might die of a heart attack, now."

Rhett winks at Aimes as he walks past her. "Waste of perfect tits," he says just loud enough for us to hear as he passes between us. He is keeping the unsteady bridge he and Marxx are sharing steadily by holding his voice low. The moment passes quickly with Marxx following so closely behind him.

"Now what?" I ask, no longer needing to keep our voices to a dull whisper filling the hole that Rhett's comment has created. It has stunned Aimes into an unusual silence. I almost hate to let the moment pass.

"She must have cut through the house to get deeper in." Rhett is staring outside with his back to us as he answers. I wonder what look his face holds after that slip of a comment. Is Rhett back or did he just forget for a moment our civil war?

"So, we are going deeper in?" I ask him.

He shrugs his broad shoulders. "Do what you want," he says, taking the first step onto the cement porch answering my question. He's not back. He forgot.

"We've come this far," Marxx says endorsing the idea.

Rhett turns to look at him over his shoulder. For a flash, there is a look of gratitude with a smile of appreciation before it dissolves back into the stern boredom he has been wearing. "Move," he says with authority, still staring over his shoulder.

"Marxx said we would come. No need to go all drill sergeant on us." Aimes rolls her eyes with the mood swing and crosses her arms to further punctuate her own mood swing.

"Move, now," Rhett says again with the same brash tone and dead eyes, but he is not looking at Aimes and myself. Something about how he is staring makes me turn in that direction.

I wish I hadn't. "Marxx, move." My voice is back to a whisper as if it could help us now. It can't.

Marxx doesn't even question us as he strolls up to where Aimes and I are standing. It's a slow walk as if he is in some park enjoying the weather while my heart pounds in contrast to his steady steps. When he is near us, only then does he allow himself a backward glance and the first look of apprehension over what was just inches from him.

There standing with the utter stillness she never possessed in life, is a small child. She still wears a cotton turtleneck and a brightly colored skirt with so many matching colored crinolines a ballerina would be envious. Her dark tights have runs showing her pale skin tone between the spider webs of lines. One shoe is missing, and with her damp hair, she looks more lost than a murderer. Those glazed eyes of hers though give all the warning to her nature that we need.

"I'm a little teapot, short and evil," Aimes sings softly, pulling the child's dull eyes to her direction.

"Perhaps you should just be still." Rhett leans down to whisper into Aimes' blonde hair startling her with his hot breath and voice.

With Rhett and Marxx now between the demonic replication of innocence and ourselves, Marxx motions with his hand for us to step back onto the porch. I don't argue. If they can't take out one little girl, as horrible as that sounds, then we are in more trouble than I could be of help with.

I watch from the doorway as the two men work together to perfect the kill. Marxx lunges for the child, triggering her attack and while she is focused on Marxx, Rhett sinks the serrated blade into her skull. She staggers to the side from the force and it brings her eyes to me. As she folds to her knees, I watch her body grow limp. After all this time, it still isn't any easier to watch.

I know what she is now, but the wrapping of the package still stirs the same shame as it did the first day. When life leaves her eyes, there is a shared moment when we are staring at the other and I feel her slip away, taking another piece of me with her; the piece of me that desperately wants to go with her.

"Let's go," Rhett says, cleaning the dark blood from her skull on a curtain near the doorway. "If there is one, there are most likely more around. I want to find April before they do."

I nod, still staring at the crumpled, discarded child on the ground. This is someone's "April" who we are now just turning our backs on, leaving her to be destroyed by time. She is just as precious to a mother somewhere as the kid we are looking for now, but we have come to not even glance back at the ones we leave behind. Who is really the monster?

"Hells?" Aimes is tugging on my arm to bring me back to the present. She doesn't know the dark halls of the past that I roam, but my face must show their horrors.

"I'm good," I tell her concerned face. "I'm good," I echo again to myself. With how she continues to stare at me, I figure at least one of us should try to believe the lie.

"Where are they, Hells?" Aimes whispers to me now that we have started to follow the two men into the street. With life's perfect timing, the sun passes behind a cloud upon her question.

I look at her, praying with every shred of belief I still cherish she is not asking about the ones I fear she is, even when I know better.

"The kids?" Aimes clarifies her question just as I feared she would. "Where are the kids?"

"Gone," I tell her, turning my eyes to the backs of the men we follow. Something on my face, or the pitch of my voice, stops her questioning. We both know it is only stalled. She is still watching me, and I can almost hear the gears turning. Her gears that will either grind the truth from me or crush me between their teeth once they have gained the strength to start to turn.

"April!" Rhett's voice bounces off the houses, filling the street with her name. It sends the heavy black birds into the air with angry cries answering his intrusion.

"Rhett," Aimes hisses shocked by his outburst, "why don't you just ring a damn dinner bell?"

"I don't plan on being eaten." Rhett never breaks his stride or his glancing around for any signs of the little girl as he speaks. There is an almost desperate edge to him; a wanton abandonment with the risks he is taking just to have any hope of finding her.

"If you make a Selma joke right now, I swear I will shoot you," Aimes tells him

removing any chance for one of his favorite sexual innuendos.

"You don't have a gun," Rhett says. He is either avoiding their normal wordplay game of dares or simply missing the chances provided for him. Both options worry me. Rhett is not one to shy from the line. In fact, Rhett often reinvents words just to make the other person uncomfortable as he crosses the line.

"Marxx, hand me your gun." Aimes holds her hand out and I think she fully expects Marxx to give it to her.

Marxx chuckles under his breath, turning to look at her outstretched hand before turning back to the street. "Maybe next time," he tells her, scanning the melting mess for any silent clues.

"Why don't we have a gun?" she asks me, and I shrug. It is a question I have often found myself asking when cornered with nothing but the knife and a giggle from a little girl.

"I think they are worried we would shoot them when they let their little male egos get the best of them." My statement catches Rhett's attention. He gives me a second of a look before returning to his search for April. The grin carves my lips before I can hide it.

"Most likely, you would end up shooting yourself," Marxx answers with his eyes still downcast, searching for the invisible trail.

He and Aimes begin a volley of the pros and cons from each perspective. He shuts her reasons down as fast as she can multiply them. When she begins the debate over rabid teddy bears attacking in the middle of the night, I tune them out. Instead, I let my eyes scan over the homes we pass with their black windows and wood covered doors.

There is a feeling of defeat here. The homes stand too empty as if the occupants were stolen, not evacuated. Cars sit abandoned in their driveways unused in escape attempts. The lawns are littered with debris that looters would have no need to steal. The televisions, game consoles, fine china, and other such items all sit under the layers of weather, smashed and broken. Looters would not have taken the time to cause such destruction or risk bringing the attention the noise would attract. This was deliberate. Like the black windows and the wooden attempts for security, this was all planned. I just don't understand the logic.

I don't understand what is ahead of us, either. It's the noise that draws my eyes to the direction. It's a soft sound, a constant motion of a sound. Like a child on a swing, it ebbs and flows with the pattern of the breeze. The sound sets the hair on my neck ridged like I should be shivering from the cold. It's one of those sounds that sets your whole body on edge before your mind can catch up to the warning.

When we turn the corner, the large oak has more than just the black crows in its branches. The tree was once used as a park centerpiece, but now it's cloaked with something sinister. The sight steals the air from our lungs and stalls our brains, slowing the pieces from being put together over the confusion of what we are seeing.

Hanging from the many thick branches are small children. Their eyes are wide and bulging from the pressure of the rope. Those who still have eyes. Those who don't are left with black cavities that somehow stare at us deeper than those who do. The birds have been relentless in their scavenging. Grooves of flesh are missing, exposing bones or darker spots along the bodies. The cold winds of winter stir them, swaying them with the creaking ropes and ruffling their clothing. They sway like broken piñatas among the branches that someone sick has taken their stick to.

All around the base of the thick trunk lay the burnt remains of people. Their skin is blackened and contorted from the flames of the fires which once burned them. The fingers of their hands are twisted, locked in an outstretched cry, begging for help. Their faces tell the horrible tale of being burned alive. Around the many circular piles is the word "IXOYE" in something dark enough to be blood.

There is no snow here to cover this. Mother Nature wants this to be seen and there, sitting in one of the many piles, is April. Her blonde head is bowed as she sits by the remains. Her clothes are now stained from the ashes she must have disturbed and the soiled snow she has run through. If she knows we are here, she makes no move to signal it.

"April," Rhett whispers the little girl's name. He whispers it softly as if talking loudly around such a massacre would be sacrilegious. He might be right. "April," he whispers it again, stressing the short name into something longer. She still doesn't move.

My feet have a life of their own. They always seem to move without my consent, landing me in situations I would have rather avoided. They are doing it now. I step past Rhett whispering her name and gingerly make my way to the child. My eyes land on the bodies around me and bounce to the bodies above me with small jerks. I'm too nervous to not keep either set in my vision for too long. If either set were to move right now, April would be back to being Rhett's problem and dry pants would be my problem.

"April?" I call to her, carefully placing my feet around the burnt bodies to reach her circle. "April, it's not safe here. We have to go, now." She still doesn't acknowledge me. There is not even a twitch of her body to show me she is listening. The way she sits limply by a body speaks to me. I take a different approach. "Did you know them?" I ask her, kneeling down beside her, and watch silently for her to speak.

Her voice is cotton soft. It is weary and worn in a way no one of her age should possess. "My mommy," April tells me, and I watch as her fingers flex with the need to touch the ruin of a woman.

I'm scared to ask the next question with so many piles around us, but I do. "Where is your dad?"

I watch as she finally lifts her head and points to a pile beside this one. There is something different about his pile, but I don't stare long enough to make any connection. "He couldn't do it," she says.

"Do what?"

"Be saved," she says this, as if I should understand. She tells me something that to her is a simple fact, but to me it is more of a question.

"Saved from what?" I ask her, trying to grasp some understanding of what is around me.

April looks at me, cocking her head, trying to gauge how serious I am in my misunderstanding of her answer. Before she can answer me, Rhett is here scooping her up like a doll. Her eyes never leave me though as she still tries to answer her question in her mind. She doesn't flinch in Rhett's arms or try to escape from him. She is a child who is used to being carried by many arms. The way her brown eyes stare at me, she is used to keeping many secrets, too. Brown eyes, not blue, and my soul aches in a different way.

I watch Rhett walk away with April's eyes studying the remains of the swaying children. She looks to each pair of dangling feet as Ashley looked to the fallen in the gym. In her mind, she is placing a name to each of her former friends. Names that have already been forgotten by the ones who did this, whereas for April they will remain with her forever, like stains on what was once a perfect childhood; like the red stains on once-perfect white clothes.

Chapter 19

"Where the hell have you three been?" Dolph's accent is heavy with his anger. Marxx is obviously not the only tracker in our happy little homestead. Dolph was waiting for us in the woods we once thought of as thick and encompassing. It was just another illusion we allowed ourselves to be lured into.

"Happy to see you, too," Rhett tells the man, as he passes Dolph. The sight of Rhett holding April must be as unnerving as I imagined with how Dolph watches the pair. "Guess the math skills weren't important growing up?" Rhett asks as they pass him.

Dolph smirks at the attempt of an insult. He says to Rhett, "Sorry, man. I was just counting the ones who matter." Dolph waits, half-tensed for the inevitable return from Rhett for his insult. All he receives is a smile.

"What was all that about?" I ask, being the only one confused by the exchange. Dolph has never been a fan of the men of the MC, but he has never so bluntly dared one without provocation.

"You've missed a lot," Marxx mutters. He seems to be unsure of which side of the little tit-for-tat he should stand.

"Your two other boys are tearing the place apart looking for you." Dolph ignores my real question and launches into a different explanation. "Law seems to think that since this one here was missing, along with the other guy, something went down and took you and Aimes with it. He's even got that preacher guy worked up."

"Chapel?" Aimes' famous eyebrow is arched again as she helps Dolph out with names he is either omitting or forgetting.

Dolph shakes his head for a moment in a short, controlled act. "Nah. The other one."

"Travis?" Aimes offers again.

"Yeah, that one." Dolph swings the rifle he held close to his leg back onto his back. I hadn't even noticed the gun, but Rhett had. He had purposely cut ahead of me so he could pass Dolph on the side of the gun. With the two being so close, Rhett would have had time to disarm the long-barreled weapon if the need would arise. I don't know if I am grateful or alarmed by Rhett's ability to spot such things.

"Let's get this over with." Marxx begins to walk towards the high school. He is no longer huddling against the cold wind and floating ice crystals. He has pulled himself tall for the fight he knows awaits us.

His shoulders will bear most of the anger from Lawless who has begun to see everything as a personal insult. Even to offer the truth that it was my fault he found us outside the walls, that it was my fault we went after April, the blame would still be Marxx' to hold. Chapel, I'm sure, has done his best to diffuse the mounting anger Law has used to cover his fears. There is only so much that can be done though when a man has become as consumed as Law has with his emotions.

"Let the good times roll!" Aimes mockingly replies, as we begin to file in behind Marxx.

It always amuses me how the men will naturally pick one to take the lead while one will always volunteer to follow last. Like some sandwich of protection, Aimes and I often find ourselves in the middle of this pattern like we are now. It's amusing because when trouble does arrive, I'm often one of the first to rush in. Only later, do I find myself thinking just how once I'd like to be on the sidelines.

It's amazing how we only stop to think about how stupid our choices were when we are neck-deep in them, or worse, as we sit and think about them. People wear rubber bands to snap themselves with to break bad habits. I wonder if there is a band big enough for all of my habits.

We hear Lawless before we enter the courtyard. His voice is raised and heated in conversation with someone. The high walls keep the words being exchanged private, but the volume is enough to give an idea of what is being exchanged. Especially since most of it seems to be one syllable at that and 'you'. I think I hear a lot of 'you'.

"Anyone else thinking perhaps we should have beaten Rhett back?" Aimes asks, catching on the stream of conversation faster than the rest of us.

"Shit," Marxx swears under his breath, with the thought of what must be happening. "I do, now."

The four of us stand transfixed by the two voices rising over the grey, thick walls. The wooden doors of the entrance loom tall, being the final barrier between another battle of the civil war happening on the other side and us.

"Paper, rock, scissors?" I offer, since no one has volunteered to be the first casualty.

Dolph leans against one of the walls, crossing his arms still listening to the exchange. "I say we let them have a little longer," he says with complete seriousness.

"Yes, let's just let Simon clean up the mess again while we all stand back. You and Richard seem to do that well." My words pull him off the wall with a power I hadn't meant for them to have. I wanted to sting, not bite him. Being the coward I am when it comes to admitting I'm in the wrong, I walk into the courtyard to avoid his stare. Any wound Lawless and Rhett offer me are better than standing here and looking at the wound I have placed on Dolph.

Aimes is quick to follow me in and what she whispers reminds me of just how horrible of a person I am. "You do remember Richard is dead, right? When you were attacked in the shower, turns out that wasn't the only loner left standing," she tells me.

I can feel my stomach drop so fast I am afraid for a moment I may trip over it. No, I hadn't remembered. I didn't just bite. I may as well have amputated a limb with the misjudgment I have made. Let the good times roll, Aimes had said. No one throws a good time quite like I do.

The creaking of the wooden doors with their opening was like a signal for a play to start and we just walked onto the stage. The shouting and its muffled counterparts become a vacuum of silence. Lawless is standing across from Rhett with a semi-circle of the town's folk surrounding them. The nervousness on their faces shows how ugly their fight was becoming. Now that we have entered, all of those faces are turned to us. If their stares had weight, I would lie broken under so many eyes.

Chapel and Paula stand across from one another with their own line drawn. Their line doesn't cause them anger. Their sadness is plain to see with how lost they are in this war. Either would gladly step across the line if the other would ask them to. With so much outside willing to destroy us, here we stand inside doing it ourselves.

"Sup?" Aimes asks, being the first one to break the tension.

"Sup?" Lawless asks her, mocking her very question. I'm starting to think she should have chosen a better entrance. "What's up?" he asks again hovering between rage and disbelief. Now I *know* she should have picked a better one. "Why don't you tell me, "what's up"?" he asks her, and I can hear her answers choking her as I look in his eyes.

"We went and had tea with J.D.," I start with my plans fully aimed at being a bigger ass than Lawless is being. Aimes picks up the path of my plotting and eagerly joins in.

"…then we went through the woods to grandmom's house."

"…where we crashed a birthday party."

"…killed a little girl for good measure to be sure we aren't ever invited back."

"…went and saw a tree decorating event."

"...rescued a little girl to even out the karma for the dead one."

"...and then followed the breadcrumbs back home."

"I don't know who keeps requesting there be more Risen action in our lives, but I could really use a nap." Aimes finishes the volley with a head cock and a forced pout.

"Cute." Marxx's disapproval is not only with what we have said but also with how we are handling the bomb of a man by dancing on his tripwires. Well, I'm dancing. I think Aimes is just jumping in place on them.

Law's eyes are bouncing from Marxx to Aimes and myself as he tries to pick the one to yell at first. With each person he sees, his hand clenches into fists before relaxing again to repeat the process. At least his anger is showing. If he was holding himself to the mask of disinterest, I might be more worried. This I can handle. I have become a pro at cleaning and handling the toxic mess from the explosions of their male egos and the way they leak all over everything they touch.

Rhett has not turned to completely face our little grand entrance. He keeps a side view of Law as he studies the man's face. Whatever Rhett is seeing there softens the hard lines of his mouth and relaxes his posture. "Nothing was going to happen to them. We wouldn't have let." All the anger from whatever was said is gone from Rhett's voice. He sounds tired, deflated, and almost sympathetic. His tone brings down the wall of aggression between the two men, but for Selma, it does the opposite.

"How do you know?" Selma asks Rhett. She isn't really concerned with Aimes and myself. She is more concerned with keeping the male animosity thriving. "You could have been injured, or worse, and no one would have known where to find you. The woods are a dark and evil place. We've talked about how they should be avoided at all costs. The risk is just too high."

"Good thing we didn't think so since you allowed April to go play in them," I say to her, and I can watch her response filter through the many levels of schemes she is building. What she really wants to say to me, she can't. It would ruin her perfect, shining example of holy righteousness. Not many people can pull off a, screw you and praise the Lord, at the same time. I don't think she is one of those few.

"Yes, a tragic mistake that will be taken into hand. It's a good thing you and yours continue to be so reckless with your safety so she could be returned home to us. Thanks be to our Lord," Travis says, wearing his best smile. Now, he is one of the few.

"Can I be taken into hand, too?" Aimes asks, with the excitement of a child on their birthday. "It's been so long since I have been taken into hand. A good strong hand, or a soft, firm hand? How about a good tickling hand?" Aimes continues to rattle off the many types of hands she would prefer to be taken by as she makes her way through the courtyard with the same excited voice at every idea which comes to her.

Her patience has worn thinner than mine, but she is better at her wordplay. The audience smirks and tries to hide their laughter as she walks by them to the stairs. By the time I have followed her in, she has gone more than just the fifty shades with her thinking.

"Cute," I mock Marxx, but Aimes' strategy has worked. With the situation so destroyed to hold any anger now, the groups separate into their respected corners like the sea rolling back out; all but one, anyway.

Rhett stands alone in the spot Lawless left him, his head lowers until it is bowed with each step Law and Marxx take away from him. Chapel only lingers for a moment in between the space which has occurred. I'm not sure if he is waiting for Rhett or for Paula, but when neither turns to him, he follows our path inside. He follows us now for the same reason he followed us then. He doesn't do it because he wants to, not really. He does it because this is home. As dysfunctional and mind battering as it is, this is home.

"We should go to him." I'm watching the man who was once our enforcer, our nightmare, stand-alone and fragile with so many staring at him. Selma stands a few feet from him with the same uncertainty that I am feeling.

"We should what?" Lawless asks, but I know he heard me. He's just daring me to say it again.

"We should go to him," I say it again. I do so love to dance.

Aimes has never stopped walking in her rambling path to the stairs. She calls back without even looking at me, "He made his bed, Hells. If he wants to change the sheets, he has to do it himself."

"Exactly." Law agrees with her. He passes me so closely that he has to walk sideways. We exchange looks before he moves by and I know that he is waiting for us to reach our little second-floor loft before exploding again.

"Anything you do now, will just set it all backward." Marxx has wrapped his arms around me and is whispering in my ear as he pushes us forward with his body. "Those two have to work this out, themselves. You can't fix this one."

"But –" I start, before he cuts my sentence short.

"Leave it alone." He slides to the side of me so he can look into my eyes. His voice is so low the bass of it vibrates me. "Why not, just for once, try fixing your own messes. You might be surprised at how much will fall into place once you do."

He leaves me with that gut-punch of a thought. My head still swivels to where Rhett is standing behind the safety-glassed windows on his own accord. I really do have a problem standing up to my own mistakes. Muddling with others' problems is so much easier than having to face your private demons. Especially, when your demons don't wear horns or sharp teeth, but the faces of the ones you have failed.

Aimes is waiting at the heavy, metal doors for us. Lawless enters the stairwell first and she follows him with me right behind her. The sandwich of protection forms again. Let the good times roll.

Chapter 20

"What were you thinking?" Lawless has either completely spent his anger on Marxx, or he is keeping it hidden well as he asks me the first question that comes to his mind. I'm not sure which I hope for.

He and Marxx had walked away from us when we arrived at our private floor. Whatever was said between them was kept tight and refined leaving us with no real sense of the conversation. It had ended abruptly when Lawless had walked away and still Marxx kept his face blank. Law had pointed at me and then into the room we shared, summoning me without a word spoken. My pride had first refused to answer, and if the truth were to be shared, I would still be sitting out in the makeshift loft if it were not for Chapel's gentle nod encouraging me to come here. In my mind I didn't obey Lawless, I answered Chapel's request. See how much better that sounds?

"…about the little girl." I shrug as much as the hug I am forcing on myself permits. My hands slide along my arms to hide my nervousness with the impression of being chilled. Without the winter coat, for some reason I feel vulnerable. "I was thinking about that little girl out there alone."

"We don't even know her." Lawless is trying to understand my reasons instead of shouting. I have to give him credit for that small step. I just don't know how to help him understand them.

"Does that matter?"

"Yes. Yes, it matters."

"Why? Why is her life less important because we don't know her?"

I watch as he searches for the right words. His eyes betray his thoughts by swaying back-and-forth. He is weighing his answer with hopes of controlling the conversation.

"It just isn't," Lawless says, forgiving his lack of an explanation with blunt honesty. "You, Aimes, Marxx, Chapel – those are the ones who matter now. We keep taking these risks for people who wouldn't do the same for us like we owe it to them, but we don't. We don't!" He begins to pace in front of me with the attempt to control the rising flood of his emotions.

"And Rhett? Does he still matter?" My question halts the pacing, but he still isn't looking at me.

His head shakes slowly, and he half laughs before saying to me, "You just won't let it go."

"You're not the only one who lost J.D." I know I am traveling through a dangerous landscape. Like hidden quicksand, I could sink neck-deep before even realizing what I have stepped on. "Rhett buried him that day, too. We all did." My courage falters with the truth of it pulling my voice this deep into private thoughts. This was meant to be a speech to reach through his walls, not mine.

"I was the one who pulled the trigger. I'm the one who has to put us back together." His head is lowered under the weight of his self-enforced shame. His voice comes slowly as if the words are too heavy to form. "You've almost died twice. We almost lost Aimes, too. Marxx was going down right along with you. I've almost killed over half of us, Helena, with the plans I have made. I've helped turn our home against us. I don't have a clue what I'm doing. I just keep thinking that if he was here, it would all be different."

"J.D. lived in the moment. The furthest plan he ever made was maybe ten minutes into the day and that was before half the world went cannibal. You really think he would be doing any better right now?" His head half turns to me as I speak. There is a flicker of hope in those amber eyes and I want to see it catch fire. "Not even J.D. could keep me from doing the things Aimes and I do, much less the things that I do on my own." I smirk at him, knowing how correct I am. His lips turn upward with mine carving a similar smile on his face.

"We need Rhett, don't we?" he asks me, still wearing his smirk. It looks more sad than amused though, like the joke is on him versus it being humorous anymore.

"Rhett needs us. It's kind of a package deal."

"Parasitic deal." He pinches the bridge of his nose before running his hand over his short dark hair that has replaced the once close trimmed mohawk that has been his trademark look since I've met him. "Shit," he exhales the word with the deep breath he took. "I don't even know where to begin with him."

"A nap." My answer is completely not what he was expecting, and it shows on his face.

"I'm not sleeping with Rhett. I have my lines."

"Good to know." My voice has more venom than I meant for it to before I could bite back the thought. I'm tired. My stomach is an even deal of fire and pain with a topping of nausea. My tongue has a power of its own without my mental leash to control it. "I meant mine."

As soon as I admitted my weakness, his whole demeanor changed. The worries of the world slip from his shoulders as he comes to me tenderly. "Paula said you were supposed to be taking it easy," he says, helping me onto the cot.

It's amazing how hard it is to move when your stomach is the cause of the suffering. "I think we already covered how well I listen to people." I remark trying not to wince with the movement.

"I'm just wondering how much you have to go through before you start to listen to people." He meant it as a jest, but I noticed the undertone despite him trying to hide it. He pulls the timeworn boots from my feet and rubs the life back into my cold toes. His mind is already somewhere else. I can see his thoughts roaming with the shadows they make across his face. "Sleep," he tells me, never turning to me but feeling my stare just the same. "I'll keep watch."

"Keep watch for what?"

He does turn towards me now. His smile is genuine making me realize how long it has been since I have seen it. "In case you try to do something stupid again."

"What could I possibly do now to top my record?"

He laughs a deep male sound before saying, "I've learned not to ask that."

"Jerk," I answer his idea of charming, but I have to smile. He has a point. "If I start sleeping, walking, and fighting at the same time, then we have been doing this for way too long."

"Fair enough." He shrugs and winks at me as I succumb to sleep. It's a soft drifting of darker and darker shades as I fall under the waves of exhaustion letting the pain slip away. Like a moon-driven tide, each wave pulls me further from the shore I have left until I am completely afloat in the arms of sleep.

There is a campfire near me. I can hear the crackling of the wood. The heat from the flame warms me, surrounding me in the scent of the fire. I watch as the sparks soar into the darkness above me. They weave their way into the dark night sky with pairs or partners like dancers. It's spellbinding.

There is no fear here. I have no urgency to glance around me for things moving in the darkness. I'm not straining to hear any slight sounds giving clues of danger approaching. It's just myself, the fire and the soothing darkness filling the space around us.

Turning to stare into the bright flames, I watch the colors meld into one another and apart again as the flames flicker. I am transfixed by the light show it's providing. The shadows sway like palm trees on a beach. The heat it gives is almost tropical with how easily it penetrates my clothing to touch my skin. This is peace, and closing my eyes, I just want to cling to this moment.

The wind shifts, pulling the flickering flames and their dancing sparks in a different direction. The scent of the warm wood changes. It has a more acidic smell as the wind washes over me. It steals the heat that was holding me, pulling my attention once again to the peaceful pyre.

The wood is no longer the stacked glowing red logs but long, white rows. The subtle cracks from the logs giving under the heat are now replaced by the fast-burning sounds of cloth. Stack upon stack of white sheet covered small bodies burn before me. They scream from the flames devouring their skin. Long wails for help for parents who will never come fill the night.

The sheets twist and kick as the children they contain try to escape from the torture. I can smell their flesh cooking, gagging me, but there is no way to help them. They won't die. They just continue to scream for help with their little bodies fighting to be free. With the intense heat from this new fire, my tears evaporate before they can frame my face. My peaceful escape has turned into a torturous imprisonment.

"Nice and toasty," J.D. says from beside me, startling me with his sudden appearance.

I quickly turn to see him and the sight of him locks my throat, removing all the air in my body. His skin is blackened and skeletal taunt in places. In other spots, it is flicking off into the night like the sparks I was so mesmerized with earlier. His eyes that stare at me are still the steel coloring I remember along with the wide grin he wore.

"Why is it that kids always burn so well?" he asks me, with grinning lips that crack and bleed, like the tears the heat stole from me. "You going to bring me more wood?" He laughs softly at first, with each laugh building in volume until he is as loud as the screams from behind me, as loud as my screams that join them.

I jerk awake with the trembling from the dream still clinging to me. My body vibrates with the fear it has left upon me, making my stomach spasm with pain. Slowing my breathing, I glance around the now dark room to find myself alone.

Way to keep watch, Law, but honestly, I'm grateful. He would be curious and want to know what the dream was about like all people are when it comes to nightmares. It was just a pile of burning kids and J.D. enjoying the glow from the fire, nothing unusual about that. Although now, I do think I will be skipping naps for a while.

Chapter 21

Chapel and Aimes are alone in the recreated loft area. Either the men did their best to prove that it doesn't bother them to be a floor down or they are doing their best to further grind the dagger in the new group's collective back. With such a display, it's really hard to tell which idea is the real truth.

Chairs have been collected from the former music room and painted black. Arranged to allow a path of sight to the stairwell doors, they sit on a long deep red rug, making the black paint appear a darker shade. The biggest proof of their new space is the artistically painted grinning skull of theirs on the wall. Its black void of an eye stares out at those same double doors defiantly taunting any who enter this space who do not belong. Seeing as how none of the men could master a flipbook of stick characters, this has Aimes' name all over it.

"Nice drawing." I motion with my head to the artwork hovering above us.

She shrugs, ignoring the teasing of my voice. "I was bored," she says, slumping in a rather uncomfortable position in her chair. My stomach aches just trying to imagine myself attempting such a poise.

"What are you now?" I ease into a chair near me, ignoring the watchful eyes of Chapel. The way he is studying me, I know he has been given the chore of keeping track of Aimes and I. It also explains the pouting from my partner-in-crime.

"A prisoner," Aimes says, sticking her tongue out at Chapel. It confirms my suspicions and I feel pity for the man who has been stuck dealing with her angst. She looks at me with large, exaggerated eyes telling me, "Seems we are a flight risk. Runoff into the dark, possibly Risen infested, woods one time chasing a stranger's child who wants us gone and poof, welcome to solitary."

"You know that solitary is when you are all alone, right?" Chapel asks her.

"…and poof, welcome to isolation!" Aimes counters, without a pause.

"Isolation is where you are kept away from everyone," Chapel returns.

"…and poof, go away," she says to Chapel, and receives a smile from the man.

"It feels more like a lockdown," I offer, squirming in my chair to find some position which doesn't make me want to squeal with pain; so far, no luck.

Chapel nods, pressing his lips taut with thought. "That would be fair," he says and a part of me knows if I wasn't in such a pathetic state, he would unleash his own lecture about our choice of behaviors. I guess he thinks the agony I am in is a better life-lesson than anything he could put into words. It is, for now, but it's amazing how quickly we can forget things once wounds are healed.

"Did you really get stuck watching us?" I smirk with my question; amused someone felt such a need. I can guess who the someone was.

"We can't even go down to eat." Aimes doesn't hide her dissatisfaction with our predicament.

"That's not what he said." Chapel stretches his long arms into the air, exhaling to let his mounting frustrations escape before they can turn into verbal weapons. "He said not to go down to eat until Hells is awake."

Aimes attentively turns to me, peering at me as if I am a stranger. She asks me, "You awake?"

I'm sure as hell not taking a nap again is the response I bite back. Instead, I tell her, "Yup. I'm very wide-awake."

Aimes stands, finally wearing a smile. "She's awake," she tells Chapel, with a moment of glee.

"She's awake," Chapel concedes, leaving me feeling like an awkward third party to their conversation. It's one of those all too common moments where you are included, but not as a participant, but as the topic. The good times just keep rolling.

If Aimes could skip down the stairs, she would. There are only a few things that make it to her list of things she considers are never going to happen and expecting her to sit still for longer than a few moments, tops that list. Expecting her to be quiet quickly follows it. Myself, on the other hand, dreads each stair that pulls on the assaulted flesh of my stomach as I climb down them. I might paint my own mural with happiness over being moved to the second floor instead of having to climb the extra set of stairs from the third before I am fully healed. If Chapel keeps being told to keep an eye on us, the boredom will definitely be there to further inspire me.

The smells rolling from the cafeteria would send professional chefs to investigate with envy. My stomach responds with complaints over my lack of good eating habits. Considering what happened in the shower, a lot of my habits are about to become rearranged. No more naps. No more showers. This should free up a lot of time for a few extra meals. The strong scent from a passing male completely calls my bluff on the shower theory.

"I know that look," Chapel says from my shoulder. "You're thinking again."

"I do that sometimes. Shocking, I know," I reply back, wondering when my wonder bitch mode was activated.

"Yeah, just normally trouble follows it." Chapel pats my back as he walks past, and I know he is just jesting but my tongue swells with the retorts it wants to unleash. Chapel has done nothing to earn any of it. I want to hurt him just the same. He is correct and maybe that is what is encouraging my mistreatment. One man shouldn't be your warden and your confessor. There are too many things that could be wrong with that much information about a person stored in one genie bottle.

I continue to follow the other two into the room chewing on my tongue to keep all of us safe. Judging from the room's inhabitants' stiff silence, it's not my tongue which is the threat.

Lawless and Marxx are already sitting at a table. There is an almost carved space between them and the rest of the room. The men pay no mind to the stares and poorly covered whispers. Nor do Aimes and Chapel hesitate to enter the room to join their table. Not even high school was this childish, close, but not completely.

"Travis suggested it would be best if we ate on our floor as well as lived there until we could learn to accept our sins and become one with God." Aimes doesn't whisper the explanation. She pretty much shouts it just for the amusement of seeing the shocked looks. "Law agreed and had Marxx start packing up all the food that was our donation from the runs they have been doing. Travis suddenly became very Christian after that and forgave us for our transgression as we are learning the wonders of His love."

"How very charitable of him," I answer, mentally picturing the snake oil of a grin Travis must have worn while declaring their imperfections as a mere stepping-stone. How anyone continues to believe in the man is a mystery to me. Like the mystery of why those children were put in the tree, both are dark and brutal with their hidden agendas.

"She's awake. Can I eat now?" Aimes accents her bluntness by resting her hands on her hips. There are no wide eyes or cock of her head to soothe her bite. She wants to fight and has thrown the first stone at Lawless.

"By all means…" Lawless stands, bowing in a grand gesture of days long lost. It's not her that uses this moment to strike.

"Please, let her eat. She's losing inches of ass by the day." Rhett plops himself down with his tray in the barstool like seat by Marxx. He sits as if he never left, proudly displaying the vest again. Jaws just don't hang; I can hear the sound of them as they bounce on the surrounding tabletops. Supplier of food, protection, and hours of entertainment; you're welcome.

"What do you think you're doing?" It's Chapel who recovers the quickest. Or at least it is Chapel who has the nicest way to phrase the question first.

Rhett never pauses from his dinner, but says with no volume of amusement between mouthfuls, "Eating." It's a simple answer and sometimes it's the one-worded ones that inflame their anger the fastest.

"That wasn't really the question and you know it." Marxx leans in lowering his tone, but not his volume. He is purposely invading the other man's space to insult him.

"He told you, he's eating. Let the man eat." Lawless settles back on his stool not looking at either man as if the discussion is beyond boring. He motions with his head for the three of us still standing to go. Since I have no desire to watch, I do just that.

Only Chapel hesitates as if he is trying to figure out where his calm head is needed more. Should he stay at the table to try to rebuild the bridge or stay with the walking, and sometimes lethal, duo of good intentions? I guess, Aimes and I are the bigger threat because he follows us. I'm not sure if that is a compliment or an insult. Seeing as how the men keep picking fights like spoiled toddlers jealous of the others toy, I'm hovering on insult.

"So, what is in the apocalypse cookbook for today?" Aimes twirls her tray on the metal counter looking for Paula.

"Apocalypse is kind of harsh." I start the mind-numbing chore of separating the utensils to hand down our chain.

Aimes shrugs her normal *I guess* gesture. "People are eating people while they scream. I guess I just have a different idea of harsh."

"Good to see you're keeping your spirits up," Paula says, with her biting, sugary tone overhearing our conversation from her side of the barrier. Her smile matches it.

Like a child scolded for cussing, Aimes looks down at her feet as she takes the plate of food from Paula. I raise an eyebrow at Chapel asking silently over Aimes' behavior. It's such a simple retort; she should have had a volley of wit to return. Instead, she is walking away like a whipped puppy. Walking away was never something she would have done before. Trust me, I have wished for it more times than I can recall.

Chapel doesn't offer any clues with his blank face. He doesn't greet Paula either. I watch as he and Aimes both retreat to our area; make that two whipped puppies.

Paula vanishes as quickly as she appeared, leaving me to stand alone, lost, and confused. I never enjoyed silent movies. I never really understood what was going on in them. Now I'm living one as a part of the main cast with the same overacting and washed shades of greys to set the mood. Lucky me.

Rhett still sits by Marxx when I finally make my way back. Lawless is watching over everyone while chewing like a teacher with a table of naughty children. His arms are tense, ready to spring if one of our toddlers steps out of line. With heads bowed, deeply invested in the plates of food, the only sounds are their metal forks tapping the plastic plates as they eat. I'm equally impressed as I am amused, and I have to bite my lower lip to keep the laughter restrained. The Prince has proved he can be King. They don't hide the way they would if it was J.D.'s steel eyes upon them, but it's a start.

Being the suicidal flirt that I am, I break the standoff with my own questions as I take the seat next to Lawless and across from the rest of them. The silent movie has grown dull. "How did we earn the privilege of a private floor?"

The tapping slows and the eyes look to Lawless to answer for them; make that four puppies. How many do I need for a full litter?

"It was best," Lawless says on the topic, leaving more unsaid than answered.

"Are we really that hated?" I push the conversation with just eyes swinging from Law to myself.

"Depends on who is around. Mostly we are just avoided."

"…unless they need something." Marxx finally joins Law and I in conversation.

Lawless nods still pushing around what is left of his dinner on the plate. "Unless we are needed," he says, agreeing with Marxx.

"What do Travis and his crazy crew have to add to this place?" My question brings their eyes to Rhett. He sits oblivious to it with his thick barrier of skilled uncaring.

"Whore and prayers." It's Aimes who takes the first swing when the men were trying to figure out how to play nice. I may have just lost a puppy as she finally finds her wit.

If her statement bothered Rhett, he doesn't show it. He simply puts another full fork load into his mouth ignoring the room.

"…and our area upstairs?" I ask, setting her up to continue to keep playing.

"Travis took over the "satanic symbol of our separation" for their prayer groups," Aimes answers. Her smile showing, she is growing braver by the question.

"Satanic symbol of our separation?" I repeat the phrase, dumbfounded by the quote.

"Yup. Afterward, I wanted to go pick a peck of pickled peppers. I was so moved by his speech," Aimes says and when she leans forward to address the man at the extreme opposite of the table from her, Lawless reaches over to lift her face to him.

Whatever he shows her in his eyes is enough to bring the pixie back to perch. His thumb gently taps her chin before he releases her, and it humbles her even further as she swirls the food before her with her fork. It was such a simple and gentle act that only the silence of her lapse of conversation brings the other men's heads up. By then, the show is over, leaving them unaware of what took place. Lawless has already returned to his food as if nothing has happened. Only my own visible reaction leaves them a clue.

"Where is Simon in all of this?" I ask, trying to recover the flow.

It's Chapel who picks up the broken pieces of the conversation sensing my need to talk. He says, "Simon is a broken man. I had thought he may recover from losing Shelia and Kira, but once we lost Richard like that, he retreated deeper. Only Dolph really keeps him going now. If Dolph were to quit, Simon would be content to stop living. He would just sit up in his room and let himself wither."

I remember what I told Dolph in my moment of anger-inspired weakness. The look on his face has a deeper meaning to me. "What happened to Richard?" I ask, not wanting to talk about Dolph right now.

No one offers to go first. I look to each person across from me waiting for someone to answer me. All I see is deeper bowed heads and hands clutching unused utensils. I should take it for a warning, but for me, if the warning isn't flashing a neon red with the long list of dangers scrolling past, I always rush forward ignoring it. "Well?"

Rhett sighs, finally proving he is aware of what is going on around him. "The same day you decided to take a shower with a new friend, Richard stumbled into one as he was in the kitchen looking for something for Simon to eat. You fared better, barely."

Images of Richard's playful smile and his teasing nature consume my memories. He was always a constant wall for his friends. He was the first to step into the peaceful option when possible. It's understandable why Simon is not surviving the death and why Dolph has picked up the banner of caretaker when it was stolen from Richard.

"Travis used it as further proof of our neglect," Rhett continues, slipping the word 'our' when before it was 'yours'. "If we had been more invested in the whole place instead of just our own, it never would have happened."

"People really bought that?"

"They wanted someone to blame. Someone to place their hatred and anger on about losing so many so suddenly. Travis provided that for them," Rhett answers me without the bitterness he would have once felt towards such an outcome. I'm not the only one who takes note of it.

"Like you did?" Marxx asks, never looking up as if he couldn't be bothered to.

"Yeah, like I did." Rhett's answer does bring everyone's head up. He doesn't say anything more about it and no one pushes it. Not even our chihuahua.

"I just can't believe they have swallowed all this religion hype," I sigh, remembering the many Sunday's that Carol would rush us all to mass under the umbrella of spiritual guidance. It only took one service to understand the real reason we were there was to show how well she was doing in life. God doesn't care about how many diamonds you are wearing or the labels on your clothing. He doesn't place any higher value on your soul because of the car you drive. Somehow though, everyone always arrived displaying their finest.

"In man's weakness, there are always those who use the good book as a weapon instead of a bomb. Now, there is a lot of weakness with so many afraid of what it all means," Chapel explains and of course it would be him to try to make us understand. The rest have no more grip of religious understanding than I do. "Everyone has lost someone if not more. Travis has them convinced his answers are the way to be reunited with them. To not obey him is too heavy of a risk with the fears of what if he's right constantly on their minds. Add that to his natural charisma and it is how men like him have always snuck from the darkness to overtake the world. That same charisma has led them to be wary of us."

"J.D. set up the start of it. Law not backing down when Travis started the war didn't help," Aimes says, finally recovering.

Lawless smiles as if she gave him a compliment. "I think you helped," he says, and she returns his smile.

I imagine her help has more to do with Selma than Travis by Rhett's return to mute.

"What are we going to do?" I ask the question they have each tossed around. The sighs combine as one and they couldn't have better timed it if they had tried. Their eyes are back to staring at Lawless now.

"We are still working on that." Lawless gives the best answer he has. To leave now would admit defeat or scared and neither have ever been on the men's list of words. They are not willing to add it now. "Why don't you help me understand what happened in the neighborhood you found?"

I'm confused by his question. I know he has already had Marxx tell him everything so what does he want to hear from me?

"The tree," Marxx says, when I don't answer right away.

"What about it?" Aimes asks, as lost I am as to why I am being asked about it. "You mean, other than the kids or the burn piles?"

"The letters," Marxx answers again, and I'm starting to feel like a child being led through a conversation. If I am given enough hints, then perhaps I will be able to say what they want to hear.

"I X O Y E?" Aimes puts the clues together faster.

Chapel twitches to attention. He looks as if he was just hit by lightning. "What?" he asks Aimes, as if he doesn't trust what he thinks she said.

She nervously says again, "I X O Y E."

"That was on the tree?" Chapel still has the shocked look on his face.

"No, it was under it on the sidewalk." My voice pulls his attention to me.

His shocked look is fading into one of pain. The way Lawless and Marxx tag-teamed this conversation into action, and are now silent, they must have known how it would affect Chapel.

"Tell me about the tree?" Chapel asks, but everything about his voice says he really doesn't want to know.

"There were children hung from it. Under it were burned piles of bodies," I answer as delicately as possible.

"Not all the piles were burned, though. Some were just like in a ring of fire where the grass was burnt, but the bodies were fine," Aimes recalls a different scene than I remember. To be fair, I was more interested in April than what was around me.

"Only children in the trees?" Chapel asks, as he cringes waiting for the answer.

"Yeah," Aimes and I say in unison.

Chapel swears under his breath before rubbing his forehead with his hands. "Follow me and I will make you fishers of men."

What Chapel says pulses that same invisible lightning out from him that struck him with such shock. Lawless and Marxx are no longer just the neutral spectators to the conversation. Even Aimes' jaw drops with her deep inhale. Once again, I am left confused and annoyed.

It was sudden. There was no time for Lawless to stop it. I never saw Marxx strike Rhett, but the proof is flowing from the cut on Rhett's face and how Marxx is towering over him.

"Did you know?!?" Marxx is shouting at Rhett, as he stumbles to recover from the blow. Marxx doesn't allow Rhett to answer as he hits the man again, doubling Rhett over. Marxx continues to try to reach Rhett as Lawless and Chapel do their best to pull him back. They strain against the man's rage and it shows on their faces and taut arms.

Rhett doesn't fight back. He doesn't encourage Marxx or answer him. The defeat of their knowledge deflates him faster than any insult or fist Marxx might land. With that defeat visible on his face and shoulders, Rhett walks away. One painful backward step at a time, Rhett walks away with his shame reducing him to lost words and apologetic eyes. He's watching the recreated bridge crumbling beneath his feet as he retreats.

He glances at me and we both know there is no life-saving device I might throw him now. The wind is shifting again, and the flames are consuming more than just the small bodies in their white sheets. They are determined to consume us all.

Chapter 22

"Anyone want to explain to me what just happened down there?" I ask, as Marxx paces our new loft with his anger still unspent. "Other than giving them something more to fuel the rumors of how dangerous we are?"

"I really don't care what they think anymore." Marxx stops to stand in front of me. His tone is deadly, and I flinch from him instinctively.

"She doesn't know," Aimes says, sitting beside me looking as lost as a disaster victim.

Lawless is slumped in a chair with his foot pounding a pattern on the floor. I look to Chapel standing at a window as he stares at nothing, looking as lost as Aimes. Whatever he is seeing is only in his mind, but it's still just as real for him as us sitting around him by the lines it's cutting upon his forehead. Aimes is right. I don't know what is going on. I'm not sure I want to know with how it is affecting them.

"It's Travis' quote. Follow me and I will make you fishers of men. It is what he says after every prayer meeting." Chapel's voice is as empty as a cavern and just as dark.

"I don't understand what that has to do with the word we saw." I don't know why I always push the topics that are sure to push back, but I do. I push my luck as if it's a giant boulder that is only going to roll right over me when I stumble under it.

"Earliest followers of Jesus adopted a secret symbol being the fish, or Ichthys." Chapel brings his voice to a tone of a teacher telling a ghost story. He tells us, "Those are the initial letters of five Greek words forming the word for fish, IXOYE. It means literally, Jesus Christ God's Son Savior."

Aimes stirs in her seat listening to him. "So, the whole fishy word is where he gets the whole fishers of men deal? Well isn't he clever?"

"Travis isn't the first to think of the connection and he isn't the first to misuse it either." Chapel sits in a spare seat as if he is weary and defeated by the weight, we have placed upon him. Law or Marxx could see us through a fight, but only Chapel can guide us through this. It's a tour he doesn't want to lead.

"Why the dead?" Marxx is still pacing with his anger. His questions are short and clipped as he fights against his rage. "Why those dead kids?"

Chapel still hasn't found an answer which suits his issues with what we have discovered.

"That, I don't know," Chapel sighs a long exhale of sadness, "I'm sure he is using it, twisting it just enough to convert and control people."

"Is he going to do that here?" Aimes' question brings a new level of energy. Each of the men take turns looking to the other, thinking silently about what it could mean if he tried. "Think Rhett knows?" Her second question increases the anxiety.

"It's what he has known as far as I'm concerned." Marxx growls with this deep voice.

"Yeah, you left that sentiment on his face." Lawless tries to smirk but the anxiety is too great.

"Do we call Travis out?" Aimes sounds almost hopeful with the expectation.

"On what? We don't have any proof he is behind it," Lawless answers, before anyone can jump to the idea.

"We might." My mouth speaks again before I have any clue what it is saying. It and my feet must have it out for me.

"What?" Marxx sounds more hopeful than Aimes did. It only adds to the risks. Aimes will bark, but Marxx, Marxx will do more than just bite if given the chance.

"April," Aimes and I say together as she puts the pieces together like I have.

"She said that woman in the pile was her mom, but Rhett said she belonged to Selma." I can almost watch Aimes putting it all together as she speaks. "She said her dad was in the other pile because he couldn't be saved."

"So, why is Selma claiming her?" I ask, and the turning gears are visible on everyone's face.

It takes us into a cocoon of silence as we each think about what the answers could be. The thoughts wrap around us, but no one is emerging as a pretty butterfly. Each thought only becomes darker with what we are imagining as the answers and it pulls our wings from our bodies instead of giving them to us.

"Do we care?" Marxx asks, and the question is such a change from his first response and I'm afraid to pursue his change of thoughts.

Lawless isn't, though. He asks, "What do you mean?" He presents his question carefully, holding his body still and his eyes neutral.

"This level of crazy isn't our problem. We have enough to worry about without adding this to it. Those deaths were recent. Which means there will be plenty of homes with supplies still in them." Marxx finally sits, leaning in to present his idea. "I say we go, stock up, and get out before this all goes bad. They don't want us here. Why stay? Why risk it?"

It shocks me to hear him talk like this. It shocks me more that part of me agrees.

"You know what may happen as soon as we go?" Chapel asks, letting the answer weigh on our minds.

"You really think if we walk up there and tell them the truth we would be believed?" Marxx counters with his own weight. "If Travis has been doing this all along, we won't even be a bump in the road to a man who can convince people to hang their own kids."

Well, when he puts it like that, it's hard to argue to the merit of staying. I'm not the only one having this thought.

Lawless is settling into the idea of leaving. If he has to weigh the weights of us compared to the weight of people who have turned their backs on us. He will vote we leave tonight. This is where I could point out that it was because one of us has doubts, but unless they are willing to listen, I would just be going against the tide of male mentality. That same member taught me that one needs more than just a life vest if willing to do that. You need a secure rope to anchor you to the shore.

Chapel and Aimes are watching me. The three of us have become our own little circle due to the past events. They are waiting for me to argue with the other two. They are hoping I won't be able to live with what may happen if we left now, leaving the risk of the children here to the torture Aimes and I have witnessed. I hate it when they are right.

"We can't go without, Rhett." I'm stalling. I hope changing the main topic will leave me time to think of something more stable than just their shared anger over what Rhett might have been hiding.

Lawless holds his hand up to stop Marxx' obvious reaction before it can turn verbal. "Save it. She isn't going to let it go," he says.

Marxx settles back into his chair with a look that is less than friendly, and he gives it all to me.

"Just let me talk to him before we make any plans. That's all I'm asking." I'm actually pleading. I'm pleading for one last chance to keep what is left of us, whole. It seems like such a simple thing. Looking into the burning eyes of Marxx, there is nothing simple about it.

"One day," Marxx tells me. "One day and then we move." He stands as if his body is attached to hot wires. He doesn't just lift from his chair, he jumps out if, making his way down to the rooms that serve as our private spaces. "Don't come to me to help you out of this one if it goes bad. You're doing this on your own," he calls as he leaves giving us all his back.

Lawless stands, arching one eyebrow at me before turning to follow his brother down the hall. He won't stand in my way, but he isn't going to help me either. I had wondered once how long Superman could handle always having to save Lois before he lost his mind over her antics. I guess we just found out.

Chapter 23

I didn't sleep well. My mind was racing with the many different scenarios that could take place once I put whatever it is, I am going to do in action. I don't want to believe Rhett has really chosen someone over our little fun bipolar family. I can't believe it and it may just be my pride or maybe my ego spinning me in nervous circles. It might be both.

Sitting on the bike that once led their club down the streets of our small town, I am not at all trying to hide the fact I'm watching the fishermen mingling on their wooden pews. Travis walks among them, keeping their rapt attention as if he is a movie star. The women blush as he passes when he acknowledges them while the ones, he ignores glare with animosity and yearning for the same attention. His smile makes the men return it instantly with some hypnotic pull. His handshakes are firm, steady grips that reinforce his hold on these people, like his hold on Rhett.

The seat of J.D.'s bike is too wide for my hips, making me lean forward some to adjust my comfort. My feet can only reach the icy ground on the tips of my boots. Leaning across the tank to rest on the handlebars, I feel like a little girl on her father's bike. It isn't that far off in its theory.

"Arch a little more and we just might have a poster," Law's voice startles me, as he catches me deep in thought. He too is staring across the courtyard at the mock church.

Aimes throws her leg over the bike near me, settling herself on its leather seat. It's Rhett's bike. If she did it to push someone's buttons or simply because it was nearest to me, it's hard to say. At least, it was until she smiled and stretched, making a show of herself. She's jumping on tripwires again and this bomb may take out the whole school.

"When did he get the new crew?" Lawless motions with his head towards the men standing near Travis as he ignores the double dare Aimes is giving Rhett. The new men are doing their best to look as intimidating as our game-master and failing miserably. It's almost comical to watch.

Rhett is aware of their actions. He randomly changes his stance and waits for the other men to rush to copy him. He smirks with each change as he toys with the men, playing with them and their insecurities. Some things never change.

"They have been here all morning," I answer, watching the show.

"Looks like Travis picked himself up a new God Squad." Aimes leans back, making a lounge out of the bike. I'm curious to see just how much of her maneuvering the kickstand can balance.

Rhett's bike is dark as pitch and seemed to always glow with the color. He wrapped his pipes long ago declaring chrome was for posers. Oddly enough, the more Rhett complained about chrome the more Lawless seemed to find a place to add it to his bike when he first brought it home. The only color on Rhett's is their skull, but even it is done in darker tones than normal. If Aimes does something to drop the large Harley on this cement, there will be no hiding the evidence of it. Knowing Aimes, it could very well be her goal. She doesn't like being ignored and has a very limited cache of what she wouldn't do to get your attention.

Lawless reaches out a hand to steady the rocking bike as Aimes flips to a new position. "Question is why?" he asks, once Aimes is momentarily settled.

"Think he knows we are on to what they did?" Aimes does arch as she asks her question. She finally has Rhett's attention, but with his neutral face, it's hard to read his opinions of her new throne. Arch your back just right on a man's bike and you could almost ask for the world if you let him watch. I'm sure her boots are helping with her game.

Lawless shrugs turning from them, removing the attempt of a church from his sights and thoughts with the simple act of dismissal. "You have your keys?"

"Always." I pat the side pocket of my winter coat. You learn quickly to keep such things handy. These days there is no time to rummage through a deep purse that would rival Poppins'. "Why?"

Lawless lets his hands stroll down the tank of J.D.'s bike as if it were a living thing under his fingers. "I want my bike back," he says.

There is a longing to his voice that I may never understand. I learned long ago these bikes are not simply a mode of transportation for them. To them, they are so much more. They are a personal extension of their own personalities in a way a car or truck could never encompass. Watching Lawless now, I am reminded of it.

"How's her keys going to help you with that?" Aimes is positioned in such a way I'm not sure how she is even balancing on the bike much less how she is paying attention to the flow of conversation.

I finish the train of thought for her. "I'm going to drive us to the store where he left it."

He smiles when I put the dots together. It takes years off of the many that have suddenly accumulated on us all. He is the playful tease of a boy who I met years ago again with the thought of his favorite toy being returned to him.

"Then, we are going to take a little spin through that neighborhood you found. I want to see this scene myself," he says.

That I hadn't expected. Aimes and I exchange nervous glances wondering where this is going, as she almost topples from the Harley.

"Why?" Aimes asks, sitting up fully with the joy gone from trying to annoy Rhett.

Lawless looks over his shoulder to where Rhett is standing with his new crew and Rhett stares right back. "I just need to." Lawless turns back to Aimes and I slowly and says, "I just need to know if what Marxx thinks is true before I make up my mind on what to do with him."

The playfulness is gone like the warmth of a setting sun. One moment I was basking in his heat and now I'm shivering in his coldness. His eyes are dull and flat, ruining the amber smolder they can contain. It's replaced by a gleam that resembles another man's eyes when setting stones to paths no one wants to walk. J.D.'s ghost still walks among us all.

"You don't really want to go down that road," I whisper to him, fearing that Rhett can somehow magically hear us. I try to caution him with my eyes in a way I know my words won't.

"You're right," he says, before looking back over his shoulder with a lowered gaze. "I really don't. But if I have to," he shrugs, "then I have to."

"You agreed to give me time." My whispering is gone. The apprehension over what he is insinuating flutters inside me. "You have to at least let me try."

Lawless says nothing as he walks from Aimes and I. He is no longer making promises or leaving any doors open for interpretations. He keeps his gaze on Rhett as he walks back towards the school. The same cold, calm look is returned to him as neither man is willing to look away first.

"Where are you going?" I call out across the courtyard, hoping to break the standoff.

"To tell Marxx where we are going. I wouldn't want for him to worry when half of us just disappear," Lawless calls back, and I know what nerve he is pulling. "Just be ready." His slamming of the courtyard door is more final than any words he might have picked.

I can feel the intense gaze of Rhett without having to look at him. I know his interest is perked with what small pieces he was able to gather of our conversation and Lawless' defiant gaze must have roused his curiosity. Either of those is never a good thing, but add them together, and it could be hazardous.

"Do you think he was bluffing?" Aimes has turned in an attempt to hide from Rhett. An almost white-blonde with pink streaks on top of the blacked-out bike stands out amazingly well in the grey courtyard making her attempt amusing.

"No," I tell her, shrinking in on myself without the same hope as she has. It's startling how often one of the guys will poke the other and leave Aimes and I swimming in the muck of the aftermath.

"What are you going to do, now?" She asks me the same thing so many ask me. I have the same answer for her that I always have – no clue.

"What we do every night, Pinky."

"Try to survive the world?"

"Exactly."

"Hey Brain," Aimes whispers, "is he looking over here?"

"Drop his bike and find out." I climb from J.D.'s bike looking at her with a smirk. "I dare you." I make my way to the large black truck I adopted long ago when a metallic crash echoes in the space that surrounds us. It cuts through all conversation leaving only the sound of Aimes' boots as she runs to me leaving me stationary with shock.

"Run!" Aimes shouts as she passes me faster than I knew she could move with her laughter trailing behind her. I don't look back. I run. The muck just deepened by meters.

Chapter 24

"I can't believe you dropped his bike," I repeat the mantra I have been saying since Lawless came running to climb into the truck with our escape.

"You told me to!"

"I dared you to!"

"What's the difference?"

Rolling my eyes, I look at her shocked all over again when I think of what she has done. The only contribution to the conversation from Lawless has been random chuckles and the shake of his head.

"I'm glad this amuses you," I say, after hearing his most recent laugh.

"You really just dropped it?" Lawless asks her, with a smile so wide it causes small wrinkles near his youthful eyes.

"Do not encourage her!" I scold them both like an exhausted mother. "We are going to have hell to pay when we get back." I watch her mimic me while mockingly rocking her head back-and-forth. "Really?" I ask, completely exasperated.

"So, I dropped his bike? I think you're making this a bit more doomsday than it really is." Aimes smiles sweetly at me, which does nothing for my battered nerves. "You know, since the doomsday preppers' official holiday has already come and forgot to go, I think the worst-case scenario has already played itself out."

"Law, if Selma dropped your bike, what would you do?" I match Aimes' smile with my question and watch as his amber eyes sway from me to Aimes with caution.

He doesn't answer me, and it swipes the smile from Aimes' pink lips. I let the silence and the new guarded mood permeate the truck's cabin with an I-told-you-so smug manner. I would love to let it carry for the full trip, but I have no idea where we are going. We were in such a hurry to find the freedom from Aimes' stunt that we never held the discussion of where I am supposed to take us.

"Where are we going?" Aimes breaks the silence, with the same thing I was wondering.

"You're heading in the right direction." Lawless scans the landscape looking for familiar sights to help him navigate our path. The new, subtle touches of winter are not being helpful.

The red light ahead sits dead and dull like its surrounding area. The four-way is silent, peaceful with the thin layer of ice adding shimmer to the area. I've been around the high school for so long, this almost feels like a mini-vacation. The air is perfumed with the winter pines standing tall and majestic against the early afternoon sun. It's days like this when winter lures you out to appreciate her beauty. It's days like this when life lures you out to be her victim.

"Pick one," Aimes is watching something behind us in the rearview mirror with dread. "Pick one soon."

Lawless and I both turn to look through the back glass with curiosity. My peace-filled mindset is crushed by what I see. The road behind us is clustered with scowling faces, sunken and tight, with grey skin and decrepit bodies. They balance on tattered, flesh-bare legs and feet which are being forced to continue to travel forward. The clothing that remains is timeworn and destroyed by nature's temperament. It hangs loosely to concave features, swinging with their movement. They stalk forward with deep growls of hunger like a pack of starved wolves. As they fill the street behind us, my basic primal desire to survive flares to life.

"Pick one Lawless!" Aimes shouts, as more come from the thick pines around us.

I'm not waiting on him. We are going left.

The tires slip with the sudden command to move, shuddering the large truck before they catch on the street. Her engine roars with the command from my foot, pulling us forward as if she too fears what is coming for us.

Aimes never takes her eyes from the forms behind us. I never look back, being forced to keep my attention on fighting this beast to stay on the iced road. Her heavyweight steadies her some, but without any traffic to wear through the slick coat of ice, we are mostly sliding forward. My fear won't let me release the steady pressure from the gas pedal and the more gas I feed her, the more unstable she becomes.

"Steer into it. Stop oversteering." Lawless has wedged himself against the dash and the bench seat bracing for the crash he already sees coming. I would flip him off, but I need both hands to control the truck.

"You can slow down." Aimes clamps a hand on my thigh to reach through my panic and my mood. "They have stopped running."

I spare a glance from the road to the rear mirror for a second and see the proof myself. Whatever intelligent life operates them has seen that they aren't going to reach us. With their bodies only able to withstand so much due to their level of decay, they have begun to go back to the sleeping state as they wait for another chance. Only their eyes move now as they watch us take the bend in the road. There is no panic like we would feel if we were watching what might be our last chance for food escape. There is no sense of depression or fear over what they will do to survive, as our nature would have us feeling. They stand watching and waiting; waiting for our return.

There is no more conversation as we drive. Lawless is slumped against the passenger door with secret thoughts. Aimes shifts randomly, searching the area around us for any movement. Everyone is tense after our little not-so-subtle reminder that this isn't a vacation or mini-escape at all. It's just another day in paradise, if paradise has become the Devil's playground while God wasn't watching. With what is waiting for us with the mock wooden cross back home, he might have.

"How much further?" Aimes asks Lawless, after her latest round of I spy with the trees. "I thought you walked back?"

"We turned the wrong way," he reluctantly says.

"We have to go back?"

"We have to go back," I answer for him, coming to the conclusion of what I should have done from the beginning. I let the truck coast slowly, shutting the engine off when she finally comes to a full stop. Tossing the keys across the cabin I say, "You drive."

He nods at me allowing me to not admit how scared I am about having to turn the truck around. If the ice doesn't take us out, will what's waiting for us in the middle of the road? Let's not answer that.

He exits the cab, layering himself with resolve as he walks around the truck. That same calm numbness I pull from when walking into the fights he now uses to armor himself. By the time he reenters the truck, he is a wall as icy as the road under us. His eyes land everywhere but upon Aimes and I as he turns the truck around. His resolve is only as thick as we allow it to be, and if we were to look into his eyes, it would call that bluff.

"Plan?" Aimes asks, never the one afraid to break any layer of silence.

"We are going bowling." Lawless is shifting through the gears faster than I would feel secure doing with the hazards around us and the truck roars with the freedom he is giving her.

"I was afraid that was what you were going to say," Aimes replies, as she and I both begin to slide down to the floor with his announcement.

He laughs a devilish sound seeing us both begin to retreat from his madness. "The truck is high enough that it will clip them at chest level. We will ride right over them like weeds with these tires."

"But it won't kill them?" I ask, worried with how each one we leave alive seems to find us later for retribution and with friends.

"Some, but it won't kill us either," he calmly replies. "Might mess up your paint." He sways his eyes to me for a brief second, flashing me the smile that used to melt the hardest hearts of women and the lower areas of those not so stubborn.

"It won't kill me," I tell him, even as I feel myself instinctively sliding lower.

He smiles that dangerous smile again as he shifts into the final gear. The thunderous engine noise from the truck excites the forms in front of us. I watch as they smile an eerily smile similar to the one Lawless is wearing. His white teeth almost gleam against his natural coloring of tanned skin. He has locked his arms to brace for the first impact which is only moments away at this speed. The noise from Aimes acts as a timer with it growing louder the closer, we approach the intersection filled with what was once those who lived in the surrounding homes. I close my eyes and brace more mentally than physically to what is about to happen. The last image I let slip into my mind is their arms slowly rising to reach for the truck.

Lawless is cursing softly with each exhale and I hear him laugh as the first jolt strikes us with such force my body rocks with it. It's followed promptly by many more with each body the truck is forcing under its chrome grille. I try to convince myself that it is just large pieces of the missing road the tires are bouncing over. It's not what is left of those who I may have just walked through their homes. I try, but Lawless isn't helping to seal the mental bargaining attempt with his maniacal laughter.

The back tires start to glide. The bed of the truck fights to come around even as the grill continues to feed the tires more bodies. Lawless is no longer laughing as he fights the truck, which makes me squeeze my eyes and my body tighter, fully expecting this ride to come to a crashing conclusion. The ones not in the direct path beat against the truck as we drive past. If we crash now, they will overtake us quickly as our bodies recover. Dazed and what's for dinner doesn't sound very inspiring for a death certificate.

The smell of their destruction is filtering into the truck. The dark blood they spill carries the acidic scent of rotting meat. Their limbs are fracturing and tearing under the large tires. They spray the windows with black fluid and pieces of thicker things. I can hear it hitting with the sound of defiant rain, splattering and covering the truck. The sounds and the smells churn the small meal from breakfast in my stomach. It climbs the back wall of my throat, gagging me as I swallow against it. The jolting slows, leaving only the back tires to bounce one final time declaring our victory. The truck shudders as we escape as if she is as disgusted as I am by her new paint.

Lawless exhales the tension from his body. He rolls his shoulders, hoping to relax them from the stress of fighting the truck to stay on the gore and ice mixed road. "You two can sit up now." He is amused and smiling down to where Aimes and I have somehow managed to completely slip under the dash of the truck.

"I'm good here." Aimes is as troubled as I am over what just happened. Our minds filled in the images we hid from with each bounce the tires delivered and with each pounding of palms across and even under the truck. Add another page to the storybook of my nightmares please, Sir.

Lawless looks at me with his impish smirk and I know where his male mind is already venturing, staring at me by his knees. With a roll of my eyes, I climb from the newly invented hiding spot. He shrugs still watching me and still wearing that smile.

My stomach is aflame again. This new limitation is starting to annoy me. If we did have to run for our lives right now, I don't know if I could. I don't know if Lawless or Aimes could leave me behind either. My injury could cost us not only my life, but those who I love, too. Yet, I am still the first to jump into each new fray, even inventing a few as I go for added measures of karmatic justice.

Lawless reaches with his free hand to pull me into his space of his arm. I slide into his pocket of warmth, letting him cradle me as I fight to hide the pain. "You should be resting," he says, whispering into my hair slipping us both into another time when life was all about these moments of comfort.

"…and leave you without Zombie Barbie?" I make a joke out of my constant turn of bad luck.

"You've clocked your timecard ZB," Aimes calls from still under the dash. "Let's not go overachiever on us and try for overtime. Okay?"

"We haven't even reached the store, yet?" Lawless teases her, trying to coax her to the bench seat again.

"Exactly!" she says, retreating deeper into the small space like a startled animal.

"How much further?" I ask, fighting through the waves of flames from the flesh of my stomach.

"It's already opening up," he says.

I look to where Lawless is driving to watch the small road widen as buildings begin to appear. Abandoned office spaces expand to larger abandoned buildings where commerce took root providing a way of life for the area.

We have already learned where there are larger spaces there are larger chances that we will not be the only things around. The virus took hold of people in the middle of their everyday life. People fell victim at work, on errands, at schools and now we are driving into the heart of so many of those activities with one hiding, one injured and one growing more manic by the day. The A-Team, we are not.

In the darker corners where the sun can't quite reach, snow has piled into some spots of the larger parking lot we turn into. It's a collaboration of shared rows of white lines between the many stores that once owned this spot. The type of place most would try to avoid during holiday hours and crowded weekends because of the long row after row of vehicle torture to park. It is a different type of torture to see them all empty. Like thrill-seekers who continue to ignore the warnings around them, we drive right through the same long rows ignoring their silent warnings. It's only thrilling to one person and that person's thrills are becoming darker as he discovers more needs to vent against.

His eyes light up the way most do when seeing a long, lost friend. Sitting alone like a kid in time-out waits Lawless' pride and joy. The sun has melted the snow from the bike leaving long lines on the black demon of his. The low-profile bike waits for him, stranded and alone, as if daring anyone but its owner to touch it with its painted skull watching us from the gas tank. I know it is an inanimate object, but I fully expect a skeletal middle finger any moment from it to match the look the skull seems to be giving us. It's as if it knows somehow its owner left it behind and it's not a happy reunion. Not for the bike anyway. Lawless might just start bouncing beside me here at any moment. If you ever want to watch a mood swing from one of our guys, aim your actions towards their bikes. Unlike Aimes, just make sure it's the mood swing you want if you do.

He sits when he parks the truck, just staring at his bike. His eyes roam the long lines of it as if it were a nude woman under him. His smile matches his appreciation of the view.

"You going to stroke off while we wait, or can we please go back now?" Aimes' remark cuts through his sightseeing but it doesn't damper his smile.

Lawless wastes no time mounting his war horse once he is out from the truck. He bounces to test the tires from being exposed to the constant rise and lowering of the outside temperature and it reminds me even more of a kid on a toy. It stalls the first two times as if it is pouting, but when he finally finds the sweet spot of the throttle, it roars under him as he twists the handle revving it a few times for his own enjoyment.

"Let's just announce to the world where we are." Aimes' sour mood continues to cover her remarks.

"You knew he was going to do it," I tell her, positioning myself behind the wheel. "When have they ever gotten on them and just started them? It's a dick thing I'm sure."

"Yeah, it's a "dick thing" alright."

"You know what I meant..."

She sits, crossed arms, staring out to the rider beside us. "He's going to freeze."

"Then I guess we won't have to worry about that dick thing anymore," I tell her finally, earning a smile from her lips.

Lawless nods at me from astride his best friend and obsession wrapped in one. His sunglass-covered face still wears the half-smirk of amusement as it purrs under him waiting for the throttle again like a woman waiting for the kiss on the back of her neck to let her know the ride is about to begin.

Aimes is right. He is going to freeze, and he is going to love every second of it. He told me once that unless I was a rider, I wouldn't understand it. Sitting in the warmth of my truck, I'm okay with not understanding it and the many other things about their little toys.

He follows in my path as I lead us back to the school. I weave through the long rows as if other cars are parked around us and he follows the same path with his smile growing larger the lower he leans the bike. Even Aimes is laughing at his antics as she watches him from the mirrors. There are so few chances in the life we live now for this freedom. It's completely wasteful of our time and resources as we cut figure eights and rush at high speeds around the lot.

We should be sneaking away, not testing our vehicles' limits to robust laughter. We shouldn't be risking injury with medical supplies so low. Especially with how my luck has been running the last few months we should not be doing this, but at this moment, this small sliver of time, we are happy. I don't feel the pain of my stomach. Aimes doesn't feel the pain of Rhett's betrayal. Lawless doesn't feel the weight of the world on his shoulders. We are light with laughter and glowing with the youth which has been stolen from us. This is how life should be for us.

I wonder often when I am resting, avoiding the torturous minions of my mind, where would we be today if life hadn't been distorted so abruptly. There was talk of a wedding once, of children with his eyes and my attitude. Now, the only talk is of surviving as tomorrow is nothing more than a passing hope to discover. A hope we are about to rediscover. To reach home, we have to go back through what we left waiting for us. We have to go back through the people who have also had their tomorrows and hopes stolen.

Chapter 25

Lawless coasts from side-to-side behind me letting the bike swoop with his movement. It's almost dizzying to watch. The smile hasn't relaxed its hold on his face one inch.

Aimes is watching him as if she is afraid at any moment he will be lost forever. Her eyes dedicatedly follow his every swing. "We should have gotten his bike for him days ago." She meant it as a joke, but watching his newfound peace, I tend to agree.

"If you're not a rider, you wouldn't understand." We both spontaneously mock the line that has been forced down our throats since starting work at Grit. We can't help but also share a smile that slowly builds to laughter.

Aimes and I haven't been on the same ground as we were before. Just as reality stole J.D.'s sanity, it is stealing our pixie's smile. Her wit, which was once so abundant, is sheltered and hidden under a rock of anger. I see the same fissures forming under her that cracked the solid surface of our leader. This world just doesn't kill the ones you love to steal them from you. It can steal them slowly, robbing you of the days with them just the same while they are very alive and kicking.

Overcome with my thoughts I hear myself say, "I miss you."

It turns both our heads to each other with the shock of hearing it aloud. There is a space of dreaded time as I wait to hear her reaction, but she only has blue eyes swimming in a dammed river. She nods, shutting those eyes before the dam can break, spilling forth more than just the tears she is keeping at bay.

"It'll get better," I whisper to her the lie we are all telling ourselves these days when the thoughts become too dark and the burdens too heavy. She doesn't believe it anymore from my mouth than when it falls from hers, but she nods anyway.

"It was weird seeing you on that table like that." She is watching something in the tree line only her eyes can see. They stare with such intensity I almost imagine I too can see something. "You're always the brave one; the strong one. Nothing scares you. Whatever has to be done, you just do it, but to see you all tore up like that, I think that is when it really hit me." She turns to me slowly like an animated doll. Her blue eyes are vacant as if they are painted on and not the shining pools of mirth that normally adorn her face. She says, "We are all going to die, aren't we? They are going to kill us all and we can't stop them."

Later, when I have time to think about this moment, I will wish I had said a million different creative things; the type of things only hindsight can gift your tongue. Right now, all I can do is try to place some style of bandage over the hurt she is feeling. "That's not true. We've come this far; we can make it. We are fighters. We have our family. That has to count for something..." Even to me, I sound lame as I am rushing through the words, I think will help her. I'm the gym teacher who tries to reassure you it's okay if you suck at every sport. We all have something within us that makes us special and that is what counts. Obviously, the teacher never tells you who to see for the counting.

"Our family is falling apart. It literally is killing each other."

"The men have fought before," I say, shrugging as if this civil war of a divide is nothing but an amusing pastime for them. "They will get over it. Men do that. They will punch each other in the face, have a couple of drinks and all will be well again. Just with slightly different noses and few extra scars. No big deal." I smile at her, but only her blank eyes stare out at me.

"Not this time," she hoarsely whispers. "No, not this time."

Her shift in character worries me. It's almost alarming to see her like this. It's more alarming to know I have no idea how to fix it. Not one tiny inch of it.

"We are all going to die, and there is nothing we can do about it," she whispers to the windshield with her sightless eyes still staring forward.

"We'll be okay…" I reach for her as she turns to me, finally with life in her eyes.

She asks me, dares me even with one simple question to prove what I am saying is true. "Then where are your Angels?" As my hand floats away from her, she wins. She wins and turns back to the windshield without a smile to declare it on her face. "Here we go," she says with sorrow as if she is prepared for this to be the final stand.

She's right about half of it. We have found the greeting party we left standing on the road. Their numbers are dramatically lower, but enough still stand before me to flutter the pit of my stomach. I know the original plan will not work with Lawless behind us. We were lucky escaping from the cabin that night. The Risen were not fully aware of us as we sped through the thick fallen leaves of fall. They are aware now and our luck won't hold true a second time.

My eyes meet with the man behind me, but with his dark glasses, all I can register for confirmation is his blank face as his mind works to figure out a plan. "I'm going to shield him." I hear the first rambling of thoughts flow together. "It's going to put them on that side. Scoot in."

Aimes has already started sliding over to my side before I finish the hastily put together plan. I glance up again into the rear mirror and begin to slow the truck, coasting it to the left. As the sun slices through the bare tree limbs, it lands on the dark glasses letting me glimpse the eyes behind them. I watch them as they waver side to side as he pulls the plan into his mind. He nods, finally putting it together. His face sets to a deeper frown of concentration.

I leave just enough space on the side of the road for him to slide beside the long bed of the truck. If the truck should swerve to any degree, it will hit him, sending him under the same tires he used to destroy so many of them in a reverse karma of the act. I will have to focus not only on the patches of black ice, but also on the added weight pushing against the truck from their many defiled bodies to keep his little strip of land safe for him.

As we approach the first wave, Lawless lowers his body to hide behind the metal body of the truck. He also vanishes from the rearview mirror with the motion. He has found the truck's blind spot and it is as if Aimes' fears from earlier have materialized.

"I can't see him." Her fears impregnate my voice. "Can you see him?" I almost shout my question to her, as I work on ignoring the eyes that have made us their focus.

Aimes lifts her body, bracing on the bench overstuffed back to support her so that she may peer through the blood-rimmed back glass. "Yeah, he's fine." She steadies herself and tells me, "You watch the road. I'll watch him." It sounds so amazingly simple, but it always does. It always does.

The Risen reach for the truck with fingers so emasculated their knuckles appear to be swollen and brittle. The skin of their face is paper-thin, shredding across the high cheekbones and sturdy chins. Their eyes are more devoid of color than I have ever seen before. The hate we have come to expect is missing from the thin lips and gaunt features. It's replaced with desperation as they beat against our passing truck. Their outstretched hands remind me of beggars, pleading for escape from their suffering and not their murderous madness of past encounters.

"We are all going to die..." My thoughts escape from me again and this thought startles Aimes just as much as my last train of vocal disaster.

"Why don't we try not to focus on my little breakdown right at this high-speed moment?" She is watching the invisible body of Lawless, but her eyes are roaming back to me.

"Look at them," I tell her, trying to reassure her I haven't become any more suicidal than I have always been. "They are dying."

She turns her head, glancing quickly out the window at the many faces we speed past. It's a constant flash of images pressing against the glass as we sail past. Their open mouths omit nothing as they file in behind us, missing their chances to reach us.

"These aren't fighting nearly as hard as the first bowling-for-brains crew." She watches them with the same curiosity as I had. "We are slipping right past."

"Don't jinx us?" I ask, not wishing for anything from the evil deities who still roam the earth to call her bluff. Karma is a busy girl and I hope she stays that way for just a few moments longer.

We do though. We slip right past them with their bone-like fingers scratching along the blood-caked paint of my warhorse like limbs from a tree. Within only a few following steps they stop, tilting from their staggering like misused toys left discarded by unloving hands. Accepting their fate, their eyes close as they lose animation with bowing heads.

For some reason, I'm almost saddened to see the sight as it shrinks in the mirrors. *We are all going to die.* It's now just become a waiting game to see who will die first. Though, how do you out-wait Death's army?

Lawless throttles past us. His bike growls with our less than miraculous victory, but we celebrate it anyway. We watch as he passes us, still lowered and hugging the tank of the bike with his legs. His smile is spreading wider with the space he rapidly puts between us, and when his back tire slips on a well-disguised patch of ice, Aimes and I laugh once he recovers from his almost mistake. Karma is a very busy girl, but she is always watching.

Chapter 26

The deserted neighborhood is different from this angle. The once crisp paint declaring how perfect it was to live here is scarred by the seasons. The homes around us seem more depressing with the destruction so much more evident than of those on the backside we had first encountered. There are no black wooden-barred windows. None of the doors are Tetris styles of wooden layering. It looks as if this is where it all went wrong, rippling its way through the place like a stone thrown into a still pond.

Lawless weaves in and out of the debris scattered by past hands that I just roll over with the large tires. The homes range from every size but with cookie-cutter mock-ups. This was once a dream life of factory-built ambitions. Even the colors of the homes are repeating chants of shades. This was the American Dream destroyed by American aspirations of longevity and our obsessions for perfection.

The silence is just as unsettling now as it was then. Only our tires disturb the peace of what has become a tomb. The sun watches it all just as uncaring as she was when it happened, as she is now that we are discovering it.

The tree isn't hard to find. The building plans of this neighborhood were once to set this piece of land apart as a meeting place for the happy families. Here they could interact on grassy stretches of picnic-perfection. What it serves now is such defilement to that idea it's shaming.

I kill the engine of the truck, but neither Aimes nor I make any motion to leave the safety of it. The large windshield shows us it all again, and it's as close as we wish to explore it. The children still hang from the branches as we discovered them like fruit for the crows and the dark clouds of buzzing flies. Their tiny toes are mostly bones, pointing down to the piles of parents around them. Their clothes hang heavily to them from the weight of the water they have accumulated from the melting frost making them look even more skeletal.

Crows call angrily down from the limbs of the tree to Lawless, as he strolls along the paths of decay. Their bodies are rainbows with their black feathers reflecting the light their eyes devour. They watch him with tilting heads and half-opened beaks as he wanders their playground, disguising any emotion from what he is seeing. Aimes and I are feeling plenty. We don't bother to disguise it.

"Do you really think Rhett knew about this?" Aimes asks, grimacing as a heavy blackbird lands on one of the hanging children's heads.

"He did seem surprised by it when we found April," I say, pulling back the film on the memory as I try to focus on Rhett's reaction.

He was stunned like the rest of us, I'm sure. I remember his eyes following the trail of horrors as each sight dragged us deeper into the madness. Was he stunned to discover it or to see it? Did he finally have to put what were once only words to Kodak-colored boldness?

"He came to us last night. If he knew, he can't be happy with what they have done?" I'm asking us both because alone, I can't figure it out.

"Rhett is twisted, there is no point in trying to lie about that, but this," she stalls, as she searches for what could best embrace such cruelty, "this is just distorted savagery. Rhett would never agree to something like this?" It's another question because we both can't find the answers.

I watch as Lawless leisurely strolls along with the piles of burnt and discarded bodies. He randomly kneels to inspect what has been left behind using fallen sticks to poke or move the offerings. With his eyes shielded behind his glasses, he is a mask of boredom as his head tilts this-way-or-that to better search for whatever it is he is trying to discover. It's oddly disturbing to watch him so passive in the midst of such butchery. I find myself once again wondering how well do I really know the men I call family? Or this one whom I choose to call so much more.

He stands under a cluster of children who appear to be staring at him as well. He reaches a hand up to a little boy's hanging feet, spinning him slowly around. The sound of the rope is like that of breaking bones as it twists under Lawless' command. He leans down under the boy to collect a forgotten baseball style hat. After he fidgets with it some, Aimes and I frown at one another as he secures it on his bike.

"Is he taking a memento?" She squints, as if her eyes will help her justify his actions. "What do you think he is going to do with that?"

"Fire the first shot."

She is silent as we watch him. You don't confront someone like Travis with words and empty threats. Words are Travis' weapons. They are what he uses to defeat and conquer his enemies and forge the blind following he amasses beneath his feet. If you wish to wake sleeping dragons, it's not words you use, but the one thing that even the best of beasts can't run from. You use the truth.

He sits on his bike staring at the scenic view of Hell. His thoughts are still a hidden passage only he knows, but his shoulders seem to sag from an invisible weight pressing against him. His hand crushes and releases the tiny hat like the heartbeat of its owner that has long stopped. Whatever resolve he is plotting with finally spurs him into motion. His bike rolls slowly from this spot of defilement with paid respect to those who have suffered here. This is not a throttle-filled, throaty exit or tires skimming across the asphalt with quickened haste. We depart with our heads bowed and we leave behind another small part of our souls to keep the ghosts who haunt this place now comforted. One day, someone may be doing the same thing for us.

Silence is like a quilt on the bed of an old, well-loved relative. We wrap ourselves in it letting the familiar smell soothe the worries and fears that are plaguing us. We bury ourselves in its heavyweight from the fabric, letting it shield us from the coldness of the outside. You can't buy quilts like the ones we grew up with and you can't find silence as welcoming as we do now.

Aimes and I don't spare a word as we travel behind Lawless with the tiny hat braced under his leg. It peers out as the world flies by unknowing to what it is about to become. The youthful coloring and broad embroidered script carries a message of childhood innocence. It's easy to imagine the little boy whose head it once graced and, in that imagery, lays the hopes of Law's plan. Does Rhett know the serpents he has decided to sleep with, or like Eve, is he just a toy being tempted to anger a bigger target? Are we really ready to find out?

The courtyard gates are open and waiting for our return. It's the first sign that something has happened while we were away. The wooden gates are the last line of protection. Once the courtyard is overrun, there is no way to escape. Leaving it open like this is pretty much a white flag to the world or a middle finger tempting Fate with your boldness. Neither is something I would recommend. Karma and Fate are two very twisted twins.

Marxx and Chapel step from one of the far entrances to the school as we park. They wait for us like gargoyles at the top of the stairs with stone faces of warning and a sinister appearance. If the ice-edged wind hadn't already stolen my breath, seeing them standing there would.

"Ever just once want to come back to streamers and balloons?" Aimes asks, as we follow like shadows behind Law. "Maybe a nice song playing or cake? I miss cake. Just one small cake?" She rambles like this the entire walk through the pews and the imagined glaring eyes of the wooden cross. Where Travis stood preaching the gateway of revelations, she skips across, foretelling the glories of cake. For all the sermons I have had to endure, I'm more moved by the gospel of the missing cake.

"They all left," Chapel tells us, with fear dancing in his eyes as his mouth sets in stone. "Travis and Selma wanted to show them the "Glory of God".

"We stayed behind." Marxx smirks as he says, "Was half-tempted to shut and lock the gates. Figure a few hours left in the cold and their prayers might change."

"They aren't at the tree." Lawless lifts the precious memento into view. "It's as bad as they said."

"What did you notice?" Marxx asks him, waiting for some secret suspicion to be confirmed.

"The piles were different," he starts. "Some were just shot. Some were burned. Some were burned and shot. All of them though had fire to some degree around them. Only the kids were hung."

"...but why?" Aimes is still fragile over the sight and her voice encompasses those raw feelings.

"April said her dad couldn't be saved. That's why he was in the pile not with her mom." I recall the simple look she wore with resignation framing her slight frown.

"What pile was her mom in?" Chapel timidly asks me. His question has teeth, but the answer will hold the bite.

"The burn pile," I answer him and we both wince from the piercing canines.

"So, her dad was shot," Marxx says. Like the prince that he is, he says aloud what the rest of us were happy to figure out silently. If brutal honesty was a faraway land, he would be king. "Why is the shot pile the ones not saved? What is the burn pile?"

The answer comes to me as bitter as the wind that whispers around my ears. It coats my throat with warm bile, burning me further as my mind pulls the answers together. I pray that I'm wrong. "The burn piles are turned. They either shot their turned, or they shot themselves while the children hung. It was a judgment call; proof of their faith."

"Those bodies haven't been there that long. If they were from the shots, they have been turned for a long time. Why would they keep them like that?" Aimes has a point.

The shots that started this nightmare were given months ago. To safely keep such a person would be incredibly difficult, not only physically, but mentally as well. If having to kill the ones you know is brutal to your soul, having to keep them fed would be butchery.

The men look to the other as they try to figure it all out. Slowly, each one gives a facial look of surrender as any logic fails to come to them. It gives me further hope that perhaps I am wrong. Sister-Slasher-Savior, check. Sister-Logic Solving-Liberator, pass.

"There is one person who might know." Aimes is testing the temperature of the water toe first. She doesn't trust her whole foot to the situation, yet. "He's been watching us the whole time. You know…inside…where it's warmer…further proving who is the IQ holder of our group."

Lawless smirks at Aimes over his shoulder. His smile is the boyish charm of his edged with a dangerous dare. He asks her with slow drawn out words, "Calling me stupid?"

She returns his charm with her own, matching danger with wit. "Asks the one who just had us go out there to rescue a bike?"

They stare at one another in a locked battle of returning smiles. It's an old game of theirs and a part of me would celebrate this steady return to our normal if it wasn't so damn cold.

"Did you want us to get some decorations for Valentine's Day while we were out since your run for Christmas went so well?" Lawless' smirk never shrinks, but hers does.

"Children," I say pushing through their game of one-upping-the-other, "you two can continue to stand here and see who can make the other wince first, but I'm headed inside where it is warmer, Miss IQ." I give her a warning glance as I make my way through the double barrier of safety doors. Once inside, I almost exhale with the comfort of the hallway's air.

The school does not run the heaters due to the amount of strain it would place on the generators, but the stone walls horde enough heat from the many people who are normally roaming the place to make it comfortable. Just as she said, there leaning across from the row of double windows stands Rhett staring at me. His blue eyes glow like an enchanted forest's beast as he watches our group's silent movie from the shadows of the hall's cavern.

"I have something for you," Rhett's voice calls from those same shadows, and I'm reminded of the old stories of the maiden tempted into danger by the call from the male in the dark. Lucky for me, I gave up the maiden title years ago.

"Come give it to me," I tell him. I might not be a maiden, but I've learned to stop skipping into danger.

My heart does skip when he accepts my command. Watching him walk towards me, I know why so many fears this man. I know why I fear him too, but as of late, I've seen a different side of him. I've seen what he has kept locked behind grins and masks of boredom for all of these years. I once thought their masks were made of steel or thick stone walls holding their hearts secure. I've discovered that it's only paper mâché and every day wears the glue that holds the strips together a little thinner.

He extends his arm to me and there in his clenched fist is the very thing for which I had warned Selma. J.D.'s black leather vest hangs between us like a peace offering or a twisted replica of a white flag. With trembling hands and begging eyes, Rhett is telling me in as plain as he can how much he wants to come home. He is asking with his eyes the words his mouth is not strong enough to let out.

"I made a mistake," is the only thing he says, as I take the vest. It's the only thing he needs to say.

I let my fingers pause on his. His sigh is audible and visible. It rattles his whole body with the release of the loneliness he is feeling. Lawless had told me all a man wants is something to protect and someone to love him to explain Rhett's sudden departure. Rhett thought he had found those things with Selma. He forgot he had them all along.

I watch him re-layer his mâché as the rest of the group finally comes in from the winter chill. Their rambunctious laughter abruptly stops when coming face-to-face with the one problem no one wants to talk about. I don't even pause as I continue to take the peace offering, placing the leather vest over my own winter coat. Chapel had told me privately the reason Rhett had taken this same vest from me was because I dared to wear it. He saw it as an insult to the man it had belonged to. Once upon a time, this would have been seen as a sin. Now, we have bigger sins being committed against us and greater rules being broken to harm us. Him taking the vest, I was told, was like a hairline fracture to the backbone that supported us. Him returning it is his way of trying to cast what has now become completely broken.

"Cute," Lawless says, as I adjust the vest while he walks past. Leaning close into Rhett, he asks the man, "but where the hell is yours?"

We have watched everything burn around us, destroying us from the inside out. We have burnt our friends, our loved ones and bridges all with the intended goal to make things better. It would be so much easier to let it all burn down around me, to let the wind float the ashes to someone strong enough to carry them when the flames finally die, but it's not in my nature. I can't stand by and let the flames take us. I don't know if I will have the courage to fix this, rising like a phoenix from this disaster we have allowed to happen to us. I only know that I'm not willing to let go. Not yet. I will fight just one more time. We survive because we have each other. It's not because of me or them or anyone else alone. It's because we take care of each other. Rhett taught me that in a blood-soaked hall when the weight of my doubts was enough to crush me. I had warned Selma that I always take back what belongs to me. Standing in that same hall, Rhett very much belongs to me and to mine.

Chapter 27

Finally, we are sitting as one again in our hidden little room. The men are spread out around the room like beasts weary of the other being in their space. They watch with just as cautious eyes as we graze on the stashed food they have been hoarding from their runs. Aimes and I sit in our own little area relishing the chocolate bars they found on one of the last runs. We are keeping our heads low fully expecting the shrapnel to be sharper than the actual blast when the first rounds are fired. Men forgive easily, but it is one hell of a battle to wade through first.

"So," Marxx is the first to break the silent standoff. His voice is rough with the anger he has over Rhett's latest actions. It's not surprising when Marxx steps up to the gun range first. It's also not surprising to see Chapel slowly adjust himself between them and us. "Did you know what they do?" Marxx asks. It's the only question he really cares about.

Rhett doesn't move to acknowledge the question asked of him. He fidgets with the wrapper to whatever imitation of nutrition he picked from the pile. Every second he stalls the room grows that much more dangerous with tension.

"I asked you a question." Marxx is standing now, not taking kindly to being ignored.

Lawless pushes from the wall he was leaning on. He is either ready to join Marxx or poised to intercept them both. He also could just be trying to get a better view of the show.

Rhett answers with his attention still rapt to the shiny wrapper. "I heard you." The room waits for more, but that is all he is giving.

"Did you?" Aimes asks, before Chapel or I could stop her. She has her own answers she needs him to answer for her sanity, but this is the only one she can ask publicly.

Ignoring the men for Rhett is most likely a source of enjoyment. Ignoring the tiny voice of Aimes, shielding the real questions they both know will be asked at some point, robs his composure. The wrapper is not nearly as interesting as it once was. "I thought it was more Jesus' play. I didn't think it was literal." Rhett sighs leaning back into the plastic chair making it moan around him as if it knows what story he is about to tell. "Travis said something about rebuilding the world with just the strong and the devout. It made sense. I'm tired of having to carry people who don't want to carry themselves. Like J.D. said, we do all the stuff around here and they just sit back letting us take the blame when it goes wrong. Travis said they have a way to prove it by using the "love of family". He puts the children's fates in the hands of their parents. If the man is brave enough, strong enough, he will prove it." His head hangs low letting his dark hair cover his shame. "I didn't know it was real."

"Where are they now?" Chapel asks. He isn't very interested in what has happened as much as he is worried about what might.

"Hunting demons." Rhett smirks as he recalls something that was said. "They think of those things as demons; people that are possessed by the Devil. Killing them is how to prove you are in the Army of God. Here I was just thinking it was a fun past time." Rhett isn't exactly exaggerating. He very much enjoys having free reign to kill as he likes. It's just another layer of his ever-disturbing charm.

"So, it's started?" Chapel asks again, tempting to once again be bitten.

"Yeah, it's started. Once we brought April back, Selma and Travis became very secretive. They knew we had seen the tree and their time was running out. I guess they like to go a little more slowly with the whole mind game theme. When you three left this morning," he pauses giving Aimes a steady look over our rapid departure, "it really set Travis to task. I didn't even know that black book of yours had so many chapters until this morning's preach-a-thon."

Chapel's mind is already skipping ahead to the days that may come, but replies anyway. He says, "Maybe you should read it sometime."

Rhett laughs an amused chuckle telling the man, "Nah. It's all a bunch of words left only to interpretation by the one reading it out loud. The articles in Playboy, pretty much straight forward."

"Glad to see you're admitting to your reading level." Aimes isn't content with how well this reunion is appearing to go. Her posture of crossed arms and her pressed lips further tells how disappointed she is in the lack of male angst.

Rhett's gaze swings back to her with his searing blue eyes, "I'll admit to many things if you'd like."

His dare drops her jaw and pulls the strings of her spine straight. Their little play has the whole room's attention now.

There isn't a way she can deny his sentence without admitting to the subtle warning. The way the other men's eyes twitch from Rhett to Aimes, I don't think she has a chance either way. When their eyes come to rest on me, I realize that I don't have an escape either and my wrapper is very interesting. You just can't find shiny paper like this anymore.

"You two finally are going to admit it?" Lawless is smirking from his wall, upping Rhett's dare.

Aimes' eyes grow wider as the male's smiles take over the room. They say women kiss and tell, but no one brags like a room full of bored men.

"The whole time?" she asks the room, that has become filled with mirth.

"He never said the name, but with Hells being out and the school being thin, it wasn't hard to guess," Marxx offers.

She flops back into the chair aghast at being a source of their male-tinted banter. "You told?" If her eyes could grow any wider, I'd be worried about socket damage.

Rhett smiles fully now. The smile that sends shivers to all the wrong places, or the very much correct places depending on your feelings towards the man. Watching Aimes melt in her chair with his smile, I think everyone in the room knows what's really melting.

"Sweetheart," Rhett starts, pulling the words out into an almost syrupy drawl. "I didn't tell them anything then and I didn't admit to anything now. You did that all on your own."

He has a point, and you can almost hear the light switch turn on as it hits home with Aimes. "So, wait," she says, with the furrows framing her forehead with her thoughts, "you're saying since Hells was not available, then it had to be me? If Hells was up and around, it never would have crossed your minds it was me?"

My wrapper is just levels upon levels of interest, and I stare at it, lost in the amazement. I might have to slip lower into my chair to fully enjoy the sight of it.

"No," Lawless' voice is deep with menace, "it being Hells never would have crossed my mind one way or another."

I'm still staring at the wrapper of long-gone chocolate, but I can still feel the weight of the room. I slip a little lower into my chair pleading with the pain it causes me to be understanding. Searing stitches or the focus of many stares? Sorry, but the stitches are out of luck.

"Now if Dolph were to mention something, he might have concerns." Rhett stands under the disguise of stretching, but he's really prepping for a reaction from Lawless.

Lawless doesn't jump on the bait, but he's ready to and he lets the other man know it. "Is that really smart from a man whose fate hasn't been decided yet?"

"It's not my fate I'm warning you about, Brother." Rhett looks at me and I have no idea where he is taking us now. "Since we are holding confession, are you going to tell him?"

"Tell him what?" I'm not being sly. I really am without a clue as to what he is asking about.

"Selma saw you and Dolph. She told me all about it."

"Her and Dolph what?" Now, Lawless is jumping.

I'm still scrambling. "I don't know what you are talking about."

Rhett stares at me as well as Chapel, my keeper, as he tries to read me. "You told Dolph no, but not until after you let him do some exploring."

"Why did she tell you this?" Chapel has stood, placing himself closer to me as he asks his question.

Rhett shrugs, but the motion doesn't match his expression. "She said she had proof that Hells wasn't the girl we think she is. We all think of her as being our little combat doll, but the whole time she's making her own way on her back."

"You think that's true?" Chapel asks the room letting his eyes stop on each male. I guess I should be thankful he didn't feel the need to look to Aimes even as I do.

"Payback is a bitch," Rhett says, recalling a little domestic meltdown inspired by J.D. 's plot.

"Men are really this stupid?" Aimes is asking me, as she rolls her eyes over their indecisiveness. "Just climbing out on a wild limb here, but did she tell you this the day you hit Hells?"

Rhett pauses and the look of his gears having to turn to remember is slightly comical. "Yeah, I guess."

"The same day that Hells threatened her?" Aimes pushes further.

Rhett stands silent knowing where his ship is finally taking him – sinking.

"You idiot, Hells is her only real threat. She knows that. She saw how it affected you when you hit Hells and took the chance to weave this tale while you were being stupid. She wanted you to have a reason to be mad at Hells to keep you from talking to her. It's basic high school reindeer games. Now let's all laugh and call you names." Aimes looks to Lawless who still stands rigid with his imagination holding him prisoner. "And if you believe it, then you are even more stupid than he is. So much for not running anymore?" When Lawless looks shocked by her words she wears a smirk similar to the one Rhett was adorned with when the ball was in his court. "Yeah, you boys aren't the only ones who talk."

"If their plan is to do this thing of theirs," Chapel pauses, not even able to put words to the evil, "they would have to make sure we were out of the way for it to really work. We don't have kids for them to use against us."

"We are the only ones not swallowing the punch, too," Marxx adds.

"…and if Travis really believes that Hells is the root of us, it would make sense to try to dissolve our trust with her. It would divide us pretty fast." Chapel continues to debate more to himself than for anyone else in the room. Lawless still remains silent.

"Maybe, but I still think she is just playing the jealous new girlfriend." Aimes clings to her ideas, not from pride, but from fear of how much deeper their plans might reach if Chapel is correct. "Leslie was right there with her. I'm sure she's very sharing her opinions on the matter since she is still trying."

Law's eyes swing to me again and I only arch an eyebrow to serve as my question. We have the world trying to eat us, a group trying to hang us, so I really don't care about the daily telephone game Selma has tried to play. He softly shakes his head and for now it's a good enough answer for me. Perhaps, I'll help Leslie into a circle under a tree.

"So, nobody is sleeping with anybody and everyone is sleeping with someone. Great, glad that's all worked out. Can we just figure out what we are going to do before they pick a tree?" I ask, fully bored with it all and fully expecting to hear anyone's voice other than the one that answers me.

"Since the last tree in this place provided such happiness, who would be willing to pick another?" Selma asks, spinning the room in her direction. She is framed in the doorway with her simple blue jeans and white sweater offering a sweetness of the all-American girl.

"Why are you here?" Rhett starts to walk to her with the training she has instilled in him. J.D. would have had a field day with them two. Sometimes, I really miss that man.

"I was looking for you. I was starting to worry when I couldn't find you," Selma says, placing her palms on either side of his face when he reaches where she is standing. She is melting with worry and it smells like burning plastic.

Rhett is very aware of us watching him. He is being forced to finally declare a side and like I said, J.D. would not have missed this chance to make the big man break if he were here. The prince isn't going to either.

"Let one disaster into your door and more follow. You can also follow her back out. Don't worry. We'll come to find you to tell you the results of the vote." Lawless folds his arms across his chest as he relaxes back against the wall.

This is Rhett's last chance for survival with our group. If Lawless declares him dead, dead he will become. I've seen the missing person report showcasing members of their club and their shrugs with blank stares that accompany when the police asked about it. I just never wanted to believe it. It's easy to look away when your back isn't shoved into a corner.

"Last time I checked, this school was ours. That includes this floor and this door as well." Selma smiles at Law and I have the spider sensation crawling along my arms again.

"Last time I checked, this school belonged to Simon," he tells her, still a relaxed gentle stance upon him.

"Simon really isn't in the position to be running anything. You should know that since it was your circle here that made him that way." Selma spins her webs again trying to reopen sores that have since tried to scab and heal.

"Even they don't play that card anymore. You're going to have to try harder than that," I hear myself say in defense of the man and it brings me right into the middle of her attention.

"Helena, how nice to see you up. Dolph was just asking about you," she tries, and I can't stop the laughter from erupting from my throat. Aimes is right.

"That's nice. Rhett here was just asking about Aimes." I stand letting her see the token I am wearing. "We were all just having a nice little chat about sinners, shooters and hangings."

To be as manipulative as Selma is, you have to be smart. The colors almost change in her eyes as she figures out what has happened. Her sugary smile never slips.

"I told you," I continue to nail the coffin on her hopes. "I always take back what is mine. Once, twice and now three times, just as Travis said." I have given Rhett his chance to come home wordlessly. He can simply just step back letting the line be decided upon, but he stands frozen with his thoughts or his doubts. Both might get him killed.

We wait in complete silence for Rhett to make his decision. His hand trembles, flashing my mind back to the other times he let this little slip of emotion show. I can say all the words in the whole English language, but they would never reach him. Selma's poison has rotted away too much of him and my words do not have a strong enough antidote to heal his pain. This fight is for someone else to win.

"Go to him," I whisper to Aimes. "If you want him, prove it to him."

Aimes looks at me with the doubts clearly expressed on her face. Her feet begin to slowly slide forward. The weight of her fears are making them heavy to lift, but slowly she gains speed as she defeats her demons that whisper to her of failure.

She slides up to Rhett, entwining the tall man with her arms and smiles. He straightens with the heat of her body looking to her with blue eyes fighting to keep their thoughts hidden. Rhett is hearing his own demons and they are shredding him as his belief in himself is being destroyed by the evil of Selma in front of him.

Aimes gives him her best pixie smile. The warmth of it is contagious as it crawls up his body and onto his own face. "Throw the trash out, Rhett-stein," she says.

Rhett trails her small face with his fingertips, spreading his smile to the furthest corners of his lips. He tucks the smile away as he slips from the warmth of Aimes to take the arm of Selma. The two of them exit the room, but I have a feeling only one will be reentering. The most perfect couples aren't always built around love, but those whose demons understand the other's the best.

"How did you know?" Aimes asks me, as I come to stand beside her.

"Sometimes," I whisper to her. "they just need to be reminded where home is."

I can hear J.D.'s dark chuckle, but it doesn't scare me. J.D. was what he was, but without him, I would not be who I am. Like conjoined twins, we are responsible for each other the same way he has molded every man in this room in some way. They all have his strengths, his weaknesses, and his fears, but mostly they all just need to be reminded who to fight for just as he did. If I had learned that lesson sooner, could I have saved us all from him?

"Now what?" Lawless asks, not as moved as I am by what just happened.

"No clue. We let him change the sheets on his bed, I guess. I'm going to go check on Simon." I tell the room with sincere worries over Simon's mental state outweighing their needs.

"Tell Dolph hello for me," Lawless says, still wearing the scars from earlier.

My annoyance with him bubbles up to feed my anger. "Don't worry Larance, it's hard to purchase white roses these days." I let the feel of my words rest in his mouth and he frowns at me. I let it twist that smile of his into a deeper taste of anger. I hope the taste gets stuck in his throat. I hope the acidic bile gags him. I hope it gags him like the way the scent of roses gags me to this day.

"You sure you want to go out wearing that?" Chapel calls from the back of the room, where he has stood guard. I can hear how anxious he is over Aimes and I away from his side.

I don't look back to answer him. My answer is the slamming of the door leaving it all behind me. The subtle thing is completely overrated but the shrapnel is still just as sharp.

Chapter 28

Aimes and I travel the corrupted memory lane of the third floor. Flimsy ghosts float around us with their memories haunting us. Every corner, every tile, holds a corner of our mind we have fought to forget. It's easy to see how the people are so twisted against us when they are stuck in this loop of remembrance. To them, it happened just yesterday and not over a month ago because they still live in the middle of it like a memorial.

Simon's "apartment" isn't hard to find. People cross its open door with bowed heads and quicker steps than normal when they pass. Knocking, I cross through the threshold so many others fear. It's kind of my thing. Bravely going where no smart person would go before. I'm like bad sci-fi without the T&A to promote it.

I can still smell Shelia. Her perfume clings to the plaster haunting the room in it's own way. It's so real I expect to see her come from behind the false wall someone put up to section off the classroom into a living room. She doesn't, but Dolph does.

"Dun dun duunn," Aimes sings the classic song for trouble in my ear with his arrival.

He doesn't offer a greeting, a question, or an accusation as we stare at each other. Leave it to our resident smartass to break the deadlocked conversation.

"I heard you two made out," she says, tilting her head with mock curiosity.

"I heard we had sex," Dolph replies with his eyes a shade so like my own bearing down on me.

"Nah, you're too cranky for the sex rumor," Aimes says, and I could hit her – with a bus.

"I've heard Simon isn't doing well." I stop the train before it goes any further off track. As it is, there is a sharp turn ahead and there is no telling how well the wheels will hold.

"A lot of people are talking about things they shouldn't," Dolph answers, still blocking the manmade entrance.

I kick the door closed with my foot letting force slowly seal it. "You done?" I ask him, with just the three of us now closed inside the room. I've had about all I can handle with male drama. Their egos are softer than fresh baked bread and are almost as much fun to tear apart.

Dolph relaxes some once the door is closed. While our group has been managing our own fall out it seems there has been one up here as well. "Just tired," he says, trying to excuse his behavior towards us. "I'm tired of it all."

"Choir, man," Aimes relaxes in one of the chairs arranged near us, "and the refrain is getting really old."

"How bad is it?" I follow Aimes' lead and take the chair next to me.

Dropping his guard, Dolph joins us and I see how weary he is. "Travis has them all riled up about the end of days, and only those who are "devoted" will survive to see the world restored. Some are completely lost in his mess while some are over it." He leans into the little sitting area lowering his voice as he shares his fears. "I'm not a leader. I never wanted to be. Richard and I, we came from another group before we found this place. I've seen what happens when no one knows who to trust. Once everyone starts turning on each other, there is no stopping it."

"...and that is exactly their goal," Aimes shares the conclusion we have reached upstairs.

She fills the gaps with what we have heard exhausting every avenue before Dolph finally caves. It doesn't matter who we are, we all try to desperately believe the best of people. We hope to see in others what we can't find in ourselves and we are always so bitterly disappointed when they show they are just as faltered as we are ourselves.

"I haven't told Simon any of it. He is barely even aware anymore. He lives in the past, constantly recalling things they did as a family or things we did as friends. Travis uses it as further proof of how dangerous times are now and how only the strong will survive." Dolph lets his head hang low. This is not the man who met us at the gate with sharp words and watchful eyes. I don't know who any of us are anymore.

"How do we snap him out of it?" Aimes is twirling a strand of her white-blonde hair with her thoughts. It's never a good sign.

"You mean to snap him out of losing his wife, daughter and a good friend back-to-back?" Dolph asks, putting the irritation back into his voice.

"Exactly!" She smiles at him. Aimes is going to need more than just a little snip to back down. She's slowly crawling her way back to her inner-self and her attitude is blooming again.

"We have to get him out of this room. He's surrounded himself with what he has lost and forgotten what he still has," I suggest, remembering how hard it was for me to walk down the hallway. I can't even begin to understand the pain he must be feeling with it constantly pressed to his mind.

"Where?" Dolph asks thinking about what I have said. We both know where the only place is for them both to escape and it just might be a different ring of Hell.

"There is only one place in here where Travis isn't brave enough to visit and has no memories for Simon?" Aimes is asking if she's thinking of the same place as I am without having to actually say it. She is. "Do you really think that is a good idea?"

I arch my eyebrows with the question. "Why not?" I ask. I know why not. I just don't care about the tiptoeing around egos and property anymore. Another boxing match might do them all some good. We are running out of bikes to drop or to find.

"I agree with her. Do you really think that would be wise?" There is something hopeful in Dolph's eyes when he asks me his question, something that stirs my heart just a little too well.

"You scared?" I ask him. Whenever you want a man to agree with you, doubt his manhood. It works like a charm and I wear it like a favorite bracelet.

"No." It's one word, but his body is filling in the rest of the sentence. He might not be scared, but he isn't happy either. He walks with a new resolve as he leaves the chair. "I'll meet you down there later." He doesn't ask for help and we don't insult him by offering it. I've done enough damage. At least, I have until the real fun begins.

"What have you done now?" Aimes asks me, as we leave the room.

"If we are going to stop hiding then we have to start fighting."

"You really think Dolph and Simon are going to take up the banner of Hell-no-we-won't-go?"

"You really think they have a choice?" I leave her silent as she thinks about my question.

None of us have any choices left to us. If this is truly our home, then we are going to have to fight for it or we might as well run now and watch it burn as we abandon it. I don't run well and I'm not just talking physically.

Fighting, I have learned to do very well. It's not a matter of who is right or who is wrong when the truth can be blurred with a simple tilt of the candle. Truth is a personal virtue. It's something of importance only when laying in the dark with your mind as your only companion. I'm not scared of the dark anymore. I'm not impressed with people's truths either. I just want to survive. Even if it means letting go of the virtues I once fought to keep.

I know the reindeer games I am going to have to play to bring us all together. I know the road I will have to travel. I also know the person I will have to become. I'm not proud of any of it. I only pray I don't succumb to the darkness as J.D. did. I pray when everything has settled, I can still call my soul my own. If I can't, I at least pray it goes somewhere where I can find it again when this is all over. Now I lay me down to sleep. Should I die before I wake, I pray that someone's life it doesn't take.

Chapter 29

Dinner was blissfully uneventful. Aimes sulked without Rhett making a villain-defying return. I had a feeling he wasn't ready to let the ship named Selma sink. Knowing Rhett, he's going to go down like the Titanic; iceberg and all. Travis sat with his new God Squad, as Aimes dubbed them watching us and of course the men had fun with that. I wasn't even aware they knew so many versions of "Kumbaya", and when they did run out, Lawless was more than happy to apply his gift of wit to a few lines. I'm pretty sure the Lord never did such things with strippers as Lawless hinted with his new renditions.

The after-dinner show, now that was a bit more climatic. Dolph and Simon were waiting for our return in our assembled loft area. I felt the mood shift like a sudden burst of static in the air. It set the hair on my neck on edge and my stomach fluttered before I could swallow against it. With one look from Law's golden-hazel eyes, I knew the thoughts circling him. I saw his tongue slide across his teeth under his clamped lips. I heard a sudden inhale. This is act one of the play I have been dreading since I cast the actors earlier today. Lights. Camera. Execution.

"Not running," Law whispers to me even as he closes down around the edges. He is not going to run, but he's not going to be cooperative, either.

"Wasn't my idea," Dolph tells him, as Law takes one of the seats near him.

Law lounges, putting on a show of contentment. He sits with complete disregard for Dolph and I suppose it's one of the more polite roads he could have taken, even if all of it is obviously just for show.

"Do we get the tape now, or later?" Aimes asks, with a mockery of a whisper. She is teasing them about their last attempt at being friends and how long it had lasted.

"Wasn't my idea, either," Dolph says again. He wears a half little smile this time as he looks to Lawless. Law returns the smile with a bit more menace.

"It was mine." Simon's voice is a husk of what I remember. All of his confidence has eroded, reducing him to a sliver of the man he once was. "It seemed like something that would have helped at the time. I didn't think your group would be so willing. A few of my ribs still hurt." Simon smiles wistfully with the memory.

It's as Dolph had mentioned, just more tragic now that I see it before me. This was a man who could have out charmed Law if he had wanted to. He stood up to J.D. with grace where so many before him had shrunk with fear. He had navigated the waters of leader, husband, father, friend and foe only to end up on a distant, deserted shore.

"Shelia had a much better bedside manner than Paula did over that." Chapel is hoisting the white flag between the two sets of men. It's just what he does.

Simon stares at the gold cross on the chain around Chapel's neck. It might as well be flashing a private message to him with how he watches it glow from the many-lighted candles. "Shelia liked to save the verbal beatings until we were alone. Once that door shut, all deals were off." His voice is monotone. It never climbs in pitch or lowers to accent any of his thoughts. He just stares as his mouth moves reciting the memories. "How is Paula?" he asks Chapel as if the woman has been gone for some time and not just downstairs preparing for breakfast tomorrow.

"We don't talk much anymore." Chapel lets us glimpse his not-so-secret secret.

"No one really does," Simon's words drift off like a toddler fighting sleep. He wants to stay in the now, but his mind is fighting to let go.

Aimes walks to Simon, kneeling in front of the man who stares right past her as if she were a ghost and not the family he is longing for. "I miss Shelia, too," she tells him, and his eyes do move to her.

A single tear travels along his face. It falls along the contours of his dark skin highlighting the path it takes. He doesn't say a word as he stares into Aimes' eyes. His face expresses more than any string of vowels he could form.

"I'm so sorry," she whispers to him, pulling him deeper into his unspeakable dictionary.

"We all are," I tell him, as he stares at Aimes. "They didn't deserve what happened to them."

"You don't know how this feels," Simon whispers his first string of words with emotion. "You don't have the right to talk about them. They would still be alive if it wasn't for you." Simon sees us. Simon sees the whole room and he's not happy with anyone in it. Dolph hangs his head with shame too.

"I might not have the right, but everyone here knows how it feels," I keep my voice a steady line of volume. If I am to bring them together, to really break past this male ego of dominance, I am going to have to break more than just their pride. "Chapel lost his family. Aimes lost her parents. Lawless lost his dad. We've all lost someone, somehow since this started."

Marxx retreats into his chair deflating his chest with whatever memory he has yet to share with us just as I have kept mine hidden behind locked doors. Those doors rattle now with excitement with the hopes of freedom. Pandora's box held just a fraction of what I might unleash if their curiosity pushes me.

Lawless becomes unsettled as Dolph stares at him. It's hard to remain tough with your scars exposed. It's harder still when the scars are still fresh and red-rimmed sores.

"What's your story?" Lawless asks, when Dolph refuses to look away.

"Richard and I worked construction. It paid the bills and left time to do what we wanted if we didn't want the job." Dolph melts back into his chair. His southern drawl is soft as he recalls how this nightmare started for him. "We were doing this one job, a new office space or something, and this man just walked right onto the site. One of the guys went over to tell him he couldn't be there, and the guy just bit his face. He tore the guy's nose clean off. After that, they were everywhere. People were being attacked all around us. We got in Richard's truck and we never looked back. We were on our own for a bit but hooked up with this other group. It was good for a bit until it wasn't. One night, the guy who was supposed to be on watch just upped and left. When they came, everyone who could run did, including Richard and I. I kept hoping we'd come across some of them. Haven't seen any. I keep thinking, what if we were the only ones who made it out?"

"No family? Wife?" Aimes gently asks.

Dolph shakes his head with his lip a thin line of tension. "Wasn't that guy," he says.

Simon looks to me with a flicker of life behind his eyes. He asks me, "What did J.D. lose?"

I know what he is after. I know what he is asking with a hidden innuendo of an idea. Before I can answer, Lawless does.

"His life," Lawless answers with a voice that dips low with a warning.

The tension in the room escalates with the abundant dare. As Dolph becomes protective of Simon, Marxx mirrors that attitude over Law. Trust was a long, hidden hope, but a truce I thought was attainable. Watching how easy they can set the other off, I'm not sure anymore. The common thread I had hoped to pluck to unravel their hate is holding strong in its weaving and of course Fate with all of her antics sends Rhett into the room at this moment.

The metal doors scream as they open with so little being said around us. A slow smirk-like laugh spreads across Rhett's lips as he becomes the center of attention. "I took care of the trash. Now I'm going to bed. Fill me in on this later?" Wearing the same smirk, he simply walks past the showdown, but when he pauses in front of me, I should have known he wouldn't let this chance slip past him. "So," Rhett leans into me with a sly smile, "whose bed are you in tonight?"

"Whose bed did you just leave?" my voice escapes like a whip.

"Damn, I've missed you," Rhett says, laughing as he continues on his way down the hall. It echoes along the walls making him sound louder than he really is.

Dolph stands, helping Simon with his still lost mental state. "Going to call it too." He wants to escape from whatever Rhett's words have left. He understands how much he needs this truce as well as I do. Sitting here would only layer more damage to that hope, risking its complete destruction. It's not hard to throw the first punch. It's hard to walk away from it when it's thrown. Watching Dolph walk away now, I have no doubts which role he has silently played in his life.

"Why are they here?" Marxx asks the question Lawless is too afraid to. Law's face might be blank, but his eyes are burning.

"We owe Simon." I'm exhausted and hurting. I'm too much of too many things to go into the depths of the plan I hope will unfold itself for me. Because I said so, would be such a wonderful thing to be able to say right now.

"He totally needed to get out of that area. It's like a wake up there," Aimes says, from the chair the man we are speaking about just left.

Marxx nods, understanding but I can see his thoughts still forming. He asks, "You think we can give the man some kind of closure? He blames us."

I laugh, not out of joy but from the irony. "How do you give someone closure? If we knew how to offer that, a few of us right here wouldn't be such the mess that we are."

"We?" Law asks. I'm not sure if he is asking if I meant him or me. I meant us both and I don't mind letting him know.

"Yeah, we," I say again, closing my eyes as the exhaustion covers me like a heavy blanket.

"Do I need to remind you about the little list of theirs?" Lawless leans in, almost whispering his concerns as if Dolph or Simon may be listening. "You really think you can trust them?"

"Do I need to remind you about our little O.K. Corral act? If anyone should worry about who to trust, it's not us." I close my eyes again. "I think you guys have proved time and time again how well you can handle yourselves."

"So, we are the monsters now?" Lawless grows defensive with my lack of empathy.

I look to Marxx and watch him as I quote him. "No Law, we're not the only monsters. We're just more honest about being the monsters. We are going to need that honesty if we want to survive this."

"Survive what?" Aimes has one eyebrow cocked in her normal fashion.

"Everything. If we want to survive everything," Chapel answers for me. Of all of us, it's Chapel who has learned this truth the most. He started out the passive viewer of the club to now becoming one of the main voices of reason. If anyone has learned how to embrace the truth of what this world makes of people, it's him.

"You're up to something," Marxx says, half amused and half worried. I can't blame him. I'm not known for stellar planning skills.

"Who, me?" I ask, lacking the strength to open my eyes, but my lips still curl.

I hear him chuckle and Lawless sigh. They stand on two different sides of my adventures. Somehow, I always end up dragging one with me and the other I always leave to cope with being left behind. I don't plan it that way. It just happens. I did mention how wonderful I am at this.

"I noticed how you didn't offer up your own story?" Marxx asks, and he sounds miles away as I drift.

Sleep comes for me in hues of greys and silvers with the flickering of the candles. I haven't reached the pure blacks of the abyss yet, but I crave it. "I noticed how you haven't offered yours, either," I tell him, from my rocking boat of slumber.

"Nope. You can't offer me closure anyway." He uses my own words against me to keep his secrets. He's right. I can't. So, I don't try to argue with him.

"Just promise that you'll clue us in on what you are plotting before you go running into any Risen? Your track record isn't holding as strong as it once did," Chapel asks, and I hold up a three-finger salute mimicking another all-boys' club from the past.

A shadow blocks the dancing, darkened hues and I hear Lawless say, "Let's go Sleeping Beauty."

"I've upgraded from Snow White?"

"Yeah," he says, "we are down a few dwarves."

"Don't worry, Lawless," Aimes says, with a retreating voice from somewhere behind me down the hall, "you'll always be our Grumpy."

"Ask me what your name is!" Lawless shouts over my head. His only answer is high-pitched female laughter.

I let Lawless help me from the chair that has grown rather comfortable with its plastic arch. I even let him help me down the same hallway everyone has retreated through. I think this is what is worrying him the most out of the whole day.

"How hurt are you?" he asks, lowering me to the cot.

I smile, trying to cover the truth to shield some of his fears with how bad it really is. "I'm just tired," I tell him, even as I wince with my movement. Guile is not my strongest asset.

"Right," he answers, and I know how thin my attempt was.

I let him slide off my boots and roll the thick socks to fight against the winter's strength from my feet. I don't even argue as he nonchalantly removes the jeans or when he pulls the vest and shirt from me. I watch as he stares at the long gauze on my stomach with pain leaving me finally feeling vulnerable.

"I can put one of your shirts on..." I leave the offer hanging between us. Sleeping in his shirts has always been soothing to both of us. He enjoys seeing me in them and I enjoy the feel of them on me as they wrap me in his scent, allowing me to feel that much closer to him.

"No," his voice is hoarse with the thoughts he is hearing. I can see the guilt boldly written on his face and I know exactly where his mind is taking him.

"It's not your fault." I reach for him, touching our fingertips together. He is still too overcome to allow more.

His eyes watch our hands with their gentle game of entwinement. "You asked me to join you," he says with his voice still burdened from his thoughts. "I told you no, but if I had put my own petty needs aside, I would have been there to save you. It would never have happened." His eyes float to my face heavy with his guilt. "I keep failing you and I can't help but wonder if Dolph could do better by you."

"Shut up," I tell him. It's the world's worst pep talk, but I am not feeling very peppy. "I would have walked into trouble eventually if you were there that night or not. It's my gift. You have your smile to get you out of trouble and I have my luck to attract it."

He smiles, crawling to hover over me. "It's a curse I swear," he says and smiles the very smile I was talking about at me. I feel it returned as I mimic it. "You up for this?" he asks me with hope and so much more in his eyes.

"It's been a while," I smile, ignoring the fluttering of my heart with his question. "But from what I remember, I'm not the one that has to be up for it."

He lowers his lower body to touch mine, keeping his torso suspended with his arms. A moan pulls from my throat when I feel his body's response to the same possibility that has my heart racing.

"Covered," he tells me, as his voice becomes deep and husky.

His clothes come off slower than mine had with his further attempts to seduce me, and when I feel his skin to mine, the heat overtakes us both. The room fills with our voices crying for the other as he gently takes me. Ice is tapping on the window and it sounds like the soft sounds of applause for the love we have salvaged tonight.

Chapter 30

"I guess you figured out how to make Lawly okay with Dolph hanging around last night?" Aimes asks me, as we shift our way through the crowds around the cafeteria. With the weather growing colder by the day, most have started lingering in the hallways for their social interactions. Sounds of their conversations, and the few remaining children running around, make the air feel more claustrophobic than it should.

"What are you talking about?" I ask her, battling against my nerves that seem to be shorter than normal.

"Really?" She looks at me with a look of disdain. "You two weren't exactly very shy. Either he is very good, or you are very good, or it was one of the amazing flukes that leave us wondering why it can't always be like that."

I want to blush. I just don't want the teasing that will occur if she knows how embarrassed I am. I had forgotten about our close quarters last night under the skilled body of Lawless as easily as he had lost himself in my abandonment. We had fed off the other until the sensations were too much, bringing us clinging to each other with hungry hands and mouths. None of this is what I want to share with her as she stares at me with searching eyes and a devilish smile.

"It was a fluke," I tell her, leaving her curiosity with more devil than searching.

"I guess that is why we snuck away so early to eat and shower?" Aimes asks, still unrelenting with her smirk.

I smile, merging into the small spaces left by so many pushing into the hall. "His morning gloating is a little annoying," I lie to her. The early morning hours are when he is the most himself, but I couldn't bear it this morning. I'm not running. I'm just mastering avoiding. I need a new gold medal to wear with my other medals.

"Just tell him it was a fluke." She shrugs, making her grin even more lopsided with her mischief.

"We never tell him that."

"You're right. They are so much worse when they have their little sexual egos hurt."

"Words of advice or experience?" I ask her, returning the mischief back to her.

Aimes sticks her tongue out at me as we finally make it through the congested room of the library to an open, private corner. She pauses, looking to me with honest curiosity. She asks me, "Why do they always think they are God's gift?"

"Because we never tell them about the flukes."

She laughs as we take the two overstuffed reading chairs in the corner. From here, we can see most of the room and the conversations are a mixture of volumes and moods. It swirls in the room combining the different elements like a recipe of life. No one is really happy, and no one is really depressed. It's a flat line of facts that once again the sun is upon us and another day is here to survive, which in itself sounds pretty depressing.

"Glad to see the morning finds you two well," Selma's voice slithers from a spot beyond us. Like magic, or voodoo, the crowd parts right at that instant to reveal whom we missed when we picked this area to sit.

Like a viper in the tall grass sensing its prey, I'm pretty sure she saw us the whole time.

"It had. Now, not so much," Aimes answers, sounding a lot like her old self.

Selma isn't phased by Aimes' remark at all. Her smile is stuck on sentimental, and with how she is watching me, I have a sickening suspicion Aimes is not her target today. I have the privilege with all the earned bonuses of psychotic that goes right along with it. Lucky me.

I sigh, bracing myself for the attempt of a mind screw I know she is plotting behind her smile. "Need something, Selma, or did you just get lost on the way to the punch?"

"I hear strawberry helps hide the taste of crazy when serving bullshit to the masses." Aimes is twirling a strand of her white-blonde hair with a relaxed poise Lawless would be proud over. If she could stop tapping her foot with the energy of a toddler on a sugar bender it would be a lot more convincing.

Selma doesn't even flinch with the remark. Her dark chocolate-colored eyes are locked on me with a death grip. She could be chiseling my tombstone by hand with her intensity. She most likely is doing it mentally.

"It must be hard to always be the strong one; the one they always look to. Especially, when your friend just skates through life, living behind their adoration to keep her safe," Selma says, reopening a book I have closed. She is a few chapters behind for her to reach her goal.

I say nothing, giving her not the least little nibble of which way to dig her talons into me. It's more fun to watch people like her try to grasp at air than to give them an avenue to skip down. I want to see how well she can play this game before I return her pitch.

She isn't discouraged with my lack of concern. She just finds a different swamp to wade through. She says still wearing the artificial smile, "Rhett has spoken so often about you. He really admires your strengths and how bravely you are always putting *them* before your own safety." She pauses with hopes the compliments will take root so that her next move may bear fruit. "He also mentioned how awful your parents were to you. How they never really loved you like you deserved to have been loved. You've lived your whole life trying to earn someone's love and now you are searching to fill that same void with *their* respect."

I'll give her points for getting closer to home with that one. I continue to stare at her, waiting for her attempt for a homerun, which worries me some since that last pitch was so close to the plate.

"He told me about Law and Leslie as well. I was very ashamed of her actions when I found out. I feel like a fool to have trusted her." She lets her smile fade to a forced frown as she tries to play the an-enemy-of-my-enemy-is-a-friend-of-mine card. It's cute, but not the home run she was hoping for. "The shame *you* must have felt when you found out trusting Lawless to such a degree. Then to find out it was all a plot by the man who had sworn to protect you, how heartbreaking!"

That one flew right over home plate, but I'm not taking the swing. I have two more strikes before I'm out.

"You deserve so much more, Helena." She looks at me the way a mother is supposed to look at her child when discovering they are hurt. With how starved my heart has always been to have Carol look at me in such a manner, I can feel my resolve cracking. "Tell me it wouldn't be nice just once to let someone else carry the weight. How nice would it be just once to be the one just accepted and not the one who is always tested?" she asks me, with a face I have craved and I feel myself finally give under her skills.

"What are you trying to get at, Selma?" I ask her, forcing my voice to fill with contempt and not the cravings.

"It's okay to be tired and scared, Helena. It's not fair for them to force you to always bear their faults. You have your own needs. You have just as much right to be comforted as they do," she implores me to understand.

Aimes laughs with a tone of amusement. She says, "You obviously didn't hear her last night. She was comforted just fine."

"Flukes aren't very satisfying for anything the heart needs," Selma says, entwining me in my lie. To disagree now would unravel the web I have spun. A web she has used to trap me to be devoured later.

"Is that how you've become this person, Selma? Has a lifetime of flukes left you a puppet master for Travis? Or, is that just an added plus of this new role of yours? You lure them in, and he makes them sign on the dotted line?" I told myself I wouldn't take the bait, but once again my mouth is moving before my brain can stop it. My mouth and my feet once again with a plan of their own - shocking. Obviously, it is not self-preservation.

She melts back to her self-assured smile. We both know I have taken the poisoned bait and now she just has to wait until it's fully digested to win. Her silence is provoking as she reverses the roles we were playing. She lets me sit and wait for her answer showing her smile as she climbs under my skin.

With a nod she begins her story, sharing some small glimpse of the woman before us. "No, I was blessed before all of this. I had a good husband. He was my first love, and we had the perfect fairytale. A few years after being married, we had our son, Beau. Our blessings kept growing, and like most people, the more they grew the more we forgot who to thank for them. We became so busy with our perfect life that we soon lost track of our beliefs. Church became something to do only on holidays and then slowly, not at all. We would tell ourselves we were going to change, but we never did. We never did until we were forced to." Her smile is finally free from its cage and I see the real woman.

I know the twist her story is about to take before she says it. It's the same twist that all of our stories have.

"There I was on the floor holding our son's dead body, hating the Lord and ranting about how unfair for Him to take Beau and not me as well. I promised everything I owned if He would take me, too. I wanted to be with my son more than I wanted to live. I just never thought the Lord would collect."

I watch as her memories take the slyness from her face. I see her stripped of all of her programmed manuscripts and manipulations. Her heart is blistering, and I can almost understand why she is the woman she is as I watch her suffering.

"My husband came in and started to try to revive him. He kept screaming for Beau to breathe and I kept screaming for him to let me hold him. When Beau came to, we were both so relieved. My husband picked him up and held him and that is when the real screaming started. Beau killed his father while I watched. I watched while my little boy murdered my husband like a monster and then he came for me, too. God did as I asked. He gave me the choice to live without him or to die with him. I killed my little boy for God and God took everything I had just like I had offered. So no, I am not the woman I am because of flukes. I'm who I am because of truths, simple black-and-white truths. When you're ready to live with your truths, I'll be waiting." Selma stands, pressing her palms down her jeans to smooth imagined wrinkles with a nervous habit of a lifetime ago. She doesn't glance backward as she leaves, but I'm sure she feels Aimes and I staring at her retreating back just the same.

"It doesn't change anything," Aimes carefully says. It almost sounds more like a question than anything else. My weakness for the child story is not exactly a secret. Just the reason why I am so susceptible to it is.

"No, it doesn't change anything," I tell her with a voice as unsure as hers. "We all have our stories. You don't see Chapel going all medieval crusades, so why should it make it okay for her?"

"Wonder what's Travis' story?" Aimes asks off-handed. Curiosity, cats, and her have a shared theme.

I call her on her question. "You want to find out?"

I watch as her eyes grow and shrink from shock to uncertainty to shock again before she can finally find her voice. "You're serious?"

"Come on, no one loves to talk about themselves more than Travis does. We'll just tell him we are looking for repentance for our naughty, naughty ways."

"The sounds Lawly was making last night, you might have to."

"Jealousy is such an ugly shade," I tell her with false airs.

"Yeah, but whore isn't. You're just so purdy, remember?" She returns and I mock a gasp before playfully hitting her arm.

Hiding behind our laughter we are both nervous, if not outright afraid, of walking into the den of snakes. We have seen their handiwork and how their forked tongues can convince people to do such horrible things to the ones they love. Adam and Eve were God's chosen. They had paradise to themselves and all it took was the whisperings of a single snake to bring them to ruins. What chance do we have against a whole den?

We continue with our completely inappropriate jokes as we make our way to the third floor. The more lewd the joke, the larger and deeper the looks of disapproval we gain from those we pass. By the time we reach the metal barrier of the top floor, I have verbally done more sexually in the time it took to climb the stairs than I have my whole life. Shockingly, Aimes tops my every joke with her own falsified escapades. If this gossip does reach our group, we will have a lot to try to explain and a harder time keeping a straight face as we do.

The floor is much as we left it yesterday, dark and emotionally stagnant. The same hollow eyes stare at us as we enter. Those same eyes watch us as we travel down the hall looking for the man who brags about having the ear of our Maker. Their depression hangs in the air like accumulated cobwebs. I can almost feel the shivers of walking through their wraithlike strings. Their sadness clings to me like a living thing, attempting to devour my life and laughter. Conversations aren't just hushed here. This is where they go to die.

A man sits in the hallway letting his daughter invent her own version of the game duck-duck-goose. She's been "ducking" the whole time we have been walking towards them, and by the smile on his face, I don't think she ever reaches "goose". They are an oddity of light and joy in a place devoid of any such sensations.

"Travis?" Aimes asks, reluctantly disturbing the private world of theirs.

"Ryan," he says, momentarily distracted by his daughter.

Aimes cocks her head over the misunderstanding and asks again, "No, Ryan, where is Travis?"

"Oh," he replies, still bewildered as to why we are talking to him, "down the hall. It's the room holding the meeting. They have been doing that a lot as of late."

"Any clue why?" I ask. I toss my hat into this almost one-sided conversation with the chanting embedded between the attempted words.

"Nope. I don't have a lot to do with that group. They have names all written down like there's a giant roll call going on." He pauses as his daughter's never-ending circle loops in between us. "Besides, I have my hands full as it is." He smiles a proud beacon of fatherhood letting us know exactly what he speaks of. Not that we really would have had to guess.

I pass him, leaving him and his little girl to their game. "Thanks, Ryan," I say, as I watch them. I do have to applaud his constant stream of peace. I have only been in the hall for minutes and I am already starting to hate the word, duck. Some people are not cut out to be parents. I'm raising my hand for that line, please.

Travis is easy to find like Ryan had said. He, and his collection of God Squad, are in one of the few rooms with life actively happening within it. It's a hustle of running to-and-fro with some urgency of lists. There are many names and just as many lines connecting them. Names are circled in either red or blue ink leaving purple ink to underline the rest. Unsettling as it is to watch, I feel that same numbness coating my insides with a reverse act of climbing up instead of down. It settles my stomach, steadies my heart, and slows my breathing to the calm space I crawl out from each time I step into something I really want to run from.

"Tell me Travis," I hear my voice, and it's a rock of solid strength from my throat, "did I make the naughty or the nice list this year?"

As if playing musical chairs and my voice was the signal to rush to a seat, the room was upheaved in the duty to hide what I had mentioned. It's charming really that a woman as small as myself can cause such stress with one simple sentence. Wait till they see me on a bender.

"Helena." If Travis could glow with his self-importance, he would. As it stands, his smile and unnerving eyes will have to suffice. "I was wondering when you would honor me with a visit. I didn't expect you to have the club's sidekick in tow though. It's a shame really the people we align ourselves with sometimes."

"What is this? Did I forget a holiday? Hallmark invented a new card while I wasn't looking? Happy Kick the Blonde Day everybody!" Aimes shouts, outstretching her arms to further add to her exaggerated angst.

"It's like kick the can, but with better tits." Rhett's dark voice is shocking and seductive at the same time from behind us.

To say we spin to see him would not fully explain the motion I made to quickly see behind me. If I could learn to move this quickly always, I might not keep finding myself at the bottom of a pile of Risen.

Travis chuckles a sound of reprimand. He says, "Now Rhett, we have talked about that mouth of yours. Sinning starts with the mind and follows the tongue. You must remember this."

Rhett stretches along the doorframe like a lazy cat. "It's not my tongue I want to sin with, Reverend." He couldn't give Aimes a more poignant look and she couldn't turn any more pink even if she were competing with the streaks in her hair.

"Rhett!" Travis snaps his voice, but Rhett doesn't flinch. His eyes ascend from Aimes to Travis with deadly precision. My numbness falters being so close to his mood swing. Even Travis has to recover some of his dignity under such a stare.

"Rhett," Travis starts again, calmer with a more respectful edge, "perhaps, it would be best if you left your inner-demons elsewhere. With consideration to the girls' feelings, of course."

Rhett smiles an instant beam of teeth. "Of course," he replies, but the smile never penetrates the ice of his eyes. With the same lazy cat-like attitude, he watches Travis and the men around us but doesn't say anything more.

Travis walks towards me with one arm extended in a mockery of sincere friendship. I fight against the shudder my body wants to do as he wraps it around me, engulfing me in his cologne as he pulls me from Aimes. A stale cologne that is too sweet to be male and too musky to be female. It eats at my numbness as my skin crawls.

"What can I help you with, Helena?" Travis asks me. He has dialed down the smile to that of one a good friend would wear when greeting one another. He sounds almost sincere with his desire to help me. I can hear the hinges being pulled back on the trap and yet I still find myself putting my neck out.

I don't try to lie to him. Someone such as Travis has too much skill in doing that himself. He would see through it before I could see that he had. Honesty is the best policy someone once lied to me. So, I try it now.

"I want to try to understand," I start, leaving no ambition in my voice, "I want to know what happened to start this mission of yours."

Just as I had suspected him to, Travis stares at me, trying to read my face. He nods, his face a serious look of stillness when I pass the test. Just another sheep to the flock, that's me.

"It's always been my mission to bring the people back to their roots; to their very foundation of religious beliefs, if you will. Now the people have no choice but to see their way back to Him. It's glorious!" He exclaims that last part like a man in love. Maybe he is. "I saw what was happening all around us. I saw the sinners being contorted with their black souls. They became the evil that lived inside them." Travis cups his spare hand in front of me like he's holding something precious and fragile. "In one fell swoop, God picked his survivors, his namesakes, and showed us the proof we needed of His glory. The proof so many had dared to forget."

"Why? Why did you take up the call so unwavering?"

"As I said," he inhales, as if I have insulted him, "it was my duty as a man of God."

"Melanie," Rhett remarks in his boredom.

Travis' hand tightens across my shoulders, squeezing me, keeping me from looking over my shoulder.

"A woman?" Aimes asks, with a little more interest than Rhett had for the topic. "I thought you Holy Rollers couldn't double-dip?"

"You must ignore Rhett." Travis is dripping with charm to cover the fact he is losing his poster-boy perfection. I felt his hand clamp reactively on my arm at the mention of the name. "He has been misled by the gossip of the Devil."

"I'm not sure Selma would appreciate such characterization," Rhett says, with his face still a map of boredom. I know better. He can't look at Travis or I or his smirk will ruin the game.

I watch the muscles by Travis' mouth twitch. Seems Selma likes to share everyone's little secrets in hopes of keeping her bedmate.

"I'm sure it was just a mistake on how you interpreted the topic." Travis is forcing his smile. His voice comes from behind clenched teeth.

"Maybe." Rhett shrugs one shoulder, not even investing his whole body into the conversation. "Something about how she was a member of your church. You two had a little thing going on. When her husband found out he was going to let the church know what kind of man you were," Rhett pauses to look at Aimes and me, "Oh, yeah. Travis has a thing for other men's women. When Travis here found out his gig was up, he shot the husband, claiming he was possessed by demons that made his tongue foul with lies."

Travis pivots losing the composure of his facade. Before he opens his mouth, he exhales his smokescreen, letting it replace the charm he momentarily let slide. With a smile that reminds me of the woman who has let his secrets slip, he looks back to me with an attempt to ignore Rhett completely. It's too late. Travis has shown his hand and now Rhett knows just the cards to deal to forever undermine him. You never let Rhett know the kinks in your armor. Rhett only has one rule for a fight and that is to win. Once he knows how to beat you, it's playtime for him and his smile is matching the man's who is trying to ignore him.

"Was she at least pretty?" I ask, forcing Travis to stay on the topic. If Rhett wants to play, I'll shuffle the deck for him.

"You shouldn't listen to idle gossip, Helena." Travis' eyes do not reflect the harmless man his face is trying to cast him. "If one were so inclined, just imagine what they might think about you?"

"I'm not the one shooting my flock," I evenly reply.

"…or screwing them," Aimes points out, still irked with the new declared holiday.

I'm the main target for his eyes. They stare at me from behind the curtain he keeps between the real man and the ones he wants to feign with his holy act. No one in the room can see him as I am seeing him now and this is the window I have been waiting for. This is the stage I wanted us to stand upon.

"She got the shot, didn't she? She became the very thing you now have declared war on. Now you see her face on every one of those things you kill, don't you?" I whisper to him, making the room grow restless with our hushed conversation. "The children in the trees, she was with child, wasn't she?"

I watch my words hit home. I watch his eyes flash a dark warning while his smile still beams his white teeth. I have played the room to our drama by whispering to him. They strain to hear any shred to satisfy their curiosity. They are staring at our little huddle with watchful eyes trying to read our locked expressions. Even Rhett who was so bored a second ago is fully standing as he tries to guess which way this will go.

"Or, did you just want it to be? You didn't shoot him because he knew the truth. You shot him because you knew. You would never have her or the child she carried. She was going back to her husband leaving you the fool, and everyone who saw you for the pillar you wanted them to, would also know the truth. You're not holy, Travis. You're just another sucker being played by the lonely housewife."

I never saw his hand reaching for my throat. He was upon me before I could brace for the attack, blocking the wind from my lungs that my shock was gasping to attain. I did see his fist coming for my face though, but I didn't try to block it. I let him connect as Rhett fought to get through the God Squad. I let him strike me as the room began to fill with the people from the hall. I let my body go limp, lying at his feet for all to see when he dropped me. Travis isn't holy. He's just another sucker being played.

"Remove them!" Travis is smoothing his hair back to its slicked style as I cower from him on the floor. I can read the satisfaction on his face. Pity for him, but so can the rest of the room.

"I wouldn't." Rhett only glances once to the few men still following orders. He kneels to lift me to my feet, and as he examines my face, I have my first hint at how bad it really is.

He props me up against the wall, slowly turning my face this-way-or-that as his eyes become veiled. Helping me into the arms of Aimes, he turns to lead us from the room. I never saw Travis' hands and he never saw Rhett's fist.

Rhett doesn't even slow in his exit. He doesn't exchange a look or a word – just his fist. Travis stumbles and falls backward from the blow and Rhett still just keeps walking right past him. He leads us through the hanging jaws, the whispering behind palms, the hands that reach out to comfort me, and right past Selma. She reaches for Rhett with a look of shock and confusion, and when he dodges her outstretched hand, her mood simmers to anger.

Ryan is still sitting on the spot on the floor where we met him. His daughter has been joined by April. They skip in unison creating the perfect loop around the father figure. As we approach, I hear his daughter shout, "Goose!" and watch her run as April chases her with their own rules for the game. For a moment, the hallway has life again. Their laughter thrives as they run. It pierces the veil of mourning that has shrouded over this place.

I feel the first splash of my blood from my face. Staring at the red drops on my hands, I am reminded of another place where I watched children laugh as blood pooled around me. They skipped and played as they waited to escape from their imprisonment, an imprisonment that I caused. I remember how their blood covered my hands as now mine seeps into the same lines and crevices. I spilled their blood entombing us in the nightmare we can't be free from. Now, I will spill my own so these children will not become victims, too. I will spill all of it if I need to. There will be no more tiny bodies swaying from protesting ropes. No more burn piles. Hopefully, no more added pages to my portfolio.

Let Travis come for me. Let him try his best to do his worst. I will be waiting. With blood-covered hands, I will be waiting.

Chapter 31

"What the hell happened to you?" Lawless explodes, as Aimes and I follow Rhett to our loft.

"She was texting while riding her broom again," Aimes tells him, helping me to one of the plastic chairs we now claim as comforts.

It's no surprise they turn to accuse Rhett with our history. Before I can say anything to defend him, Dolph comes through the screaming doors with Paula right behind him. He's holding the same bag she carried Christmas morning. A bag no one can look at and still have the power of speech. I might have to get one of those for myself.

"I didn't think I would be seeing you so soon," Paula says, tilting my head back between her strong hands. She repeats the same tilting process as Rhett had. She just isn't as kind about it.

"I guess news of religious upheaval travels fast?" I ask, as the headache grows to nausea.

"No, Dolph does," Paula says, not in the least bit interested in me personally. She has switched to a professional role turning off any amount of friendship.

"I actually went to get her for Travis. I didn't think Rhett would stop with just one." Dolph's southern voice comes from somewhere to my right.

"Travis did this?" Marxx cautiously asks. I don't have to see him, to know he's putting the pieces together. "What did you do to him?"

"Would you believe me if I tell you nothing at all?"

"No," all the men say with almost perfected timing.

"Nothing at all," I say it anyway.

"I thought you were going to let us know before you went and found any more trouble?" Marxx asks with a touch of parental reprimand in his words.

Paula saves me from answering him that it was Risen I told them I would warn them about, not crazy preachers. She says, "I don't think the nose is broken. I'd clean out the lacerations on your cheeks, but with how often Travis washes his hands, I think you'll be fine. How's the stomach?" Robotically, she tries to lift my shirt before I can squirm from her inspection.

"Fine," I say, pushing against her hands. "It's fine." Thanks, Paula, let's just keep pointing out how skilled I am in ending up broken.

She hands a stack of the never-ending supply of gauze to Dolph. "Put pressure on her nose until it stops. If it keeps bleeding, let me know and I'll take another look at it," she tells him.

He automatically hands the stack to Aimes not wishing to be involved in the drama that will erupt with putting his hands on me with so many male egos still leering.

"Whatever you are up to, Helena, think it through. Really think it through," Paula says, leveling me with a knowing look that I bend under. I turn my eyes from her, and she turns to leave. One sideways glance to Chapel, and she exits with the same air of authority as she had entered.

It leaves a vacuum of stressed silence. They are all waiting for me to explain and I'm not sure I really know myself. Luckily, I don't have to.

"How many saw?" Marxx asks. He has moved so he can see my face over Aimes' hands. Marxx would figure it out first. A sound resembling a laugh from Chapel and I know he has put it together as well.

"Enough," I answer from behind the packed gauze.

"Enough to talk about it?" Chapel joins in, leaving Dolph and Lawless still doing the math.

Rhett laughs, "You provoked him on purpose!"

"I'm not the one that brought up the woman," I answer defensively. "You provoked him, too."

"Rhett could have taken the hit." Lawless is finally on the same page and he doesn't like the words written before him.

"Oh, she took the first hit fine. It was the third and fourth that put her on the floor." Aimes doesn't even hint that she is aware of how much she has stirred the cauldron as she checks my nose. The bleeding has stopped, leaving only the feeling of congestion in its absence. "Don't look at Rhett like that, Lawly. The God Squad had him pinned. Took seven of them. I think a few were just trying to look like they were helping though."

"Helena may not have a broken nose, but Travis does," Dolph says.

Rhett looks to Dolph with neither appreciation nor friendship saying, "Didn't know you were there."

"Wasn't for the whole thing," Dolph starts seeing where he has landed himself, "Ruby, one of the more gossiping women, stopped me saying that she saw Helena and her blonde friend-"

"What, Ruby didn't get her holiday card either?" Aimes interrupts.

"She said they were asking about Travis. Knowing Helena, the way I do, I knew it wasn't going to end well," Dolph continues, not taking the bait from Aimes.

"So, you *know* Hells now?" Rhett doesn't relent with the pressure. A part of him is still hearing the evil whispering of Selma in his ear just as she wanted him to.

"Everyone knows she's not exactly afraid to step in it." Simon is leaning on the wall near the room he and Dolph have taken. "Well, everyone but Travis."

"He knows now," Aimes tells Simon, and they both share a small laugh.

"You really think that will work? You provoke him to lose it and the whole place suddenly is over him?" Law asks, reclining in his chair trying his best to not look at the damage on my face.

"No. I think it's just the start," I answer honestly. "Between my face and what Rhett suggested, he is going to have a lot of doubts now. He told them we were the dangerous ones. He said we were the ones to fear because of our dark ways. I think he is going to have a hard time spinning this into scripture."

It's Rhett's turn to be stared at as they wait for another explanation. It's kind of nice to be part of the staring contest and not the one being stared at, for once.

He sighs, sliding down their wall to the floor instead of taking a seat. "Selma mentioned that before Travis took the freak show on the road, he had an affair with a married woman. He killed her husband and blamed it on the guy becoming possessed."

"She found out she was pregnant with her husband's baby and was going back to him. I believe Travis shot him because he was jealous. I don't think he ever really feared what his church might say," I finished the explanation.

Marxx has been watching me the whole time. I really have to find a way to keep him and Chapel apart with how fast Marxx is picking up the unnerving habits of the other man.

"I guess your face is all the proof of that?" Marxx asks, with his serious eyes watching me still.

"Surprise!" I say, beaming a mockery of a smile. "She became one of the Risen after that. He's been hunting them ever since and destroying the happy family life from behind the ruse of God's work."

"…and you had to figure all of that out with your face?" Simon asks, from his spot behind us.

"If you want to step back and lead them, my face may thank you." My mouth moved on its own again and I wince from its honesty.

"She's right," Dolph shockingly agrees. "Those people are going to need you. They are stuck right now between Travis and the MC. You can help stop it all before anyone else has to get hurt."

"Like I stopped J.D.?" The amusement has faded from Simon's voice with his question.

"If you don't move past it, they won't." Dolph is staring at his friend now. I have a feeling these are things he has wanted to say for a long time. "What happened is done. It's no one's fault who is still alive. Letting it go doesn't mean you have to let Shelia or Kira go. You're not betraying them by living. You're betraying Shelia by letting our people get hurt. If she was still here, it would have been her in that room demanding answers from Travis."

We don't speak. Our heads swivel watching someone else's drama. Being at the center of it for so long, it's almost uncomfortable to be sitting here between them.

"Aren't you tired, man?" Dolph continues. "You can't keep going like this. It won't bring them back, not Shelia, not Kira, not Richard. They are gone and we are still here. It's just the way it is."

Simon is a wall of silence. He doesn't speak or move. If he is digesting what has been said or simply daring more to be said, I can't tell.

"Hey guys, not to interrupt life lessons, take bazillion, or anything, but we might have a problem." Aimes has turned to stare out the window in an attempt to escape the tension around us. Whatever she has seen has made her normally pale coloring even lighter.

"Sit," Lawless says, gently pushing me back into the chair when he walks past me to see what Aimes is seeing. It's insulting and my feelings must have flashed across what is left moveable on my face with how Rhett chuckles.

"Well Pres," Rhett mockingly asks Lawless. "What did we get?"

"I see dead people," Law says, watching the show from the window.

"I hated that movie," Rhett answers, pulling himself to stand in preparation of what lies ahead.

"Then you are going to have a very bad afternoon." Lawless doesn't explain as he turns to leave. They don't wait for an explanation either. With the sound of clips being checked and blades being adjusted in their holders, the room clears before I can even ask for one.

"So what, give them ten minutes, and then we follow?" Aimes asks. She knows me so well. She knows I won't sit here. I just want to wait until they are far enough away so they can't stop me.

"Exactly," Simon says and there is a new tone to his voice. It's a familiar tone that I have missed. "I guess you don't have the keys to the stockpile?"

Simon is talking about the room where he has collected and stored the many scavenged guns and their matching ammunition since they declared this place theirs. It's what this floor was originally intended for and ironically made it perfect for the men to take as their own.

"Keys are kind of overrated these days," Aimes says, with her normal mischief. She leaves out how she has always found keys to be overrated. I'm not going to point that out. I'm finally going to get a gun.

Chapter 32

I didn't glance out the window as we were breaking into our private armory. I didn't look as we made our way back through our hall. I didn't ask Aimes what was waiting for us as we went down the stairs. I don't want to know what is unsettling enough to set Lawless' jaw as he left until I have to. I might not be able to fool myself into thinking I am brave otherwise. My courage might fail me if I knew what awaits us.

The sound of their guns ripples through the courtyard. It's a constant thundering like drums shoving their vibrations into my chest. There are too many shots to be something simple to remove. Each vibration moves my feet a little faster than the last with worry over what is beyond the wooden doors of the courtyard's final defense. The same worry is filling the cement space with people. They watch as Simon, Aimes, and myself make our way through the crowd, weaving our way to the exit. Some are silent as we pass them. Some wish us luck. It all makes me that much more nervous. Stitched like a rag doll, face bruised and self-esteem withering, here I go right back to "step in it" again.

"How many?" I finally ask Aimes, once we have exited and shut the doors behind us.

"You don't want to know," she says with eyes glued straight ahead with the attempt to bolster her own confidence.

"You're right. I don't. Tell us anyway."

"Enough to be able to climb over the fence," Aimes answers, and I can't help but swear under my breath.

"They can do that?" Simon asks, finally speaking since Aimes broke into the room.

"They can do anything you or I can do. They just make it look a lot creepier," Aimes tells him and she's right.

Once they figure something out, there is no way to stop them unless you kill them. They are thinking, fully working creatures. The virus stripped them of their humanity and somehow that has made them even better at being clever. There is no guilt, just the pure need to kill at any cost. There isn't any barrier which can really stop them once they have found you. Now, they have found us – again.

The men are fanned out, focusing on each section of the chain-link fence surrounding the grounds of the school. A few of the Risen's bodies lay on this side of the fence proving to Simon what Aimes had said to be true. The rest are climbing over the fence like ants, bending it with their combined weight. As soon as one is shot, another climbs into the space the missing body made. Their growls and screams in such a large number are mind shattering. Any hopes I had wished to use to strengthen my desire to face this have faded.

"It's pointless," Aimes voices the same thing I have been refusing to think. "We have to get back inside."

"If we do that, the school is lost. This is the only way out. We will be trapped until they figure a way in." Simon walks away, leaving Aimes and I here staring at the impossible.

Impossible is what I do best. I reach down to that numb spot and spread it through my mind. I let it kill the doubts and the fears clouding me. I use it like a shield as I march forward.

Lawless' eyes twitch to me sensing movement beside him before returning his focus on the fence. "You've got to be kidding me," he mutters, adding a few extra words under his breath to make sure his annoyance is completely understood. It is, all four letters of it.

"Focus on the bottom," he says to me, and I don't understand the logic behind it. The barrel of my gun rises back to the top of the fence as the male I am targeting gets tangled in the barbed wire. "The bottom, Helena. We have to stop them from climbing. Marxx has the ones that make it over."

I watch the male shred the skin from his face and hands as he pushes himself through the sharp teeth of the wires. He lacerates his scalp, peeling the hair from his skull. He never flinches nor does his growls slow as he mutilates himself, pouring the dark blood from his exposed skull down on the metal links.

"Tell me you brought more ammo?" Marxx asks, as he suddenly appears behind me, breaking me from the trance. I motion with my head to Aimes who waits with one of our black duffel bags stashed with various items that Simon picked out. Nothing was pink, so nothing called to Aimes to pack.

"When you run out, let Marxx know," Lawless says, already taking aim again.

"Why isn't he on a section?" The gun's recoil jerks my hand as I ask my question encouraging more four-letter words from Lawless.

"His arm won't let him grip a gun for long. Now focus before you take your own head off."

It feels pointless. There are so many of them that I don't even see them slowing despite the growing piles around the fence's bottom. They have amassed in such numbers that the smell of them wafts towards us without any wind to help spread their scare tactics. In their eagerness they step on each other, they chew on the metal of the fence as they climb, and a few have lacerated their faces or arms as they try to press through the metal diamonds. The fence buckles and moans under their abuse. The round posts are even vibrating in their cement homes.

It isn't hard to pick a target since they never look up as they climb. They focus on us and it seems their hands and legs work on their own accord. Their faces are almost dragged up the links as an afterthought.

They can do anything you or I can do. They just make it look a lot creepier, Aimes had said and now more than ever is the proof. I instinctively look for her to find her and Marxx running up the "battlefield" reloading empty clips or handing off the guns completely. Everyone understands that if we lose this space, we lose everything and we are running out of time.

There are too many of them for this to work. They will wear down our supply before we can stop them. What felt like an armory is quickly depleting. We have to think of something else.

Removing what is left of my clip, I place it into the pocket of Law's jeans. He only gives me the eye twitch again before returning to the fence. He doesn't bother to question me. Half of me wonders if he's just too afraid of what my answer might be. Tucking the gun into the line of my pants, I turn from him to find that mysterious solution I haven't yet grasped.

Rhett doesn't share the same fears. "Where are you going?" he shouts, as I begin to run.

"Getting a faster solution," I shout back, still working out the details in my mind.

To claim I am rationalizing a plan would be a lie. I'm going on autopilot, hoping some part of me has an idea which I don't consciously yet hold. When I find myself running to the generators, both parts of my mind finally connect. Too bad I am not the only one here.

It's not only the front gate they have made as a source of entry. On a smaller scale, the same scene has started on the far side of the fence as well. Twenty or more heads snap in my direction as I come running around the corner. The growls start low and deep before swelling to almost screams. Unlike the ones we left on the road, these Risen are almost as fresh as when it started. Their bodies are whole, showing none of the signs of exposure due to the changing seasons. All of their outfits are the basic styles of life, not the combination of lifestyles we have become accustomed to seeing in their collection.

The ones still stuck on the mechanics of the fence; they show the signs of the others we have been fighting since the start. Two groups. It has to mean these are two different groups, but it doesn't make any sense. As they start to run for me, I don't have time to debate the meaning.

I race for the gas cans as they race towards me. Their excited screams almost seem to mock the ones still stuck on the metal barrier. Their slower counterparts scream with their frustration with their fence-embedded bodies. All they can do is watch, being too damaged for the task of breaching the metal line of security. A few hang, thrashing in the barbed wire topping off the fence. They scream with rage as they continue to shred their bodies with their frantic movements, much like the man I had watched earlier. Their dark blood makes the fence slick, resulting in the ones who haven't figured it out to continue to slide down the links with the blood coating their hands like oil. Sometimes, Karma is on your side, but she is still going to make someone amuse her.

I reach the cans, leaving almost no room between them and myself. My heart is screaming my fears through my body as it pounds inside me. It's the pure adrenaline from those fears serving me now. It keeps my body moving in ways it shouldn't be able to. I run faster than I could if it were just a jog around the building. The cans are awkward, but I don't notice their weight, as I should. Only my ragged breathing and the jolt of my feet hitting the ground are registering on my mind. I block out the screams from those behind me, refusing to accept how close they are to me. I pant through my mouth with hopes to not let their acidic rotting overwhelm me. I even tell myself the sharp stabbing of my lungs is nothing as winter rapes them.

I'm Zombie Barbie, Rhett's little combat doll. I can make it. I can make it back to them and hope one of them can finish the plan. Right now, I still don't really have one. All I have is monsters behind me and I am running for my life.

I turn the final corner with hell on my heels. Marxx runs to meet me when he sees what I have brought to play. Taking one of the cans from my hand, he opens the spout letting it pour as he runs backward beside me.

"Don't stop," he fights to say between his breathing. "Run to the fence and spread yours along the line."

I do as he says, too scared to add anything to the conversation. I don't have to. In their typical skills of mind-reading, Chapel has started towards us, flicking a lighter just like the one they all keep in remembrance of their smoking days. I coast past him letting them work out the details. Without thinking, I enter the firing range sprinkling the flammable fluid on the hands that reach for me. The ones climbing the fence turn almost upside down, suspended on the fence, watching me in resemblance to the monsters they have become.

"Heads up!" Dolph shouts, as I cross his section without thinking and one-by-one the shooting stops.

I'm arching the can up, dousing every inch to which I can make the fluid cling. They scream like it's holy water as it lands on their bodies. When I finally make my way to Lawless' section, I walk backward, extending the flammable trail to him.

"Heads up," Lawless says, with less enthusiasm than Dolph had. One flick of his metal lighter that has traveled with us for so long and not even the damp winter ground can prevent the path of flames.

It gains speed and heat as it travels toward the fence. Like flaming dominoes, one-by-one they catch fire as the gas fuels the flames. The fire climbs higher and higher, fed by the fluid, and the bodies are still racing to reach the top before it is too late.

It's the same scene behind me as Marxx and Chapel wait to see which ones will escape their flames, breaching the line of fire they have made. Flames surround us, and if the ground wasn't so winter-kissed, I might hold concerns.

The smells of their burning flesh and their screams of anger also surround us. They don't feel any pain as the flames devour them. They don't pass out from it, as we would have. The missing limbs the fire removes goes unnoticed in their attempts to reach us. They crawl, climb or almost slither until the heat finally cooks their brains, popping the glaring eyes staring at us. They hang from the fence with their bodies trapped by those burning limbs as they roast. Some fall back to the ground, feeding those flames as they snap and pop like dried kindling.

My body is foretelling the pain I will feel soon. Each inch that returns to life has its own complaints. I let myself sink to the wet ground, watching the burning line of the fence.

"You make it hard to be a man," Lawless says, staring down at me.

"You mean because she is always doing the "saving"?" Rhett asks, as he joins our little resting spot.

"Every hero needs a sidekick," I pant, still battling my lungs for control.

They both laugh a laugh as if to say, *never going to happen.*

"Remind me to look for marshmallows the next time we do a run," Rhett says, as he watches pieces of the burning bodies fall. "If we are going to keep burning stuff, I might as well get a snack out of it."

"You're so twisted!" Aimes shouts to him from what would be the closest thing to the middle between the two groups.

"Don't," I say, stopping him before his smile can reach its full potential. "Just don't." I know what that smile hides and I prefer to keep it that way – hidden.

"Did you see any other spots?" Lawless asks.

"There are some stuck on the side fence. That's as far as I made it." I watch the clouds float overhead. Like the laughter of little girls running down a bloodstained hallway, their puffs of white innocence seem so out of place looking down on the burning bodies we have caused.

Extending an arm, Lawless pulls me off the ground to him. His brown eyes churn with concern for me. "If I ask you," he stresses the word "ask" with an effort to appease my own ego before he continues, "to go inside and stay there, would you actually do it?"

His voice is soft but it's what his eyes hold that splinters my stubborn wall. I nod, accepting my limitations and his needs. Mostly, I am accepting my limitations and letting him think it's his needs. It's like the fluke thing, but more self-serving. I will never admit to either.

"Do I have to go too, Dad?" Aimes is already reaching to help me, but she can't resist a chance to climb under Law's skin.

"Just leave the bag. That's actually useful," he responds, then places a soft kiss to my forehead telling me good-bye.

Lawless whistles a sharp sound gaining the men's attention. He makes a circular motion with his finger and those mind-reading skills kick in again as they fan out to inspect the rest of the grounds. To me, he points at the courtyard entrance before returning to the task he has set into motion.

"I bet you never thought you'd see this day," Aimes says watching them walk away as I am.

"What? The end of the world or its half-dead people trying to kill us?"

"Nah," she says, tilting her head that serves as a warning for her sarcasm, "that's just every Black Friday. I meant the day that Law would be leading. Our little playboy flirt is actually in charge. It's kind of scary how much he has changed."

It's not scary. It's depressing. The smiling, good-natured boy I have been convincing myself I didn't love all these years is now a sullen, reserved man. On a rare, private moment I get a glimpse of who he once was. They are few, short, and treasured, but they happen.

Truth be told, we have all changed into different people in some ways. Little things have amassed and built new holes from the pieces we weren't aware of having inside of us. Well, all of us but Rhett. He's still the scary, bucket of crazy he has always been. It's just splashing over the edges now.

Chapter 33

Aimes and I didn't stop in the courtyard or pause at the cafeteria to answer any of the questions shouted to us as we passed. I didn't exchange glares with Selma or compare grins with Travis. I did avoid Paula's shaking head as she rested her hands on her hips. I didn't need to hear what she was thinking. Her frown and tightly pressed lips were plenty to provide the clues to her thoughts. If I look an inch of how I feel, she will be upstairs soon enough with her miracle bag of silence.

Aimes and I walk to our space, watching our growing family dispatch the small pockets of Risen from the windows. They started using their knives once they discovered the few that are left. The way they each kill tells about their personalities. It's not surprising Chapel is the least engaged in the clearing. He, like myself, often wonder who these people were before becoming what they are now and if any of that still remains inside them. If they can think and work as a group to attain their goals, surely, they must hold some small fragment of their former lives.

"You're doing it again." Aimes pushes my shoulder letting my body rock to awareness.

I look at her using my face to ask what she means instead of my voice.

"They aren't human, Hells. You know that, right?"

"Paula said they aren't dead. The virus just takes over like a switch to the programming. If that is true, could there be a cure?"

"It's not some super flu that some horse pills and three glasses of juice a day will get rid of. The fever cooks the brain, allowing whatever it is to take over. You can't cure it."

I watch Marxx, my personal Superman, put one down with his blade through an eye socket. It doesn't phase him when the gore backsplashes upon him. He easily moves to the next one, repeating the same action through the links of the fence. It bothers me some that it doesn't bother them anymore. I'm not ready to accept this is our life now. Wake, dress, kill a handful of people, rinse and repeat every day? No, I'm just not ready to accept the life we once had is over.

"What happened to you?" Aimes asks another version of the question she has already asked me several times. "Where are they, Hells?"

A thousand answers clot in my throat like a wound that keeps bleeding with the slightest touch. "I killed them," I say, with a voice as hollow as my heart. "It was my job to keep them safe and I failed them."

"Oh, Hells," she barely whispers. "One day, I will ask to hear it all and you will tell me so we can nail this coffin shut."

I nod, watching the show end below us. "One day." One day I will have to answer all of their questions, just not today.

"Come on," she says, rubbing my arm with an attempt to remove the ghosts that are haunting me. "Let's go down and meet them. If Lawless comes across Travis anytime soon, your face will just go to waste. It will be hard to keep playing the "good guys" if Law is smacking around the holy guy."

That's not exactly true, I want to tell her. Nothing makes a bunch of middle-aged, over-romantic women flusters faster than a man defending the wrongs done to his girl. It's the middle chapters of every sappy romance book I have ever tried to force my way through with worries that something might be wrong with me for hating every book of that style. If the women really lived in a life where the guy was always avenging wrongs, they wouldn't find it so romantic. Sweeping up broken glasses and bottles night-after-night at Grit became less romantic by the hour. I'm not trying to appeal to my sense of heroics though. It's to the ideas of the people living here we have to cater. I need the home team to change back to us and everyone loves a good comeback story.

"Think Travis is already preaching?" Aimes asks me, as we take the stairs two at a time to reach the show.

"He's going to have to think of some way to spin it all." I wince with every forceful step now, seeing as my body has rid itself of the superpowers given by adrenaline. "He and his people keep staying safe behind the walls while we and our heretic-selves keep going out there. He can't risk letting those thoughts start forming in people's heads."

"Isn't that the point though?" she asks, with a toss between excitement and curiosity.

"Yes, but not for him."

I reach for the metal door on the first floor as it flies forward. My fingers slip from the cold handle as it is forced past my hand and Aimes jerks me towards her, saving my face from any more added colors being distributed.

Selma looks as shocked as we are to be suddenly face-to-face. "You better hurry," she tells us. She recovers from the shock faster than we can, but she has the skill of plastic with her face that we lack.

"Hurry where?" Aimes asks, feigning an innocence that would make a true priest proud.

You can't fool the puppet master. Selma doesn't answer. She pushes her way between us, refusing to play our game. I hate poor sports. As Aimes skips down the last few steps behind me, I guess she enjoys them.

"You know that woman needs a whore-fax, right?" Aimes asks, as we walk towards the room, serving for more than just an eatery. "One owner, my ass."

"You don't think she wore white?" I smile with my questions as we both begin to build our confidence.

"Everyone wears white. It doesn't mean they should."

"So, I guess you will be wearing white?"

She gives my question the very special one finger acknowledgment. From here we can hear the shouting from the cafeteria is all male. The deep pitches of the voices are colliding with random louder noises as if the room is divided and cheering for each side.

I have a moment of weakness letting my feet slow. Normal people don't have this amount of constant drama surrounding them like a black plague. Normal people don't have this constant fighting to navigate through, never knowing which step will be the one that finds the landmine. The things waiting outside for us, those sadly have become normal and even that I can't really handle. I'm not sure what it really says about me when I would rather fight hand-to-hand with the undead monsters than to walk into a room fervent with male angst. I would rather be risking my life than to have to once again step into the middle of the flying fists and words. Bruises from words often last longer than any damage fists could cause. Bruises heal, but the words never leave you.

"Here we go again," I sigh, before pushing through the last set of protective doors.

The noise explodes without the metal to dampen the flaring tempers. Tempers are burning hotter than the many candles being used to combat the early darkness of the season. The voices flicker back-and-forth as fast as the light being cast upon the walls. Right in the middle of it all, is shockingly not a single member of G.R.I.T.

G.R.I.T. stands like tall pallbearers along one side of the fighting. Dressed in their black vests and wearing serious faces, they stand watching and waiting as Simon and the God Squad exchange verbal beatings. Travis is firmly behind the row of protectors wearing the same slimy smile as always, being the constant instigator who he is. For a man of God who believes He will protect him, Travis is never standing anywhere to test the theory.

"That's Horrence," Leslie's voice slips behind me, giving a name to the man battling with Simon. "He is the newest one trying to prove his dedication."

"Why are you telling me this?" I ask her, without turning to look at her.

"Why are you talking to us at all?" Aimes asks, taking her discomfort a tad bit further than I had.

"I thought you would want to know," Leslie says. Her red hair is a deep mahogany with nothing but the soft candlelight casting on her loose waves. It's hard to not hate her. Or maybe, it's just hard for me not to hate her. Her natural perfection just makes it more justifiable. I am a woman. Hear me compare.

"So, what is the deal, Miss Helpful One?" Aimes asks, with the sincerest attempt to be nice I have seen her put forth yet.

Leslie accepts it for what it is – sarcasm. She explains, "When your group came back in, Selma made some offhand comment about Rhett changing sides more than Lawless changed partners. I guess she thought something so simple would get under Rhett's skin, or Law's skin, but Rhett just laughed and asked her if she missed him that much. He then said something about her wanting other people's toys more than Travis does. The rest was really kind of hush-hush, but whatever was said aggravated Simon enough to start defending your crew. It's been going back and forth ever since." She made motions with her hands to help separate the events as she was telling them. It was a mistake. We have had our own little past dramas, and with the one raging on in front of us, the room is waiting to see if ours is about to reopen, thinking her hand motions were more than what they really were.

"How long do we let them ego it out?" Aimes whispers to me. "I mean, welcome back Simon, but this could go on for a while."

"You mean, because they won't throw a punch like yours would have by now?" Leslie wants it to sound like an insult, but she has a trail of longing at the end of her sentence that ruins her intent.

Aimes just smiles at her with the normal cocky expression, which often adorns her face. "Try to keep your vagina from your voice if you want to try to be insulting. Otherwise, you're just being pathetic," Aimes tells Leslie, as she turns to walk towards the commotion.

"I don't even know what that means?" Leslie looks to me for help and I just laugh.

What else can I do?

I listen to the shouting match as I follow Aimes into the thick of it. I'm not sure what they are fighting over. I'm not sure if even they know at this point. In every fight, there comes a point when it's just venting and no longer holding to a true path. I think not only has this one reached that point, but also it has gone past it, resulting in almost random insults. Now it's just whoever can shout the loudest will win.

I can feel Travis watching me like the snake he resembles for me. I can almost hear the warning rattle and it adds more of a glide to my steps. Other women feed from his hands offering them compliments and whistles. I graze from the looks of contempt and whispering judgments. At least those are honest.

Every step I take towards them, Travis copies in a mimicked attempt of provocation. The room begins to grow still seeing the new drama unfolding. Everyone knows the main event is about to start, and like those who bet on a fight, people are debating which side to place their faith on.

"Helena dear," Travis calls to me from behind the security of his lesser-than-stellar-brain-powered security team, "where have you been? You've been lacking in your duty to keep the peace."

"I had to powder my nose," I call to him, without turning my head to see him. "The shine was contrasting with the bruising."

"Hmmm," Travis almost moans the sound, as he stalls to collect his thoughts. After all, it's going to take something creative to make him sound like the good guy now. "Yes, that was unfortunate the way you made me defend myself. It takes a brave woman to initiate a fight between herself and a man, as you can see, it's not always a wise thing to do."

Reaching the wall of the men I have come to trust with my life, I finally give Travis my full attention. "It's sad you felt the need to have to use your fists to defend yourself from me. I was just a girl asking … questions." I pause, extending the last word, letting it hint to what he really hit me over. "Good thing Rhett has better self-control than you do, Travis. Your face might match mine otherwise."

"Want it to?" Rhett almost purrs the question and the men softly laugh.

"Violence. That is all your people know!" Travis exclaims and it doesn't take any brain power at all to know he is about to start preaching to distract from what has been said against him. "They bring violence. They encourage violence. They live it. They wear those vests declaring it!"

Aimes makes a grand show of a yawn while staring straight at Travis. Leslie was wrong. It's not the men who always swing first. Aimes just doesn't use her fists.

"We have been safe behind these walls this whole time. They go out one time and look at what follows them back?" Travis is spinning now using the cafeteria like a stage. "You call them heroes for going out there to destroy the demons when the demons came because of them. Like calls to like!"

"Or deer meat calls to hungry." Paula's voice silences the room. She doesn't need that little bag after all. Who knew? "Someone's been dumping the remains left from cleaning the meat by the fences. Oddly enough, the same spots where they climbed over today."

I notice how Paula calls the Risen, them and not things or demons, like Travis has trained the place to do.

"Isn't it Dolph who hunts for us? Now he stands among them. Rather fitting wouldn't you say?" Travis feels like he's played his ace. Too bad he's playing cards with a woman like Paula. She knows that the ace is never played first. You hold that card until you have more than one to boast.

"Except that it's your man in charge of removing such things, as per your order," Paula says, crossing her arms to wait for his answer.

"If someone said that, it was untrue. I never placed such a suggestion." Travis wears his smug grin. I've come to learn that the wider that grin becomes, the deeper the lie. Right now, he's lying through his perfect white teeth.

"Yes, you did," the one named Horrence says, before he can stop himself.

The corners of Travis' mouth actually rise higher. I didn't think that was possible.

"Like I said, a misunderstanding," he says.

Horrence shakes his head, still not understanding the subtitles Travis is doing his best to spell for the man. "No, Boss. You said to be sure to take the unusable meat and place it along the fences. I understood just fine." His words spill forth with the worry Travis might think his every command wasn't obeyed.

I relax into the arms of Lawless as we watch the comedy hour. Horrence is a large man; someone who would live in a gym as long as that gym was walled in mirrors. He most likely used to catch every woman's eyes with his extremely toned body but lost their attention just as fast when he opened his mouth. The more he opens his mouth now, the more attention he gains. Not all of it is good.

Travis' eyes hold the same gleam I saw when I was at his feet while he was holding that perfect smile.

"You just have to hate it when a plan almost kills people," Lawless says, while resting his head on my shoulder. He reaches into his vest pocket and pulls the baseball hat from its hiding place. "Unless that is the plan."

The room is in an uproar of hushed whispering over the little memento of a tragedy still unanswered. Travis shows no sign of recognizing the hat, but one of his Squad does. The man pushes through the line ignoring their looks of disapproval. He reaches for the hat like a starving man stretching for one final sip of decadence. His fingers tremble as they slide over the stitches and the many worn spots from years of wear. Each discoloration holds some memory for him and his smile flashes before it fades with each spot he remembers.

"How?" he asks as his tears start to glide.

"We found it under the tree you left your son in," Lawless says. He doesn't mince words or try hiding his disgust for what the man has helped happen.

The man turns to Travis with shock. It steals his breath and his chest rapidly rises and falls with the emotions coursing through him. "You said you buried them. You told us you would honor our sacrifice." The man steps towards Travis with clenched fists. The line of protection Travis depended on steps aside from the man's anger. "Our wives? Did you leave them too?"

The room starts to ring out with questions over what they are watching.

"What tree?" comes from one side of the room.

"Leave them where?" comes from somewhere else.

"What sacrifice?" comes from somewhere deeper in the room.

Travis's eyes bounce from each section which calls out. The mounting panic radiates from behind those eyes.

"What is Selma doing out there?" Leslie is staring out the fogged windows with squinting eyes. Set after set of eyes join hers as they try to peer through the hazy windows at the woman standing by the cross outside.

"She has Cole!" a woman shouts, shaking her husband's arm as she points.

"Is that Harper?" another woman asks, with the same shaking of fear as the first woman.

If the room was electric before, it's pulsing now. Rhett grabs Aimes as the bodies force forward to see what is exactly happening outside. I want to stop them. I want to warn them, but I have nothing to offer and Travis' smile is growing.

It's a different smile this time. He's not nervous anymore. He's not the least bit worried about what the people think of him or his. I watch as he takes out a small red beaded necklace with its gold cross and brings it tenderly to his lips. He closes his eyes as he kisses the flesh-warmed metal. I know it will all be over soon. I'm about to bleed.

Chapter 34

The dropping temperatures of the night has allowed the snow to float again. It's the start of a winter paradise and the children dance and run under the frozen flakes. They extend their tongues, trying to capture the flakes in the centuries-old tradition of winter fun. Their laughter is the soundtrack of innocence. The unease that was shared inside the cafeteria dissipates watching them celebrate the snow.

Selma is winding the handle of an old-style record player. The needle plays the ancient strands of *Amazing Grace* with the white noise only a true record player can produce. The melody mingles with the laughter, and what was originally composed to inspire faith, only paints an eerie backdrop.

"What the Hell?" Chapel mutters, but we all have an idea of exactly the Hell we are about to witness.

The missing members of the Squad stand between the line of people and Selma. Her hands temple in prayer with a mouth silently moving as she recites whatever message to God she hopes He is listening to. A large crate sits by her feet. Its wooden structure hisses a warning no one is listening to with their eyes locked on the children they can't reach. Panic with the event they just narrowly escaped a month ago inspires their bravery. I watch as the man named Ryan pushes against the men blocking them and he is shoved to the ground with an answer to his attempt to reach his daughter.

The barrels are lit one-by-one around the yard while Selma continues to pray, oblivious to it all, or either very well aware and ignoring it. The members of their community pour the sharp smelling gas from the generator's stockpile into the barrels. The flames catch with an almost hell-like heat. The crowd winces from the mini-explosions of light, settling their voices and their fight to reach their kids.

As if the sudden blaze was a rehearsed signal, Travis walks solemnly from another exit of the school directly across from the amassed crowd. What rests across his arms sets my knees to water. His head is bowed over the long stretches of rope. Their nooses sway with his steps like silent chanting and I am chanting in my mind. As I watch Selma praying, I can mentally hear my repeated refusal of what is about to happen and my own prayers to not let it happen.

The men are loading the chambers of their spent guns with stealth-like movements. They hide each other as golden bullets are passed between closed fists. Their practiced moves are normally calm, but now they hold an air of urgency making their cold fingers clumsy. Like the Risen that was held hostage by the fence, I could scream at them with my frustrations.

"Give me my clip." I try to shield my voice from the crowd watching Travis' painfully slow procession.

Lawless only shakes his head, answering me, and ignoring me at the same time.

"Larance," I clip between my teeth, "give me my clip."

He lifts his head only high enough to look at me. "No," he tells me, returning to slipping his clip full of the little golden cylinders. "You're going to, for once, since this thing has started, stay out of it."

"You really think that is going to happen?" Aimes asks him, and her amusement is audible in her whisper.

Lawless lifts his head again to stare at me. Our breathing becomes a pattern that echoes the feelings in our eyes. Every fear he has laid behind his tall walls is now bare to me. I can almost hear the beat of his heart.

I forget sometimes the man behind the mask. I have lost him to the weight he now bears on his shoulders and the strength he has to summon to endure it. I begged Truth for his life. I fell to her feet with her black gown engulfing me. I wore my misery like a widow wears her scars, but he was returned to me on a night much like this. As Mother Nature kissed the earth, he was returned to me and all I have done since is throw myself at Death.

"Please?" Lawless asks me, in this bubble of time we have captured.

I nod. I nod because my voice wouldn't hold the strain of my thoughts or my regrets that constantly encase me. I nod because to put the agreement into words would be a lie.

He holds me in a tight embrace and now I can feel his heart just as I imagined hearing it. He is frightened of what this night might bring. In some tragic way, it's all repeating.

He kisses me and I let him gather his strength and the belief in himself from my lips. I let him hold hope in himself to do what has to be done. All a man wants is someone to love him and someone to protect. I give him that and I let him take it from me.

"I love you," he says against my lips, and it sounds heartbreakingly like a goodbye.

"I love you, too," I whisper, frail and frightened of what he must imagine tonight to entail.

"You ready?" Marxx asks, crashing us back to the present like a meteor to the ground.

We both nod, still holding to the other with the last moments of our bubble dissolving into the cruelty slowly becoming true; a cruelty we have seen swinging from large tree branches and left in ashes in the many rings upon the ground.

Aimes pulls me to her knowing I won't be able to let go of them on my own. I will march right through the crowd beside them if left of my own will.

"Congrats," she whispers into my ear, as we watch them walk away, "you get to be a girl. It kind of sucks, but you'll get used to it."

"Don't cry," I tell her, hearing her voice quiver.

"I'm not crying. This is totally my game face." She sniffles with the secret knowledge of what Travis is about to do. "I'm just really sad about the game we are going to have to play."

Travis has made his way to the front of the wooden cross and the area that has served as his pulpit. Selma stands beside him with a look of rapture on her face. As she calls the children to her, she almost glows with the compassion of motherhood. Her smile is the sweetest I have yet to see upon her face. Selma may very well have a sweet side, but it is coated in cyanide. One smile she gives to the children and they run to her. One smile she shares, and their lives are hers with the strands of Amazing *Grace* floating around her.

"My friends," Travis shouts into the night air, "not all of us are made to walk in God's glory. Only the most refined, the most tested by temptations, can truly know the suffering of reclaiming their lost divine grace. Only when we are stripped from all we cling to with false declarations, can we truly see the power of salvation. Tonight, I will show you that grace. You will feel that power and a few of you will even rise from the flames."

Travis kisses each rope, bowing his head as he anoints them with prayer before handing them over to a member of his Squad. My heart breaks hearing the children still laughing as they run in circles around a playful Selma with the music enhancing their joyful steps. The snow looks like magical fairies again as it twirls around them as if it's marveling in the children's beauty.

Time slows as we watch the ropes being secured from the extended arms of the cross. Voices begin to rise with curiosity and anger over the obscenity of it. Little feet prance and the ropes begin to sway in time. Travis watches it all from above on his self-built stage.

Aimes holds me in a reverse style of a hug. Her arms are draped around my shoulders, pulling me to her so that my back is to her chest. We can't look away, but we aren't strong enough to watch alone. Her arms tighten every time I instinctively pull to rush the stage. She swears under her breath with each new rope hung and I'm not completely convinced she is keeping me here for my good or for the good of her sanity.

"We just can't watch this happen," the man from earlier says. I never saw him come to stand by us. My focus has been torn between the children and the nooses, letting the rest of the courtyard slip away. He is holding the blue hat in his hands, twisting it between his fists as he stares at me. "They have to be stopped."

"We can't do anything until he does something," Aimes tells him, still watching it all unfold. "If we rush him now, he will just use it to convince them more of his God-power."

"It's not us who have to stop him. Simon has to lead us all now." My voice is a strained whisper with my doubts.

"If he waits too long, it will be too late." He steps towards us with a threat and yet pleading with his eyes for Aimes and me to listen to him. "I won't let him do it again. Not again." He is gone in the mass of moving bodies before I can do anything. I have no name to call out to stop him, or to regain his attention. I send a prayer, if anyone does still listen, for the man. My prayers are more riddled with demands than questions though as of late.

Paula finds Aimes and me in the cluster. Her face is blanched, and it sets my stomach deeper into a pit of rolling sickness. She is saying something, but I can't hear her over the screaming of the crowd. I turn my eyes from her as Aimes whispers another pretty little syllable behind me.

Selma has the children now lined up and still playing like this is a game. Each child stands under a rope, reaching for it on their tiptoes like the brass ring from an old merry-go-round. To the children, it's a fun game, but to the parents, it's proof of what the lengths mean. Selma is showing us all that their tiny little hands can't reach the ropes and their tiny little feet won't reach the ground, either.

Paula is shouting again. I can hear the sound of her voice, but the words are just melodic with the amount of chaos now inspired around us. Women wail for their children as the men scream for blood. Both sets are lost as to what to do, not wanting to risk any harm being brought to the smiling faces watching them.

"It is time to prove to the Lord how thankful you are that He has kept you safe. He has saved you and your families when so many others have been brought low. He has guided you here, as He has us, to rebuild in His name. He will purify your souls so you may truly know His love for you. All He asks is that you believe in Him and He will grant you everything," Travis says. He is pacing along the wooden beams nearest to the crowd. His fists are raised, shaking to accent his words with a religious passion to draw attention to the syllables and to hide the definitions. "Are you ready to believe in Him? Will you give everything to prove it or will you let your everything be taken from you because of your fears? All He has ever wanted is your trust, your belief, and your love. Can't you give that to Him? Do you have the courage to prove your beliefs?"

The crowd is shouting every possible phrase of "yes" they can remember. I bet the crowds always do as they watch their children make toys out of the tools of their deaths.

"Bring me the mothers. Mothers, come to me. Come to your children who God has blessed you with," Travis demands, and turns his back to solemnly stroll to the far side of the stage to not block the show.

Paula is screaming now. She is waving her arms and pointing to the forgotten crate with its hissing warning sitting by Travis. I still can't make out her words and my curiosity doesn't hold strong enough to try.

Women shove their way to the stage. Some don't even bother with the steps, hauling their bodies onto the wooden platform with assistance from the men behind them. There are no manners as they rush to make it to their children, pulling them away from the ropes they saw as swings.

Travis and Selma let the moms touch and hug their children as the line of God Squad fights to keep the men back from the stage with frightening force. I can see random flashes of the grinning skull on its black leather moving through the area like shadows. They are attached to the drama, but adrift from it as they keep their own plans to heart. If they could give me some hint to what those plans might be, my heart might climb down from my throat. It also might climb right out of my mouth if I knew.

"Are you listening to a word I have been saying?" Paula shouts into my ear, as yet another person sneaks up on me. The bell threat from before comes back to mind.

"I can't hear a word you've been saying!" I shout over the crowd's anxiety, keeping my eyes to the stage.

"That crate. I know that crate," Paula says, as if that is the most important thing up there. The look on my face must have expressed my doubts. "I was there, in the meeting at the lab, when the Ice Queen, as we called her, told us the truth. She told us the vaccines were corrupt and causing side effects we hadn't prepared for. As I was leaving to take this assignment, we were being told there was another strain of the vaccine that had been released to humanitarian workers. It was designed to be faster and stronger to help combat the illness that seemed so abundant in third world countries. It was supposed to have been confiscated, but some were shipped before it could happen."

"Wait, you're telling us this isn't just local? This… thing… is global now?" Aimes' eyes are the size of saucers as she is shocked at what Paula is trying to say. It was depressing to think this had become our life, but it's terrifying to know it could be everyone's life, everywhere.

"Yes, it could be, but that isn't the point," Paula says, sounding colder than I have ever given her credit for. The "Betty Crocker look" is long gone. "That is one of the shipments of the vaccine. I would know the crate anywhere. We called them Pandora's Boxes and Travis is about to open it right here in the middle of the school."

"Why would he have it? How could he use it?" Aimes asks, releasing me from her grasp with her habit of using her hands and arms when she speaks. "Oh, and when did our nurse-slash-cook become some secret spy? Can we officially freak out now?"

"You can," I tell her, with my voice dipping into the numbness that always brings me trouble.

"You can't go up there Helena." Paula grabs my arm with as much awareness as my family has for my suicidal habits. "If he is going to use those shots, you'll become infected."

"He is going to use them. It's why some of the piles weren't shot. He let them burn once they were infected. He purified their souls." I'm putting the pieces together and the puzzle is looking nothing like the box it came in. The box was shiny and promised hope for the future. It wore smiles and charm with lies about being our saviors in our time of need. It still is wearing the same smile, but it's killing us now with our naivety.

Some silent moment let the members of the Squad who stand on the stage know to pull the women from their children. The screaming starts anew with the action. Children reach with fully extended arms to their mothers as they are dragged back to the ropes. With their rough hands, they force the women to kneel as they fight for their kids. A few are even slapped when their struggles start to become unmanageable. Travis winces with each connection in a mockingly amused manner and it brings the men watching to a boil.

"My friends," Travis shouts, bringing their angered focus to him, "there is nothing to fear!" His voice is an intervention of comforting. He says, "The lives of your children and women are yours to save. If you are a true believer, if your soul is worth saving, you shall live tonight to claim your place by God's side. Haven't every single one of you told me how you have wanted to survive this nightmare with peace and comfort for your remaining days?" He stops, staring into the crowd of men while his words sink in. "Why now do you throw arms against us as we bring what you have desired to you?"

Travis was so intent on his show, he too was snuck upon. Selma wasn't inside to see the man's face when Lawless handed him his son's hat. She never knew the danger she let stand beside her, as he was once one of their own. When the click of the safety being turned off sounded behind Travis' head, she discovered too late the truth.

"Tell them what you are about to do," the man demands. His over six-foot frame towers behind Travis. He glares with eyes holding the anger of a man possessed. "Tell them what your salvation means for them."

"It means a chance to weed out the non-believers. We can rid ourselves of the weak ones who only mean to bring us down with their weight of doubts." Travis' explanation sends chills down my spine as it echoes so similar to J.D.

"Tell them the truth!" the man shouts, pressing the barrel of the gun forcefully against Travis' head making him tilt with the pressure.

"Eugene," Selma calls from behind the man, and somehow, he knew that Selma wasn't the only one who let danger slip past their awareness.

Eugene pivots his weight, pushing Travis to the ground as he turns to Selma. Their guns lift at the same time and the echo of their timed shots shudder the walls. There is a moment when everything is suspended. Time retreats to an almost stop as everyone holds their breath.

The small, blue hat falls to the space between the two like a leaf taken by the breeze. Selma watches it fall as her knees crumple under her. She presses a trembling hand to her upper shoulder with shock. She stares at her blood-covered fingers with disbelief while Travis crawls across the stage to where she has fallen. Instinctively, I look for Rhett and find him leaning on his black warhorse in the shadows of the yard. The glow of his cigarette highlights a face filled with a lack of care as he watches the stage. The shadows take him with his exhale like the comforting arms of a lover.

Eugene is bent over, leaning on his knees, on the stage when I return my attention to him. Selma's shot didn't miss. The tall man is clutching his stomach as he watches with eyes of burning coals the two in front of him. Their mouths move in whispers lacking the strength to reach our ears.

"They will stop you," Eugene seems to say, and it only makes Travis smile again. "I let you kill my son, my wife. I might not have stopped you, but I'll take your whore to hell with me."

The women on stage scream as Eugene lifts his gun again with shaking hands from the pain of his wound. He's too slow with that pain. Travis has Selma's gun lifted and fired before Eugene can pull his first shot. Eugene's body bounces with each round that lands until his body falls limp on the stage. His last moments are spent staring at his son's blue hat. A hat his wife most likely purchased what feels like a lifetime ago to him. His fingers reach for it, crumpling it in his hand before those same fingers fall as still as his body.

Travis stands, letting Selma recline on her own accord. His pressed dress shirt is covered with her blood. The dark mass ruins its perfection the way the scowl on his face ruins the precision of his earlier performance.

"It starts now," Travis tells the men by him, even as the two lean to help Selma from the stage.

The theatrics are over as the real show begins. The children are lifted on the shoulders of the men. Seven men, seven children, seven ropes are waiting for Travis while seven women beg at his feet. He is beyond any showmanship now. The depiction is over. The truth is about to begin.

He kicks the lid of the crate open. It flies to the cement floor below the stage with a violent sound. He pulls the first pre-measured dose from the crate with a sick look of glee. He has lost his mask. He has lost his care to wear the mask. The moment he has been setting into motion is finally here and he doesn't need to pretend anymore.

"He can't be allowed to do this!" Paula hisses beside me. "That is not the normal strain. I don't know what will happen to whoever receives it."

"You promised!" Aimes says on my other side.

Like two waging wars, Paula and Aimes both stare at me for different reasons. I never imagined Aimes to be wearing a halo any more than I pictured Paula wearing horns, but the children on the stage, I always knew I wouldn't allow them to become victims.

"I promised two little kids I would keep them safe. I lied then, too." I let that guilt propel me into the crowd. I feel what were their last moments because of me. I see Ashley staring at me with resignation. I hear Conroy screaming my name in agony and fear. The sing-song chant of the children at play overshadows any hopes of "Amazing Grace". I love Lawless, I do. I just love my guilt more.

"Will you give your life for what God has given you?" Travis asks the women before him, casting the vaccines into the wind to be harvested by desperate hands. "Will you put your trust in Him to redeem you both?"

Each woman agrees, grappling for the liquid death threats rolling around the wooden beams. The children are crying now as they watch their mother's desperation with confusion. Their innocence keeps them from fully understanding how close they are to death. Some say ignorance is blind. Watching the children so close to the nooses that seem to constantly sway, I consider ignorance to be bliss.

An arm becomes like a vice around my waist, jerking me to a strong chest. Chapel's voice is dangerously low in my ear. "What are you doing, Helena?" he asks me, with the aggravation that I normally find in abundance from Marxx.

I try to turn around to look at him, but it only finds me forced tighter to him.

"Paula says what's in those shots is twice as potent as the original shot," I tell him, with some small explanation.

Chapel is gone as quickly as he came and I almost stagger with his exit. It leaves me stunned for a moment, losing the momentum I had built for myself. He leaves me with something else as well. He had aimed his arm precisely to land across the wound of my stomach. The burning pain is almost crippling where his fingers dug across the stitches. I'm on one knee before I even have the time to exhale and I'm standing again before I can inhale.

Horrence is smiling into my cringing face. He tells me with no hidden amusement, "Travis says we have a special spot for their little savior."

Chapel had meant to leave me in pain to keep me from venturing further into the line of fire. Now, Travis will have me standing in the middle of a ring of it.

I'm forced up the stairs by Horrence and dragged by another. Every pull I make to free myself only pulls deeper at the wound, until I am gasping and broken of my will. It's just how Travis now likes his women.

What were once dark shadows roaming the crowd have become a fighting force. I can hear their shouts through the white-haze of my pain. We had no reason to be under Travis' thumb. We have no children for him to ply us into obedience. We have no need to seek for someone else to protect us or to provide for us the guile of safety. We take care of our own and fend for ourselves. We have accepted what this world is and what is to come, but Travis found a way to make us dance just the same – me.

I fight to stand, refusing to play into the show he has conducted. My bravery is rewarded with a knee to my already fragile stomach. I drop, never feeling the ground through the agony already cascading through me. I'm lifted by a fist of my hair from the ground sending waves of pain through my scalp, but I won't cry out. I won't give Travis the erection he is seeking from this torment.

Bruising hands guide me backward. I know what death sentence he has declared for me. In his little game, he wants to take out as many of us as possible; one for the money, two for the show.

An eighth rope is hung. Its length is shorter than the rest, and as I stare up at it, I know only the tips of my toes will reach the ground. Travis isn't after a fast death for me. I will hang. I will suffer. I will feel every second of my death. Somewhere, Truth is watching with her sisters the twins, Karma and Fate. I thought I had escaped from them that Christmas morning, but they were just waiting. Feeding me fables, they waited for my perfect suicide.

"Seems we have something a little bit different here," Travis says leaning side-to-side in front of me with a wide smile. "I don't guess you have a mother in the audience to save you?" he asks me, with a whispered sense of joy.

"Nope," I tell him, smiling into those cold eyes of his. "I killed her."

He shrugs, pressing his lips together to match the body expression. "…a dad, perhaps?"

"I guess you could say, I helped kill him too."

Travis lets out a long whistle of fake shock. "I guess, you deserve the rope more than most," he says softly to me before shouting, "Rig her up!"

The hands that were holding my shoulders now lift me from the waist, keeping my arms locked to my sides. Their squeezing sensation makes me feel as if my stomach will escape through the tender stitches, leaving me too limp to fight against the man who places the rope around my neck. I'm hovering between the squeezing hands and the grey void of my vision.

"Who will save Helena?" Travis screams into the night, with an excitement that curdles any strength I may have had left to fight him.

The noise of male shouting is abundant, but there is one who never makes a sound. Just like Eugene, Chapel takes the back steps one steady foot at a time. "I will," he says, and his voice is flat with fact. I know he feels the guilt as tightly as I feel the rope. He never thought his attempt to keep me safe could become so misguided. He will give his life to correct that wrong, and when it is done and he is standing with his family again, he will tell them it was a beautiful suicide.

Travis isn't shocked to see Chapel, just disappointed. He wanted someone else in the ring, but he still has one more trick snarling from his sleeve.

"Well, the party is all here!" Travis spins slowly with his arms spread over the stage. The guise of religious fervor has vanished as it does with most cults when the deaths start. When people are already motivated to do as you say, there is no more need to herd them.

A corresponding rope is placed over the children and synched tight. The sight is enough to bring the women back to wails. The sound of the noose sliding taunt brings the whole yard to an uproar. The children's sobs bring those who are mere onlookers with no children of their own to their knees.

"Round up the fathers," Travis says, skipping along the unintentional path the women have made. Chapel's glare as the path winds near him brings Travis back to his disguised senses. "Oh, and Rhett. Bring me Rhett. Let's see if we can still save him after all," he says this to Chapel, but it's the God Squad who moves into action. Chapel doesn't give him an ounce of concern.

"Now, gentlemen, you will have a choice. I leave it in your hands entirely. One-by-one you will come forward as we come to your child and their matching mother. These ropes are very real, as Helena can assure you, and if the mother does not inject herself with the very shot which has turned so many into their true forms, who now hunt us down for our purity, the man next to your child will pull their little legs," Travis boasts and I was wrong. He is still going to stick to the Holy Roller façade for the whole crazy train ride.

A few mothers are looking for the first time at what is in their hands with fear. A few are staring at their kids as they chew to open the plastic wrappers that contain the shots. The remaining are lost in the disbelief over what is even happening.

They remind me of my mother, Carol, lost and waiting for someone to take them by their hand and tell them how pretty they are. My mother never would have risked her life for us. She would have had us killed and at her end, she did try to kill us. She tried to eat us.

A little girl is the first to be chosen. I know her and I know it is Ryan who will be the first father put to this test of faith. The matching mother has already chewed her way through the protective plastic bag. She doesn't wait for any instructions for this game. I don't know if she would have waited if her child was the first or not with the anguish on her face. She starts stripping the winter layers from her clothing to expose her arm. When finally, she is in nothing more than her bra and pants, she pulls the cap from the needle and aims for the muscle of her arm.

"Vein, dear," Travis says, as he eagerly watches her show. There is a lust in his eyes that has nothing to do with carnal needs.

She doesn't even question him. Finding the pulsing blue tube, she pushes the liquid into her body. She looks to Travis fully expecting him now to free her little girl. She doesn't understand this is just the first phase of his evil.

The females of Travis' cult pour a ring of gas around the women. I have to wonder about the logic of this on a wooden stage. I shouldn't have. Travis had it all planned long before the first pew was placed.

Other than the men holding the children and the one now hugging my waist, the cult has departed, leaving only the victims to the flames should they spread. One quick step backward and the executioners will be safe, too.

"Now," Travis calls from one of the pews. He has taken a front-row seat for the bonfire which is about to occur. "Drop the child."

The little girl is shoved forward from the man's shoulders by the one who placed the rope around her neck. They don't want to run the risk of her neck breaking. They let her swing from the rope-like the toy she thought it was. Her gasping sounds as she swings forward steals the air from everyone else, leaving the yard in shocked silence. The fire is lit at the same time as the girl begins to swing. It keeps the mother in place, yet still she runs towards it, testing the heat as if it might be a mirage.

"Who do you save?" Travis calls to Ryan, "Do you take God's work into your own hands? Will you prove your faith in Him to save your family because of your love for Him?" Travis stands, lost in his religious disease. "Will God let your wife be turned into a demon or will He keep her safe, saving them both? Do you feel God's hand Ryan?!?" Travis is screaming. He is shouting into the night air with his voice steaming the area around him.

Ryan reaches for the offered gun. He can kill his wife before she turns, or he can kill his child to save her from the slow death of suffocation. His last option is to wait and see if God loves them enough to save them all.

The roar of a motorcycle is building as it races towards the courtyard. At this point of the night, it wouldn't surprise me if it were J.D. riding back from Hell with a new set of minions close at his wheels. I'm not exactly wrong.

Dolph tears into the courtyard astride Lawless' pride and joy. He doesn't slow to avoid the crowd of bystanders and they scatter amid the new threat. The Risen are running not far behind the roaring bike. In the confusion, Simon rushes the stage to hoist the little girl back into the air with Ryan running up right behind him, but Travis won't be cheated that easily. Horrence raises his gun and I shout desperately to warn Simon. He turns to hear my drama, but it's too late.

Simon twitches twice as he is hit with the gunfire. His chest explodes with the content of his coat spreading around him in a mockery of the snow floating in the air. I watch as he falls from the stage. He is gone before his body bounces on the ground, but his name still tears from my mouth with denial.

Dolph is off the bike and running to open the double metal doors to herd the screaming people inside. They follow his commanding shouts, and once his side is secure, Dolph shuts the doors, locking his side down. He never saw his friend fall. He was never aware he just lost the last of the family he built under this roof.

"Drop them! Drop them all!" Travis shouts, as he runs with his pack of protection bearing Selma in their arms.

They do. I feel my body weightless for mere seconds before the rope catches my throat. Its knotted fingers grip me as I stretch to touch the stage with my toes. My boots slide, slipping on the beams pulling me tighter against the rope as I sway. I can already hear my blood rushing as my lungs empty their last reserves of air.

Marxx is first on the stage but only a breath behind him is Lawless. As they reach for the children who dangle with kicking feet, Rhett and

Chapel have put the ring of fire out, freeing the women from their prison before they rush to the cross to help free me. The women help each other lift the choking children who still remain in the ropes.

The fleeing executioners are the first to be overtaken. Their dying screams mix with the religious hymn adding yet another twist to the song. The screams of the dying have never sounded so sweet.

We run to Aimes and Dolph who stand at the nearest door, beckoning us to them with motions instead of sound. The men slide to a stop on the iced cement, waiting for the women and children to be ushered in before sealing the door on those who thought tonight, they would be the ones dealing death. How sweet the sound that saved a wretch like me.

Chapter 35

Husbands rush to find their wives, to find their children. They fall into embraces with gratitude to find their family still alive. Half-hugs and handshakes are shared among the men who have once again risked it all to save this group. No one acknowledges the fact that right on the other side of the safety glass are men being devoured while their screams die in their throats or the fire that has mysteriously restarted. It eats the wooden beams faster than before, charring the wood of the cross with its still swaying ropes.

Lawless stares at me where I rest against the wall panting from pain. His eyes hold me with the same fire that blazes in the background behind him. We should be holding one another, spreading words of reassurance over us both with our lips. We aren't, and when he turns from me, I fear the rope hasn't fully left my neck.

A screaming woman has thrown the crowd back into a panic. Ryan's wife is convulsing on the floor. Her body fights against Ryan's grasp as she continues to slam herself against the floor. Paula watches with detachment as her name is being chanted to help the woman.

"Get away from her," Paula says, pulling the crowd further down the hall. "Get away from her!" she demands, as the nature of human curiosity slows their response to her command.

As quickly as the convulsing started, it stops. Now the crowd begins to back away from her knowing what follows from their own experiences. I don't want to watch what has to happen next.

"Let's go," I tell Aimes. I turn my back as Ryan remembers the gun he was given, and I remember those who gave it to him are still here.

"Shouldn't we stay here?" Aimes hasn't forgotten a thing.

"You want to watch him have to kill his wife while his child watches, go ahead," I tell her as I walk. It's a half-truth, but it's a completely good cover.

When phrased like that, of course, she isn't going to stay. With the sounds of boots following us, our escape has not gone unnoticed. They don't call out as they follow us, and we don't glance back to see who it is following us.

The candles have been blown out in the stairwell. The only light comes from the cloud-covered sky. It floats in with patches before fading us back into the shadows.

Aimes bumps into my back as we take the first corner, startling us both. She says with mild annoyance, "You know, life would be so much easier if it had a background track playing. At least then you would know when it's about to suck. Happy music, we live! Violins and drums, kiss your ass goodbye!"

"Keep moving," Marxx says, from the shadows ahead where he forced his way past us.

"Keep moving, right. Why didn't we think of that?" she hisses into my ear, not brave enough to give it a full voice.

"Because they have the guns and we don't," I whisper back, with less success than she had.

"Keep moving," Rhett repeats, with the same coldness from behind me.

Who's the most hated woman on death row? I'm the most hated woman on death row! Three cheers for the home team!

Marxx nudges the door to our floor open with his foot. We listen for any welcoming noise. With nothing making an obvious introduction, now the hard part has come. Marxx has to enter the dark hallway with us right behind him.

The once familiar length has become a dark cavern of unexplored dread. The windows of the many classrooms cast a subtle glow into the hall. Nothing moves making the stillness as captivating as a charmer to a viper.

"I don't think they are here," Marxx calls back to Lawless. He is standing between the doorways. His attention is divided between our floor and the stairwell behind us.

"If it were me, I'd be upstairs packing to make a run for it," Rhett says and finally Lawless acknowledges something with other than a glare in my direction.

"Rhett, Marxx," Lawless almost barks the names, motioning with his head for them to follow him out. "Watch them as they pack. Grab as much as you can, as fast as you can," he says to the only man left with us.

Chapel understands and starts pulling us to action. "They aren't going up there to clean house," he says, as he hurries us down the hall. "They are just going to find another way out with the courtyard full now."

Chapel clears the first room where Lawless and I stay. He nods as he walks to the next room that belongs to him and Aimes leaving me to pack.

When rushed, everything feels twice as slow as it is. Hands become clumsy and drop things with ironic glee. Feet will trip over invisible things and yet you will still stop to look as if to find something reaching for you. Bags won't unzip, and then once packed, they refuse to zip. Irony – the ultimate leveler of life.

Hauling the duffle bags despite the screaming complaints of my stomach, I pause as I enter the hallway to wait for the other two. My heart stops when a shadow breaks the lighted square projecting into the hallway from the empty room across from me. Lowering the bags,

I stare at the square mentally demanding for it to prove what I saw was true. It does and I gasp.

Aimes comes running from her room with enough noise to make a drum line envious of her skill.

I wave my arms, motioning for her to stop. She looks at me with confusion, enlarging her eyes before calling out into the hallway, "What?"

She's about to ask another question when once again the same shadow streaks across the square at her feet. She doesn't ask any more questions as I make my way to the entrance of the large room. She follows behind me like a living shadow. At least one person is appreciative of my knack for trouble.

"Any chance it's Chapel?" she asks me, with a glimmer of hope in her words.

"You saw him last. You tell me," I whisper back still trying to see into the room without having to fully turn the corner yet.

"He said he was going to the armory." She leans to look down the hall before becoming one with my back again. "Any chance he got lost and didn't want to ask for directions?"

"It's not Chapel. Chapel has no reason to be lurking in an empty room," I tell her. Plus, I have never been that lucky.

Crouching low, I look through the opened doorway waiting for a hail of gunfire to explode around me like it always seems to happen in the movies. It doesn't happen. This isn't a movie. If it were, I would have rejected it long ago and left a scathing review as all people who are safe behind a keyboard do.

The room once served as a science lab, containing row after row of tables for someone to hide behind. To one side is a little room where the teacher would have taken anyone who had the misfortune of messing up their experiment. I know rooms like those well.

"Hello?" I call out creeping along the room like the wall is my long-lost best friend.

"What are you doing?" Aimes shouts as soft as she can.

"Seeing if anyone is in here."

"You think they are going to answer you? Yeah, over here around the corner. I'm waiting with a very large and sharp knife. Come on over. I'll make you a sandwich."

"Is this really when you want to start pointing out the lack of logic in my actions?"

"You're right. I should have started months ago."

I have been watching the room as we held our little exchange. Still, nothing moves. I'm about to chalk it up to something passing by the window when a little head peers around one of the table's sides.

"April?" I call to the little girl who is staring at me.

"What are you two doing?" Rhett asks behind us and we both scream. He chuckles bending down to extend his arms to the little girl who is already running to them. "Hey, Pet," he whispers into the girl's hair, still smiling at how easily he frightened us. He leaves us panting from the shock while we lean against the wall.

"They are fine." We hear Rhett tell someone who our screams must have alarmed. "Just a case of overactive imaginations."

"Jerk," Aimes says, but I know the real word she wanted to use is taking a little longer to grace her tongue.

"Let's go!" Chapel shouts from the hallway, and when asked so nicely, how does one refuse the request.

"Did you find them?" I ask Rhett when we catch up to him and Chapel.

"No."

"Did you find a way out?" Aimes asks, more interested in our well-being than that of a cult. I suppose she has a point.

"Yeah."

"Want to share it with us?" she asks, a little kindly.

"That's why I was sent back," Rhett answers as if she should have already figured it all out. I guess our imaginations aren't as vast as he mentioned because we haven't.

We follow the men out into the bottom hallway. Our bodies are laden with the many duffel bags that carry our humble belongings. Rhett is whispering encouraging words to the little girl who hides her face in his broad shoulder. It's odd to watch, and at the same time, my nonexistent, biological clock starts to tick.

"I wouldn't head that way," a voice purrs from the darkened library.

It stops us all with fear-filled curiosity. Rhett hands April to me as Aimes strips us both of the bags in preparation for running. No matter how it begins, there is always running.

Aimes and I melt backward with April as the shadow steps forward. Ahead of its entrance rolls shot vial after empty shot vial like the ones we saw brought from the crate.

"God works in mysterious ways," Travis says as he emerges into the dim hallway. "Selma and I thought we would add to our flock here, but here we find our flock was added to the damned."

"What have you done?" Chapel's voice vibrates with shock. We know what he has done. Sometimes you just have to hear, or see, the evil to really believe it.

"Cleansed the world," Travis says, with the complete belief in his actions.

Something inside Chapel finally breaks. He reaches for Travis, pulling the man to him with the strength only rage can provide. "There is nothing holy about you." Each word is clipped, spoken behind locked teeth.

"I never said there was," Travis says.

The low lights catch the flash of the blade one second before we can shout the warning.

Chapel recoils with each stab from Travis. The knife slides in and out of his stomach and I scream with each motion. Chapel reaches for the neck of the man, but his hand finds only the red beaded necklace holding the cross he wears. I'm staring at the floor when the red beads drop to the tiles at their feet. Each ruby, red bead hits the tile before it slowly rolls. Before long, they are cascading down and rolling as a cloud towards me. I back away from them as if they are what my mind has made them. Holding April's head to my shoulder, I step from their path as the imaginary blood from Chapel spills past me.

I glance up in time to watch Travis' head explode from the side exit of a heavy-caliber gun. Chapel staggers backward into Rhett's arms when Travis' body falls. Dropping the gun that ended the life of the man who has stolen so many lives himself, Lawless runs to his fallen friend.

Marxx is blocking Aimes from making her way to Chapel. She is fighting and screaming to get around him. I stand, dumbfounded in the middle of it all, clutching a child who isn't mine and avoiding the red beads still rolling around the tiles following the many worn grooves of the floor.

"Come on, man," Rhett says, pressing against the torn flesh bleeding freely from the knife's damage. "We are almost out of here."

"Rhett is right. We have the way cleared. Get up." Lawless tries to tug on the taller man to motivate him to move.

Chapel only stares at them both knowing the truth of what is going to happen.

"We have to move," Marxx whispers, placing his hand over Aimes' sobbing mouth.

Turning to see what he has found; Travis' promise comes from the direction of the gym. His flock who once found a reason to murder so many behind their hate for the "demons" are now the very things they led a holocaust to destroy. They stare at us, locked in their stalking state. They are newly turned and not starved enough yet to push their advantage. Their new minds are still learning how to use the new extensions they have. Like the children from the school, they will wait until we give them a reason to pounce.

"Go," Chapel says softly, but the many eyes still rotate to him with the sound of his voice. "Go on. I'll hold them."

"You can't even hold yourself. Get up!" Lawless demands, and the eyes roll to him.

Chapel reaches for the back of Law's neck, pulling them forehead-to-forehead. The misery in their eyes is synchronized and reflecting in all of ours who are watching.

"Listen," Chapel says to the younger man, whose heart is breaking behind the walls trying to hold it together, "take care of my girls. I won't be around to do it anymore. They are a handful, but they love each of you in their own way. You remember that. Those girls are your humanity. They always have been. Don't become him. Don't let this world break you the way it did him." Chapel winces from the pain, shuddering him. "I'm not going to make it, Brother. I'm ready to go home. I want to see my kids again. I want to hold my wife."

Lawless reaches for the gold chain around Chapel's neck. He fishes the cross from behind the bloodstained shirt, snapping the chain to wrap it around his friend's hand. Chapel grins as his hand closes on the metal effigy.

"I got this, Brother," Chapel says, pulling his gun from the holster on his side.

The same holster that once winked at me with encouragement. The same gun that had once seduced me into action. I saved a group of strangers with that gun. Now, it will once again face an army to secure a group's safety, but this time, its owner won't be the one to leave.

Lawless pulls slowly from the shared embrace. His face is wet with tears even as his face sets with resolve. He walks backward from Chapel as if afraid to turn his back to what is about to happen. Marxx is lifting Aimes off the ground as she fights to stay. Waiting eyes flip from one pair to another as they debate what is happening.

Rhett turns, scooping the mute April from me as he moves past. The glass beads turn to dust under his boots. The red powder is ground underneath him and deeper into the marks on the floor.

Chapel's mouth is already moving with his silent prayers as he stares at his death. My feet move forward to him as he pushes from the wall.

"Not this time," Chapel tells me, seeing me move towards him. "Don't let me be another haunting, Hells," he tells me, bringing a conversation to life which centered on an evergreen serving as the North Star that night. "I want this."

"Let's go," Lawless says, taking my hand. His fingers wrap around mine, pulling me away from the man who once laid everything on the line for me. He pulls me from the man who stood beside me when nobody else would. The preacher's son is going home.

Aimes is screaming his name from the cafeteria. Chapel smiles when hearing it.

"Run," Chapel says, turning to the fray who has become animated.

Lawless and I turn and run, stopping only long enough to scoop up the spare bags as they rush forward. Law tells me to not look back. It's a warning we are all told when something horrible is happening. We never listen, and like Lot's wife, I look back.

I watch as they reach him despite the few rounds, he was able to fire. I watch as they pull Chapel down into their madness. I watch as the grinning skull disappears, slowly swallowed by the things that it had meant to represent. The silver tear catches the light at the last moment as he falls, and I turn to salt with mine.

Chapter 36

It requires Dolph and Marxx to haul the shrieking Aimes from the cafeteria. The courtyard has been cleared of the Risen Dolph lured in to act as a distraction. The men never went upstairs. They came below.

The windows of the top floor explode, sending flames erupting from their casings. We flinch from the explosion. The safety glass glitters in the air as it cascades down around us. Travis had set fire to the floor before infecting his people. Now it is fully engulfed in the man's one last attempt to purify those who have escaped from his grasp.

Only a small handful of those who lived on that floor before we arrived are gathered under the cold rays of the moon. They stare with gaping mouths as their home becomes a cauldron of lost hopes. There should be more, so many more, standing here.

"What happened?" I ask Lawless. He still has a death grip on my hand as if he fears I will run back inside with one final attempt to rescue Chapel. He needn't.

"Ryan's wife turned faster than she should have. She killed a few before she was stopped. The rest ran out the door not thinking."

"Ryan?"

"Shot her after she attacked their daughter. Then he shot himself."

The horrors keep mounting and we haven't yet made it out of the gate. Paula races towards us thinking that Aimes is hurt. When she hears the name Aimes is screaming, her running stops. Aimes is hurting. She isn't hurt.

Paula's eyes look to me and what she sees there sets her jaw to quivering before she can regain herself. Something cold overcomes her face as she stares behind us. For once, I don't look back. Let someone else become the pillar of salt.

"Jesus Christ," Marxx says, seeing whatever Paula has, "you people just won't die."

With one hand Lawless turns as he pushes me forward, reaching to draw a gun from his waistline with the other. I still don't look.

"Leave her," Rhett tells Lawless, pressing the barrel of the gun to the ground. "She's got nothing."

Collecting Aimes, I finally spare a look behind me and I lose my grip on our violent pixie.

"Kill her, Law!" Aimes is screaming across the span between them and us. She turns to me, forcing the duffels I carry open. "Give me a gun. I'll kill her!"

Selma limps towards us coated more in blood than clothing. She still bleeds from an attempt to bandage the gunshot. Her arm is torn and dripping crimson like rose petals thrown from a flower girl's white basket as she walks, but her smile is still as sweet.

"Rhett," she calls out, "you wouldn't just leave me here?"

Rhett says nothing to her. His face doesn't even twitch with her quilt-laden question.

"I'm sorry," she tries again. "I love you…"

"Where the truck is a gun?" Aimes is muttering beside me, as she turns the bags inside out.

She isn't watching Rhett the way the rest of us are. She isn't holding her breath, fearing what he may or may not do. He only stares at Selma, and as he hugs April a little tighter to him, his hand doesn't tremble.

"April," Selma calls to the little girl, who nestles deeper into Rhett's arms hearing her name, "come to Mommy. Come here, Sweetheart."

"Like I said," Rhett tells us, as Aimes still ransacks the duffels. "She's got nothing." He turns from the woman he once placed his faith in. He lets her stumble and fall the way she made his soul stumble as she tore him apart mentally. "Let's go."

Marxx lifts Aimes again and she fights to be released, still screaming about finding a gun. Paula helps me quickly repack the bags. Her hands tremble in tempo with her jaw.

"You can ride with us," I tell her, knowing she would never ask for the comfort she needs right now. I know because I wouldn't ask either.

"I'd like that," she tells me, with a voice holding steadier than her hands. "You might need me to sedate Aimes."

I smile, believing the woman completely. Aimes is mute as we climb into the truck. The men have deposited our bags in the truck's bed, but I can't start the truck yet.

Climbing back out, I walk to where Rhett is starting his bike. I don't ask him for permission. I simply lift April from the back of the bike as he watches me in the side mirrors with a grin.

"Idiot," I tell him, carrying the girl who is more like a doll than a human to my truck while Selma screams her name.

Sliding her into the lap of Paula, I climb back into the truck and start the large engine. It roars, threatening the vehicles in front of me. Paula laughs a soft chuckle as the cars pull out of my way with such a simple act. I lead the exit from what we had hoped would be our safe refuge. We leave behind the many bodies of our loved ones who will forever live in the rooms of our hearts. With every beat, their memory will be reborn inside of us. We will search for their faces in our dreams. We will hear the sounds of their voices sometimes when the wind blows just right. We will mourn them, but the words we never said to them, we will mourn the most.

I watch in the rear mirror as my wishes fade away in a parade of painful pride. Their floats are decorated with the flashing décor of lost dreams and I wave as they go by like a child marveling at their wonder.

I wave at every desire I once cradled in those walls as smoke takes it from sight. What else can I do but once again drive into the night with no knowledge of what tomorrow might bring.

The loud bikes fall in behind me. I'm amused to see Dolph astride the large beast, which once belonged to J.D. I can almost hear J.D. cussing over it and my smile grows larger. Dolph has lost everything as we exit the place, he fought to keep secure. It feels fitting that the men now should adopt him.

As we reach the road, I see the right blinker flash from Law's bike. So, I turn right just as another man had once instructed me to. The cars following us pull off in different directions as we come to intersections. Each lost car signals their final goodbye with short waves as a salute.

We can't promise them a safe future. No one can. Each must find their own path now for better or for worse. Finding it is the heart behind what it means to have courage.

Courage is not a goal set in the dark throes of desperation. It's the need to survive. It's the need to push through the fears and find the strength to face the perils ahead. It's not a brass ring to be claimed or a trophy to boast over. It's the personal level of discomfort we all must face when no outstretched arm is there to help you. Travis was right about one thing. Only a soul lost to the deepest pit of despair, void of any other option but of fighting for each new day, can truly understand what it means to claim life in its shaking, defiant fist. Courage isn't something you are born with. It's something that life carves out of you along the way. To say one has courage is to say one has been through Hell and back so many times they have grown bored with life's attempts to break them.

"She wasn't really my mommy," Aprils says, from the warmth of Paula's arms. "My mommy was turned into a monster and tried to eat my daddy."

"Mine, too," Aimes says, as lifeless as April. "Mondays just suck."

I can still see the smoke towering into the night sky behind us. It curls its way into the heavens where I hope Chapel is at peace. I hope he is standing with the family he never truly let slip from his mind. I hope he can find the forgiveness he longed for from the actions he had no other recourse. I hope he does, because one day, I hope I do too.

Flames flicker through the trees as it buries more than just the memories we leave behind. If I listen hard enough, I can still hear the strands of the hymn being played.

Through many dangers, toils, and snares I have already come. 'Tis Grace that brought me safe thus far and Grace will lead me home.

Chapter 37

It isn't long until we find ourselves behind the line of skulls as the road widens before us. Once, there were five that would stare back at us with their threatening eyes. Now, only three remain.

April has long since fallen asleep and Aimes drifts in-and-out with her dreams sabotaging any hope for rest. I battle against my body's fatigue with better efforts. I can only imagine the toll being taken on the bodies riding through the cold night in front of me.

"You could let me drive," Paula offers. It's the first sound to disrupt the silence of the cabin since April and Aimes had their little moment of bonding. "I know your stomach has to be hurting you. I wish you'd let me check the stitches like I have been asking you to."

"Been a little busy with the whole death camp thing."

She snorts to disguise her laughter. "Well, you ain't busy now."

"Obviously, you have never driven a large truck without power steering."

"A list of excuses as the day is long."

"- and I'm not even trying."

"She's really not," Aimes mutters, resting against the passenger door.

I know Lawless and the men are searching for any place to pull over that might hold a hope of safety. Our bodies are too tired from the past day's events to trust ourselves to be alert to danger and assigning someone to look out would just be cruel. It's just mile after mile of open road on this small town's highway and it feels hopeless as the miles continue to stretch on.

Only a few times have we come across a cluster of wrecked or abandoned cars to navigate through. Well the men navigated. I played bumper cars with my large grill demolishing the compacts in my path. It was a sick release of the frustrations to watch the metal fly in shrapnel-like pieces as I pushed the truck through the clusters.

Lucky for me, we have found another one. This one might not be as easy, though. A large Jeep sits parked across the road ahead of us. Behind it sits another car and I'm already mentally lining them up like a game of pool.

The men slow their bikes and I slow as well, just a little further back. I know I will need a decent amount of speed to topple that Jeep.

"You could just go around," Paula says, with a touch of motherly disapproval.

"Where is the fun in that?" I smile at her and receive an eye roll for my excitement.

"They are stopping," Aimes says, sitting up with her concern.

"They just need to stretch their legs," Paula still uses her motherly voice.

"There are people out there." Aimes is squinting to make out the moving shadows.

The men are stretching, but it's to cover their motives as they reach for their guns. Aimes is obviously not the only one to have spotted the moving shapes. When the first shape comes around the corner, I highlight him in the brights of the truck. His hands instinctively come to cover his face, showing he is unarmed and now blind.

More men come around from the back of the Jeep. They each shield their faces from the burning light from my truck. Knowing any risk of danger has passed, I climb from the cabin to see what the people want. Mostly I just need to stretch too.

The sounds of their voices float to me in the night air. Fog forms from their breath as they speak, giving proof of who is speaking when. One voice, one voice from the circle ahead of me, makes the hairs on my neck rise. I have goosebumps and it has nothing to do with the weather.

I listen as he introduces himself with good-natured intent, but I can't really trust what my ears have heard or what my mind is screaming. I couldn't believe it until Lawless turned to look at me, squinting into the high beams of the truck. I didn't want to believe it until Rhett and Marxx also cast their eyes my way. I wouldn't believe it until the man, sensing something is wrong, stares trying to pierce the glowing veil that conceals me.

My whole body is trembling with a rush of emotions that for most I don't have a name as I stare at him. Memories tumble through my mind and the door I have locked bursts open. I say the one name I never thought I would say again. I cast it into the winter night as Truth, Karma and Fate clap with distorted elation. "Dad?"

Epilogue

Selma sits in the blue minivan left behind by those who once lived in the forsaken school. Her shoulder throbs, her arm feels as if it is blistering from an invisible fire, but it's her head that is sending her into tears of agony.

Pressure thrusts against the walls of her skull. It ruins her vision as a fever-like fire blazes inside her body. A part of her knows what is happening. She has seen it enough times in the past. She has caused it to happen to every small neighborhood in their path as she and Travis played out their personal vengeance for what had happened to them. She, of all the people who are still cursed to walk the earth, should know what is happening. It just doesn't make sense.

She never injected herself with the shots she and Travis had convinced the remaining believers to take. She sat, watching them self-administer the doses marveling at how Travis could so easily twist people to his plans. Plans which had involved their mathematical-like destruction of every pocket of life they discovered, until now.

Selma stares at the gaping, torn flesh of her arm where one of the believers had bitten her when he awoke. She stares at it as the first convulsions rattle her skeleton with the force of the contractions.

It doesn't make sense. It doesn't make sense! Are her last thoughts as her mind is destroyed by the very evil, she had used to destroy so many others? If she had only taken a moment to learn what was really in the create, it would all make perfect sense.

Extras

THE SIREN SERIES BOOK ONE
CROWN OF BETRAYAL
Daggers will kill you,
but the cloaks will
destroy you.
MARIE F CROW

Verona has lived in the safety and bliss of the palace and the luxury of what being a Siren means. Content to live her life in the shadows of her beautiful mother, Ostila, and the enchanting, dark beauty of her aunt, Morlena, Verona never thought about what life would be like should they be taken from her. At her mother's coronation, these once impossible thoughts become shockingly real.

Corander has lived his life in the shadows of his father, Kurt. At the head of the Empradar bloodline, Kurt holds no mercy for those who fail him and even less for those he distrusts. When the palace falls to madness, it will be Corander who is tested by his father's desires and torn by his own.

Together, Corander and Verona must discover who they really are, and who they are truly meant to become, before all is lost to hidden plots and crowns of betrayal.

Continue Verona and Corander's story here!

About the Author

Marie F Crow weaves her stories around the human element of the horror verses the 'monsters' themselves. She believes that the real horror of life does not come from the expected, but from the unexpected responses of the human nature and what depths of trauma a person must survive in certain situations. She began writing The Risen series when feeling that the popular genre was slipping too deep into the realm of pure 'slasher' and forgetting what the horror of zombies can mean for a story.

Now, with her children's series launched, Marie hopes to use her favorite 'monster' as a teaching tool to inspire children to understand that not everything that looks scary, is scary. With

Abigail and Her Pet Zombie series, Marie hopes to further spread her love for all things "that go bump in the night" with small children showing them that it's okay to be different and to embrace those same differences in those around them.

Social Media Links
Facebook: @MarieFCrow.Author
Instagram: @authormariefcrow
Twitter: @MarieFCrow

Additional titles by Marie F Crow:

The Risen Series
Dawning
Margaret
Remnants
Courage
Defiance (Coming Soon)

The Siren Series
Crown of Betrayal
Crown of Remorse (Coming Soon)

The Abigail and her Pet Zombie Series
Illustrated Children's Books
Abigail and her Pet Zombie
Zoo Day
Spring
Summer
Halloween

The Abigail and her Pet Zombie Series
Beginner Chapter Books
Abigail and her Pet Zombie (Coming Soon)

The Great HEXpectation Series
The Little Lies (Coming Soon)

About the Publisher

Kingston Publishing offers an affordable way for you to turn your dream into a reality. We offer every service you will ever need to take an idea and publish a story. We are here to help authors make it in the industry. We've been hurt by publishers in the past and we want to provide a positive experience that will keep you coming back to us.

Whether you want a traditional publisher who offers all the amenities a publishing company should or an author who prefers to self-publish, but needs additional help - we are here for you.

Now Accepting Manuscripts!
Please send query letter and manuscript to:
submissions@kingstonpublishing.com
Visit our website at www.kingstonpublishing.com